A Carri[illegible] of Misjustice

Charlie Cochrane

Riptide Publishing
PO Box 1537
Burnsville, NC 28714
www.riptidepublishing.com

Cover art: L.C. Chase, lcchase.com/design-portfolio.html
Editors: Veronica Vega, Rachel Haimowitz, Carole-ann Galloway
Layout: L.C. Chase, lcchase.com

ISBN: 978-1-62649-929-4

First edition
May, 2020

Also available in ebook:
ISBN: 978-1-62649-928-7

A Carriage of Misjustice

Charlie Cochrane

With thanks to my daughter Ros, whose misspeaking gave me the saying "Carriage of Misjustice." After that, the book had to be written.

Table of Contents

Chapter One

Adam Matthews turned his left hand so that his ring caught the light. It was an elegant piece of metalwork, Welsh gold in a chunky, slightly squared-off design, exactly the same as the ring on Robin Bright's hand. They'd not deliberately chosen an identical pattern for romantic reasons: that was simply how it had worked out. They'd both studied the jeweller's brochure, both written a list of three favourite choices in order of preference, put the lists into sealed envelopes . . . and opened them to find they'd picked the same one in pole position, with remarkably similar ones in second and third place.

Great minds think alike and all that.

"Are you still admiring your wedding ring?" Robin said, from over the other side of the lounge, where he and Campbell the Newfoundland were having some bonding time. Nothing better than watching the Sunday lunchtime game on the telly, especially when it featured Liverpool against Spurs. Campbell in particular seemed besotted with Harry Kane.

"I'll never stop admiring it. Even the kids in my class think it's cool, and they're hard to please." Adam took another glance at the ring, then picked up the Sunday paper to flick through the sports pages. He wasn't really reading, though—it was more of a prop to cover the inane grin that was about to break out all over his face and for which Robin would take the micky out of him. A grin he couldn't help producing every time he thought about *it*. The fact that they'd gone and tied the knot at last.

What a day it had been: a small civil ceremony out at a local upmarket pub, the Sporting Chance, with only close family and friends, their mothers wearing enormous hats and looking stunning.

But the star of the day had been Campbell, outdoing everyone in terms of style with a white bow tie around his neck and stealing the show as he trotted up the aisle with the rings in a bag—waterproof to avoid the slobber—in his canine jaws. He'd dropped them at Adam's feet, then returned to sit on a blanket at the back of the room with nonchalant ease, as though this were the sort of thing he did every day. His presence had proved to be a bonus, because when the guests were fussing over the dog, they'd been leaving the groom and groom in peace.

The newlyweds hadn't gone off on honeymoon, given that Adam couldn't have got away during term time, so they were saving their leave for a proper holiday later in the year. So just a celebration that weekend, then straight back to school for Adam and the nick for Robin, on Monday morning.

That had caused comment at both workplaces—as had the fact they'd opted for a small, restrained ceremony rather than the big lavish do some people had expected. They'd made it clear that they'd been making a stand against the commercialisation of weddings, believing that so long as there was a ceremony, a photographer, a good meal, and a bit of a knees-up, all boxes had been ticked. Anybody who'd suggested they were being tight wads had got subtly reminded that they'd made sizeable charity donations in the names of those who hadn't been invited.

Now, they'd been an officially linked couple for all of a week and the sensation still felt as shiny and new as it had the previous weekend.

"I could do with a few weeks to recover from all the excitement. Wha-at?" Robin paused, frowning. "Why are you making that *stop it* gesture? What's the problem?"

"Don't say anything about time to recover. Don't tempt fate into arranging a surprise Ofsted inspection for me or a cold-case murder that rears its head again and means weeks of you working all hours God sends." Adam touched the wooden table. He wasn't really superstitious, but sometimes you were trying to appease your own conscience as much as some nebulous source of fortune, good or bad. *Like wearing lucky socks to play sport: your brain tells you it made no difference but your heart won't believe it.*

"Okay. Do you want me to wish that a horrible case drops in my lap on the principle that it'll ensure life's nice and quiet?"

Adam grinned. "Don't say anything. Put your mind to whether we want to have a religious ceremony to go with the civil one."

"That's trickier than solving a murder case."

Both were regular if occasional churchgoers, and both would say they had a degree of faith, although they didn't make a big thing of it. And both appreciated that only certain parts of the Christian communion wouldn't turn their noses up at the union between two people of the same gender.

"Would Neil do us a blessing, do you think?" The vicar was pretty broad-minded and he'd never shown any disapproval towards Robin or Adam.

"Privately, maybe. If we asked for something small—smaller than even the wedding was—and maybe not in the church itself. I don't think he's got a problem with homosexuals but there are a few folk on the PCC who'd throw their toys out of their prams if they knew we were standing in front of the altar at St. Crispin's making vows in the presence of God."

"And the fear of the congregation?" Robin said, which was an old joke if still a relevant one even now.

"Some of them, but that's inevitable. You know who I'm thinking of." Like any parish, Lindenshaw had its share of people who would prefer it if there were no women priests, the only prayer book used was the one published in 1662, and everyone lived by the parts of the Levitican law that didn't apply to them but stopped everyone else having fun. "I remember a few folk getting the hump on when Neil first arrived here and made them share the peace at the ten o'clock communion. They couldn't have been more outraged if he'd taken the service in drag."

Robin made the kind of face he produced when he had to clear up after Campbell had relieved himself in the garden. "Sounds like they're due to be outraged again, then. Shall we make an appointment to see Neil?"

"Works for me. Although he probably can't do anything till late spring. Lent coming up, and I've a feeling the church doesn't do weddings then. I guess a blessing would come under that umbrella."

"Our mothers would welcome deferring the event for a while. It would mean they can get new summer hats to go with the winter ones they wore last weekend." The local milliner must have made a small fortune out of the Matthews and Bright womenfolk.

"Right. Before we start planning any of that, we have work to do this afternoon. Our good deed for the day."

"So we have."

The cottage three doors down was owned by a fiercely independent lady in her seventies, whom they'd told that if she ever needed anything done round the house or garden that didn't need technical skill, just a touch of brawn, she shouldn't hesitate to call on them. It would have to be serious for her to call in that offer, and the loss of three fence panels in a storm two days previously came into that category. They'd take Campbell—Mrs. Haig doted on him—and the pair could supervise Adam and Robin while they repaired the old panels and shifted them back into place. The fact that Mrs. Haig's boiled fruit cake was legendary turned an act of kindness into a positive pleasure.

They got into their working clothes and set off.

An hour, a cup of tea, and a large slab of cake later, the old panels were out and the new ones ready to be installed.

"You're doing a grand job, there," Mrs. Haig said. "I don't know what I'd do without you."

"It's a pleasure. Better than marking books or catching criminals." Adam gave his husband a wink. "Neither of us take enough exercise."

"I used to watch you running with Campbell." She scratched the dog's ear. "I suppose you're too busy for that these days."

"You're right. We tend to take him for a walk together, don't we?"

"Yes," Robin replied. "It makes sure we spend time together too." They had no need to hide their relationship from their hostess. Her brother was gay, a stalwart of musical chorus lines in London.

"You could join the church choir," she suggested. "They always need tenors."

"I'd love to, but I'd always be ringing Martin up to say I couldn't make the practices. Armed robbery to sort out or whatever."

Adam hid his grin in his teacup. The choirmaster fancied Robin and barely hid it.

"Yes, I suppose so." Mrs. Haig frowned. "You work too hard, the pair of you. And here's me eating into your weekend."

Adam shook his head. "This isn't work, it's play." And the sight of Robin in an old T-shirt, muscles rippling and working up a sweat was a sight to enjoy. Adam gave him an affectionate glance, which was immediately returned.

"These panels won't install themselves," Robin said hastily, perhaps with half a mind on some less strenuous but highly enjoyable activity that could go on later, assuming they weren't too tired.

An hour later, they were home, tired but happy. Adam cleaned himself up while Robin brushed residual crumbs off the dog, then *he* could head into the shower while Adam had a well-earned sit-down. As he was getting dressed, Adam thought he heard Robin talking on the phone. Please God it was only Mrs. Bright touching base rather than work calling the bloke in. The fact that Robin wasn't leaping up the stairs apologising and changing out of his old clothes so he could report for duty had to be a good sign, surely?

"What's up?" Adam called over the banister, heart sinking when Robin entered the hallway. "Anyone would think you'd lost a tenner and found five pence."

"Not quite. Not an ideal situation, though." Robin weighed the phone in his hand like it was a piece of ordnance he'd like to chuck as far away as possible.

"That's what Brits say when it's the end of the world."

Robin grinned. "It's not as bad as that. I have to go off on secondment, as of tomorrow. Hopefully it'll be a short one, but you can't tell with murder. Or with peritonitis."

Adam made a *that's gone right over my head* gesture. "I'm sure that's supposed to make sense, but you've lost me. Secondment to where?"

"Hartwood. It's a town between Oxford and Birmingham, east of the M40. There was a murder there about ten days ago. Don't know if you saw the story—bloke found dead in the loos at a rugby club."

"I was a bit preoccupied last week, if you remember, but yes, I did see the story on the BBC site. Why can't the local police handle it? Test Valley or East Midlands or whoever covers the area?"

"That's a long story. Can I come and clean myself up and then I'll tell you everything?"

"Might be an idea. You're slightly fragrant." Adam forced a smile. Going on a secondment? They really shouldn't have tempted fate.

While Robin showered, Adam pottered about in the kitchen. He always found that a calming place, somewhere he could think clearly. No doubt that was associated with the house having originally been owned by his grandparents: many happy hours he'd spent there as a child, helping his granny to make the Christmas pudding on stir-up Sunday or learning firsthand the way to make a perfect Yorkshire pudding.

As he transferred from fridge to oven a defrosted casserole—courtesy of their domestic help, Sandra, who'd insisted on stocking the freezer when they'd been knee-deep in wedding preparations—Adam cast his mind back to the news story, but nothing much had registered about it. Still, it was easy enough to refresh his memory by researching the story on his phone. By the time he'd followed a few links, he'd built up a reasonable picture. Hartwood Wasps Rugby Club had used to be exclusively for gay and bi guys, but had decided to welcome everyone, initially because they'd had a bit of a crisis in terms of player numbers. They'd been so successful that they'd carried on with the strategy and were now heading up the leagues, making a tongue-in-cheek thing about their equality policy ensuring that straight players didn't get given a hard time.

The Wednesday before last, a bloke called Nick Osment had been found dead in the changing room in the clubhouse, and so far the police had shown no signs of making an arrest. Plenty of appeals for help, though, and some noncommittal statements about following a number of leads.

Had they hit a brick wall so early in the investigation and needed a fresh pair of eyes? Robin had built up his experience of murder cases over the last few years, and he'd been a hundred percent successful on leading his team to finding the culprit, but surely he wasn't the most experienced officer they could call on if a case had stalled? Or was there another reason, given the history of the club, that the local force had picked on this particular officer?

"This secondment," Adam asked, as soon as Robin appeared, "they've not called you in because you're gay? Rainbow rugby and all that."

Robin shrugged. "On the surface, no. They needed to call somebody in, though—right bloody mess up at the local station—and I used to work with the detective superintendent there when I was a snotty sergeant and she was my inspector. Rukshana Betteridge. I've mentioned her."

"You have." They'd also discussed the fact that some people muttered behind her back that she'd only been fast-tracked because she was a woman, and mixed race to boot, but Robin wasn't having that. She was simply a better copper than most of the blokes she worked alongside, and he'd learned a hell of a lot from her. "I particularly remember a story about you, her, and the nuclear-strength chicken vindaloo. Three hours on and off the loo, was it?"

"I was hoping you'd have forgotten that." Robin gave Campbell a pat. "Your dads can't get away with any misdemeanours, can they? Cowdrey rang me, and he says Detective Superintendent Betteridge—I'll never be able to call her Rukshana to her face—got in touch and pleaded to have me help out. I'm hoping it's my skills as a copper and my track record with solving murders that was the key thing, rather than who I bed."

Adam nodded. He'd already got out and opened a couple of bottles of beer: Robin looked as though he could do with one. "So, what's this *right bloody mess* you've got lumped with sorting out?"

"The detective inspector who reports to her, Robertson. His appendix went haywire back end of last week, and he's developed peritonitis on top of appendicitis. They've operated successfully, but he won't return to work anytime soon, no matter how much he wants to be. This bloke was running the investigation, and there's nobody local to take his place. Even his sergeant's been working nonstop on an abuse case."

"Bloody mess is no exaggeration, then."

"Yep." Robin scratched Campbell's head distractedly. "Cowdrey says it'll be great for my career, but he also understands it won't be easy, hard on the heels of last weekend."

"I should have applied to the school for unpaid leave. We could have headed off to the back of beyond, in which case they couldn't have got hold of us." Adam put his arm around Robin's shoulders and held him close. "It'll work. We'll make it work."

Robin nuzzled into Adam's chest. "Yeah, I know. I really wish I didn't have to, but Betteridge was a good friend to me, and I feel I owe her. And there's some poor dead sod who deserves justice."

"Don't apologise. Just catch the bloody killer quickly so you can get back here. This is not the sort of honeymoon I imagined having." Adam chuckled, gave him a kiss, then had to pretend to give Campbell one too, as the dog was clearly feeling left out.

"I could tell Cowdrey to stick it. Politely, of course, because I'm neither that brave nor that stupid. He told me to take an hour to think it over." Robin glanced at his watch. "I've still time to decide."

"Hey, I was only kidding about the honeymoon. You go. It's not like I'm some blushing bride and we only had our first night together once you'd put a ring on it. As far as I'm concerned, the honeymoon started ages ago and it's never stopped." Adam gave him a lingering kiss. "It would be worse if I'd fallen for a soldier."

"You soft bugger. I'll get onto Cowdrey right now, and put him out of his misery. He'll be grateful, as will Betteridge."

"Anything I can do to help, let me know. When does he want you to travel?"

"Tomorrow, preferably." Robin grimaced. "I'm glad Sandra got all the washing and ironing up-to-date. I need to get rummaging in the airing cupboard and get a suitcase packed. There are other phone calls I should make too."

"Make one to your mum and another to Pru. Subcontract all other communication to them." Mrs. Bright and Robin's favourite sergeant would be able to handle any task set. In fact, the maternal information network would ensure the news would be halfway across the county within thirty minutes of Mrs. Bright being told. Adam wondered if she stood on her roof using semaphore flags or an Aldis lamp, depending on the time of day.

"The first would work, but Pru's likely to be too busy. Cowdrey said he'd like her to go with me. DS Betteridge wants me to have an officer I'm used to working with on my team, and it'll be good experience for her." Robin was clearly warming to the positive aspects of this assignment. "I'm sure that if I give young Ben a call instead, he can pass on the news to the team. He always hints he wants extra responsibility."

"Will you still be calling him young Ben in twenty years' time, when he's in his forties and losing his hair?" Adam snorted. "Maybe then he'll regard you like you regard Betteridge."

"If he does, I'll be pleased." Robin returned the kiss, grabbed his phone, and went to call Cowdrey.

The casserole wouldn't be ready for a while, so Adam nipped upstairs to get Robin's clothes out of the airing cupboard; he laid them out on the bed, trying to be helpful and also gathering his thoughts.

It had to be a good opportunity for both Robin and Pru in terms of career development. Showing their willingness to help out even if it meant personal inconvenience, the chance of working with a new team and a new area, and maybe learning things they could bring back and apply in Abbotston. Adam felt a swell of pride at the confidence Robin's old boss clearly felt in her protégé, whatever other considerations might have come into play. Adam wasn't going to get sidetracked into thinking about whether this might herald a move to Hartwood itself, with Betteridge taking Robin back under her wing in a police variation on the January football transfer window. Robin would certainly enjoy working with her again. He'd never expressed anything but praise for her and the way she'd fought her corner firmly but politely at so many turns.

Adam would have loved to have been a fly on the wall the day when she'd charmingly pulled up a young sergeant who'd referred to her having had an attack of feminine intuition with the words, *"If a bloke made a leap of reasoning like that, you'd call it a hunch, so that's what we'll call it in my case, eh?"*

Heavy pawsteps on the stairs, accompanied by snuffling, heralded the arrival of Campbell, who wasn't usually allowed upstairs except on special occasions, of which this had to be one.

"Come to make sure I'm laying out everything your other dad needs? He doesn't want that, thank you." Adam wrested a small stuffed toy—albeit not horribly slobbery—out of the Newfoundland's jaws. "I'll get him to FaceTime you every day so you'll know he's safe."

What would his colleagues say if they saw him having an earnest conversation with a dog? The children wouldn't bat an eyelid, naturally. They'd understand such things were important.

"We'll both miss him, only don't let on too much, eh? I don't want him giving up the chance simply to stop us being upset."

Campbell glanced up, big brown eyes full of what might be interpreted as understanding, then nuzzled his nose into Adam's hand. It was going to be just the two of them again for the next few weeks, and they'd need to take care of each other. Although there was a plus side to the situation: the murder having taken place so far away, the investigation of it really couldn't draw him or Campbell in this time. Could it?

Adam stretched over to touch the wooden bedside table, aware they'd tempted fate already that afternoon.

Chapter Two

Robin didn't set off first thing the next day, not least because the traffic was always a nightmare on Monday morning. Reports on the morning travel news of an accident blocking the M40 and causing huge delays in the area left him feeling smug at making the right choice. He went into Abbotston station, where he could ensure a proper handover of active cases—Robin suspected Cowdrey was quite looking forward to rolling up his sleeves and being operational for a while.

Pru and he also got their heads down for half an hour to familiarise themselves with what had happened so far in the investigation. As expected with anything organised by Betteridge, the initial enquiries had been methodical, painstaking, and had left no obvious stones unturned. Cowdrey having passed on an updated mobile number for her, Robin had sent a brief message to his old boss saying that he was delighted to be working for her again and received an answer along the same lines, with the intriguing addition, *Something doesn't add up in this case, and I can't spot what it is. Fresh eyes welcomed.*

"It has to be out of the ordinary for Betteridge not to have put her finger on it," Robin said, after sharing the message with Pru. "Sharp as a razor, that woman."

"It does seem an odd case all round on the face of it, sir."

That was an understatement, given what they'd learned reading the case notes.

"Okay, Pru. Talk me through this like I know nothing."

"Last Wednesday evening bar one. Hartwood rugby team holding their regular practice session at the ground they share with the local athletics club. One of the players, Greg, gets badly hurt in a tackle, and the ambulance is called. Dave, the bloke he tackled, and his mate Andy both go into the changing room to clean up so they can head off to hospital, where they'll keep the injured man company until his girlfriend, Dawn, can get there."

"Dawn's the one who's providing an alibi, right?"

"Hey, you're getting ahead, sir."

"Sorry. I'm finding it complicated, trying to take it all in at once, rather than organically." He'd not appreciated before how important the normal slow accruing of information was. "And don't say it's wedding brain."

"Never crossed my mind." Pru grinned. "Right. Dave and Andy go into the changing room, then Dave goes into the loos on his own. He notices a pair of feet sticking out from one of the cubicles, nudges the door open and finds a man lying in there, stone dead because somebody's walloped his skull. It turns out that the victim, Nick Osment, is the husband of the woman Dawn's currently having a girls' wine-and-chat evening with. As you say, she's giving the alibi."

"If we believe her."

Pru wagged a finger at her laptop screen. "It says here there's only one obvious way into the changing rooms—straight off the pitch—because the other door, connecting to the clubhouse, has been routinely kept locked and bolted on the other side unless the bar staff are in. Because of a spate of thefts a year back."

"People would have had keys to those doors, though. Maybe a set of master keys to the whole site." Robin recalled the sports club where his dad had played football in the winter and cricket in the summer. A bloke they called Codger—Robin had no idea what his real name was—had a great big ring of keys that Mr. Bright had said included one for the Tower of London. Robin had believed that for months until his mother had put him straight. "We need to follow that through. Easy enough to enter from the bar, then bolt the door behind you when you'd used it to escape."

Pru nodded. "Unlikely the victim's wife, Melanie, would have been in that position, but that's me making assumptions. On the face of it, she has that unbreakable alibi for the time of death. Unless Dawn's lying for her. Same goes for the people involved with the training session. They all account for each other at the time the murder is supposed to have occurred."

Robin shrugged. "I'll have more of an idea about that when we've talked to some of the key people face-to-face. I trust Betteridge, but I have no idea how robust her junior officers are. You ask the wrong questions, you get incomplete statements."

"It's going to need all our tact, sir. Witnesses won't be happy to go through everything again, and they'll be suspicious that the local force has somehow cocked up, which is why they've had to call us in."

Pru had a point. "Betteridge says she's happy for us to be upfront about Robertson's illness. But yes, we'll tread carefully." Robin glanced at his watch. "Traffic should have eased. Let's hit the road."

The sooner they got on with things, the sooner he could get back to Adam.

By the time they arrived in Hartwood, Pru and him sharing the driving, Robin had set up the first of their interviews. He'd wanted to nab the man who found the body, Dave Venter, but he wasn't available until the next day, although his mate Andy—the one who'd accompanied him to the changing rooms—was happy to meet them as soon as they arrived. He worked around the corner from a Hilton hotel, so suggested they all meet in the bar there, which he reckoned served good coffee and had plenty of places where they could chat without being overheard.

Robin and Pru drove straight there before going to the police station, both wanting to get something on this case firsthand. They'd soon, no doubt, be bombarded with the opinions of the constables already working on the murder. Robin had advised them he'd be there late afternoon for a meet-and-greet followed by a briefing. He toyed with offering to take them out for a beer, but held that in abeyance until he got a feeling for what they were like. He was there to do a job, not to be flavour of the month.

Andy was waiting for them in the foyer, as they soon established after a bit of *Are you waiting for us?* type mime. He was ready to get down to business and seemed happy at an opportunity to rehash things. Maybe too happy, given the puppy-dog grin he kept flashing Robin. Somebody else who fancied him, like the choirmaster seemed to? Adam would be threatening to lock him up at this rate.

"Thanks for meeting us," Robin said, straight-faced. "Sorry to have to make you go through all this again, but we're new to the case and I'd like to hear everything straight from you, not via someone else."

"I get that." Andy nodded. "Word got around that the inspector who'd seen us had appendicitis. I wouldn't wish that on anybody. As for repeating stuff, I'm a customer service manager at an insurance company, so I know how information can get garbled if you don't hear it direct."

They ordered coffee, then got settled in a quiet corner.

"So, can we hear direct what happened at the training ground two Wednesdays ago?" Pru asked.

Andy winced. "God, I'll never forget that evening. Bad things happen to other people, right? I'd never have thought me and the guys would get caught up in something like this, but we got a shit-ton of crap dumped on us."

"You certainly did," Pru said, soothingly. "You'll still be in shock."

"We all are. Sorry, I sound like a whiny teenager, all sorry for myself, but it's really got to us. And I feel guilty because it's Greg I keep thinking about, rather than the bloke in the loos." The sentiment sounded genuine.

"Rugby's a dangerous game. Anyone who's played it appreciates the risks." Shontayne Hape had suffered so many concussions he'd not been able to remember his PIN.

"Yeah, we've had that drummed into us enough. You should hear Coach. 'Not like the old days where we pretended not to be hurt and walked round in a daze half the time.'" It must have been an acceptable impression of a Welsh accent given that Pru didn't appear to object. "Now we have proper protocols for head injuries."

Pru, being a valleys girl, was even more enthusiastic about rugby than Robin or Adam. "Coach misses the old days, does he?"

"Yeah. He always says nobody can sidestep like they used to back then. But all joking aside, he doesn't miss the injuries. Seen too many good blokes affected for the rest of their lives. Like Greg might be.

Up to now we've had nothing worse than a few broken noses and cauliflower ears. Trouble is none of us believed that the big, bad injury was ever going to happen at Hartwood. Until it did."

Time to bring this back to the matter in hand before it became a rugby heart-to-heart. "Coach? Was he leading the training session?" Robin asked.

"Yeah, he always does. Oh, and his name's Derek Preese but nobody uses that."

"Ah. That name rings a bell from the statements. Right, imagine we know nothing about what went on at training. Talk us through it." Much as Robin wanted to get through the rugby stuff and get onto the finding of the body, they needed to set the scene. The action on the pitch was all going on at the same time as the victim was being attacked, which made the matter of who was where, and doing what, vital.

"Okay. It was a normal training session, almost."

"Almost? Want to clarify that?"

"Well, such a bad injury wasn't normal, was it? Before that we were all on the pitch, running through the usual moves and practice plays. Then Greg Holmes, who plays on the flank meaning he's pretty nippy despite being muscular with it, got his angle wrong going into a tackle on Big Dave and caught the side of his neck on the bloke's shoulder." Andy paused for breath, having delivered all that at a lick. "The pair of them went down awkwardly, and Greg didn't get up."

"Take your time," Pru said. "We know it's not easy."

Andy nodded. "Greg was out for the count, so our scrum half Joe—who's first-aid trained—came running over, meaning to put him in the recovery position, but Coach said it was best to leave him alone. Somebody, Gareth I think it was, called an ambulance, while Joe kept an eye on Greg to make sure he was breathing okay."

Greg, Gareth, Big somebody or other. Robin was glad that Pru was keeping a record of all the names to compare with their notes. The arrival of a waiter with coffees a few seconds later was very welcome, letting Robin get his head round the characters and emotions involved that night.

Once the waiter had gone again, Andy continued. "Eventually I took Dave off to the side of the pitch, because he was getting himself into a hell of a state. I kept telling him it had been an accident, and he kept saying that he hadn't meant to dip his shoulder as he went into the collision. He was rambling, going on about how he wished it had been him who'd been injured, how he'd never forgive himself, and how Dawn was going to kill him."

Robin wasn't unsympathetic. He could imagine what Dave had been thinking, wondering if things would have turned out okay if he'd taken the tackle at a different angle, or whether it might have made things worse. Wanting to go back in time and replay the moment, changing the outcome. "We've not been to the ground yet. Could you draw us a rough sketch of where everything is, and what part of the pitch the accident happened on?" He produced a notepad and pen.

"Yeah, of course." Andy set to, talking as he drew. "Typical multipurpose place. Athletics, rugby, training. There's a stand along the home straight—there's the rugby pitch touchline running alongside. The bar-cum-clubhouse takes up half the bottom of the stand and the changing rooms are at the back and side. You get to them through this tunnel, right by the twenty-two. Go down there, then turn right. There's no external door to the changing rooms, but there's a direct door though to the clubhouse."

"Is that the only door to the clubhouse?" Robin asked.

"No, there's three altogether. One out the back and another into the tunnel. You need them to cope with the postmatch rush."

Robin bent his head over the paper. "Can you see the bar from the pitch?"

"Nope. The bar area windows are mainly at the side, with a row of small ones facing the pitch, but they only really let in a bit of light. The bar seating area is under the spectator seating, if that makes sense."

Which meant somebody could go in there and hang about, unnoticed.

"Where did the accident happen?" Pru asked.

Andy placed his finger on the diagram. "Greg went down here, five metres in from the far touchline, roughly on the twenty-two that's farthest from the tunnel. The bar end. When I took Dave off to talk him down from the ledge, we came over to the grandstand, to get him away."

Robin was impressed. Both the map and the explanation were clear and concise. Here was a witness you could put into the box and a jury would believe him.

"I guess you were all pretty distracted at that point?" Pru asked. "Could anyone have got in or out of the tunnel then? Or the bar?"

"The bar's kept locked, so unless they had the keys, they'd have no chance. We might not have seen them, though. When you're under the lights everything off the pitch is rather fuzzy."

"And the tunnel?"

"Nobody could have sneaked in or out after Dave and I went and stood by where we'd all left our kit. I know that for a fact. It's possible they might have done previously, given that we were preoccupied what with training and then the accident. I've had a think, since, and I'm pretty sure I can account for me, Dave, Coach, and Greg from the moment we went out to practice until the point Dave found the body. Nick's body, although we didn't know that at the time. I couldn't swear to where any of the others were, though. Coach would have noticed if they were skiving off training, but once Greg went down, everyone's attention was focussed on him."

Apart from the killer's, presumably. Shame that the medical report couldn't tie the time of death down to a more specific window than between seven and eight o'clock, give or take a few minutes either way—although there was corroborative evidence concerning when the changing room had been empty. Vacated by seven and occupied by around a quarter past eight, all of which Robin would double-check now.

"I'd like to get the timescale clear. What time was the last person out of the changing room and onto the pitch for practice?"

"Seven o'clock, on the dot." Andy grinned. "I know because it was Big Dave and he got the traditional fine for being tail-end Charlie. And before you ask, there was nobody in the loos before the rest of us came out."

"Okay. At what time did Greg have his accident?"

Andy's brow wrinkled. "Somewhere around eight o'clock, I guess."

That chimed with the 999 call that had been logged a few minutes after then. As suspected, something like an hour's window for both victim and murderer to get into the changing rooms.

"I have to ask," Pru said, "why do you call him *Big* Dave?"

"He's been my mate since primary school. I used to get picked on, but then he moved into the area and we became besties. He was built like the side of a barn even then—hence the nickname—so nobody was going to be stupid enough to get on the wrong side of him, although he's actually as easy-going as they come. Gentle giant."

Robin had his own gentle giant at home. Campbell might have been large and imposing, but he was soft as a goose feather.

Andy frowned. "You know, I've been kicking myself. Thinking about what we know now that we didn't then, things might have turned out different, because we almost went back into the changing rooms earlier. I'd grabbed Dave's arm and said it was no use freezing our ball— backsides off hanging about, but he wasn't having it. He wanted to stay until the paramedics arrived, because he was determined to tell them exactly what happened. Said he knew Greg would have wanted him to wait there. Daft sod, but there was no moving him. I got us our track suits from where we'd left them by the side of the pitch, and we put them on. Then the paramedics arrived."

"Did Dave go and talk to them?"

"No, I managed to stop him from going and describing the tackle in detail. Joe was already miming the impact, demonstrating where and how Greg's head had been hit. Dave nearly fainted when he saw that. I asked him if he wanted me to get the paramedics to check him over too, but he said he was fine. Simply a jolt to his shoulder."

Last out of the changing room, reluctant to go back in there: Dave's actions might have been entirely innocent, but they'd bear further investigation. Was it possible that his coming over faint at the reconstruction of the accident was less about the tackle than the fact he'd bashed someone over the head earlier that evening?

Pru's thoughts were clearly going down the same lines. "I know he's your mate, so this is going to seem a pretty harsh thing to ask, but did you believe him? I mean, did anything strike you as suspicious about how he was acting? Or anyone else was acting," she added, hastily, as Andy's face had turned thunderous.

"You lay off Dave. I've known him long enough to realise he's no actor. What you see is what you get. And what I saw was him wanting to go in the ambulance with Greg because he reckoned he needed somebody with him until Dawn got there. It was only when Dave said that we realised nobody might have rung her, yet."

Was that an honest assessment of the situation or a neat sidestep of the real question?

"Did Dave want to make the call?" Robin asked.

"You've got him sussed. Yep, insisted he should be the one to relay the bad news, but he was in no state to ring anyone. I decided to ask Coach if Dawn had been contacted."

Robin glanced at the diagram Andy had drawn. "Did Dave stay by the grandstand?"

"Nah. He tagged behind. Short of tying him to one of the railings, I couldn't stop him."

"Who rang the girlfriend?"

"Coach. He's got the knack with these things."

"Which means?" Pru asked.

"If there's a shitty job to do, he steps up to the plate and does it better than any of us would. He gets on with all the partners—female or male. Coach bats for the same team as me, see, and while he's never said anything much about his private life, we all know that his lodger, Steve, isn't only his lodger." Andy rolled his eyes. "Shame that generation didn't have the same freedom to come out as we do."

"Same applies to some people in this generation. You don't have to be in a third-world country to risk everything by admitting what you are." Robin halted, aware that he was preaching to a pair of people who least needed it. Also aware that he was at risk of coming out himself and that wasn't relevant to the situation.

"You're right. I don't know what pressures Coach has on him."

Pru gently brought them back to the matter in hand. "Mr. Preese rang Dawn? Given what we now know, it's important we have all the details."

"Yes, he rang her. He walked off a few yards, so that Dawn wouldn't hear all the hoo-hah, which means I don't know precisely what was said. He just told us she'd be going to the hospital as soon as she could. That she'd been having a couple of glasses of wine at a mate's house and didn't want to drive until she'd got some coffee into her and no longer risked being over the limit."

Again, that could all be true or it could be part of an elaborately constructed alibi for Melanie. Robin asked, "What happened then?"

"Coach got to work on Dave. Persuaded him not to go driving off after the ambulance as he'd be another accident waiting to happen. Asked me to run the bloke to the hospital." Andy frowned.

"Ye-es? Is there a problem?"

"I was trying to relive what happened next. I remember suggesting we go and have a shower, and Dave insisting that we should go to the hospital straight away. Coach put his foot down and said he'd make sure one of the players went with Greg in the ambulance. He also told me to get the smelly bugger—his words, meaning Dave—to have a shower and get changed before we went."

Again, Dave not wanting to go into the changing room. And *he'd* wanted to be the one to ring Dawn: evidence of collusion or evidence of the workings of Robin's oversuspicious mind?

"Okay, to clarify, again, Mr. Preese was the one who persuaded him to go and clean up first?"

Andy nodded. "The rest of us were being pretty useless apart from Joe and his first aid. Anyway, Coach said that the accident and emergency department staff wouldn't appreciate having a muddy, sweaty lump of lard hanging around trailing grass across their nice clean waiting area."

Robin grinned, imagining some of the rugby coaches he'd known saying the same thing. He nodded for Andy to continue.

"I took Dave off to the dressing room where we had a quick shower, then changed back into our normal clobber. Before we left, Dave said he wanted to use the loo. I wondered if that was an excuse, if he needed some time to pull himself together before we went to the hospital. I got a hell of a shock when he screamed, because I immediately assumed he was having a nervous breakdown or something. I hared in there, asking if he was okay, which is when I saw it too. Saw him, I mean."

The body sitting slumped on a cubicle seat: Robin had seen the pictures from the crime scene. No wonder Dave had screamed when he'd swung the door open. "Can you do me another diagram? One of the changing rooms and where the showers and loos are?"

"Yep." Andy took the paper again, sketching it out. The tunnel took a sharp bend to the right, with a door into the changing area. Right turn from there into a small area for cleaning boots and storage. Straight ahead had you facing the entrance to the showers, with the changing area on the left, occupying the long part of the room. The toilets were at the far left, two cubicles needing a right turn to get to them. The door to the bar was at that end too. "We try to keep all the mud and muck up one end, but it doesn't always work. You can't see into either the showers or the loos from the changing area itself, which is why we didn't see . . . him . . . until we went in there."

"That's different from when I was playing."

"We got a lottery grant to update the facility a few years back, and one of the considerations was ensuring privacy if people wanted it."

"And where does the opposition change?" Pru asked.

Andy pointed at an area just to the right of the tunnel entrance. "Their changing room and showers are here. There's a door almost by the tunnel entrance. Home and away teams separate for the rugby, male and female for the athletics."

Robin was starting to get a clearer picture. Plenty of places for somebody to hide in if they had the right keys. "What did you do when you found the body?"

"Manhandled Dave out of the toilet area, for a start, before he puked on the crime scene. Then I got my phone to ring 999 while I sent Dave out to warn the others. I hovered at the entrance to the changing rooms, making sure nobody went in, then Coach came up the tunnel and told us not to move anything until the police gave us permission. He always knows what to do. I thought it was lucky that I'd brought mine and Dave's bags out already."

A case of either luck or good thinking. Robin hoped the officers on the scene hadn't let the pair swan off without having those bags checked.

"Did you recognise the victim?" Pru asked.

"No, although I've got to admit I didn't take a proper look. I'm rather squeamish when it comes to blood and gore and when I saw his bashed-in skull, that was it. Couldn't get away quick enough." Andy gave Pru a sheepish grin. "Typical rugby player. All brawn, but a big, wet lettuce with it."

"What did you notice near the body?"

"Nothing. They asked about that before. Seemed to be searching for a phone, but I didn't see that." Andy shrugged.

"What happened then?" Pru asked.

"The police arrived. Good timing, because we almost had a riot on our hands. The paramedics had got Greg into the ambulance and the other players wanted to get changed. Even Coach was struggling to control them. We could have opened the other changing room, but that would have been no good without people having their gear." Andy shrugged. "Then Dave and I showed the police the dead bloke and they took a brief statement from us about how and when we'd found him. Then they went into a conflab with Coach about how to get the mutiny quelled."

"Not an easy task." Robin recalled dealing with a similar situation when he was a junior officer. Taking a list of names and addresses, doing a quick search of bags to make sure no weapons were being sneaked off the premises. The most galling part was the fact it had been a bunch of old ladies who'd caused the most trouble and had complained the loudest.

"I didn't envy them it. I only had Dave moaning at me, wanting to get to the hospital and find out what was happening with Greg. They had best part of forty blokes causing a fuss."

Robin hoped that the officers in charge had been effective in managing the situation—he'd get Pru to delve into that little matter—so nobody had slipped through the net or managed to conceal something. Although only the most stupid of murderers would have left an incriminating article in the changing room when the dead body was so easily discoverable and a clampdown on the site would inevitably follow. Didn't most people have a good idea of what happened at crime scenes given how often they were depicted on the telly?

"You definitely didn't know the dead man?" he asked.

"Nope." Andy peered at the diagram again, as though the answer might be found there. "Mind you, there have been so many pictures of him in the media since then, I've begun to doubt myself. I might have met him once, but his face didn't ring a bell at the time we found him."

"But he was connected to your group of friends, surely?" Pru said, with surprising determination. "Through Greg and Dawn."

"Yeah, well, that was a shock. We had no idea. He doesn't—didn't—hang around with us. Melanie didn't, either. She was Dawn's pal, not Greg's."

There didn't seem to be much further to be gained from the interview. Robin concluded it with the usual reminder that if Andy remembered anything else that might be significant, he was to get in touch.

"I'll do that." Andy made a sheepish grin. "Look, I know this is being cheeky, but can I give you a flyer? We're fundraising for Greg and Dawn, and I thought maybe you could put this up in the station canteen, if there is one?"

"I've no idea if there is or not. We've not been there yet. But I'll take it." Robin cast a glance at the sheet, which listed the range of activities planned to raise money. He passed it to Pru, who raised an eyebrow, then carefully filed the flyer in her briefcase.

Back in the car, Pru had barely started the engine when she said, "What did you think of that? Is it me or did that interview raise a heap of questions?"

"It's not only you—I've got half a dozen. I've been wondering whether it's possible to plan a rugby accident. Seems rather an extreme way either to create a diversion, or delay the body being discovered, though."

"Callous, as well."

"Unless Greg was faking it, although that would make the fundraising a smokescreen too." Robin gazed out of the window, watching the unfamiliar buildings go by. "We're probably running before we can walk, but I've a list of things I want checked. Greg's condition. What happened at the scene on the night, and whether Dave's and Andy's bags got checked properly."

Adam would have called that his rozzer's nose twitching. Robin had told him it was experience, the subtle signs you had to keep an eye out for, like Adam would be aware of what signals children gave off when they were up to no good.

"There certainly seems something odd about Dave not wanting to go into the changing rooms and Coach insisting he did so."

"Derek Preese, not Coach. You're showing your natural leaning towards the rugby crowd." Robin chuckled.

Pru deftly manoeuvred a tricky roundabout, showing an expertise in her driving that Robin's previous sergeant had never managed. "Dave was last out of the changing rooms too. And what about Mr. Preese himself, worrying about a spot of mud being dragged into the hospital? They've seen it all in casualty, so a bit of dirt wouldn't bother them. Why was he so insistent Dave and Andy went to clean themselves up?"

"Maybe he was thinking of Greg. If Dave was fussing like an old biddy, he might have thought it better he had time to calm down before travelling. Not that I haven't wondered if he meant them to find the body." Always knew what to do and always in charge. "Here, is that the rugby ground?"

"I didn't notice. Eyes on the road." Pru snorted. "Want me to do a one eighty at the roundabout ahead?"

"Please." Best to get a clear view of the crime scene in their mind. "I thought I saw somebody cutting the pitch, so we might get a look around."

They did better than a look around. The groundsman had driven his mower over at their approach, wearing a face like thunder, although as soon as they'd flashed their warrant cards and made an introduction, his attitude had transformed.

"I thought you were the press. If you were, I'd have chased you off." He held out his hand. "Call me Tom, everybody does. I hear you've taken over because the other officer is unwell."

"Yes. Word spreads here, doesn't it?"

"Blame Derek, the rugby coach. He knows everything. Want a tour of this place?"

"Just a quick once-over," Robin said. "Have you had much trouble with the media, then?"

"On and off. I caught one of them—he'd nipped over the gate—trying to get into the clubhouse so he could take pictures of where that poor bugger was found, but I saw him off. Whacking great bruise on his leg with it." Tom gave Pru a pleading smile. "You won't do me for assault?"

"Not if he hasn't complained. Only don't do it again." Pru flashed him a smile and they set off.

Andy's sketch had been spot-on, so they got their bearings quickly. It also became apparent why the house-to-house enquiries locally had yielded nothing. The only nearby residential properties were behind the sports ground left of the clubhouse and would only have had a view from their upstairs windows, given the high conifer hedge that ran along the boundary of the site. The wrong side to see anyone getting in and out of the bar area. Roads on another two sides and an industrial estate on the fourth, which was likely empty in the evening.

As he, Pru, and the groundsman entered the tunnel, Robin asked, "How many people have keys to here?"

Tom blew out his cheeks. "There's a question. Too many, probably, by the time you account for both the rugby team and the athletics section. Coaches, volunteer bar staff, Uncle Tom Cobbley, and all. I could get you a list, if you gave me a few days, but I can't promise it would be a complete one. Plus, it wouldn't take account of anybody who'd made themselves a key or two on the q.t."

"Indeed. We'd appreciate that list, though. Thank you." Robin felt a twinge of surprise that the police hadn't already asked the groundsman for a list of keyholders, but he'd give the team the benefit of the doubt on that one for the moment, because they might have made the request of somebody else. He pointed at the away dressing room. "Can we examine this changing room, please?"

"You can examine where you like." Tom unlocked the door. "I'll admit I've had a good poke in all the nooks and crannies since we were allowed back on the premises. I expect your crime-scene people do a good job, but they don't know this club like I do. Didn't find anything unexpected, though," he added, with a grin. "My pals at the pub say I've been watching too many detective shows on the telly and fancy myself as Hercule Poirot, which is probably true, because I've been thinking this out all ways up."

None of Robin, Pru or the wannabee detective groundsman found any surprises whilst on their tour, even though they visited all the parts of the clubhouse and kept their eyes peeled.

"If I wanted to get in and out of here without being seen from the pitch, I'd have to come through from the bar, wouldn't I?" Pru said, as they reached the toilet area where the body had been found. "And I'd need a key to open the door."

Tom rubbed his chin. "Not necessarily. I've been having a think about this. Assuming that the rugby lads have got it right when they say nobody slipped into the tunnel while they were practicing, the obvious thing is to think somebody used the connecting door. Two people, if you count the victim and the murderer. You could have hidden in the away dressing room if you had a key to that, then slipped up the tunnel once all the players had gone out to practice. Unlikely you'd be seen from the pitch. Although why either of them would have wanted to go into the changing rooms in the first place beats me."

"Maybe one of them was caught short." Pru didn't sound like she was making a serious suggestion. Robin could think of other reasons blokes hung around in loos, but there'd been no hint of recent sexual activity in the postmortem report and anyway, if you were cottaging, wouldn't you pick somewhere you wouldn't be interrupted by a couple of dozen burly rugby players?

"Maybe. But if they needed the toilet, why not use the ones that are accessed off the bar area?" Tom shrugged.

"What about robbery?" Robin proposed. "There was a spate of it in sports clubs around Abbotston, where we're based. Some toerag waited until everyone was occupied out on the pitch learning the line-out calls for the next weekend or whatever, then nipped in and helped himself to cash and mobile phones. They only caught him because one of the devices had the Find My Friends app turned on. The police never seem to think of that on the telly, do they, when they're trying to track someone down?"

Tom chuckled. "I bet you shout at all the TV cop shows."

"I threaten to kick the television. Anyway, this player's girlfriend thought he was cheating on her when his phone showed he was three roads away rather than at the ground. Sergeant, would you like to finish the story?"

Pru, who'd been grinning, said, "She stormed round to give him what for and ended up helping to make an arrest, having taken her pal with her for moral support. Me."

Tom shook his head. "You must have a few tales to tell. Take your time in here, then we'll visit the bar area when you're done. We'll have to go the long way, out of the tunnel and round the building, as the only door to the bar that's not kept bolted is the one leading from the outside."

Tom took himself off, leaving them to it, although apart from getting their bearings, visiting the scene hadn't helped much.

Pru idly turned the handle of the connecting door to the bar. "Locked doors don't always signify much, in my mind. Easy enough to get your hand on keys and make a copy of them if you're determined on getting access. Or nick a set. If this is like the sports clubs I grew up knowing, some of the keyholders never have any cause to use the things but refuse to give them up after twenty years of possession. Point of principle. One of those people might easily have misplaced theirs and been reluctant to own up to the fact."

Robin had been thinking much the same. "Nothing much else to see here. Let's see if Tom knows when the locks were last changed."

It turned out that the locks had all been replaced three years previously, when the buildings had undergone the major refurbishment Andy had told them about. That narrowed the timescale for accessing keys and put the long-term forgetful keyholder out of the frame.

They made their way round the front of the grandstand, down the side, and around the corner to the access door, Robin noting that it wouldn't have been in view from the car park. The bar resembled every sports ground bar that Robin had been in. "You must know this place like the back of your hand. Have you noticed anything unusual since the night of the murder?"

Tom shook his head. "Not heard reports of stuff having been nicked, if that's what you're thinking."

"What about this?" Pru pointed to a team photo, one of many on the wall nearest the tunnel. Alone among them, the glass was cracked.

Tom peered at it, then said angrily, "Nobody's owned up to doing that."

Probably because they didn't want a kick up the backside.

"I suppose someone was arsing about and it went too far. I need to take it down and get it mended." He was reaching out when Pru's hand on his arm forestalled him.

"Please don't," she said firmly. "We'll need to do some tests on that. Any idea when it happened?"

Tom shrugged. "Might have been months ago. You can't see the cracks unless they catch the light."

"We'll get something to wrap it in and take it away." Although what it might tell them, Robin couldn't say. Unless, he realised, it related to the abrasions that had been found on the victim's fingers, according to the post-mortem report.

They finished in the bar, then circled the building, noting what must be the groundsmen's shed and an equipment store. They passed a bench that bore an engraved plate. "Who's that for?" Pru asked.

"Young rugby player, killed in an accident. Sorry, I find it all really difficult to talk about." Tom took a deep breath, clearly unsettled, and who could blame him at the thought of a life cut short? "It used to be at the front of the stand, so that players or coaching staff could use it during matches. But some mindless twat—or twats—got in here a few weeks back and knocked it about. I'm going to spruce it up again."

"Good man." Robin hated that kind of idle vandalism. Although what if the relocated bench had been an unexpected aid to gaining access? "Is there any way into the changing rooms from out here? Windows or whatever?"

"Not unless you can jump like a kangaroo and you're shaped like a beanpole, as you can see." Tom was right. The only windows were ten feet off the ground and their shape defied access through them.

"This has obviously upset you," Pru said, pointing at the bench. "Were you friends with the young man who died?"

"More than that. He was my son." Tom ran the back of his hand across his brow. "Come on, I'll show you the rest of the place."

He set off, Robin and Pru exchanging glances in his wake. No wonder the bloke had been dismayed at the vandalism.

By the time they'd seen every one of the nooks and crannies the groundsman had mentioned, Robin was convinced that you could only have got in and out unseen if you had keys, albeit then it would have been relatively easy.

"What are the chances the rugby lads would have missed seeing somebody entering the tunnel, given they'd have been busy working out line-out calls or whatever?" he asked.

"Slim but realistic, especially if they were working on a move on the other side of the pitch." Tom nibbled at his bottom lip. "But you see, as Poirot might say, the getting in and out is the easy part of the puzzle. People aren't as careful with their keys as they should be."

On the way back to the car, Pru said, "Poirot might say that, but as far as I'm concerned, it's all about *why* both victim and killer came here, and why they went in those toilets. That's the key question."

Robin had to agree with her.

Chapter Three

Hartwood police station was located in a spanking new, purpose-built building, making the Abbotston equivalent—1960s build and thought of as cutting edge at the time—look like it came out of the Victorian era. Cowdrey had told Robin and Pru not to get too comfortable working in these flash new offices as there was no prospect of *their* station being upgraded anytime soon. The old Hartwood building had outlived its purpose and the money needed to upgrade it had been better spent on starting all over again. Especially as the old site was prime building land, so they'd made a profit on selling it. Some of the original structure would apparently be retained and made into executive flats at eye-watering prices; welcome to the twenty-first century.

Betteridge was there to meet them, beaming with delight—most likely at seeing Robin again—and apologising for not having kept in touch beyond a card at Christmas.

"Loved the one with the dog on. Does he really have five legs and a tail?"

"Artistic licence." Robin grinned. Last Christmas, their card had been designed by one of Adam's pupils and had been an enormous hit.

"I'm afraid I can't stay long. Got this big county lines drugs bust about to go down and so I need to be elsewhere." Betteridge's expression registered her distaste. "Please keep me in touch with developments as a matter of urgency."

That seemed reasonable, given that this case had already gone nearly two weeks without any appreciable progress being made.

Betteridge was letting Robin have a free hand, but she was the one who had to deal with the media, so the more information she had before facing them, the better.

"That's part of the job I never envy," Robin said, remembering how the press had clustered around Lindenshaw school during the first murder investigation he led. The one that had been life changing on all counts, not just for his career. He quickly changed the mental subject, not wanting to dwell on Adam and the prospect of being away from him.

"Necessary evil." Betteridge jerked her thumb over her shoulder. "Let's go and meet your team. They're less intimidating."

As Betteridge took them through the building, Robin found the interior was as impressive as the exterior, although the incident room resembled others he'd known, as he found while viewing it through the internal window. The usual information board with pictures and notes and arrows linking things all on display. Around the room, an array of desks and computers and shiny-faced officers, all of them heads down and industrious, clearly trying to impress. Those heads—two male, one female—shot up as Betteridge, Robin, and Pru came through the door.

Betteridge's bright "Morning, all!" produced three responses of "Morning, ma'am."

"I'm not stopping, but I wanted to do this personally." She gestured towards Robin and Pru. "Chief Inspector Robin Bright and Sergeant Pru Davis. I'll let them introduce themselves. This is Robertson's team—Callum Keyworth, Laurence Beaumont, and Sally Cotton. I'll give you two things to mull over before I go. One is that I've seen coincidences in real life that you could never put in a book because they're too outrageous. The other is that you've maybe only got one coincidence here—the training accident. All the other strands might be linked, so not coincidental at all. I'll see you when I see you. Wish me luck."

Robin did exactly that, then gave the constables a very brief account of his background, although the young officers clearly had already heard of him, perhaps from Betteridge herself. He asked them to talk him through the case, not simply what had been found out so far, but their own impressions and ideas, the sort of things he'd pick up from his own team of constables that would be subsequently sifted through and any gems identified.

Callum—a shaggy-haired lad, facially similar to the rugby player Maro Itoje but half the size—went first, giving a logical, lucid account of how and when the body had been found and what the postmortem had shown up.

"Victim was a thirty-year-old male in good physical condition. He'd had a couple of head wounds, one relatively superficial and the other decisive, inflicted on him by an instrument of exact type unknown."

"Anything else on the body?"

Callum consulted his notes. "There were also some abrasions on the victim's fingers, fresh enough to have been done within the hours before death. Not defensive wounds, the medical guru thinks, but as though he'd been scrabbling about with something liable to scratch. Brambles, maybe, or something metal with sharp edges. It's the coincidences I don't like, sir," he concluded. "I know weird things happen in real life, but this bloke being killed at the same place as where his wife's best mate's partner is attending rugby training, at the same time as those two women are having a girl's night in. Oh, and the partner's getting a horrible injury while this is all going on?"

"You're suspicious of everything," the other male constable, Laurence, said. This officer had immediately reminded Robin somewhat of Ben, one of his Abbotston team, with the same smiling willingness to help, although there the resemblance ended. Ben had a stocky scrum half–style build, while Laurence was what Robin's mum would call a long streak of water out of the tap. He towered over Robin by a good five inches, and when sitting at his desk, the furniture appeared to be doll's house sized. Still, Betteridge had reckoned he showed promise, and Robin hoped she was—as usual—right.

"I'm suspicious about the same thing." Robin gave them all a smile. Betteridge hadn't warned him about any tensions within the team, so hopefully this was nothing other than banter being exchanged. "Sally, where are your thoughts on this?"

The constable shifted in her seat, clearly uncomfortable at being put in the spotlight. "If I'm honest, I can just about buy that Melanie could be creating an alibi for herself while somebody else did in her old man—you always start with family and friends, don't you?—but I don't see how this rugby injury comes into it. That's a conspiracy theory too far. And we don't really know how close the timings of the two are."

"Do you think Melanie has motive?" Laurence asked.

Sally flashed him a scowl. "I never said that."

Pru—thank God she was here to pour oil on what might be turbulent waters—said, "You didn't. But you were right about starting with those closest to the victim. Is there any reason why she, or anybody else in his circle of family or friends, should have wanted him got rid of?"

"Nothing obvious. Nobody's hinted at marital problems. He wasn't the easiest bloke to get on with, though, according to his boss. Type who's always itching for a fight, especially when he's had a few." Sally glanced at her colleagues, who nodded their agreement.

Time to get some input from Laurence. "What about the forensics? Are they telling us anything about the killer?"

Laurence thrust out his lip. "Not much. The scenario appears to be that the first injury to the victim's head might possibly have been accidental, then he was finished off, dragged to that cubicle, and pushed onto the seat. The weapon—of which there's no sign—could have been anything large and heavy enough. There are no indications in the wound of what exactly we're looking for, although the signs are it's something made of steel, with powder-coated paint. Not much sign of a struggle either, in terms of the victim, apart from those odd marks on his hands. There was some bruising on his backside, as though he'd been hit there too, but that was a few days old. All in all, it points to him being attacked by an assailant who easily overpowered him and could manhandle him into the loos. Although Osment wasn't that big a bloke, so it doesn't narrow the field much."

"He could have been attacked by somebody he wasn't wary of," Sally pointed out, "who got in close, then walloped him when he was down. Either knew where to hit to avoid making much of a mess or got lucky first time. If the victim cried out, there was nobody around to hear."

"Which suggests the killer knew the training-night routine." Robin turned to study the incident board, with its picture of the victim's battered head. "What if they got *unlucky*? Didn't mean to kill, only stun him, but when they realised what they'd done, they dumped the body and scarpered. Laurence, you said the first injury might have been accidental. Want to expand on that?"

"The CSI found blood and hair that matched the victim on the corner on one of the benches in the changing room, and spots of blood underneath it. He could have initially been pushed, but he might have simply fallen and he was finished off there."

"Which could have rendered him incapable of fighting back." Robin, done with the picture, turned around. "The killer must have got some blood spatter on them and the weapon they used, you'd have thought. No sign of a trail? Or discarded clothes?"

Laurence consulted his notes. "Crime scene officer reckons there were spots of blood from where the body had been dragged and then deposited. She felt that it might have been a rushed job, maybe to get him out of the changing room and buy a bit of time, but that was a gut feeling. There's also evidence that somebody, possibly the killer, had one of those heavy-duty plastic bags with them. There was a fragment of black plastic snagged on the door of the loo. Trouble is that the two blokes who found the body clouded the issue where they'd gone in to see what had happened. There was the odd spot of blood in the main part of the changing room, but that's possibly from where Dave passed through to go and get help."

Dave and his mate again. *Deliberately messing up the crime scene?*

Callum raised a hand. "There's another thing, sir. We've not had a proper statement from the wife, yet."

Pru shot Robin a puzzled glance. "Why's that? It's been nearly two weeks."

"She's apparently been too ill. Inspector Robertson and I went to question her the day after it happened, but the doctor was there with her. Said she'd had a slight breakdown, was going to stay at her mum's, and that we were under his orders to leave her alone until she was feeling better."

"That sounds a touch too convenient," Robin said.

"That's what we thought." Callum nodded at Sally. "Robertson said that when you've seen as many family members weeping and wailing about their dear departed as she was, only for it to turn out that the ones who appear to have taken it hardest are the ones who are as guilty as sin, then you become cynical. Still, these days the police always have to keep their noses clean and harassing a distressed widow wouldn't go down well in the local media."

"Especially as she appears to have an unbreakable alibi," Pru observed. "We need to talk to her, though. Any idea when she's available?"

Robin suppressed a grin: his sergeant knew as well as he did that they'd lined up an interview with Melanie the next day, Betteridge having exerted pressure on the doctor. This question was a test to see how much the team had been told or how much they'd be prepared to share.

"Anytime we want, from now on," Callum replied. "The superintendent got the doctor to agree, but we've been holding fire until you arrived. Hope that was okay?"

The test had been passed, at least for the moment.

"I'd probably have made the same decision in your position," Robin said. "We want to see all the main witnesses for ourselves, anyway. Not that we think you missed anything, but because we want to hear things firsthand. Watch people's faces while they answer our questions. Pru and I have some interviews lined up for tomorrow, and we'll want one of you to come along with each of us. We'll sort that this evening. Now," he jerked his thumb in the direction of the board, "this alibi of hers. Dawn and the wine bottle. Is it really unbreakable?"

Sally shrugged. "Seems like it. They were Skyping one of their pals who moved over to Massachusetts last year. At around the time the husband was being killed." She raised her hands. "Yeah, that looks suspicious too, but unless it turns out they're all in it together, the wife couldn't have been at the sports ground. Dawn says the timing has actually made it worse for Melanie. You know, the fact that she'd been drinking and making jokes while somebody was walloping her husband."

"Somebody that *she* could have put up to doing the job," Pru pointed out. Nobody disagreed.

The briefing wound up with some setting of standards—Robin expected people to do what was asked of them and to hit their deadlines, and in return he'd always be available should he be needed and he'd always listen to any ideas the constables had.

"Believe me," he said, backing towards the corner desk that he'd decided to appropriate in lieu of having his own office, "Pru and I are bound to have heard dafter things from our own officers, and I've known chance remarks which have been the breakthrough to solving a major case."

That might have been a slight exaggeration, but it appeared to make the team relax a bit. *What they needed.* Robin would have to forge new working relationships quickly, and he didn't really have capacity to deal with his constables' hesitancy. They had a murder to solve.

Monday evening, Adam settled himself on the settee with football on the telly and Campbell gently snoring on the rug. Robin had touched base earlier—he and Pru had arrived safely and they had some ideas to follow on the case, but seeing as he'd already tempted fate this week and been caught out, he'd not be getting ahead of himself.

Adam's phone buzzed with another incoming message.

Wanted to say good night. I'll ring properly tomorrow before breakfast.

Adam was desperate to hear Robin's voice. *That'll be great. I've had a thrilling evening poring over some updated Ofsted guidance and other exhilarating reading.* He'd done that over his dinner, not having anyone to talk to apart from the dog.

It's all thrills, isn't it? Love you.

Love you too.

Now Adam had the rest of the evening to chill out. But he was restless, in a way he'd not been restless either before Robin came into his life or when he was working late on a local case. He'd not even felt like this the odd occasions Robin had been away overnight at a conference.

You're turning into an old married man.

He'd need to find something to occupy himself while Robin was in Hartwood, something beyond work or watching Premier League prima donnas on the gogglebox.

The incoming email alert flashing on his phone brought a welcome distraction. Hopefully it wouldn't be a notification that the

Ofsted schedule had changed yet again, at the point when he'd got his head around the latest version, although chances were it was simply an advert.

Adam opened his inbox, to find a mailing sent out to what Neil the vicar called the Big List, which comprised everyone in the St. Crispin's congregation who made use of emails. It was an appeal but this one was different. Martin, the choirmaster, was on the hunt for volunteers to take part in a fundraising concert. Proceeds were going to a rugby player who'd been badly injured in a freak training accident and whose friends were trying to raise money to have the flat he was buying with his girlfriend properly adapted to his needs.

Adam read the email twice, then snorted so loud he woke the dog.

"Sorry, old boy."

Another instance of Robin's cases wanting to intertwine themselves with his life? He clicked on the link Martin had provided to the information page, prepared for what he'd find. Yep, this was the guy who'd been injured the same night and at the same place as the murder that Robin had gone to investigate, exactly the sort of thing Adam should be steering clear of. He should simply delete the email, tell anyone who asked that he was too busy, and not risk another murder case trying to draw him in. Trouble was, he'd been mulling over the idea of joining a choir since Mrs. Haig had suggested it. Martin was asking interested parties to go to the church the next evening, with a view to getting this project started as soon as possible. What better way of occupying himself while Robin was away?

He read the email a third time, then told himself not to be a silly sod. How could getting involved with this fundraising effort in any way embroil him with the case? A sharper prick to his conscience was a whimper from Campbell, who'd drifted back to sleep. He'd be bereft enough without his other dad, so what would he think of being left alone evenings and weekends or whenever Adam was required for rehearsals? Suddenly remembering a conversation a couple of months back, when Martin had been trying to inveigle him and Robin into joining the church choir, he recalled how Martin had graciously said that if they ever changed their minds about joining, not only would they be very welcome, but so would their dog, who could sit in a corner of the church and snooze during choir practice. Would that offer apply to the concert rehearsals? There was only one way to find out. Adam dialled the number given in the email and waited.

"Hello?"

"Martin?"

"Ye-es?" The choirmaster sounded uncertain, although given that the email had just gone out, surely he was prepared for folk ringing him out of the blue.

"Adam Matthews here. I saw your email about a local choir. Raising money for that rugby player who was hurt. I wanted to ask you a few things."

"Excellent." There was a distinct note of relief in Martin's voice. "Are you interested in joining us?"

"I am, so long as the timings work out. Can I bring Campbell along, if I need to? The dog."

"He'd be very welcome. Does he sing bass by any chance? And what about that fellah of yours?"

"I'm afraid he's away on secondment at the moment, hence me wanting to bring the dog sometimes. Are you doing okay for numbers? I could ask around."

"That's kind, but I think we'll be all right. I got the core of people involved before I put it out to the Big List. You know how it is, a few cautious yeses have become a definite *I'm in*. I'd say we're almost there. We're working on a set list too." Any awkwardness had now gone from Martin's voice. "As a way to generate money, it's solid. It should appeal to a different range of people, other than the rugby crowd. I'm guessing they'd support the venture no matter how awful we sound. Which we won't, by the way."

"I would hope not. Is it simply the concert we're doing?"

"No. It's a mate of mine organising this—he's the boyfriend of one of the players on the team. He's got half a dozen choirs holding concerts, and he's going to produce a CD of us all. Some tracks with only one choir and then some clever techie stuff to make it sound like we're all singing the same song at the same time. I'm not sure how that works, but Tim says it'll be stunning."

This all sounded like something Adam wanted to be a part of. "If the final CD's good enough, you could potentially get a much wider range of people buying it, not only the usual friends and family of those taking part."

"Absolutely. I know from experience that there'll be a limited number of folk who'll dig in their pockets to buy a copy irrespective of whether it turns out to be absolute pants, because their grandson's involved and they want one up on the neighbours whose grandson's a layabout." Martin chortled. "Then once they've swanked over the garden hedge, they'll probably stuff the disc in a drawer and never listen to it. If we could access people who want the CD for the music itself, not only will it bring in more money, but it'll give everyone involved a boost. You don't happen to know any pop or rock stars, to increase the potential saleability?"

"None, I'm afraid. There used to be some sixties rocker lived in the old Lindenshaw manor house, but he's long gone." Possibly literally long gone given the state he was in when Adam last saw him. "Have we got anyone with nous for publicity?"

"That's an idea. Nobody in the choir, as far as I'm aware, but I've a tone-deaf mate who's in the business. Advises charities on their social media profiles. I'll get in touch. Good thinking, Batman."

Was that a bad joke picking up on his relationship with somebody called Robin? Adam wasn't going to ask. "The email says the first meet up is tomorrow."

"Yes. Seven thirty, in the church because the table tennis league has the hall on Tuesdays. Even if we haven't got a full choir complement by then, we can make a start."

"I'll be there." As Adam ended the call, he felt a furry face land itself on his knee. "You'll be there too. You've got twenty-four hours to learn to sing bass."

Robin felt better for the short walk to their hotel and then a hot shower. The building seemed to be a similar vintage to the police station, and with the same sense of spick-and-span efficiency. His room was comfortable and the dinner menu looked interesting, and while eating with Pru wouldn't be as satisfying as spending his evening with Adam, they could discuss the case in almost the same way as he'd have done back home in Lindenshaw. Doing something else entirely and forgetting about murder for a couple of hours had an appeal, but his priority had to be getting this case solved and getting home.

As soon as they'd ordered food, Robin got Pru to update him on that afternoon. "How did you get on with the officers who were first on the scene?"

"Pretty good. Amazing where playing dumb gets you." She took a sip of Belgian beer. "I got them to talk me through what they did from their arrival to when they were relieved, and I'm fairly confident they did everything that we'd have done to secure the scene. They told me that Derek Preese offered to make a list of names and addresses of all those who'd been present at training, so they took him up on it. Mind you, they had the sense to do a headcount to make sure they got a full list. Kept a tally of the bags they checked too. Everything matched up."

"Good." Robin appreciated simple jobs done with order and method. Corner cutting rarely helped anyone and often meant you missed a small, vital piece of information. Scrupulous attention to detail might be boring, but it would have picked up the clue. "Triple-checking: that list of bags accounted for included Dave's and Andy's?"

"Yep. They couldn't remember everyone's names offhand but they recalled the two blokes who wanted to get off to casualty. The officers said they checked their sports bags *very* carefully." Pru grinned. "They found nothing suspicious, though. They seemed to think the murder weapon had been taken off the premises by the killer and then either dumped in a convenient skip somewhere on the way home or simply washed and put away in the garden shed or wherever it came from."

Easier to hide a blunt instrument than a gun or a knife. Robin remembered reading a brilliant short story in which a wife murdered her husband using a leg of lamb to beat him around the head, then cooked and served it to the investigating officers.

"We know it didn't show up when they searched the site, inside or out. If the killer had blood on their clothes, they could have been washed and put away too."

"Or allowed to dry off, get cut into pieces, put into carrier bags, and deposited in half a dozen dustbins." Pru took another drink. "Any of which might suggest that the killer lived alone or that their partner or housemates were in collusion."

"Or that the outside clothes never got that much blood spattered on them in the first place. Either because the wound didn't produce that much, or the weapon was long enough that they stayed out of range. Or what if our killer stripped to their underwear—that could have been part of the way he or she lured the victim into the loos—and then instead of indulging in a spot of hanky-panky, killed him? They then stuck the underwear in a bag, washed themselves at the basins, got dressed, and went home?" Bugger. He'd missed out an element. Let's see if Pru challenged him about it.

"So, what about hiding the weapon when you're in your undies? You can't hide a truncheon or whatever down your pants." Pru grinned. "I wouldn't say that to young Ben back at Abbotston. He'd go red."

"He might surprise you and produce a smutty answer. As for concealing the weapon and then producing it: you could say you needed to get something from your bag, a condom or whatever, and by the time the victim realises you've produced another thing entirely, it's too late."

Pru narrowed her eyes, bottom lip jutting out in thought. "That might work. It might even be irrelevant, because if Nick was concussed from the first knock he got to his head, then he wouldn't have noticed the weapon until it was too late. It's a bit too public a place to be having a spot of nookie, although some people get off on that and Nick could have been one. We'll know more after tomorrow and talking to people who knew him."

"I hope so." Robin took a swig of Diet Pepsi. If he'd been at home, he might have indulged in a bottle of beer, but he didn't feel like drinking in these circumstances.

"Tell you what else I found out. I happened to be in the ladies' loo the same time as Sally. Coincidence, honest."

"I'll believe you, thousands wouldn't."

"Pfft. That joke's too old to be allowed out. Anyway, she had that *I want to ask you a question on the quiet* expression on her face." Pru raised an eyebrow. "She wanted to know if you were as good a bloke as Superintendent Betteridge makes out. Apparently, the officer she first worked under, at another station, was rather handsy. With fellow officers and with a couple of witnesses, which is what ultimately led to him losing his job. Sally hadn't complained—too scared, I think, being relatively new to the team—but other female officers did, once it all started to come into the open."

"What did you tell her?" Was this the moment when Robin's sexuality became common knowledge here, if it wasn't already?

"That you're just married, you're a perfect gentleman, and you're squeaky clean on all counts. And that you hadn't even had to pay me to say that. She seemed amused."

"Glad to hear it."

"I also mentioned the mess at Abbotston and how you were one of the new brooms sent in to sweep clean. She said she'd heard rumours about that already but wasn't sure how you were involved, so she was reassured you were on the side of the angels. She said she'd let the other two constables know. I think they've been quite worried about what kind of officer was being foisted on them."

Maybe that would explain the slightly prickly atmosphere in the incident room. "Sally appeared uncomfortable when I asked her what she thought of the case. Did she think I was targeting her for personal reasons, trying to chat her up?"

"That's possible. Once bitten, twice shy and all that. I'll keep my eyes and ears open and if she says anything directly, I'll drop in a casual mention of Adam and which team you bat for." Pru shrugged. "Let's hope they'll settle down once they know we won't bite them."

"Amen to that. Why don't you take Sally along tomorrow when you interview Dawn and Coa . . . Derek Preese? I'll take Callum when I go to see Melanie." Robin sighed, unhappy at having to waste energy on dealing with things that had no place in the modern police force. "Will Laurence's nose be put out of joint if I don't go back to the station and swop junior officers before seeing Dave?"

"Perhaps, but he'll have to learn to lump it. If we give him an important job to do, he might be mollified."

"I'll see if I can come up with one. Ben would have been all over the internet by now, raking up dirt about the victim." Was it unfair to already be feeling pangs of regret for not having his own team to hand and knowing that he wouldn't need to spell everything out to them? Maybe the officers here would surprise him with their competency and level of initiative: he couldn't imagine anyone working for Betteridge being sloppy at their job, but other people might have exercised an unhelpful influence on these impressionable young coppers. "I wonder if any of them have done that kind of an online sweep?"

"Not that I'm aware of, although we're still learning what's been going on. You could ask Laurence to prepare a briefing for us solely concentrating on the victim, his history and character. If the work's already been done, he can draw it together, along with anything else that speaks of motive." Pru took another deep draught; clearly this was thirsty work. "What's your nose telling you?"

Robin wrinkled the item concerned. "That Dave on his own, or with his mate, had the opportunity to do the murder before the game or when they went in the changing rooms. That they also had a chance to mess up the crime scene and could have passed off any mess on their clothes as coming from the practice session. There's always somebody bleeding in a rugby match."

Pru shook her head. "Nothing doing there. Those two constables who were first on the scene say they made the two lads leave behind the kit they'd worn for training. I get the part about opportunity, though. But why make a mess on your own doorstep? If the murder was planned, why not do it elsewhere? Unless it was a scuffle that went too far because they caught him trying to rifle their bags?"

"Then why not say so?" Robin sighed. "You asked about my copper's nose, and the trouble is it can't make up its mind because it's also telling me that Andy's a credible witness."

"You know that people panic, guv, and so one little lie snowballs until you've got an avalanche."

Pru was right: they'd seen it in a recent case. Robin must be out of sorts for him not to be thinking clearly. "Okay, point taken. Let's leave work behind for the rest of the meal. Do you think the Scarlets have got a realistic chance of winning the European Cup?"

Pru grinned. "Do you want the long answer or the short one?"

"Long answer would do me." Anything to keep his thoughts from home and the two people—Campbell counted as a person in this case—waiting for him.

Chapter Four

The Osments' flat was slightly over half a mile from the rugby ground, in an area that Callum described as, "Nice enough so long as you're careful which way you walk." When asked to clarify what he meant, he'd said that if you went in one direction, the property prices rose gradually until you hit some of Hartwood's most *des res*. Walk ten minutes the other way and you were into an area of council housing that had seen better days.

When they arrived, Melanie certainly seemed like she'd been unwell the last few weeks. Her pale, pinched face was at odds with the shiny happy person in the photographs framed on the wall of her flat's lounge. Nick wore a big smile in them too; he'd been a handsome bloke, even when he'd sported a beard. Built like a whippet, he'd likely have been a handy runner and must have been useful at darts, if the trophies displayed on the old-fashioned desk—complete with bottle of ink and the type of panel that often concealed a hidden drawer—were anything to go by.

Robin and Callum went through the usual soothing introductions, apologised firstly for a change of lead officers on the case, then for having to ask a load of questions, explaining that routine demanded it and they were sure she'd understand. They also gently stated their intention of bringing the culprit to justice. That assertion had only produced a nod, not even a hint of something that Robin's mistrustful mind could interpret as guilt.

"Has his phone turned up yet?" Melanie asked. "It's not valuable, but my number's on there and I'd hate it to be in the hands of a killer."

"It's not been recovered, as far as we're aware," Callum said. "Maybe it would be best to change your number. I know it's a pain, but . . ."

Melanie nodded. "I'll do that. Odd that anyone would take it and not his wallet, though. It was just an old, crappy iPhone of ours he was using until he could get a new model. Dropped the last one when he was out running, the silly sod." She ran her hand over her face. "Right, what can I tell you?"

"Tell us about that Wednesday evening. Take as much time as you need." Robin had briefed Callum in advance that they needed to take a *softly-softly* approach, despite any suspicions they had about the wife's involvement. If and when they had evidence to back that up, they could treat her as a viable suspect.

"It was Shaz's birthday. Her and me and Dawn have been pals since secondary school, so when she moved to the States, we decided we had to still do something to mark the event, so we chatted over Skype with a few glasses of wine. If I'd have known what was going to happen, I'd have postponed it." Melanie fished a tissue out from her sleeve, then dabbed her eyes. "Mum keeps telling me that it doesn't help me beating myself up, but I can't help it."

Robin smiled and nodded, genuinely sympathetic to the sentiment. "What was Nick doing while this was going on? Or what did he say he was going to do?"

"He'd always said he was going to leave us to have our space. As I understand it, he was off for a drink and maybe a bit of darts practice. He's—he was—on a team, based at our local, the Goat and Compasses."

Callum opened his mouth, shot Robin a glance, got a confirmatory nod, then said, "One of the lads in the team—Jeff Fisher—got in touch with us to say that Nick had arranged to play a couple of sets of darts with him, but not until half past nine. It was only when he saw the news next day that he realised why he'd not arrived."

"But he left here before six," Melanie said, frowning. "He wanted to be out before Dawn arrived at seven. He must have gone straight to the rugby ground. Where else could he have been?"

Robin couldn't answer that one way or the other. Callum had told him they'd checked all the local places Nick was said to hang out and put out an appeal for anyone who'd seen him or his car that evening, both of which had drawn a blank. "How long does it take to get from here to the ground?"

"I have no idea. I guess it's a five or ten minutes' drive, but I don't go over there much."

"I used to run around here," Callum chipped in. "I'd say it's about half an hour if you stroll, twenty minutes if you power walk, less if you're a runner."

"Thanks." Now that was clear, there'd been something in the manner Melanie had spoken about her husband being keen to leave the house that Robin could explore. "How did Nick and Dawn get on?"

"Oh, you're sharp. Not very well, actually. They always rubbed each other up the wrong way."

That might explain why the Osments hadn't been drawn into the rugby social circle. "When did Dawn leave?"

"I'm not sure. We'd started on the Prosecco as soon as she got here, and we were pretty sloshed by the time the call about Greg came. I ladled coffee into her, but it was obvious she'd never sober up in time, so we called a cab to take her to the hospital."

"Why not call a cab straight away?" Robin asked.

"Shaz persuaded her not to. She's dead set against them since she got touched up by a driver a few years back. Once I'd ended the Skype call though, we could do what we wanted." Melanie's brow creased in thought. "It must have been around nine I think by the time the cab came and Dawn left, but I honestly couldn't swear to it. Not only because of the wine—I had my own shock in store, didn't I? The officer they sent round was very nice, but she couldn't bring him back, could she?" Melanie rubbed her hands together, perhaps to stop them shaking. "Worst night of my life all round. I couldn't face identifying him. His dad had to do it."

Not a task Robin would wish on anyone. "I'm sorry to make you have to go through everything a second time. Are you sure you don't want us to call somebody to be here with you?"

"No!" Melanie's hands slowed their entwining. "Mum wanted to come over, but she fusses too much. I've been staying at hers, and it's been an incentive to stand on my own two feet again. She thinks I'm seven, not twenty-seven."

"Mums always do," Callum said, earning himself a smile in response. "How's Dawn coping?"

"She's okay. She's a doer, somebody who makes things happen, so she's pitching in on all sides. Been a godsend helping me organise next week's funeral. It'll probably all hit her later on when there are no fires to fight." There was clearly a genuine fondness and appreciation on Melanie's part. "I'll be able to be there for *her* then."

"What *is* the prognosis for Greg?" the young constable asked.

Melanie blew out her cheeks. "Not great, but then at least he's alive. Good news is he has all his mental faculties, and the use of his arms. They're not so optimistic about his regaining the use of his legs. Fifty-fifty for that at the moment, the doctors told Dawn. Something to do with a legion—lesion?—between the bones in his back."

"That's awful." Robin hoped that sounded heartfelt—it was meant to be. He couldn't imagine what it would feel like for Greg not to be able to charge around the pitch anymore.

"Isn't it? He'll never play rugby again, of course, even if he's able to walk. Dawn's going to make sure of that. She'll find him a safer sport to play."

"How will he feel about that?"

"He probably won't like it—nothing's ever going to take the place of being part of a rolling maul or slamming an opposition winger into touch—but he'll have to lump it." Melanie might not have been able to tell a legion from a lesion, but she evidently knew her rugby. "Like he's had to lump it about the fundraising stuff his mates are doing and accept that he and Dawn need some extra help. I hope nobody tries telling him he's inspirational, though, because Dawn reckons they'll get a bollocking."

Now Melanie seemed to have regained her calm, possibly due to concentrating on someone else's problems for a while, they could return to the matter in hand.

"You're clearly an intelligent woman," Robin said, "and you already appreciate that we have a job to do and there are lots of questions we need answers to, no matter how painful they are. Why would anybody want to kill Nick?"

"I have no idea. Don't you think we've all been asking ourselves the same thing?"

"Was there another woman?" Callum asked.

Melanie's response—a rolling of her eyes and a suppressed chuckle—was unexpected. "God, no. He barely had an interest in making use of *our* bed, let alone anybody else's." She didn't appear to be bitter about the fact.

Callum raised an eyebrow. "Really?"

"Yes. Not everyone in the world is sex mad, you know. And before you ask, no, Nick wasn't in the closet or anything like that, and yes, the arrangement suited both of us. We were happy." She shot a glance at one of the pictures on the wall. "He had his faults, like anyone, the daft sod, but I loved him." She blew her nose, then, purposely addressing Robin rather than the constable, said, "Any further questions?"

"When you were asking yourselves about his death, did you or anyone else come up with something from his past? An old acquaintance bearing a grudge or whatever?"

"Not that me or either family are aware of. There may have been something before I met him five years ago, but his dad would have told us. He wants answers too."

"Is Nick's mother still alive?"

"No. She died when he was twelve. That's why Nick and his dad are—were—so close. If any of us can think of a name for someone who might have wanted to harm him, I promise you'll be told, straight away."

"We appreciate that. Thank you." Robin smiled. "Is there anything you've thought of since you made your initial statement?"

"Yes, actually. A couple of things. Nick used to run for the athletics club when he was a teenager, so he trained on the Hartwood track. I know he looked back on those days with the sort of nostalgia that's too rose-tinted to be true." Melanie blew her nose again. "Sorry. It breaks me up to think of him all happy."

"Take your time." Hopefully she had another handkerchief to hand because the present one was pretty saturated.

"Thank you. They say it helps to talk, and it does. Now, I can't remember if I mentioned that the mobile phone company Nick worked for was planning a reorganisation. It didn't seem important at the time, and I'm not sure it's relevant now."

"Tell us anyway. You never know what will help."

"Well, I don't know a lot. It had got no further than the consultation stage, and the staff members were told they'd probably all have a post even if they'd have to reapply for it. Still, Nick was rather worried about how things might have worked out. He doesn't have that worry now." Melanie blew her nose again, then leaned over to deposit the hankie in a bin along with several others that must have been in a similar state.

Robin guessed she was right—the reorganisation didn't appear to be relevant, and the only thing that was in the case notes about Osment's employment was that he'd got on well with his fellow workers and worked hard. Nonetheless, there was one further thing to discuss before they terminated the interview. "Can we go back to three weekends ago? We understand that Nick had suffered some bruising on his . . . upper thighs."

"No need to be coy, Chief Inspector." Melanie clearly found that as amusing as Callum's suggestion of another woman. "He had bruising on his bum. It happened on the previous Saturday evening. He was supposed to have a darts match but it was cancelled because the other team were struck with a tummy bug. Nick went out for a run instead, but he slipped over on a patch of mud and hit himself on one of those stones people have their house names on. He had to hobble home. And not the easiest place to put a dressing on."

Robin heard Callum try to suppress a titter. Time to leave.

Once back in the car and heading to see Dave at his work, Callum said, "What's all this about her and Nick and beds? There can't be anybody not interested in sex, surely?"

"Asexuality's real enough. Each to his or her own." Robin wasn't going to hand out Callum a lesson on the spectrum of human emotions and preferences now, but the issue of sexuality was worth exploring. "Some people are born like that. Or they could choose to abstain, if they've been abused or assaulted in the past."

"Wouldn't that show up in the records?"

"Not if it was never reported, or if somebody forgot to check Melanie's maiden name. I'll text Laurence and add it to his list of jobs." Distinctly a long shot from the couple's sexual preferences to a supposed sexual assault and from there to a connection with this crime, but they'd need to check every angle. Especially given the lack of other credible leads so far.

"Sir, if he was asexual, wouldn't that make it unlikely somebody lured him into the toilets with a promise of sex?"

"On the surface, yes, although a lack of attraction doesn't mean asexual people don't do it at all. Let's not rule anything out until we're absolutely sure." Robin glanced sidelong at Callum, catching him wearing a sardonic expression. "You can wipe that expression off your face. When I was your age and rank, I had to deal with a serious sexual assault in which both the victim's and the accused's sexuality were torn inside out in the witness box. We all learned that there's a damn sight more to the world than gay, straight, or bi."

"Sorry, sir." The apology sounded real enough, but they drove to the next appointment pretty much in silence, Robin trying to assess whether he was overreacting to the young constable's comments and whether Ben and Caz on his own team would have said much the same. When he'd moved stations to Abbotston, he'd had absolute clarity over being part of the team of new brooms who'd clear up the mess. On someone else's patch, especially someone he admired as much as Betteridge, the lines were blurred.

Dave worked as bursar in Hartwood North secondary school, so Robin and Callum had to go through the usual security procedures before being allowed "pupilside," as the constable termed it.

"I like that word. I'm stealing it." Robin recalled the first murder he'd led on and his surprise at the rigorous way that school site security was enforced these days, almost as rigorous as an airport. Adam would appreciate the word *pupilside* too.

Dave, who clearly fitted the nickname *Big*, came to meet them at reception, insisting they call him by his first name rather than Mr. Venter. "Only the students call me that, here." He led the way to his office, offered coffee—which they declined—then settled himself behind his desk, which bore the inevitable PC and an endearingly old-fashioned stationery organiser filled with an array of pens, including the design of fountain pen Robin's dad had liked to use. A picture on the windowsill, featuring Dave and an attractive woman hugging and looking every bit as happy as Melanie and Nick had done in their photos, suggested Dave was one of the rugby team's straight or bi players.

Robin made his usual apology for making Dave go through everything a second time.

"That's okay. Andy said you'd taken over the case and were grilling everyone again. I don't blame you."

"We hope everybody's as understanding. Andy says you and he are best friends?"

"Yeah, I've known him forever. A number of us in the team go back a way. Played for or against each other at school level or whatever."

"Nobody's bothered about being part of a team that used to be exclusively for gay or bi men?" Callum chipped in.

"Why should I be? We're all grown-up here. Nobody uses insults or calls the gay lads Baxter."

Callum gave Robin a confused glance, then turned his gaze on Dave. "Baxter?"

"As in, 'Watch out, he's here. Backs to the wall'!"

Robin groaned. Long time since he'd heard that one.

"I was there the night in the pub that Andy came out. I'd tried to set him up with my cousin, 'cos she was going to be down visiting the family the next week and she's not only fit but really nice, which don't always go together. Andy said he was sure she was a lovely girl although maybe I should find someone else to make up the numbers on a night out." Dave frowned, in remembrance of what had evidently been a tricky conversation. "He clammed up, face like he was waiting for me to punch him or something, but then everything clicked into place in my brain. I told him I think I understood and he ought to come along with us, anyway. Because my cousin would have preferred him to any of the other lads, even if it was just for having a laugh."

"And is everyone on the team as understanding? On the pitch and in the stands?"

"If you know rugby, you'll know it's an inclusive sport. There's the odd dinosaur, but you get them anywhere, and most of us at Hartwood would say it takes all sorts to make a world and so long as a bloke's a fair player on the field and a good mate off it, we don't give a toss what he gets up to in private." Dave's eyes narrowed. "Anyway, what's this got to do with that dead bloke?"

"This is going to sound a cliché, but at the moment we don't know what's relevant to finding his killer and what isn't." Robin sought for an analogy to build rapport. "In your job, you have to plough through a pile of numbers and budget readouts to see the bigger picture. You'll be working out which of the smaller numbers you can safely ignore and which of them you have to drill down into." Robin had met a secondary school finance manager a few months previously—not through Adam and his education connections for once, but at a community liaison event at Abbotston station. The similarities in some aspects of both their roles had been striking. "I do the same thing, but with facts."

Dave nodded, apparently impressed. "I stand corrected. What facts can I help you with?"

They asked for an account of the Wednesday evening, up to the point the police arrived, which Dave provided logically and in a lot fewer words than his mate Andy. His statement matched what they'd already been told, without being so identical in wording it raised suspicions. Yes, he'd been last to arrive and last out of the changing rooms but no, he'd not seen anyone lurking about then. Or subsequently.

"Mr. Preese insisted you had a shower before going to the hospital?" Robin asked, insouciantly.

Dave rolled his eyes. "He's a touch obsessive about cleanliness. His house looks he cleans it every hour on the hour, you know? He's not realised that other folk don't feel the same."

"You didn't believe the casualty staff would be offended by a spot of mud and sweat?"

"Too right."

"So, to clarify," Callum said, "Andy tried to get you to go into the changing rooms right after the accident, but you didn't want to. Nor did you want to go in to take a shower. Was there another reason for that, one you're not sharing with us?"

Dave leaned forward, halfway out of his chair, hands on the desk. "Now you hold on! I didn't have anything to do with the murder. I got the shock of my life finding the dead man."

Robin raised his hand. "Calm down. Nobody's saying you had anything to do with it. Like I said, we need the full picture to see how it all hangs together. For example, to discover whether anybody else was trying to stop you going in there," he added, soothingly.

"Okay." Dave sat down again. "No, nobody tried to stop me. Andy was all for getting me off the pitch because of the state I was getting into. I never meant Greg to get hurt. If I could go back and live that evening again, I'd take another line when I ran, and Greg would be okay."

"You can't know that," Robin said. "If he went into the tackle a different way, he might have ended up worse than he is."

"I suppose you're right." Dave was clearly not convinced, though. "I was damn close to giving up the game. The following Saturday's match got postponed as a mark of respect—none of us would have had the heart to play in it, anyway—but Coach said he expected us all to turn up for the next training session. If Greg couldn't play, we had to take the pitch for him."

"He's right. Wouldn't help anyone to let the team down." Robin sympathised with the sentiment. "Back to the night in question and events off the pitch. You and Andy both saw the dead man."

"God, yes. I'll never get that sight out of my mind. I'm just grateful the cubicle door didn't cover up the body entirely or I'd never be able to use a public loo again. Too paranoid about opening closed bog doors." Typically British laughing off a bad situation.

"Sorry to make you relive it, but had either of you seen him before?"

"If I had, I don't remember him." That was different to the categorical *no* Dave had given in his initial statement on the night the body was found, but he'd have been in shock then. Still, Robin made a note of the fact.

"And did you see anyone lurking around the clubhouse that night who shouldn't have been there?"

An emphatic no this time. "Andy and I have mulled it over all ways up and we're sure nobody went up the tunnel, either. Not even any of the squad."

"How's Greg coping financially?" The question from Callum took both Dave and Robin by surprise. Robin wasn't sure where the constable was going with it but decided to let him have his head. He could be reined in later.

"He's doing okay," Dave replied, after a pause. "He works in software for a big insurance company, where he's always been office based, so there's no implications on that front. And anyway, his company is desperate not to lose him. It's in a modern building with good access, although it's slightly different with the flat he and Dawn were planning to buy together, which was top floor in a building with no lift. Luckily, it's a new build, so Dawn was in there like a shot to see if they could transfer to a ground floor property that had wheelchair access. She's definitely missed her calling as a referee, because nobody would argue with her, would they?"

"I wouldn't know, not having met her yet," Robin said, with a grin. Funny how Dave was coming across a lot more concerned about Greg and his accident than he'd been when describing finding the dead body, but maybe that was understandable, given it was his mate and he was the person responsible for hurting him.

"But there's a fundraising campaign going on," Callum persisted. "Why does Greg need help if everything's all right?"

Dave shot him a sharp look. "Don't go thinking that because everything's all right on the surface it'll be easy for him. His life has totally changed. Rugby was a big part of his life, and now that's denied him. We can't make that better, but we can damn well make other things a bit easier for him. We're not sure what the prognosis is for him walking again, but in a worst case he might need a properly adapted bathroom, with a wheel-in shower or a hoist or whatever the occupational therapist reckons would be best for him. We'll raise the money, and we'll trust him and Dawn to know what best to spend it on. To be honest, it isn't only for his benefit."

"Whose, then?" Robin asked.

"The team's. If things have changed for Greg, then they've changed for us too. Me in particular. Anything we can do to make some sort of recompense, then we'll do it. It's helped us to cope." Dave pushed his hair back, wildly. "We've got some irons in the fire already, but frankly, I'd have put my hand up to do anything, even sponsored toilet cleaning or drain unblocking."

The nastier the activity, the better for helping him overcome any lingering sense of guilt?

"There have been fundraising campaigns at the club before?" Callum continued his line of questioning, and by the glint in his eye, he was getting closer to his goal.

"Yes. Not long after I joined the club, I got involved with running a campaign. There'd been a young player who got knocked off his bike and killed on the way home from a match with Tuckton Chiefs. They're our big local rivals, only based about ten miles from here, but they were great in terms of pitching in."

"Tuckton Chiefs?" Callum was clearly trying to sound insouciant but failing. "The dead man, Nick Osment, used to play for them, as well."

"Did he?" Dave shook his head. "I had no idea."

Neither had Robin.

"He seems to have given up playing several years ago," Callum clarified.

"If you say so. I don't remember playing against him at any point, but you don't remember everyone on the opposition, not across a season. It doesn't help that I have an awful memory for faces. Gail, that's my wife, is always telling me off about it because I blank people in the street, but I can't help it."

"It's possible you might have met him and not remembered?" Robin asked.

"Quite possibly. Rugby can get ale heavy postmatch if you're not the designated driver, so after four pints, I might have slow danced with the bloke and not been any the wiser later."

Robin frowned. That was a neat way of covering up the fact that you'd met somebody—if anybody later reported you'd been seen together, you'd say you were too tanked up to remember. Rugby connection noted, though, alongside the fact that the Tuckton Chiefs hadn't featured in any of the summaries of the case they'd read or heard.

Callum cast Robin an inquiring glance, got a nod, then continued. "Back to the lad who was killed. You raised money for a memorial bench?"

"Yes, but we also donated to an organisation that does education work with young players in rugby and other sporting clubs about the importance of keeping safe and not getting caught up in the postmatch drinking culture."

"Had this lad been drinking that night?"

"A couple of pints of shandy, if that, according to Coach, but that's not the point. He felt it important to spend some of the money on preventing similar tragedies at other clubs. Likelier to get yourself into trouble by having a few pints and driving home than being the victim of a hit-and-run. They never pinned down who was responsible."

"Was the lad who was killed—Jamie Weatherell—gay?"

Again, Dave seemed surprised at the question. "I think so. He'd been involved from the days it was purely for gay and bi blokes. He'd have been no bigger than a kid when he started out. Probably the water boy. Anyway, the club hadn't long opened its doors wider when I joined. Is this relevant?"

Robin was wondering the same thing.

Callum continued. "Thing is, I've—we've—heard that there was a spot of trouble between the two clubs dating back to when Hartwood set up as a rainbow team. Was there a homophobic element?"

"Ah." Dave raised his finger, as though about to tell off a pupil who'd been nicking from the canteen. "You're barking up the wrong tree, there. The originally Hartwood RFC folded about ten years ago because it wasn't financially viable. I don't think anybody had their fingers in the till, so the demise was probably due to years of amateur management. People with good intentions but not the right skills. Anyway, loads of the players went to Tuckton, and they were swanking it all over the county about how they'd managed to thrive when others hadn't. When Hartwood resurrected itself as a rainbow club, they were fine about it; what they didn't like was when it expanded to take a wider range of players."

"People left Tuckton to go back to Hartwood?" Robin asked.

"Yep. Although not this Osment bloke. Coach would have said if he'd ever played for us. Thing is, we've overtaken Tuckton in the league, and that's made the rivalry worse."

"Bad enough turning out for the rivals but making them a success . . ." Robin left the sentence hanging. Both he and Dave understood sporting enmity. Could that have been relevant in this case, though? An ex-Tuckton player for whatever reason taking revenge on the opposition or maybe something simpler? "Haven't you got a match against Tuckton coming up?"

"Yeah, next Saturday. It'll be even more significant, given that Greg's supposed to be allowed to come and watch, medical condition permitting. The boys will want to put on a good performance for him."

Robin nodded. Bloody brave of Greg to be sitting in the stands, watching a game he'd never again be part of. "This may seem a daft question, but does spying happen at this level of rugby? You know, watching the opposition practice so you can note their line-out calls or whatever."

Dave put his fingers to his mouth in thought. "I've never heard of it going on, but that doesn't mean it couldn't. Are you thinking that this Osment bloke came along to watch us with the intention of Tuckton getting one up?"

"Just exploring the possibilities," Robin said, aware that Callum was fidgeting in his chair: clearly this wasn't the line of questioning *he'd* been going to take.

"If you're exploring the possibility that someone on our team caught him in the act and duffed him up, you've got another think coming." Dave shook his head agitatedly. "We can all account for each other, all during training. And that's not closing ranks or covering up."

Robin hadn't suggested it was.

Callum, evidently unable to hold his tongue any longer, said, "Is it true that there were anonymous complaints about the money being raised for the bench?"

"Eh? Oh, now . . ." Dave wagged his finger, "Coach did say something about troublemakers, but it's all so long ago. I don't remember."

"Perhaps you'd remind Dave," Robin asked the constable. And enlighten *him* at the same time.

"There were letters to the local paper and a spate of nasty remarks on social media. The letters were anonymous and the comments from a sock puppet account. Saying that people should donate their money to proper causes. That it was immoral paying for a memorial bench when there were children in Africa starving to death." Callum was visibly moved at what he was saying. Perhaps he shared that opinion. "People at the time linked it to bad feeling between the two clubs. An implication that Hartwood blamed Tuckton for what happened to the lad who was killed. The fact he was not any old player but the groundsman's son making it closer to home."

Dave stared at the constable, clearly trying to take in all he'd been told. Eventually he shrugged. "Pass. The bloke to ask about this would be Coach. He knows everything about everything. Not only Hartwood but all gossip from all the local teams."

"Would he know if the person making those accusations was Osment?"

"How the hell would I know that? This is my job." Dave swept his hand over the paper on his desk. "Not reading minds."

Once back in the school visitor car park, with the usual concluding part of the interview—*"contact us if you think of anything else relevant"* and the like—conducted in a frigid atmosphere, Robin could contain himself no longer.

"All that rugby club stuff. Sergeant Davis and I haven't been made aware of any of it. Can I ask why?"

"I only turned it up last night, sir." Callum kept his eyes fixed on the car boot, seeming to take forever to put his briefcase in it. "I was scrolling back through some of the local papers for any mention of Osment, and it turned up a match report from one of Tuckton's games. He'd been sent off for a combination of foul play, swearing at the ref, and making homophobic comments. Got a ban for that."

"Okay." Robin bit back on tearing a strip off the constable as he'd clearly shown initiative and maybe this had been an ill-judged attempt to impress. "Next time make sure you've shared the info with me before the interview. What about the anonymous letters and comments stuff?"

"I discovered that last night too." Callum, perhaps aware he'd got off lightly, at last summoned the nerve to look Robin in the eye. "You know what it's like when you start following something on the internet. Half an hour later you're down the rabbit hole with Alice. There was another match report about a game against Hartwood and it harped on about the two teams' rivalry. When I put that into the search engine, I turned up some blog posts and one of them detailed all the stuff going on about the fundraising. I never necessarily believe what I read online, so I wanted to confront Dave with it, to see if he'd confirm it." Callum paused, no doubt realising he'd been a wazzock to have played this hand solo. "I should have told you about that too. I was wrong."

"You were. Don't do it again." Robin couldn't help but be amused at the hangdog expression the constable had adopted. "I'm going to ring Sergeant Davis in case she's still with Derek Preese—Coach—and update her."

Fortunately, Pru and Sally were still with Preese, and the sergeant promised to ask him about the alleged complaints about the charitable campaign.

"Anything else he can tell us about the history between the clubs would be useful too."

"Will do, sir."

Robin ended the call, then sat thinking as Callum drove them back to the station. A germ of an idea was forming in his mind. If you were the killer and wanted to murder Nick Osment, surely the most sensible thing would have been to meet him somewhere quiet, do the deed, and hide the body where it wouldn't be found for a while. Even a few days could obscure the accuracy of estimating time of death and so help support an alibi for yourself. Murdering the victim at the club itself and hardly bothering to hide the body must be significant.

What if the lingering resentments between the clubs, on whatever count, provided that important factor? What if it had been somebody from the Tuckton club who'd caused Jamie Weatherell's death? No, that wouldn't make sense, because in that case why object to the fundraising, unless it was a muddled attempt to cover up that involvement? In any case, that scenario would be more likely to result in someone from Hartwood going to the Tuckton ground to cause trouble. Which raised an important question: If Osment had been visiting the Hartwood training ground off his own back, how had he got inside the building?

What had been in the victim's mind that evening? Meeting someone, trashing the changing rooms, nicking valuables—the list could go on. And had one of those directly led to his death or had Osment simply been in the wrong place at the wrong time?

Chapter Five

Back at the station, waiting for Pru and Sally to return, Robin gave Melanie a ring about her husband's involvement in the Tuckton club. She made no secret of the fact he'd played for them.

"Why didn't you mention that?"

"I thought it was too long ago to be relevant, Chief Inspector."

Robin took a deep breath, trying to remain calm. "Why did he leave?"

"The real reason or what he told everyone?"

That sounded encouraging. People who told different people different things featured regularly in Robin's job. "Both, preferably."

"Well, the official story was that he'd suffered a couple of concussions and decided to take up something safer, namely darts. 'Concussion' would be a bit of an exaggeration. I'd call them simply knocks to the head, but he liked to overdramatize things." It was said with affection.

"But the truth was . . .?"

"That he got the hump on." Melanie snorted. "He'd been red-carded in a game because he swore at the ref. He was banned for several matches as a result, and what with that and the stick he got from his teammates, it was all too much for his sense of self-dignity. He never played for Tuckton—or any other club—after that."

"When did this happen?"

"Oh, let me think. I want to say two years ago but you know how time flies."

"Is there anything you can use to pin the date down?" That usually helped a witness. *It was before we went to Gran Canaria but after the incident with Aunty Clare and the sherry.*

"Yes. He got sent off a couple of weeks after we had our car stolen. I think those two combined were the last straw."

Once he'd put the phone down, Robin called Callum over to check the date of the red-card match against the date of Jamie Weatherell's fatal accident. If Melanie was to be believed—and Robin saw no reason to doubt her—the game when he'd been sent off had only been a fortnight after the hit-and-run.

"Who attended Osment's postmortem, by the way?" Robin rarely did that himself these days. He probably had a stronger stomach for it than his old sergeant, Anderson, had possessed, but he'd insisted the bloke attend as part of his development, as Robin had been made to be the officer present by his own boss. Pru always volunteered to be present, although whether out of a personal interest in matters forensic or because she knew Robin didn't relish the prospect, he didn't know.

"That was me, sir. Along with Inspector Robertson. He said I needed to get used to being there."

Robin grinned. "You'll be telling that to your constables when you're my rank. I've read the report, but you can't put intonation of voice into the words. What came out that I should know about?"

"Nothing I'm aware of, sir, although I have to admit I zoned out on occasions." Callum stared at his shoes. "Self-preservation."

"We've all been there, done that. Except Sergeant Davis, of course. Constitution of an ox. Ah," Robin turned his head towards the door, "and here she is. Time to compare notes."

Robin got the team together, then allowed Callum to take the lead on explaining what they'd learned from Melanie and Dave, only chipping in to clarify a point or where the constable was put on the spot, for example about what the couple did—or didn't—get up to in bed. He delivered a reminder that you couldn't make assumptions about what it meant to be on any particular part of the sexual spectrum.

"Sir," Sally said, "what if it's just a case of Nick having a low sex drive? Aren't we leaping to conclusions by labelling him?" She smiled nervously, clearly unsure about challenging a superior officer.

"You're quite right." Robin should have kept more of an open mind on that. Perhaps the prospect of his own lack of sexual outlet for the next few weeks had temporarily blinded him to other people's varying libidos. "Can you get that clarified, please?"

Sally nodded. "Of course, sir."

Robin turned to Laurence. "Has anything turned up about Melanie in the files?"

"I'm afraid not, guv'nor. If she was the victim of assault, then she didn't report it. Nothing else for her, not even a speeding ticket." Laurence flicked his eyes up from his notes, then down again. "I checked the same question for him too. The sexual-assault-victim angle. Still a no."

"Thanks. And well done for covering the Nick Osment angle. Lots of officers wouldn't have thought of that." He covered over Laurence's delighted embarrassment by asking, "Find anything for Nick?"

"The only mention of him I can find in the database is when he reported his car stolen, a few years back. We'd had a spate of thefts from vehicles and joyriding at the time, and the idiot had apparently left his car parked outside on the road, with his satnav on view. The vehicle was found a couple of days later, burned out." Laurence shrugged. "There must have been half a dozen went the same way."

The car that was stolen a couple of weeks before Osment gave up rugby for good. Robin cast a glance at the incident board. "Could the car thefts have been linked to that hit-and-run?"

"That's what people wondered at the time, but there wasn't enough in the way of forensics to link the accident to any vehicle or any of the usual little oiks suspected of nicking them." Laurence checked his notes. "We caught a couple of lads, and they got sent down for aggravated vehicle theft. Once they were put away—surprise, surprise—the problem stopped."

"Had they got previous, then, to get a custodial sentence?" Pru asked.

"No, they'd got away with any and everything they'd been doing, up to that point. But one of the vehicles they nicked was owned by a disabled young woman who needed it for work." Laurence raised an eyebrow. "Yeah, shows you how considerate this pair were. They wouldn't have known about work, but they must have noticed the adaptations. The judge went mental at them."

So, it was possible those two lads had been the ones to kill Jamie Weatherell, but short of confession, it was unlikely the police would be able to pin that on them. *Time to get back to* this *victim.* "Anything about Osment on social media?"

"Only the usual for both him and Melanie. Holiday snaps. Pictures of the car that replaced the one he had nicked. The usual trivia people fill their profiles with."

Robin nodded. What a footprint to leave behind: no momentous achievements or works of art, just a stream of posts about after-work cocktails or what people were having for dinner. He tried to shake off his sadness by asking Pru and Sally to update the rest of the team on what they'd found out.

"I'll pass it over to Sally in a minute," Pru said, "but I'll start by confessing to making assumptions. Derek Preese isn't as old as I expected him to be. I'd built up a mental image that he'd been playing in the seventies, Wales's glory days and all that. But he's only early fifties, I'd guess. And what you might call a silver fox." She gave Sally a grin.

"Stop being sexist, you two," Callum said. "You wouldn't like it if we commented on whether Melanie was fit."

Pru didn't appear offended at the chastisement; it was typical of what she'd have said if the roles were reversed. "Agreed, but I'd argue it's acceptable if it's directly relevant to the investigation."

"You think it might be?" Robin asked.

"Yes, although I couldn't link it to the case at present. It struck me that he's the kind of bloke who has an effect on you, both by looks and force of personality. If he said jump, you'd not just say, 'How high?' You'd go and fetch a fence to vault over. Would you agree, Sally?"

"Yep. You can see why his players worship him. He got them all back into training as soon as was decent after the night of the murder and the accident. Said it was the best thing for them, to stop them brooding."

"'Get back on the horse, soon as you can,'" Pru said in a gruff Welsh accent that must have mimicked the coach's voice. Nobody would argue that was inappropriate, given that she was a valleys girl. "Even Dave was there and supposedly as committed in contact as he'd ever been. Takes a lot to persuade somebody to go for it one hundred percent after what happened to Greg."

"Greg had some input to that," Sally pointed out. "The players have got a WhatsApp group, and he'd been on there saying there was no point in the team losing two players, especially with this big grudge match coming up against the Tuckton Chiefs the weekend after next. We still don't know if the timing has any relevance. Anyway, Preese reckons there's a lot of niggle between the two on the field, although not so much off it. Some of the Hartwood guys played alongside the Tuckton ones when they were still at the local comprehensive school, while others played for the private school the other side of town. They've beaten the crap out of each other on the field and drunk each other under the table off it. Sergeant Davis is keen to go and see the match."

I bet she is. I hope we'll have got this all done and dusted and be back to Abbotston by then.

"Strictly in the interest of research." Pru chuckled. She and Sally had clearly hit it off, and while Robin couldn't quite see yet how this information related to the murder, he'd let them share it, in the interests of harmonious working relationships. "Tuckton's got a huge, ugly, mean-as-a-wild-dog lock forward who's caused Greg a heap of problems in the past. He's told Dave to keep the bloke quiet, by any means foul or fair. If Greg isn't there to watch, Dawn will be, and she'll be giving him a full match report." Pru raised her hand apologetically. "Sorry, sir. You know how much I love my rugby. We'll get back to the matter in hand."

"I'd appreciate that." Robin loved his rugby too, but you didn't catch him getting distracted by huge, muscular forwards. Not on duty, anyway. And rarely without Adam to compare notes with. A pang of regret that he'd not be able to go home tonight and sit watching sport over a beer, discussing the merits of the players' thighs, wrong-footed him. He'd need to keep his mind on the matter in hand too. "Does Derek Preese's account of events match the other ones we have?"

"Pretty much, sir," Sally said. "Nothing to report there, although this should be of interest. He said there'd been a spate of thefts at the athletics club over the summer, people getting into the changing rooms and the like, so back at the start of this season he'd bought a lockable box. The players put their valuables in it before taking to the pitch, leaving it by the stands during practice and match days, chained to the railings. Then they can keep an eye on it."

"Isn't that a bit over the top?" Laurence said. "My dad used to run the fifteen hundred metres at county level and he trained at the ground. He'd leave his stuff in the changing rooms, and they never had any trouble."

"Your dad wouldn't have had an iPhone or a smart watch or a wallet full of cards, back then." Callum rolled his eyes. "My aunt was a member of Hartwood Athletics Club as well. Really useful sprinter, although she reckons she gave it up when she discovered boys. From what she says, those good old days weren't as innocent as they're cracked up to be."

"If we're talking family experiences," Sally said, "my gran reckons the reason you get all these thefts now is because there's more to nick. If you didn't own anything much in the first place, you could leave your doors unlocked."

"She's got a point. That locked box isn't a bad precaution," Robin agreed. "It also adds weight to the notion that nobody could have got down the tunnel that evening without someone seeing. The players would always be keeping half an eye on the box. What about the hit-and-run? Any hint of a homophobic element?"

"Preese said the lad who was killed in the hit-and-run wasn't openly gay, although he suspects he might have been closeted. When we probed him on that, he said someone he knew had seen him in a gay bar." Pru pursed her lips. "I think he meant *he'd* seen him in a gay bar. Having said that, Preese didn't think there was a homophobic element to his death. Simply a case of being in the wrong place at the wrong time."

"What about fundraising?" Robin asked.

Sally glanced at Pru; they both raised an eyebrow and then laughed.

Scowling, Callum said, "What's so funny?"

"Us." Sally jerked a thumb at Pru. "Remember we said what a charmer Derek Preese is? He's touched us both for a tenner towards Greg's fund. We couldn't resist."

"I'll make sure I don't have my wallet if we have to interview him." Callum snorted. "Sounds like he's the man to have rattling buckets."

"He'd make a fortune," Pru agreed. "The way Preese talked about Greg—how he'd always been a proud bloke and a generous one, first up at the bar, last out of door after training if any tidying up needed to be done—really got to us."

"I bet his being fit didn't hurt," Laurence muttered.

"I think we'll put Mr. Film Star Preese to one side for the moment," Robin said, although he'd made a mental note that he needed to get a gander at this bloke and see what all the fuss was about. "Anything turn up about the current fundraising drive that might be relevant to the case?"

"Only in terms of an insight into Dawn's character. To quote the coach as near as I can get"—Pru put on the gruff Welsh voice again—"'I can imagine what Dawn would say if we offered money towards their wedding. She'd tell us where to stick it, probably in the kind of language that would make a prop forward blush.'"

"They clearly grow them tough around here." Robin gave the team a smile. "What about the previous fundraising effort?"

"He said he'd always suspected Osment was behind the complaints about collecting for a bench. Reckoned the bloke was a trouble-maker and rugby was better off without him. Preese then went on to say the usual stuff about that not meaning he wanted Osment dead." Pru glanced at Sally, as though encouraging her to chip in.

The constable agreed. "I felt the same. I wouldn't be surprised if there was a touch of personal niggle there."

"How did he know Osment? The bloke didn't play for Hartwood, did he?" Callum asked.

"No, but Preese had trained him when he was a schoolboy. Preese used to help with the under twenties, and apparently Osment was quite a promising player when he was young, although he lacked application. Gobby, with it," Pru added.

"Sounds like the type of bloke who rubs people up the wrong way all round." Robin changed tack. "Okay. What about Dawn?"

Pru took the lead on this one. "She's putting on a tough front and she knows it. Says she'd never want to go through an evening like that ever again and reckons in a month or two when everything's calmed down, she'll probably give herself a treat and go to pieces for a few days."

That was entirely understandable. "What's her account of the time she spent with Melanie?"

"Broadly the same as what we know from the original statements. The wine, Skyping their pal, seeing if she could get somebody to give her a lift to the hospital as she'd had one too many to drive. She reckoned she was beyond filling herself with sugary coffee and borrowing Melanie's car. Said she didn't want another accident that evening. Feels a cow for leaving Melanie to get the bad news on her own, but says she couldn't have known about Nick."

Callum raised his hand. "I know it's only a small thing, sir, but somewhere in the statements, it says when Derek Preese rang Dawn from the training ground, she told him she was going to drive. I don't remember reading about her cadging a lift. I bet one of the players would have been glad to go and get her."

"Perhaps she didn't realise how far gone she was until she got off the phone to him," Pru suggested. "Worth noting, though, sir?"

"Absolutely. Did you get anything out of her about Osment himself? They didn't get on."

"If that's a nice way of saying she couldn't stand him, that's right. She didn't hold back, did she, Sally?"

The young constable, visibly growing in confidence, said, "She did not. Said she wouldn't trust him as far as she could throw him and didn't think he was good enough for Melanie. She'd been ready for months to support her pal if their relationship fell apart."

"That's not the impression we got," Callum said. "Any concrete reason why she felt that?"

"We asked but she was evasive. 'Just a feeling.' It's possible she's been persuading Melanie that he was bad news." Sally consulted her notes. "She reckoned he'd been up to no good that Saturday he came home with a bruised backside. She was having none of the falling-over story."

Robin swivelled so as to scrutinise the picture of Nick Osment displayed on the incident board. He had an idea about what had happened to the bloke that Saturday, one he'd sleep on and then test the next day. He turned to find four pairs of eyes fixed on him, clearly waiting for a word of wisdom. He wasn't sure he had many to offer, though, given how few tangible leads they had in the case and how the people who might have had a slight motive to kill the man all appeared to have unbreakable alibis for his time of death.

"Right," he said, "we're building up a picture of the dead man. He was unpopular and seems to have made a nuisance of himself.

He must have put other noses out of joint, over and above the ones we know about. Pru and Sally, can I assign you to follow up the Tuckton Chiefs angle? Callum and Laurence, I want you to talk to people at his darts club. I know Sally already did that, but it's the fresh-eyes angle we need at the moment. If you can't get to see them today, then spend this afternoon making appointments and collating what we have. Any further anomalies like the stuff about Dawn getting a lift, I want to know. I'm going to go back to the sports ground, now."

Aware of Pru behind him explaining to the others that Robin liked to get away and think sometimes, away from any distractions, he left the office, got in the car, and headed for the sports ground.

Once in the car park, and having caught sight of the person he wanted to talk to, Robin got out his phone to message Adam. He did his best thinking when at home, and this was the next best option.

Hiya, my favourite deputy headteacher. Things going slowly here. Not optimistic about a swift return home. Sorry.

He had one leg out of the car when his phone registered an incoming call from the man himself.

"I'm on PPA and got the staffroom to myself," he said. "Want to chat?"

"Yep. I'm on my own and not in the station. Needed some space and thinking time and seeing as it's an open-plan office, I can get precious little of it there."

"I bet. Sorry to hear things are going slowly. Take all the time you need, though. Campbell and I will have to cope somehow."

"What about me coping? I didn't realise how much I'd miss you two daft buggers."

"Same here." A door being shut sounded in the background before Adam continued. "Bed's too big and too quiet without you. I've resisted letting *himself* sleep up there so his snoring can make up for the loss of yours."

"Ha ha. I could say the same about the hotel bed. Definitely too big, though. I miss your cold feet in the small of my back. I keep thinking about you."

"Is this going to get dirty? If Campbell were here should I cover his ears?"

"Pillock. Phone sex does nothing for me. I'll wait for the real thing. You can cover his ears then."

"Promises, promises. Right I can hear someone coming—I'll nip down to the car and ring you from there. Won't be a moment."

Robin waited, having to imagine Adam's journey from staffroom to car, not knowing the school at all well apart from what he'd seen at the PTA fete. There must be some significance in his wanting to continue the chat but best not to speculate over what that might be. Eventually Robin's phone sounded again.

"Sorry about that. I didn't want to simply ring off, given that we can't talk tonight. I'm off to try out that choir, so wish me luck."

Robin, relieved it was nothing more significant, said, "Is that the one that's part of the fundraising for the injured rugby player?"

"Yeah. I'm looking forward to it. Gives me something constructive to do."

Robin wished he had something equally interesting to look forward to, rather than staring at four hotel walls.

"So, this case. Is it the usual story? Victim allegedly didn't have an enemy in the world?"

"You've got it. At least he didn't according to initial statements, but things are starting to emerge from the woodwork."

"Nasty earwig-type things?"

"Yeah. Good description. Apt to be too much of a bruiser on the field, homophobic comments in the past, possibly caused trouble about some charity fundraising. Makes me suspicious about why nobody mentioned it initially." Robin relished, yet again, how good it was to talk a case through with Adam, away from the police station. Explaining it to someone who had no preconceptions made *him* see it clearer.

"Could be the old 'Don't speak ill of the dead.' Like when somebody gets killed and everybody says what a wonderful person they were, even though you get the impression they were a right tearaway."

Robin snorted. "Oh yes. The code. 'Rough diamond. Cheeky lad. Full of life.'"

"Tell me about it. I could add half a dozen others I've heard from parents defending their little darlings who've got into trouble at school. Like saying in a *Daily Telegraph* obituary that somebody never married, back in the days when you either couldn't state that they were gay but you wanted to imply it and not risk a libel suit."

"Oh, yes. I'd forgotten that. Anyway, I don't get the impression that Osment's homophobic comments were that other cliché, the smoke screen for his actually being gay. His sexual relationship with his wife was out of the ordinary, though."

"In what way?"

"There wasn't much of one. She seemed happy about it."

"Might be that one of them—or both—had a bit on the side that satisfied them."

"Not turned up anything on that front. Yet." He'd get the team at the station onto that as well. Had the low libido aspect blinded them to that possibility? *Low* didn't mean *nonexistent*. "We need a proper hare to chase."

"Keep your pecker up. You've had cases before that have felt stuck. Something will turn up to oil the wheels. Right, I really have to go now. Love you."

"Love you too. And Campbell. Kiss him for me."

"I will. Not as good as kissing you. Although almost as slobbery."

Before Robin could come up with a riposte, Adam ended the call.

He rang Pru to get the team investigating Nick's—and Melanie's—private life. Maybe someone in the darts team would be able to dish the dirt. Meanwhile, he wanted a word with Tom the groundsman, who was freshening up the pitch markings and who waved cheerily at Robin's approach.

"Hello, Mr. Bright. What can I do to help?"

"Tell me again about that vandalism."

"Happy to. Hold on." Tom carefully took his line-marking equipment off the pitch and removed his gloves. "Fire away."

"You admitted to giving a bloke from the press a thump. He's not complained so I'm not bothered about that."

Tom nodded. "But you want to know if I did the same with the vandal, given that it was Jamie's bench? Has he made a complaint?"

"Not that I'm aware of, but he may not be in a position to." Robin remembered the bruising on Nick's backside and the feeble way he'd accounted for it. What if *he'd* been the vandal, taking it out on the bench he'd objected to the fundraising for?

Tom looked blank. "Sorry, not with you. Being dim."

"Okay, let's take it in instalments. Did you catch the vandal in the act and tackle him the way you tackled that press bloke?"

"Ah." Tom sheepishly raised his hands. "I guess he's told you. He probably thinks he was unlucky, because normally nobody would have been here that evening—there hadn't been a home fixture. I only dropped in to the ground because I'd lost something valuable and was searching everywhere for it."

"Go on."

"He must have seen me coming—I had a torch—and started to run. The silly sod tripped. I kicked him up the jacksie a couple of times, but that was all. He'd have had nothing worse than a sore arse. After that I told him to eff off and not come back, so he did." The groundsman jabbed at a stone with his boot. "I shouldn't have done it, I know, but that bench is precious to me."

"Glad to hear that you're remorseful. You seem fond of taking the law into your own hands. The pressman, this vandal. We don't want that to happen." Robin hated sounding preachy, but in this instance, it was needed.

"Sometimes you have to do it yourself because the local police are sod all use." Tom launched another stone with his boot. "Sorry, you might do a great job down where you've come from, but round here some of them are worse than useless. They didn't even bother about the vandalism when we reported it. Not a priority."

"I can only apologise for that. I realise it must be frustrating." A case where Robin could sympathise with both parties. Police resources were pretty stretched at times and the expectations raised by television drama of the forensic tests and personnel readily available didn't help.

"This place feels like my manor, you know?" Tom made a sweeping gesture with his hand. "I'm happy to make a statement about what happened that evening. Put down my side of things."

Robin wasn't sure he should identify so strongly with that view, but he did, especially when the bench had been dedicated to your lost loved one. These were the times that impartiality had to be an active process. "Did you recognise him? The bloke whose backside you kicked?"

"No. Should I have done? It was dark, he had a hoodie on, and his face was partly covered."

"We believe it might have been Nick Osment, the man who was murdered here." As Robin spoke, he kept his eyes fixed on the groundsman's face, studying his reaction, but the only response appeared to be one of genuine surprise.

"No." Tom shook his head. "I mean, I'm not contradicting you—I'm just stunned. If I'd known, I'd have told you that time you were here before. With the young sergeant."

"Would you have recognised him if his face hadn't been covered that night?"

"I doubt it. I'm not sure I'd ever met the bloke. You said you *believe* it was the dead man. Is there some doubt?"

That hit straight at the crux of the matter. "The evidence we have is purely circumstantial. If there was anything you could tell us that might help to positively identify him, that would be useful."

Tom paused, gazing towards the corner of the stand, where the kicking might have happened. "The only thing I can think of, apart from any bruising on his arse, is that the hoodie had a tear along the back. I guess it could have been done that night."

They could search through Osment's clothes for an item matching that, although some less circumstantial would be preferable. "Can we take a stroll along the perimeter fencing? It's a slim chance, but maybe that tear happened climbing into the ground."

"I've always wanted to play CSIs." Tom abandoned his line-marking machine and led the way.

Robin wasn't confident they'd find any new evidence, given that the crime-scene team had gone over the clubhouse with little success, although their search might not have extended as far as the fencing. Three-quarters of the way round he'd almost given up hope of stumbling across anything other than litter, which Tom insisted on picking up and stuffing in a bag. Robin said he'd take it back to the station, although what he hoped to get out of it, he wasn't sure. Apart from some wisps of straw to clutch at.

"What about this?" The groundsman pointed at a small strip of black material snagged on a protruding piece of wire.

"I'll take it. Could be useful." Robin got out the kit he'd brought in case they found anything worth sampling. Donning gloves and carefully removing the material into an evidence bag, he scanned the area for other fragments that would be useful but without any luck. He could get the crime-scene team out here to scour the area again—if they'd done so in the first place—but it had been exposed for over a week, and a fresh search was going to be a long shot. Even this scrap of cloth might end up being a red herring.

"That could be from the hoodie," Tom said. "The fence is lower here and you could easily get over."

Robin sealed the envelope, labelled it, then scanned where they'd been walking. "To be honest, you could find a place to get over most of the way round, if you were determined."

Tom shrugged. "We can't make this place Fort Knox. Some of the local troublemakers would probably see it as a challenge, anyway, if we upped security."

"Do you get a lot of trouble with intruders?"

"We used to. Go back a few years and there were some right tearaways in the area but it seems to have calmed down. Want to examine the rest of the perimeter?"

"Might as well." Robin carefully tucked his envelope away. "Did you find it, by the way?"

"Find what?"

"The valuable item you lost."

"Oh, yes. Turned out it was at home all the time and I hadn't realised. I must have dropped it, and the thing rolled under the settee. I only found it a couple of days ago and I was fuming." The groundsman grinned. "I'd been running around like a headless chicken."

That reminded Robin of something he'd heard in one of the vicar's sermons about a woman hunting high and low all over the house for a missing coin. "It must have been important."

"It was. My late wife's wedding ring. I used to carry it in my wallet, but I won't in the future. Not after this episode."

"No. I can imagine." Robin surreptitiously fingered his own wedding ring. To lose a wife and a son. Had Weatherell recognised the vandal and been angry enough to come back and kill him at a later date? Although why would Osment return to the sports ground if he'd been caught there before and if the visit was planned, would he have agreed to meet the man who held a grudge against him?

"There's no easy way of putting this, but I suppose you'll guess what I need to ask." Not a part of the job Robin ever relished. Still, evidence had to be gathered.

"I've been expecting it. Ever since you told me who the little scrote was that I chased out. Sorry to speak ill of the dead but I don't believe in hypocrisy."

Robin, with years of experience of knowing when to speak and when to keep quiet, waited for Weatherell to continue. And odd that he now thought of him by his surname rather than as Tom; he'd crossed the nebulous line between likely innocent and potential suspect.

"That Wednesday, I'd been up here in the afternoon doing some maintenance. I went home and that's where I stayed. Couple of beers and the football on the telly."

"Can anybody vouch for that?"

"Definitely the box, because I shouted at it often enough." The groundsman wrinkled his brow. "I'm pretty sure that was the night I almost missed the start of the game because my mate Archie rang to talk about going out for a pint. He's recently lost his wife, so I said if he wanted to get together anytime, I'd make myself available. Now I won't swear to that being the Wednesday, because I watched the game on Tuesday night too, so it could have been then. You'll find your memory goes when you get older."

Robin gave a sympathetic grin. "I'll need his full name and contact details."

"I'll find them." Tom pulled out his phone, flicked on it until he found what he needed, then showed Robin the display. "Here. There's both his home number and his mobile. He'll be at work at the moment so he won't appreciate being rung there. Touchy about that. Amy—that's his wife—used to give him terrible stick about it." The groundsman got out his hankie to blow his nose. "Sorry. Amy dying's brought it all back about my Lulu. That's Louise, my wife. I should man up, or whatever they call it, but it's not that easy."

"No, it's not. I'll ring Archie this evening." Robin noted both numbers. "Much obliged."

Tom stuffed his handkerchief in his pocket. "You're all right for a rozzer. Good luck with getting that scrap of cloth matched up."

"Thanks." Robbin involuntarily patted his pocket. "We were going to walk the rest of the perimeter. Let's get that done."

They completed the circuit without finding anything other than a collection of trash to stuff in the groundsman's black bag. He carried that to Robin's car, heaving it into the boot, then wiping his hands. "Good luck with that too. Better you than me going through it all."

Robin eyed the bag, remembering how nasty looking some of the contents were. "I've got constables to do that. It'll be character building."

"One last thing." Tom kicked at a stone again. "Will you let me know if it turns out the dead man *was* the one here that Saturday?"

"I'll do that. And I won't get one of my constables to deputise this time."

Chapter Six

Adam arrived at the church in good time, picking up Campbell en route from work and wolfing down a sandwich Sandra had left in the fridge for him. He felt guilty about taking the car when it was such a short walk, but if the dog misbehaved in church, he'd then be able to take him out and put him on the back seat. That would be punishment enough to ensure there was no repeat of the misdemeanour. He also felt guilty about Robin, who sounded like he was having a wretched time of it, although there was nothing he could do about that.

He spotted Martin's car as he turned off the road and into the car park, suddenly remembering the strange reaction there'd been on the phone the previous night. Living with a detective—not to mention a large dog who was determined to get his wet nose into everything—had awakened Adam's natural sense of curiosity, and made him oversuspicious, with it. Why had Martin sounded so relieved that it was only Adam calling him? Or had it simply been relief that he'd been ringing about the choir rather than demanding the choirmaster stop chatting up *his* bloke?

He tried to put that to the back of his mind as he entered the church, or else the evening would be no fun at all. He found Campbell a comfy spot at the back of the church near a radiator, then tied his lead to a chair, more for effect than efficacy. A group of people were already there and others arriving by the minute, so after some informal introductions, they got down to business. Martin quickly and efficiently shared the key dates and times coming up, then asked everyone to spread the word about the concert as effectively as they could. Every bottom on a seat counted. People nodded and took notes, which gave Adam time to assess the rest of the group.

While his gaydar wasn't the most reliable of indicators, he'd have said the odds were good that the majority of those present were gay, which was in part confirmed when a group of them mentioned knowing each other through Kinechester LGBT choir and offered to use their mailing list to pimp the concert.

One of these, Brad, explained that the choir itself hadn't been in a position to raise money for this particular cause because they were already committed to a different charitable project, but the choir leader there had given her full support to any of the members wanting to get involved with the Lindenshaw effort. Matters nearly got derailed as another Kinechester singer tried to start up a debate about what the choir should call itself, but Adam, aware that such a discussion could in itself easily eat up all the rehearsal time, suggested that he and Martin could come up with some names and hold an online poll to choose the most popular.

Martin's glance of gratitude for this immediately morphed into his business face, the serious expression Adam recognised from Sunday services. Rumour had it that one or two in the church choir were a bit of a handful, and he managed to keep them in line, so the choirmaster should have no trouble with such a willing group as this.

Another of the Kinechester lads, Jonny, had volunteered in advance for piano duty, so they started with a simple rendition of both "Happy Birthday" and the surprising choice of the first part of "Bohemian Rhapsody." Presumably on the principle that everybody should know the words and tunes. During these, Martin went around the group listening to each singer in turn. Disconcerting it might have felt, but it certainly worked, because at the end he rapidly sorted them into groupings of voices that he said would work together, not just in terms of register but some sort of mysterious musical fit. A quick sing through of "Jerusalem," with everyone standing where they'd been put, proved what an instant difference the reorganisation had made.

"Excellent!" Martin rubbed his hands. "Now I've got a batch of material here to run through. You'll have to share the music until I get all the copies made, but that should be by the next rehearsal. Most of the songs will be familiar to you."

Adam grew in confidence as the person he was sharing music with flicked through it. A number of songs he already knew pretty well by heart, while a few—like "Bread and Roses"—wouldn't need much practice to be word perfect.

"Let's start with 'One,'" Martin said brightly, and the pianist launched into the familiar introduction from *A Chorus Line.*

At the end of the song, the sound of the church door opening caught everyone's attention.

"Sorry I'm late," the newcomer announced. "Saw the call for volunteers via my brother's rugby club. Didn't have a chance to make contact before now. Have I missed out?"

Everyone waited for Martin to answer, but he seemed to have turned speechless. Adam knew he was a stickler for punctuality, parish gossip reckoning that the only time the man lost his temper was when people turned up late for rehearsals. Probably this bloke rocking up forty minutes late and strolling in like he owned the place had put the choirmaster's nose out of joint. Eventually it was the pianist who suggested that the latecomer slip in at the end of the row and simply join in.

"We can take your details at the end." He turned to give Martin an encouraging glance and let his hands hover over the keys, awaiting instructions.

"'Bread and Roses,' please, Jonny." Martin raised his hands, closing his eyes briefly as the introduction began.

As they sang, Adam noticed that the choirmaster remained slightly on edge, and that he didn't bother to slip across to listen to the new arrival's voice. Perhaps he'd decided to give the bloke the heave-ho quietly at the end of the evening, as a point of principle. If you couldn't keep to time, by the musical beat or by the clock, Martin wouldn't want you in his choir. At least one person at the church had fallen foul of that dictum. The bloke concerned didn't seem that bothered about any fuss he'd caused, joining in the singing with gusto in a pleasant tenor voice.

"Look at that pair," the singer next to Adam whispered. "Our newcomer's giving the choirmaster the glad eye."

"You could be right." Understandable, though. Martin wasn't a bad-looking bloke if you liked them scrawny.

The choir sang for over an hour, running through most of the planned programme for the concert, and at the point voices were starting to feel the strain, Martin called it a day.

"Well done. I'd say this session's been a great success. I'm already confident that the performance will be a credit to us all. On the evening itself, we're leaving space in the programme for a set from a local band who've expressed interest in helping. They've got quite a big fan base, which should boost ticket sales. Give us a rest midway through, as well." He confirmed arrangements for the next session, then started to pack up his stuff.

Adam lingered to help put everything away, as they didn't want to incur the wrath of the flower ladies who'd expect the church to be left spick-and-span. He also helped encourage people to leave—gossip groups were already forming, and he had to subtly suggest to them that if they wanted to chat, they should do it in the car park as the church needed to be locked up soon. The guy who'd been last in had been noticeably first to leave. By the time Adam had ushered the last of them out, with Campbell acting as his wingman, Martin was coming down the aisle, studying the contact list, which he then folded and placed in his jacket pocket.

"Lights off?" Adam asked.

"Please. I'll need to get my keys. Hidden down the bottom of my briefcase as usual."

As they stood in the porch, both of them ensuring the door was secured, Martin said, "I know teachers are ridiculously busy, but would you have an hour or two tomorrow evening where we can go through some planning stuff? Like suggestions about names or a proper set order for the concert?"

Adam thought of refusing, but that would be both oversensitive and un-Christian. *He* wasn't the one Martin was supposed to fancy, so surely this wasn't an attempt at a date, and anyway he would have the dog present to act as chaperone. Campbell's slobbery chops poking themselves in Martin's face would act as a real passion killer if needed. As a project, this was for an admirable cause, one Robin would support, and it would keep him from being bored or mopey. He should be grateful to be able to pass the evening so constructively—watching sport on the telly curled up on the sofa with Campbell for company used to be fine in the pre-Robin days, but it had lost its appeal.

"Okay. At mine? Then I don't have to worry about Campbell being alone and fretting."

"Is Robin still away?" Martin was clearly trying to hide his disappointment if the answer was "yes".

"I'm afraid so. Did you know he's at Hartwood?" Adam wasn't surprised at Martin's startled reaction to the name. "Yes, the same place as the bloke we're fundraising for. There was a murder that night at the club, and the officer investigating it's been taken ill."

"So, they called in the cavalry?" Martin patted Campbell's head. "You'll be missing your dad. Want me to pick up fish and chips on the way tomorrow?"

"Are you asking him or me? He'd lick you to death for a portion of pea fritter." Cod and chips would make the evening bearable, though.

Martin laughed. "Sounds like a done deal." He headed off down the path, Adam and dog in tow, but as they reached the car park, he said, "This murder business. If a member of the public were to come across anything relevant, it would be their duty to take it to the police, wouldn't it?"

Where was this leading? "As I understand it, yes. A moral duty, anyway. I think it's only where it concerns child protection that you get into the legal-duty area. Mind you, Robin would say that he'd want to hear about anything, whether members of the public think it's relevant or not. The police build up the bigger picture and can work out what fits and what doesn't. Why do you ask?"

"Just something I came across. I'll sleep on it." With that enigmatic statement and an uneasy smile, Martin gave Adam a nod and made for his car.

As they drove home, Adam couldn't get the conversation out of his mind. Had Martin's awkwardness been to do with the latecomer or concern with the murder, and what inside knowledge did he want to share?

"I guess we'll find out tomorrow, eh, boy?" he asked Campbell, but the only response he got were gentle canine snores.

Chapter Seven

Some of the team were out when Robin got back on Tuesday afternoon and others had appointments scheduled first thing the next morning, so he organised a team briefing for later than usual on Wednesday. That would give him the chance to update Superintendent Betteridge with the slight progress they'd made. He didn't have the chance to talk to Pru about what he'd learned, as she was taking the opportunity to catch up with an old mate who lived in the area. He found a note on his desk from Sally, who said she'd been in touch with Melanie and confirmed that Nick had a low libido. Robin felt some relief at that—he didn't want life replicating the television cliché of the quiltbag character always being the victim or the killer. He went to add that detail to the incident board, but Sally had already done so. At a loose end, he decided there was nothing for it but to go back to the hotel, get dinner, watch a bit of telly, attack his emails, and generally have a miserable time of it.

The next morning's skies were bright, the weather lifting Robin's spirits as much as the prospect of a better day ahead.

The meeting with Betteridge started in a more positive manner than expected. He gave her a full update, then waited to get the *hurry up* speech.

Instead, she said, "Don't beat yourselves up. You've only been on the case a couple of days and the potential link of Osment to the vandalism is a step further forward than any the team managed with Robertson at the helm. That's not me knocking him, by the way, because he's a good officer, but I wonder if that bloody appendix was niggling and pulling him down for weeks."

"Could be." Robin should have been pleased with her confidence in him, but he still felt dissatisfied. How good it would have been to have offered his old boss some really tangible progress on the case. Although maybe that wouldn't have been politic: turning up and finding a solution almost instantly would have smacked of showing that the local force couldn't do their job properly. Probably best that it was taking a few days to bring this to a close. Irrespective of how every night away from home—had there only been two of them?—was absolute torture.

"How's the county lines stuff going?"

Betteridge rolled her eyes. "Glacially slow, although I think we're making some progress. Shame I can't clone you to work with me as well as on the murder."

"Leave off, boss. Adam will give you a rollicking for making my head swell."

Once it was time for the briefing, Robin started by thanking everyone for the effort they'd put in so far, then he asked Callum to talk hoodies. The constable said he'd been early that morning to Melanie's flat to pick up all three of Nick Osment's hooded tops.

"She said she wasn't sure which top he'd been wearing the evening he'd gone out for a run and supposedly fallen over, but the fact one had a rip up the back narrowed the field. I took them all, anyway, to be on the safe side. It'll take a while for the forensics team to make a comparison, but the odds seem good on linking the bloke to the vandalism. Or at least to his clambering over the fence at some point."

"Good work. Anything turn up out of the bin bag?"

Sally shared a glance with Laurence, conveying her disgust at the task they'd had to do. "Nothing that seemed relevant, sir."

"Thanks for doing it, anyway. If that's the nastiest job you're faced with in your career, you can count yourself lucky." He studied the incident board, where a picture of the groundsman had been added. "I spoke to Weatherell's mate Archie last night, and he backs up the story. He knew he'd rung on that Wednesday because he'd been to the co-op on the way home and got a lottery ticket for the midweek draw. He didn't win."

"Could he pin the time down?" Pru asked.

"Yes. He said it must have been around half past seven, because he had the Channel Four news on the telly. He particularly remembered that because they'd featured an article about an army wives choir who were putting on a concert. Seems like everyone's doing that to fundraise." Robin pressed on, aware that Adam had come to the forefront of his mind. "Archie says they broke into a song that used to be one of his wife's favourites and he'd had to put the call on hold and turn the box off."

"That fixes the time, but does it fix the place?" Laurence pointed out. "If Weatherell was on his mobile, he could have been at the clubhouse."

"He could. But Archie rang him on his landline; the call was completed somewhere between twenty and quarter to eight and it takes half an hour to get to the ground from his house. He couldn't have killed Osment, then gone home because that would have been too early and he couldn't have had the call and gone to the ground because that would have been too late. Another person with an alibi for the time of death. If I were ultra-suspicious, I'd be having kittens about that. Oh wait," Robin rolled his eyes, "I *am* ultra-suspicious."

"It sounds like one of those Agatha Christie books," Sally said. "Everyone in it together and covering up for each other."

Laurence snorted. "That's not what you said before, about a conspiracy theory too far. Are you changing your tune and suggesting they set up everything and it'll turn out that Greg's injury was faked as well?"

"I don't mean that at all." Flashes of scarlet flared on Sally's cheeks. "I only said it *sounded* like something Hercule Poirot would investigate. Not realistic."

"We're all getting rather worked up here," Robin said, in as soothing a voice as he could muster. "I don't think a mass conspiracy is likely—not least because the more people involved in covering something up, the greater chance there'll be a weak link who'll give it all away. Anyway, I'm not sure you'd get the little inconsistencies in the statements right, unless they're all bloody clever. But"—he raised his finger—"don't discount the notion that there's been collaboration between people, before or after the event."

Duly chastened, Laurence folded his arms and clearly tried not to scowl. The effect was comical rather than threatening: he'd have to learn how to develop a better "hard man" persona.

Robin pressed on. "Sally, the darts team. Any progress with them?"

"Yes and no. I spoke to a couple of them, and they said they felt sorry for Osment. Reckoned his wife had led him a bit of a dance before they were married, knocking about with another bloke. One of the team said he wouldn't be surprised if it carried on postnuptials. They didn't have a name for the bloke concerned, but they thought he might have been a rugby player because he was supposed to be built like an outhouse. I mentioned it to Sergeant Davis, and we reckoned it was worth going to see Andy again rather than the coach. That's where we were this morning."

"That's a brave call. Isn't he likely to stick up for his mates?" Robin hoped Pru had thought that part through before dashing in. He needn't have worried.

"We considered that, sir, and decided it was worth the risk. It struck me that he was a decent bloke who wanted to do the right thing. We went in soft, used the old gentle persuasion that if there was dobbing to be done, it was better for him to do it rather than us find out later that people had been keeping back relevant information and us being suspicious about why they'd done it."

"So long as you didn't use thumbscrews, I'm happy," Robin said. Watching Pru at work with a witness would be a useful education for any of these young officers. Gentle persuasion, with the person being interviewed sometimes thinking it was all their idea in the first place to do what she wanted.

"Didn't need them, sir. As I said, he's fundamentally a nice bloke who's found himself caught up in two horrible situations, and while I suspect he'd like time to rewind and everything to be made better, he's pragmatic about what he needs to do. Even if it means snitching on his best mate." Pru paused briefly while the penny dropped. "Yep. Big Dave. He and Melanie were going out before she met Nick. It ended when he met Kirsty, who's now his wife. Andy reckons people have been saying the fling got reignited a year or so back, but he doesn't know that for a fact, and frankly he doubts it. Says it would be out of character for Dave to carry on with a married woman."

Is that wishful thinking on Andy's part or a genuine comment on the man's character? Big Dave who'd always protected him so *couldn't possibly do wrong.* "We'll have to ask them direct. Today, preferably. Play the old *if it isn't relevant to the case, it won't come out* card. Might be worth talking to Dawn too. She'll know. Given that both Dave and Melanie seem to have unshakeable alibis, it's not like coming clean about any affair is going to put them in the frame."

"Sorry, sir, but is that necessarily so?" Callum's hunched shoulders expressed his discomfort with challenging his superior officer. "Melanie's alibi relies on her two mates, and we know how readily people cover for each other."

Robin, always appreciative of where junior officers showed a touch of spark, said, "Agreed. Although remember that I said *seem* to have unshakeable alibis. I've not forgotten that Dave was last out of the dressing room and then first back in it with his pal Andy, so he had a small window of opportunity to commit the deed and then tidy up afterwards, with or without help. It's always possible his mates are covering for him too, whether intentionally or subconsciously. Telling us he wasn't there long enough to have killed Osment before emerging."

"Also, he seems to have been avoiding going into the changing rooms until he was forced to do so."

"Shame they don't have working CCTV at the ground, sir," Callum observed.

Robin agreed. "You're right, there. Proper cameras, as opposed to dummy ones, could have provided the key piece of information we need. Now, remind me. Has anyone of the key players got a criminal record at all?"

Callum shook his head. "Dave got done for using his mobile at the wheel last year, but apart from that, it's simply a case of a couple of them having points on their licences for speeding. Preese included."

"What about the Tuckton Rugby Club angle? Any luck with that, Laurence?"

"Still pursuing it, sir. So far it seems like nobody kept in touch with Osment. Nobody admits to it, anyway. Builds up to the picture of him being unpopular and a bit of a troublemaker, though. Over fond of beer after the game."

"Isn't that true of all rugby players?" Sally snorted.

"Probably, but they usually have the sense not to drink four pints and then get in their car." Laurence shuffled his notes. "I spoke to a guy this morning—Livingstone, team captain when Osment was playing there—who said he had a near miss once on the way home, nearly taking out a lamppost. After that Livingstone insisted that he get a lift to home games with a bloke called Howarth, who lived nearby and who was teetotal so happy to help. Do you think it's worth talking to him, sir?"

"Why not? If they shared a car, they'd have chatted. Maybe Osment let something slip. Might be worth exploring that near miss he had too. Somebody might bear a grudge." Robin jerked his thumb towards the door. "Pru, can you see if Melanie's available to talk to us today? I'm going to ring Dave. The sooner we can see them, the less time they'll have for getting suspicious about what we're after and putting their stories aligned with each other."

The sergeant nodded. "Will do. Although if I were a betting woman, I'd have a fiver on that already having happened."

Which was likely true and extremely frustrating.

Robin felt a pang of guilt at not bringing the constables along for the two key interviews late that afternoon, but he wanted the reassuring presence of Pru at his side. They worked well as a team, and if this was a turning point of the investigation, they had to make the most of it. The others had plenty to occupy them, not least the delicate task of establishing whether there was any chance that Greg's injuries could have been exaggerated.

Melanie was at home, though she had apparently returned to work part-time because, as she said to Pru when she phoned, it wasn't doing her any good staring at the same four walls or being reminded of Nick at every turn. The funeral was booked for the next week and after that, she was going to have a weekend away.

"If we let her," Pru added, as they drew up outside the block of flats.

"I'm not sure we have much choice, as long as we have a contact number for her." Robin stared up at Melanie's flat's window, which had a clear view of the car park, so their arrival would likely not go unnoticed. "Come on. We've had trickier things to deal with."

Once in the flat, they went through the usual pleasantries, refusing a cup of tea even though Robin was gagging for a drink. He'd have to make do with a bottle of water back in the car.

"I'm sorry to have to ask you something so delicate given the circumstances," he began, "but you'll appreciate that we have to follow up every lead, no matter how unpleasant."

Melanie, face drawn and tired, perhaps exhausted by the half day she'd worked, blanched. "What's this about?"

"Dave Venter. You two were going out before you met Nick?"

"Yes. Although if you want to be accurate"—Melanie nodded towards Pru's notebook—"it was when Dave met Kirsty that we split up. It was for the best. They're as happily married as we were."

Did that sound over defensive? What Robin's old rugby coach would have called *getting your retaliation in first*?

"Did you get back together afterwards?" Pru's soothing voice held steel within its velvet softness.

"No! Of course not. What kind of woman do you think I am?"

"We don't judge anyone. We're only interested in the facts and how they relate to your husband's murder." The steel was out of the velvet sheath now.

"Well, the facts are that people have dirty minds." Melanie rose from the settee, crossing to the window—although whether she was looking at anything, Robin doubted. "Dave and I have sometimes met up for coffee and a chat. We understand each other. Somebody must have seen us, put two and two together and got five. All we ever did was talk."

"Nick didn't believe that, though, did he?" Robin stated, rather than asked.

Melanie still wouldn't face them. "Truth is, Nick sober believed it, but Nick aled up didn't. He didn't drink that often, but when he did, it was like someone flicked a switch. That's why I was pleased when he stopped playing rugby: the darts guys keep—kept—him on the straight and narrow."

Robin couldn't remember alcohol being reported in the dead man's system, but he'd still ask. "Had he been drinking the night he died?"

"Not when he was here. I suppose it was possible he went and had a couple after he left."

"You said it was like someone had flicked a switch. In what way?" Pru asked.

Melanie swung round. "He didn't get violent, if that's what you're thinking. My mate Shaz—that's the one who moved to the States with her new bloke—was in an abusive relationship previously, so if Nick had started anything like that I'd have been out. He had a habit of getting silly things into his head and making a fuss about nothing."

"Like he made a fuss over the fundraising?" Pru cut in.

"Yes. Exactly like that. He'd come home from a rugby match and go secretly snooping around in case someone had been here. Then half an hour later he'd have started sobering up and get all apologetic. One time he even followed Dave after training, in case he was meeting up with me. Silly sod. He'd been better since he took up darts."

"Why did you put up with it?" Pru's tone suggested that would have been beyond the pale for her.

"Because we loved each other. I took it as a joke most of the time, despite the fact that others couldn't. That's why Dawn didn't get on with him. She—" Melanie's mouth snapped shut.

"She what?"

They waited as Melanie wrestled with an answer.

Eventually she said, "She always says she'd have preferred it if I'd married Dave," then burst into tears.

"Did you buy that, sir?" They were on the way to see Dave, who was amenable to seeing them—if not happy about it—once the school day had finished. "Could anyone be so saintly that they'd willingly put up with Osment's crap?"

"You know the answer to that as well as I do, given what we have to deal with." Time and again Robin had found himself wondering why people didn't up sticks and walk away from toxic situations. "The story adds up, though. Explains his leaving Tuckton Chiefs and the troublemaking."

"To an extent. You can see why he got strange ideas about Melanie, but not about this memorial bench. Unless it was to get back at Dave somehow."

"Maybe it was Dave's idea. We'll ask him."

In fact, it was the first question they posed, being an easy intro to another tricky conversation.

"The bench? Yes, that was me, although not alone. You can imagine the scene: the pub, me, Andy, and Coach. After a few pints, we had the whole thing planned. That's why it's been relatively easy to get the fundraising for Greg going. Some of the groundwork's already done."

If Dave had received prior warning about why the police were visiting, he was showing no signs of it.

"We know he was the Hartwood club groundsman's son."

"Yes. I'd not been playing for Hartwood that long when he was killed, although I knew Jamie already. He was a pupil here, and I've always helped with the after-school rugby club, so our paths crossed. He was a promising player." Dave shook his head. "Such a waste. Why do you ask?"

"Connection to the case. Why Osment had a bee in his bonnet about the memorial bench and the money it cost." Pru smiled sweetly. "We're trying to build up a clearer picture of him and his relationship to the people we've spoken to. Like you, for example."

"Me? I'm not sure I knew the bloke very much at all. Heard a lot about him, obviously, and I think I met him once or twice in the past." Dave shrugged.

"But you knew his wife," Robin cut in. "You and Melanie were an item before she married."

"We were. I don't deny it. Then I met Kirsty and everything changed." Dave glanced at the photograph of his wife.

"Yet you didn't recognise his body when you found it?" *Or pretended you didn't recognise it.*

"No. Back then he had a beard. I remember that because Melanie told me she'd made Nick shave it off just after they were married. Made him look like a paedophile."

Robin held his tongue. The bloke worked in a school—surely he knew that paedophiles came in all shapes, sizes, and genders? "So, to be absolutely clear, you never associated the dead man with Melanie's husband?"

"Never." Dave crossed his arms over his midriff. "I haven't seen him for years. It's Melanie and I who've remained friends. *Just* friends."

Just friends. Robin's gran used to sing a song about how Samson and Delilah—and other famous couples—used to say they were simply friends. When he'd asked her about it, she'd told him that was the phrase people used about relationships in interviews to cover the fact that they were having a fling. Since then he'd heard similar denials, particularly at work.

"No more than that?" he asked.

"No more than that," Dave stated.

"Nick believed your affair had started up once more."

"He had. And he was wrong."

For all that Dave's responses were produced without emotion, Robin couldn't quite believe them. Copper's nose twitching again. "He wasn't the only person to believe it, though."

"I can believe that." The same objective, bland reaction. "If Nick got it into his head that we'd rekindled the old flame, he'd have told other people. It's like when you get some fake news buzzing round the internet. It starts in one place, then pops up everywhere."

This sounded increasingly like a prepared set of answers. Maybe it was worth trying a few questions to try to get under Dave's skin. "Did Nick Osment ever threaten you?"

"No. Why should he?"

Exasperated, Robin sniped, "Because of either or both of the things we've been discussing. If he wasn't hurrying home from Tuckton games to catch you and Melanie at it, then who *was* he trying to catch with her? Has she got a whole string of blokes?"

At last they got a reaction. Dave slammed his hand on the desk. "Now, you watch it. Melanie's not like that. She's not like some of the rugby groupies you get hanging around players. She was a good wife to Nick, and he should have appreciated the fact."

"Did you ever tell him that?" Pru asked.

"What? No. I told you. I didn't know the bloke."

"You wouldn't need to know him to talk to him." Pru would know how far she could apply pressure, given the constraints of an informal interview. "We've got your original statement with all the timings of what happened the night Osment died. Do you want to change any of that?"

"Of course I don't. I've told you the truth, and the rest of the team can back it up."

Robin pondered for a moment. He could press Dave about being last out of the changing rooms and how that would possibly have given him enough time to commit the deed, but he'd need to formally caution him before he asked the question and at present there wasn't enough evidence to justify taking that step.

"Two further questions," he said. "You and Melanie have been meeting up again, is that right?"

"Yes. I'm not denying it. But only for coffee and a chat."

"When did you last meet?"

Dave raised his hand to his neck, as though about to run a finger round his collar but thinking better of it. "The Monday of the week before he was killed. I was working late so was going to go straight to training, after grabbing a bite to eat at Morrisons. Yeah, haute cuisine, I know, but it's en route and convenient. Melanie happened to be in there shopping, so she had a coffee while I ate."

Pru and Robin shared a glance. Quite a coincidence, them both being in Morrisons—or did Melanie regularly use the store at that time and Dave had deliberately gone there to catch her?

"If you and all the rugby boys can vouch for each other, who killed Osment?"

"That's three questions, Mr. Bright."

Robin, wishing he could grab a rag and wipe the smug grin off Dave's face, gestured towards Pru. "I'll let Sergeant Davis ask it, then."

She leaned forwards. "Who killed Osment? You must have been discussing it with the rest of the team. And with Melanie."

"I've not spoken to her about it. Do you think I'm a callous bastard?" It appeared to be a genuine response. Especially compared to some of his other replies.

"But with the team," Pru pressed on. "A guy gets killed in your changing room while you're on the field and nobody's talking about who did it?"

Dave, eyes briefly closed, steepled his hands to his mouth, then took a deep breath before saying, "Hard as you may find this to believe, we've more important things to discuss. Greg's unlikely to walk again, and he's the one we're spending our time and energy on, rather than gossiping like old women."

Which was quite likely true, but left the same taste in Robin's mouth as the whole interview had. That they were being fed a version of events that was certainly accurate in parts yet overall unconvincing.

They ended the interview with the usual formalities and returned to the car with Pru texting the police station to see if there had been any developments and Robin wrapped up in his thoughts. While they were approaching the truth, it remained no closer than on the horizon. Along with the prospect of getting back to his own bed and the person warming it.

Chapter Eight

Wednesday evening, Adam got home as early as he could. Given that it seemed increasingly unlikely that Robin would be home for the weekend, he could defer some of his planning and other school work until then, which would be a better use of time.

He'd asked Sandra to get in a few bottles of beer—in case Martin had walked from the chip shop and wasn't driving home—plus fizzy fruit drink in case he'd brought either his car or his bike, both of them likelier than Shanks's pony given that speed was of the essence in keeping the chips warm. The sound of a motor pulling up outside suggested they'd be opening the nonalcoholic option.

The food and drink went down accompanied by local and church chat, both having agreed that they'd keep the business for afterwards, with a side portion of two doggy eyes fixed on them.

"You'd think we never fed him," Adam said, jerking his fork in Campbell's direction.

Martin chuckled. "Yes, he looks thin and neglected, poor child. Do you think of him like he's your child, by the way?"

"No. Never have. He's just... Difficult to describe the relationship. Our mutual best pal, perhaps."

"You seem such a nice couple. I can't help feeling a touch envious."

"We were very fortunate to meet each other." Adam didn't elaborate on the strange circumstances in which they'd met. It had been part of parish gossip on and off, so chances were Martin already knew. *They met over a dead body in a school kitchen. Like the plot of a book.* "I guess you could say we're soul mates, me and Robin."

Martin sighed, a touch too dramatically. "I thought David and I were soul mates too. I've been in a bit of a rut since he upped sticks, not really making any sort of an effort to get out and find myself another proper relationship. It's all too easy to say, 'I'm hurting too much, I'll leave it until next month and then I'll get serious about seeking a date,' and then you find you're six months down the line and nothing's changed."

"Yeah, it happens." Adam hadn't expected quite such an outpouring of personal stuff, and he didn't fancy showing too much sympathy. He couldn't be sure how Martin was going to interpret things, especially if he was feeling lonely. He was also half-expecting some follow up from the previous night's comments about passing on information if it was relevant. No sign of that coming from Martin yet.

"I have Baggins, who keeps me warm on cold nights, but a cat's not quite the same as a bloke. You'll find that with Campbell, with Robin being away."

"Yes. We're both missing him." Adam glanced down to find—as if on cue—Campbell had sidled over and was gazing up at him with doleful eyes. "At least I have *himself* to cuddle up to. Robin's not so lucky."

Martin nodded. "If and when I find someone to share my life, they'll have to accept whisker-features and get his seal of approval as well. He sets a high standard."

Adam could sympathise with that. If Robin had been a dog-hater, then they'd not have made it past the fancying-each-other stage. But Campbell—despite the fact that generally he was such a tart he'd be anybody's friend for a dog biscuit—had taken to the bloke from the start. He'd kept up the affection after any suggestion of cupboard love had passed, so it must be real.

"Trouble is I don't like the round of cruising and casual pickups," Martin continued. "Never really been my scene, and there's something about all your pals getting into serious relationships and then starting to live together or tie the knot that starts to make you feel you're missing out. I haven't got a biological clock, so I can't hear it ticking at me. I'm probably feeling lonely."

Shut up, shut up, shut up. Adam felt guilty about his thoughts, but it wasn't as if he and Martin were bosom buddies, used to having these kinds of heart-to-hearts. The fact the bloke clearly had a crush on Robin made the situation all the more uncomfortable.

"I'm sure the right bloke will come along," Adam said, in exactly the offhand platitudinous way he hated other people using. "Maybe this choir thing could be the start. There's bound to be guys in a similar position."

"Let's hope so." Martin scooped up the last chip. "Anyway, thanks for doing this. Not only the planning stuff, but the singing. I didn't realise what a good voice you've got. Never had the chance to pick it out from the congregation."

"Thanks. I wouldn't say it's good enough for a solo, but in a choir you don't notice."

"Don't undersell yourself."

"It isn't underselling, it's simple fact. If you'd heard my rendition of 'Delilah' in the university bar after a rugby game, you'd understand. Just as well you didn't hold auditions or you might have rejected me. I feel self-conscious when I have to sing solo, but I can go along with a crowd."

"I did think of having auditions. Had a few tunes in mind. 'Yellow' would be a good choice, for example. Type of song that can be sung acapella and nobody expects you to sound like Chris Martin. Shame you don't have time to sing in the church choir."

Adam shrugged. "Well, you know what it's like for teachers. Especially for deputy headteachers. I agree about it being a shame, though. I used to sing in the choir at secondary school and it was fun. Never got shouted at by the conductor, anyway, unlike some of the lads who got it in the neck regularly for growling instead of singing."

"I never shout. I gently encourage. It gets the best out of people. Have to say, it's rare that somebody can't carry a tune at all." Martin gave Campbell—who'd sidled over—a tickle behind his ear. "If they do, they're likely to know the fact. I've only once had to deliver the whole truth to somebody who had no voice at all but thought they were a budding Pavarotti. Anyway, kindness and encouragement, that's my philosophy."

"Great approach. It's the best way to teach anyone—adult or child. Talking of which"—Adam glanced at his watch—"we need to get on. Have to be ready to face my eleven-year-olds tomorrow, so I can't let tonight go on too late."

"Oh, yes, sorry. I should have thought. Shall I help clear away?"

"Please."

As they tidied away the remains of the meal, loaded up the dishwasher, and put on the kettle, the conversation continued. "Will Robin be away for long? Any chance he'll be back for the weekend?"

"I doubt it." Adam couldn't make out if the choirmaster was pleased or disappointed at that response. "Not unless they have a miracle breakthrough in the next forty-eight hours. Can you add that to your prayers whenever you next say them?"

"I will." Martin hesitated. "But only if you'll add a sentence to yours for me."

"Okay." Adam was reluctant to open up another heart-to-heart session, but his conscience wouldn't let him metaphorically pass by on the other side of the road. "I did wonder if something was bothering you yesterday. Like you'd seen a ghost."

"You don't miss much. I got a shock when that chap walked in after we'd started singing. Thought it was somebody I'd had a disastrous date with, but it wasn't. It's actually his twin brother. I'd forgotten he had one until I saw he'd written Sam on the contact sheet. Such a relief."

"Okay, you've lost me. Say that again slowly while I make a cuppa."

"About a year ago, I had the date from hell with a guy called Joe Woakes." Martin made a face like he'd got a lemon in his mouth. "It was when I was living in Banbury. We were introduced by a mutual friend and went out for a drink and snacks. We hit it off pretty well, helped by a couple of bottles of white wine, so we almost got to the my-place-or-yours part. Then he went green at the gills, dashed to the loo, and appeared ten minutes later looking like death. Turned out he'd been in contact with norovirus and it had come on like a train. Total passion killer."

"I can imagine." Adam offered him a mug. "Do you want to sort out your own milk and sugar? Then if there's more to this horror story, tell me it in the lounge."

"What about getting down to choir business so you can have an early night?" The question didn't sound that pointed.

"I can manage an extra ten minutes. Got to be better than the book I've got on the bedside table."

Once they'd sat down, Martin continued his account. "So, *norovirus Joe.* I called a cab, got him back to his place, and then left him with his flatmate to nurse. *He* was the one who supposedly gave him norovirus in the first place, so there was poetic justice in making him do the mopping up when the Catherine wheel started again. After that we didn't manage a second date. I guess he was too embarrassed, and I couldn't get the thought of *d and v* out of my head."

That couldn't be the whole story. Martin would have flushed red rather than gone white when Joe's brother walked into the church if it had been a case of embarrassment. "Did you catch it?"

"No. Iron guts, that's me. Left me wary of blind dates, though."

That made sense, although it still didn't explain the horrified expression on Martin's face; this story was the sort of thing you laughed at afterwards.

"Two ships that passed in the night without docking, if you like," Martin continued.

"Very poetic. And when you saw Sam you thought that fate had tried to get you to dock again?"

"Something like that." Martin didn't sound convincing. "That ship—excuse the pun—has sailed, though."

"Has it? I got the impression last night that he liked you. It might simply have been his friendly nature, but my money's on him eyeing you up."

"Was he?" The dismayed expression returned.

"Okay, feel free to tell me to wind my neck in, but if I'm to say a prayer for you, shouldn't you tell me the whole story?"

"Doesn't Neil say that you can pray for someone without knowing all the details, on the principle that God knows what's needed? Having said that, I'm glad you asked. In case something crops up with Sam. I had a lucky escape, and not just from *the runs*." Martin stared into his mug. "I've kept in touch with the pal who introduced us, and about a month ago he messaged me to make an apology. He'd found out that Joe had been cautioned a few years back. Beat up an ex-partner. *He* wouldn't press charges, but the police made sure Joe knew he'd better not repeat the offence. Ricky—he's the mutual friend and incidentally the person who told me about the appeal for the injured player—said he'd have never forgiven himself if I'd got involved with Joe and the same thing happened."

"Hell. Why didn't the boyfriend proceed with his complaint? I guess he was embarrassed." Adam had heard of a man—friend of a friend again, so the story might have grown in the telling—who'd been beaten up by his male partner and had been too ashamed to go to the police about it.

"No. He felt there were mitigating circumstances, I believe. Joe had got himself into a state because of a hit-and-run on someone he knew. The victim was a young lad who ended up dead and who might have survived if the driver had rung for help."

"That's awful." Whether it excused Joe's behaviour was another question but it explained a lot. "Have you asked Ricky what the brother's like?"

"I messaged him last night. He says Sam's only identical in character so far as being gay. He's supposed to be really nice."

Gay identical twins and both of them handsome, if Sam was anything to go by. The type of situation that would have set the keyboards of gay romance writers going like the clappers. Maybe this was the right time to concentrate on the matter in hand rather than the stuff of fantasy.

"Understood and filed away for future reference. Let's talk choir."

An hour—a very productive hour—later, they'd pretty well completed all they'd needed to, having worked together surprisingly well. Martin like to have a clear plan, as did Adam and their appreciation of what would make a good concert ran along the same lines, with an understanding of when to feature the solo performers.

As Martin began slowly to clear his stuff away, Adam—much as he didn't enjoy playing at agony aunts, or matchmakers—wondered if he should tell Martin to seize the day, assuming an opportunity came again, whether it was with Sam or anyone else. There was an added benefit that if he was swooning over some bloke, then he couldn't be mooning over Robin. He was about to tackle the subject with as much delicacy as he could summon up, when something from the previous night jangled in his brain.

"Martin, can you remember last night, Sam saying that he'd heard about the choir through his brother's rugby club? Was that Joe?"

Martin paused, a handful of paper midway into his case. "Yes. Ricky reckons there's only the two of them. I checked with him earlier today and asked what team Joe played for. It was Hartwood Wasps."

"Why didn't you tell me this earlier in the evening? We could have Facetimed Robin about it," Adam added, in the slow, patient tone he adopted for some of his less able pupils.

Martin shrugged. "I really am hopeless. I got wound up talking about my love life and the music and ignored all the rest."

"You are a total prat. A total prat who needs to hear this. That's not just the club where the injury happened. It's where the murder happened, the one Robin's gone to investigate."

"I know. I googled it earlier today."

Adam wondered what sort of sentence he'd get for thumping a choirmaster and whether the bloke being an utter wally was an acceptable defence. "Well, what you've told me may mean nothing, but I'm going to have to pass that stuff about Joe straight on to Robin. He can work out if his past has any relevance. He can also advise me whether I need to be wary around Sam, assuming he's got a connection to the case, given my relationship with the investigating officer."

"I could give you Ricky's details and you can get your man to give him a call. Or one of his constables could ring. Robin's no doubt too important to pick up a job like that."

Adam sensed some insult to his partner, as acutely as Campbell would have sensed a dog biscuit in the offing. "In terms of rank, maybe, but you don't know him that well if you think he's the sort of bloke who won't muck in with the team."

"Sorry, I didn't mean to be insulting. I don't understand policing, either. I know Robin's a good bloke—like I've said, you're very lucky."

"I know I am." Adam, aware that his shoulders had shot earwards with tension, tried to relax. "He'll be grateful for the lead. Sometimes it's the smallest items of information that make a difference to solving a case. And I don't think he'll need Ricky's contact number. Joe's name should be enough. I can always get back to you if need be. Right." He rose. "Sorry to boot you out, but I need to make contact with the constabulary."

"Oh, yes." Martin leaped out of his seat, shoving the last of his stuff into his case. "See you at the next practice."

"Looking forward to it."

As soon as Martin had gone, Adam got on the phone. Robin was expecting a late call, so if the bloke was lying on his hotel bed dozing in front of some awful Freeview programme, it was excusable to wake him. It turned out he'd recently got back to his room, having been down in the bar watching the footie over a pint of beer he'd made last a long time.

"How's everything?" Robin asked.

"Well . . ."

"I don't like the sound of that *well.* Should I be worried?"

"Don't think so. Need to check I'm not potentially treading on toes. And before you say that's never stopped me in the past, may I remind you that your cases want to draw me in, not vice versa?"

A loud groan sounded down the line. "I thought we were safe from that this time."

"Same here. Connection's only a loose one, though, and it may only exist in my overactive imagination." Adam went on to explain about the mistaken identity at choir practice, the story of Joe's caution, and the reasoning behind why charges hadn't been pressed.

At the mention of the hit-and-run, Robin's voice changed. Noticeably alert, straight into rozzer mode. "Right, let me grab a notepad and pen, then can you say this all again, slowly, please? I think somebody mentioned a bloke called Joe being at training that night, but it's not an uncommon name. The hit-and-run sounds significant."

Adam went through it all again, ending with, "You won't shoot me if this turns out to be nothing to do with the case?"

"Nah. Instead, I'll get Campbell to slobber in your half of the bed. I've enough experience to know what's worth following and when my chain's being yanked. Odd, though, this all turning up in Lindenshaw right now."

"I've been having the same thoughts while I was telling you about it. Sam walking through the church door almost from nowhere." It might simply be a coincidence—what Neil the vicar would call a Godcidence, where something that seemed accidental happened for a good reason. Not a phenomenon Adam really believed in.

"Well if he wants to have a tête-à-tête, find an excuse not to. At least until I know whether he or his brother are embroiled in things."

"Will do, guv'nor." Adam chuckled. "I'm taking Campbell with me to rehearsals, anyway, so he'll do the bodyguard stuff. Stops him pining, too."

"Is he pining a lot?" Robin's tone had become quiet and constrained, like a timid schoolboy's.

"A little. So am I. But don't worry about us. Please."

"I'll try not to. It's no fun, this travelling lark. I used to think it would be dead glamorous, globetrotting for work, but it isn't."

"Hartwood's scarcely globetrotting, but I take your point. One hotel's much like another."

"Yep. And nobody to say, 'Isn't the view nice?' to. Not that the view *is* that nice."

"You'll soon be home. Love you."

"Love you too. And himself."

The conversation ended with a couple of personal endearments not suitable for canine ears, after which Adam got into the bedtime routine, beginning with letting Campbell out into the garden. As he watched the dog wander around, trying to find the best place to relieve himself, Adam wondered how, yet again, he'd got caught up in a murder case, albeit at one or two removes. It kept happening. Adam didn't include the first murder case Robin had led the investigation on—the fact the victim had been killed at Adam's school had been the catalyst for their meeting—but three subsequent cases had touched him to some extent or another, whether directly or through friends. While matters hadn't quite become as bad as one of those television series where the amateur detective was dealing with death in their vicinity on a weekly basis, it *did* feel like the universe was having a laugh.

He remembered sitting with Campbell in the bedroom, smugly assuring himself that this case was too far away to draw him in, and how he'd touched wood afterwards, just in case. Well, that strategy hadn't worked, had it?

Chapter Nine

Thursday morning: the case had gone from the annoying stage where they hardly had two proper leads to rub together to the equally annoying stage where they had more leads than they needed, because all of them appeared to take them to someone with an alibi.

His update to Betteridge—by phone as she was the other end of the county—began with what he'd learned from Adam.

"Pru's subsequently found out we're talking about the same Joe Woakes who plays for Hartwood Wasps," Robin said, "and yes, he has a caution for assault, given only a few days after Jamie Weatherell was killed."

"Sounds promising."

"It isn't. He was the person very visibly administering first aid to Greg while they waited for the ambulance. Talking of Greg, Sally's got a tame doctor at the hospital who told her that his injuries are every bit as real as we've been told, so there's nothing dodgy there."

"I'd still put Woakes's name on the incident board," Betteridge suggested.

"Already done it." Even though he didn't think Woakes was a realistic suspect.

The morning briefing was lively, with everyone anxious to contribute.

Laurence had been to see Howarth, who confirmed everything they'd been told by his team captain, although it seemed there'd been a touch of exaggeration. Yes, Osment had been unfit to drive, but only the once. He'd nearly collided with one of the other players, who had been walking from the ground postmatch along an unlit road to his home nearby. Howarth had volunteered to take Osment in and out to home games to prevent a rerun of the event, as his journey took him near the Osments' flat.

"Was Osment such a good player that they bent so far over backwards to accommodate him?" Pru asked.

"I asked that," Laurence said. "Howarth reckoned Osment was promising but nothing special. Trouble is the guy he nearly hit was three sheets to the wind as well and he'd been wandering all over the road, so *he* was dead apologetic about nearly causing the accident. The club had to find a pragmatic solution."

Robin could imagine such a compromise being dreamed up over a pint of IPA. "Did Howarth ever *not* give him a lift?"

"A couple of times, but then he got someone else to do it."

"Anything emerge about Osment himself?" Robin, frustrated, kicked his heels against a desk.

"Just one thing." Laurence wore a self-satisfied smile. "Towards the end of his time at Tuckton, Osment was getting agitated that his wife might have reignited the flame with an old boyfriend. Howarth thinks it might have been the reason the guy stopped playing. Wanted to keep an eye on her. There was an instance postmatch where they'd left early as Howarth had to get home and Osment wanted him to step on the gas. He reckoned he could catch Melanie and the other bloke at it and give him a belting."

"Then the likelihood is there *was* another lover, as well as Dave," Sally pointed out. "Osment wasn't that large and Dave's supposed to be built like a Sherman tank. Why take him on in a fight?"

Laurence, smile gone and shoulders hunched like he fancied a fight himself, said, "When did logic come into consideration when you're itching for a punch-up?"

"Okay, but if it was a match day, wouldn't Dave have been playing at the same time? In which case, he couldn't have been with Melanie." She glanced at Pru for support but it didn't come.

"The fixtures don't always coincide in the top leagues," the sergeant replied. "Might be worth finding out how the lower tiers operate. We might be able to pin down a certain match day and find the start times, although that may not help. Dave might have been missing a game through injury."

Callum snickered. "Not an injury that affected his wedding tackle, then?"

"Behave." Robin couldn't suppress a grin, though. "Trouble is, thinking back to that Wednesday, would Osment have voluntarily gone to meet Dave at the ground?"

"They might not have arranged to meet. He might have decided to give the guy a thumping," Callum suggested. "Especially if he had a grudge against the club because of what had happened on the Saturday."

"Or he might have decided to get into the dressing room and either trash or nick Dave's stuff," Laurence said.

"Could be," Pru replied, "but in that case he'd be barking up the wrong tree. The players took all their valuables and left them in a locked box pitch side, remember?"

"Osment wouldn't necessarily know that." Laurence fought his corner with spirit. "He might even have been responsible for the thefts from the athletics club and was chancing his arm again."

"That's a big leap of deduction, but let's run with it. Why does he go back that Wednesday when any of Dave's mates might have come along to defend either him or their property?" Pru swivelled in her chair to face Robin. "I'm going to sound a total arsehole, but this rugby accident really complicates the whole investigation. Everybody's attention was on Greg, and it has been ever since. Things that witnesses might have noticed either got missed or they've been shocked out of people's minds."

Pru was right again. Sometimes it was the tiny things, occurrences that meant very little to the people who'd seen them, that gave the police a vital clue when drawn together.

"It's dulled their curiosity, as well," Robin said. "They've been so wound up in making sure he and Dawn are okay and planning this fundraising stuff that they've not been gossiping about the victim. Or so they say. You'd have thought they'd want to know why the bloke was killed and on their turf."

Adam had shown that curiosity when there'd been a murder at Lindenshaw school, where he was working. He'd said since that he'd never have been able to get over the incident if the police hadn't been able to identify the culprit.

"Greg matters to them," Callum said, quietly. "Osment doesn't. That may sound harsh, but it's true. Nobody seems to be fundraising for a memorial to the dead man or to support his family. And that can't just be about helping the living rather than the dead."

"He didn't seem to be Mr. Popular, apart from with his wife." Robin studied the picture of the dead man, as it stared accusingly from the incident board. He remembered telling Adam when he'd been called away on secondment that some poor sod deserved justice. The more he got to learn about Osment, the less he found the term *poor sod* fitted. Still, he had a duty to serve the law by investigating every case without prejudice, no matter how much he disliked the victim. "We've been assuming he was going to the club with a particular person in mind, but what if it was other than that? Narked at getting a thumping on the Saturday, so back to take revenge. The smashed picture in the clubhouse. Pru, you took a snap of it on your phone."

"Yes. Hold on." Pru scrolled through her photo reel. "As vandalism goes it's nothing much. Niggly rather than nasty."

"I was interested in who was in the team. Can you get it large enough to see the faces or names?"

"Not really. You'll have to check when you're chasing up the forensics. Were you thinking Dave?"

"I'm keeping an open mind." Time to add scrutinising the picture to his list of jobs. "Let's say for the moment that Osment went to the club to cause trouble. How did he get in?"

"Seems obvious." Laurence lifted two fingers and counted the options. "Either he got a copy of the keys somehow, or he was let in by someone who had a set. We got a list of keyholders from the groundsman, by the way, and it doesn't help to narrow things down, even when you take into account the change of locks. One of the barmen left two months ago and it took a couple of weeks to get his set back. I'm surprised they didn't change the locks again after that, although he only had ones for bar area access."

Robin nodded. "Can you follow that up? Get in touch with all the keyholders, including for that other dressing room as well as the bar. All their alibis for the night in question and how much chance there was that someone could have borrowed their keys. Not simply the chances of Osment borrowing them. We also have to consider whether the doors weren't locked in the first place, leaving him an easy way in either by arrangement or to lure him in if someone got wind he was up to no good and was setting a trap. After the deed, the killer simply secured everything behind him—or her—when they slipped away."

Laurence scanned down his list, then nodded. "I'll get right on it."

"Good. I'm going to go down to forensics and chivvy them up. I understand they're stretched but I'd like to see this bumped up the priority list." Robin knew—from Betteridge—that they were also handling a mass of evidence from a case involving possible sexual abuse of a child. He didn't envy them having to juggle resources. "Then I want to see Derek Preese. Callum, can you get on the blower right now and organise that for the earliest opportunity today? Pru, I'm going to take Callum with me for the interview, simply because Preese might react differently to men than women. I hate playing that card but sometimes . . ." He shrugged.

"Sometimes you have to be pragmatic." The sergeant didn't seem bothered. "What do you want Sally and me to do?"

"Talk to Joe. We've not been to see him yet, so we can still go down the *new team revisiting all the witnesses* approach. If you get the chance to talk to his brother, as well, then gently finding out what he was doing that Wednesday would be good. Usual subtlety—his name's come up in the course of our enquiries. Not easy to achieve the right tone down a phone line, but I'd rather one of us did it than get the local officers involved. Even if local in this instance may well be Abbotston." Robin jumped off the desk where he'd been perching and clapped sharply, as he sometimes did when notifying Campbell it was time for walkies. "Let's get going."

He and Callum were halfway out the door when Sally shouted across from the desk where she'd been answering the phone. "It's Dave, sir. He wants to speak to you."

"Thanks." Robin recrossed the room and took the receiver. "Chief Inspector Bright speaking."

"Glad I caught you, Chief Inspector." Dave sounded less bullish than the day before. "You asked me yesterday if I want to add to my statement. I do. On two counts."

"Let me grab a pen." Robin smiled gratefully as Sally slipped both pen and paper into his hand. "Go on."

"Right at the start, we had a team huddle and coach mentioned there'd been some attempted vandalism at the club the weekend before. I wasn't sure if you knew about that."

"We knew about the vandalism." Not about Derek Preese mentioning it, though. "What's the other thing?"

"What happened afterwards. I've just remembered and it means I wasn't the last person in the changing rooms. Joe went for a slash not long after the huddle, so maybe around five or ten minutes past seven. If there'd been a body in the toilets then, he'd have raised the alarm."

Why this convenient revelation *now*? "How can you be so sure of the time?"

"Because it's a fining offence." Dave's grin was almost audible down the line, although whether it was delight at the fine being imposed or at having got himself off the hook wasn't clear. "Ask any real rugby fan and they'll tell you there's always kangaroo courts on tour and at Hartwood we apply a similar system all the time. Money raised gets split between charity and the Christmas do. It'll go to Greg, this year."

Robin avoided getting into detail about those sporting courts. "Right, I need you to come in to the station and sign an amended statement."

"Will do. Not sure how it will help, though. Joe was straight in and out, with only enough time to take a slash, not do anything else."

"Put that all in your statement, please, with as accurate an account of the timings as you can give us. Then we can double-check it."

As soon as the phone was down, Robin said, "You need to hear this before we go." He related the conversation as close to word for word as he could manage. "Sally, can you get an amended statement ready, please?"

"Will do, sir. Odd that he happens to remember this now, isn't it?"

"My thoughts too." Robin glanced at the incident board, then back to his team, who were all no doubt waiting for him to comment further. "If Joe has a twin brother and they're as alike as two peas, then it's possible the amount of time he spent off the pitch is irrelevant. He goes off, swops outfits with the brother who then comes on the pitch, leaving Joe with plenty of time to meet Osment, kill him, tidy up, and leave, locking up after himself. A player at the club would have had greater opportunity to copy the keys than the victim would."

"Puts Dave in the clear, though," Pru observed. "Assuming it's true."

"That's a big assumption without corroboration. And as Sally says, terribly convenient that he's happened to remember it now and so show he couldn't have done it."

"Why did nobody mention it before?" Pru asked. "Or did they and somehow we've missed it?"

The constables looked at each other blankly. "I'm sure we did ask them about their movements," Laurence said at last, "but I've got to be honest and say the investigation didn't run as smoothly as it should have done in the early days. I'm not a doctor, but I think Robertson wasn't well before his appendix blew up on him. Maybe his mind wasn't on the job as it should have been. And Superintendent Betteridge was focussed on the drugs and abuse cases . . ." He shrugged.

"It sounds like we're making excuses," Callum chipped in, "but we were stretched to breaking point. That's another reason why the superintendent wanted you to come here. Not only the murder case. She says you've got a track record of sorting problems like this out."

Helping to sweep Abbotston clean of rotten wood counted as a track record, but he appreciated the notion that he could lick people into shape. "I value your honesty. Let's draw a line under this and start again. It might have been that if you'd asked, they'd not have told us, anyway."

The relieved expressions on the young officers' faces spoke volumes.

"You've done well so far on my watch," Robin added. That was true, and it helped nobody to kick someone when they were down. "Right, in light of this, there's a change of plan. Pru, I want us to go and see Joe this afternoon. I'd like to reassure the rest of you that strategy is nothing to do with what we just discussed—if we were at Abbotston, Pru and I would be handling any equivalent interview."

"You can trust him on that," Pru said, with an impish grin. "He's one of the few coppers I've ever known who struggles to tell a lie. That's why he doesn't play poker."

"That's enough of that." Robin was glad of the endorsement, though. "Instead of complimenting me, can you contact Andy and ask him about Joe nipping off for a slash. He's the only one of them I think I even halfway trust at the moment. Sally and Callum, I'd like you to go through all the other players' statements in case there are any other instances of people going off the field we might have missed. Then follow your noses about finding a connection between Joe and Osment. Or Sam and Osment, come to think of it. Keep us up-to-date with what you find. And if there's any chance of finding out whether Sam can do first aid, that would be great."

Having chivvied the forensics team—they promised they'd have all the information back by late afternoon if not before—Robin and Pru set off to see Derek Preese. Slight change to the original plan of two male officers tackling him, but the new information about Joe had meant Robin wanted his best officer at his side for this interview. Preese had agreed to meet them at the local branch of a well-known optician where he worked.

"We can add that to the list of places we've conducted interviews, sir," Pru chirped. "Never done an optician's before. Or a dentist, come to think of it."

A discussion about strange venues for meeting witnesses kept them going all the way to the most convenient car park, Pru tactfully avoiding mentioning interviews in school libraries and offices, although those had been the first ones to spring to Robin's mind. Adam's green eyes flashing across a junior-school-sized table and all the inappropriate thoughts they'd given rise to.

Once ensconced with Derek Preese in a small but private office, Robin could see why the female officers had got flustered about the man. *He* was feeling rather hot under the collar, as well. The coach must have been a stunner thirty years ago and he'd kept the aura. How many young men under his care fantasised about a May to December—or to be fair, September—relationship with him? Robin recalled something a mate of his at university had said about the rowing coach, who was in his fifties. *"He's a total silver fox."* One who'd been drooled over by all the girls and some of the blokes.

Time to get his mind back on the case or else Pru would rib him mercilessly, especially after the stick she'd received after the first interview.

He thanked the bloke for seeing them yet again, emphasising that fresh information was cropping up all the time, which meant them needing to revisit things they'd already asked about. "For example, we've got a small discrepancy the night Greg got injured. According to your statement, when you rang Dawn, she said she was going to drive to the hospital."

"That's right."

"She says she had no intention of driving because she'd had too much to drink. She needed to get a lift or a taxi."

Preese, sighing, spread his hands. "I wish she'd told me that. Plenty of the lads would have volunteered to go and get her. I can only think that she said she'd drive without thinking—she must have been in shock. Or maybe she said she couldn't drive and I misheard because *I* was in shock."

Without a recording of the conversation, Robin had no way of assessing who was telling the truth, nor whether it mattered if both were giving half the tale. Still, discrepancies niggled at him. "Okay. So, changing tack, can you talk us briefly through what you did on the evening. I'm guessing you'd start with drills."

"We start with warm-ups," Preese said, "or else I'd have a string of injuries on my hands." His voice—with a gentle Welsh lilt—flowed mellifluously through exercises and technical drills, then on to some training ground moves. They'd been working on those when Greg went down.

No wonder this man was so popular with his charges, given that he spoke with a weight of authority and what sounded like a wealth of affection for the players.

"Thanks for that." Robin pretended to consult his notes. "Thing is, you haven't mentioned that you talked to the players about the recent vandalism at the club."

"Very true, Mr. Bright. They'd have wanted to know, seeing as Jamie was one of ours and they worked so hard to raise money for the bench. I also wanted to make sure they took good care of their belongings, so I gave them a heads-up before we started." Preese fiddled with what might have been a piece of optical equipment, a small metal device resembling an instrument of torture. "I suppose I should have mentioned it on my statement but it didn't seem relevant. You're going to say *you're* the people to decide what's relevant, I guess, so you'll have to forgive me." He produced a flashing smile that would have had most people forgiving him anything.

"Did you know that Osment is suspected of doing the vandalising?" Pru asked.

"Never." Preese peered at the sergeant, then at Robin. "You mean it, don't you? What a little shite." He raised both hands. "I know I shouldn't speak ill of the dead, but from what I hear from Greg and Dawn, he's no great loss. Did Tom Weatherell recognise him? He hasn't mentioned it if he did."

"He says he didn't realise." And until they had the forensics to link Osment to the scene on the Saturday, this was still all conjecture. "The fundraising. You put half the money towards educating players about drinking. Don't take this question the wrong way, but was Jamie Weatherell a heavy drinker?"

Preese shook his head. "He had his moments, like all lads that age, but he was growing out of them. Had a lucky escape, see. Nearly came off his bike postmatch because he'd been on the sauce. Stuck to shandy after that. Sensible lad. We all miss him."

"I'm sure you do." Details noted, Robin pressed on. "Why did you insist Dave got cleaned up before he went to casualty? They're not going to be bothered at the hospital by a spot of mud."

"No, but *we* were getting bothered by Dave. He was making the situation worse, going on about how sorry he was and saying he'd never forgive himself if Greg was paralysed. Not what Greg needed to hear." Preese raised his eyebrows. "I wanted to get him out of the way."

That chimed with what Andy had told them. Maybe they could clear up another niggle while they were at it. "You wanted to get him out of the way, but he kept refusing to go into the changing rooms. You can imagine how suspicious that appears. Like he knew about the body in there and didn't want it discovered."

Preese gave Robin a long, thoughtful look. "I thought he was being bolshie. He can be, you know."

"What else has he been bolshie about?" Pru asked.

"Oh, this and that." Preese dismissed the question with a wave of his hand. "Type of person who makes a decision and then sticks by it, right or wrong. He felt responsible for Greg so he wasn't going to let him out of his sight, no matter what we said. If that makes sense."

Pru kept her own counsel on that. "Can you tell us about Joe Woakes leaving the field during training?"

"He did, that's right. He had a quick visit to the loo. Taken short, the daft sod. Most expensive slash he's ever had, given that it cost him ten pounds."

"Why wasn't that in your original statement?" Robin wondered if other titbits would emerge, the longer the case remained unsolved and as people began covering their backs.

"Probably because he was in and out like a flash—any longer and his fine would have gone up."

"All this stuff about fines makes it even more mysterious why people didn't mention his brief absence." Robin waited for an answer, but all he got was Preese shrugging and spreading his hands. "Do you know Joe has a twin brother?"

"Everybody knows that. Everybody in the squad. Sam, I think he's called. Mind you, with lads that age if you shout Sam, Ben, Tom, or Joe at them, you're ninety percent certain of getting the name right. Why do you . . . Ah, I get it. You're not thinking *he* went in the changing room but his *brother* came out in his place, giving him an alibi? Or the other way around, I suppose." Preese pushed away the metal object he'd been fiddling with. "Isn't that a bit far-fetched? I'm sure I've seen something similar on the telly."

"I've seen things in real life that trump that for implausibility," Robin insisted.

"There was a case in the news, recently," Pru said. "That bishop who was done for sexual abuse. He had a twin brother whose place he sometimes took at services. They got away with the switch."

"I remember reading about that. Point taken," Preese said, grudgingly. "Why this interest in Joe?"

"I'd be interested in anyone who was proven to be in that dressing room alone." Robin leaned forwards, ready to make the big appeal he'd been working on. "Word is you're the heart and soul of Hartwood Wasps. Everyone says so. And while you must feel loyalty to all the guys on the pitch, closing ranks isn't helping anyone. If Osment was killed by someone outside the club but we fail to identify the murderer, then people are always going to say it was an inside job. It'll become the murder that's officially unsolved yet everyone thinks they know who did it. You don't want the squad to suffer that."

The barb hit home, Preese wincing. "If I had any idea who did it, I'd say. You talk about unsolved, though, so what about the hit-and-run on Jamie Weatherell? Everybody reckoned it was those lads did it, the ones who were convicted of joyriding. Took two cars the day he was killed, but they always denied they ran him over even when they confessed to nicking the motors. I guess their lawyers told them to put their hands up to the lesser charge. Couldn't convict them of the hit-and-run because there wasn't enough in the way of forensics, but they'd burned the cars, hadn't they?"

"You seem to know a lot about it," Pru observed.

Preese bridled. "Of course I do. They covered the case in the local press, and I followed all of it. One of our own, was Jamie."

"The men weren't charged with his death, just stealing cars."

"That's right, Sergeant, but we were all interested in it. As they say, if it walks like a duck and quacks like a duck, then it's a duck. Only this duck didn't quack."

Pru's expression, as she glanced at Robin, screamed, *Is it me? What the hell does he mean?*

Robin said, "We're being thick as a seventies cop on the telly. You'll need to explain."

"What I mean is it struck me that there was nothing to link the car thefts to Jamie's death. One car had been abandoned before the accident, according to the defence briefs, while the other one—Osment's car—was supposedly stolen around that time, although there was no clear evidence of exactly when it was taken, or even if they'd taken it. Which leaves us with the question of which car knocked Jamie down and who was driving it."

Light dawned. "You think it was Osment."

"I think it's quite possible. He stopped playing for Tuckton not long afterwards. Probably couldn't bear passing the scene of the crime to and from matches. What better way of covering up an accident than getting rid of your own car, hiding it among the spate of vehicle thefts?"

What better way indeed. Why hadn't anyone made the connection before now?

Before they'd left the car park, Robin was on the phone to his team, getting one of them to drop everything else and put together a timeline of when Jamie Weatherell was knocked down, whether Osment was playing for Tuckton that day and how he'd got home after the match. Somebody else could scrutinise the statements from both Osment about his car being nicked—and whether Melanie corroborated that story—and from the two joyriders about what had happened that evening. Who did what they could sort out amongst themselves, so long as the jobs were done.

"Shame we weren't here at the time," Pru said, "or we might have already made that connection.."

"Stop reading my mind. It's spooky." Robin forced a grin. "Still no excuse. It's bleeding obvious to explore Preese's idea."

"Is it? If Osment ran the lad over, why raise objections to the memorial fund—or vandalise the bench—and so draw attention to himself? And while Preese might have a point about the accident not being caused by those two lads, the hit-and-run driver could have been someone else. Maybe even Dave, which is why he was so keen to fundraise."

"Maybe." Although what chance did they have of solving that case at so far a remove when the officers at the time had failed? Unless they'd been so convinced it was the two joyriders that they'd ceased to look for anyone else. "Sally pointed something out, though. She'd been having a double-check, and Joe wasn't at the ground when the police started to take statements. He'd gone in the ambulance to keep Greg company."

"Okay. Andy said somebody had gone along. Did we get a statement from Joe?"

"Yes. And it says he left the ground then, although he doesn't mention the earlier loo break. Nobody seems to have asked him about whether he got his kit, though." Robin concentrated on the road ahead, increasingly disillusioned at the way the investigation had been handled. Was his old boss losing her touch or had she been so distracted by the drugs case that things had slipped her notice? He'd give her the benefit of the doubt for the moment. "Let's concentrate on getting to Joe's. His flat's a new build and Google maps says it doesn't even exist."

Eventually, they managed to find the right part of the new estate. Joe had clearly recently moved in, given the unpacked boxes strewn over the carpet and freshly painted walls that greeted them when they entered the property.

"Excuse the mess," he said. "Hardly been here since I got the keys to move in. On shift."

"What's your job?" Pru asked.

"Operator at United Agrochemicals. That's the big plant near the motorway. I'm on the last day of my four off before I start four days on again, so I'd appreciate if we made this snappy. Got a lot to do."

Robin, resisting the urge to point out that murder cases didn't keep to shift-rotation systems, said, "Then you'd better tell us the truth. That always makes for quicker interviews. Any hint that you're mucking us around, then we'll take you down to the station and interview you there."

Joe, who'd been carrying on filling kitchen cupboards, stopped. "That serious?"

"*That* serious. I've got a dead man and people not being entirely honest about what happened the night he was killed. Like the fact you left the pitch ten minutes after training started."

Joe had the grace to blush. "Didn't I mention that? I just hared off, had a pee, then hared back again. There was no dead man in the loos, I promise."

Pru clearly wasn't convinced it had simply been an oversight. "Why the secrecy about that if it was so innocent?"

Joe glanced at Robin, blushed deeper, then—with eyes firmly on his shoes—said, "I had an infection. Urinary tract. The lads had been teasing me that I had the clap, but Coach put a stop to it and told them to get a life. That's why I didn't mention my sudden dash for a pee, and I'm guessing that's why the other players didn't mention it."

That was plausible. "Did you get antibiotics for it?" Robin asked.

"Yeah. Finished the course now but you can check with my GP. I'll give you her name." Joe backed towards a small dining table, where he slid wearily into a chair, picked up a notepad, and began writing. "Plonk yourselves on the sofa, while I do this." When the officers were seated, he continued. "I'm sure none of us have been deliberately obstructive. Greg getting hurt and then the dead body being found—it's knocked us for six. I didn't know about the murder until later, and I thought it was a joke until I saw the story on the news."

"Who told you?"

"Andy. He can be a wind-up merchant when he wants to be. As I say, I saw the news story on my phone, so by the time Coach came to bring the rest of my stuff and give me a lift home, I was as stunned as everyone else."

So that accounted for Joe's kit from the changing room. "The other thing people hadn't mentioned was being told about the vandalism at the club on the Saturday. Did that slip your minds too?"

"It didn't seem that relevant. I knew about it already, anyway."

Robin's ears pricked at that. "Who from?"

"Tom Weatherell, the groundsman. He knew how pally I'd been with Jamie, so he wanted me to know. He messaged me on the Sunday."

"Do you know who the vandal was?"

"Not at the time. Tom's told me since that you lot think it could have been Osment." Joe ran his fingers across the table, sweeping away dust and crumbs that were probably not there. "That doesn't surprise me. Greg's girlfriend, Dawn, always used to be complaining about him. Unreasonable git all round."

"He couldn't have been totally unreasonable or else why would his wife stay with him?" Robin pointed out.

Joe's sneer spoke volumes. "She says love's blind. We've all seen it, haven't we? People staying together when by any amount of logic they should have split up. I guess it's sometimes easier to stay than to go."

Pru went into soothing mode. "You said you were pally with Jamie. Was it other than friendship?"

"No, he was too young for me. But give it a few years and I'd have been in there, given the chance." Joe swept the tabletop again. "I'll never know, now, whether we could have got on together."

"But it couldn't merely have been a matter of age," Pru said. "You had a boyfriend at the time."

"I did, but it was always an open relationship. And yes, I got myself into bother." Joe turned his hands, palms out in front of his chest. "I'm assuming you know about the caution I got and if you don't, I'll tell you about it. Kieran didn't want to press charges. He understood where my head was."

"Why not explain to us where your head was?"

"In a bloody mess, Sergeant. Jamie was only eighteen when he was murdered. What sort of age is that? Worse still, they reckon he wasn't killed outright."

"How do you know that?" Robin asked.

"Coach told me." That figured. The source of all knowledge. "He followed everything about that accident from the very start. There was an inquest—he attended that and he said it broke his heart. They think Jamie might have got a slipped chain and stopped to fix his bike at the side of the road. His lights were dynamo operated so if he'd stopped, he'd have only been able to use the light from his phone torch setting and was unlikely to be that visible, especially if the driver wasn't paying attention. Unlit road."

There were plenty of those at home, and Robin had experienced a few nasty occasions where cyclists or animals had appeared almost out of nowhere. His previous sergeant, Anderson, had mocked him, saying he drove like an old woman down country lanes, but Robin had always argued his case. Rather be five minutes longer getting to the destination than ending up in a ditch. Or court. He nodded for Joe to continue.

"The doctor said that if the driver had at least stopped and rung for an ambulance before they buggered off it might have saved Jamie's life. Instead it was another motorist going along the road who saw the body and rang 999. Coach said he couldn't follow all the medical stuff but it was about the bleeding on his brain. He'd knocked his head on the corner of a wall, and it caused bleeding on the brain, which is what eventually killed him. They must have known they'd hit something, and even if it was only an animal surely they'd have wanted to stop and find out. That's why I said it was murder, because that's what it amounted to."

Not an unreasonable point of view. Robin could imagine how heartbreaking it would be to hear that from a medical expert, and how it would further fuel resentment towards the unknown driver. "Coach—Mr. Preese—reckons it was Osment driving that night."

Joe broke into a grin at Robin's use of the word *Coach*. "I know he does. Been saying it for years to anyone who'll listen. Osment's car just happened to be nicked the same night, didn't it? Coach reckons that was all a setup. He faked the vehicle being taken and torched it himself or he deliberately left his valuables on show to see if it would fall prey to the car thieves. His wife wasn't there that evening—out with the girls and stopping over at Dawn's, so Osment had the night to clear up any evidence. Osment knocked someone over before, and the people at his club wouldn't let him drive. Oh, Coach has got it all pat."

So pat that he'd taken dispensing justice into his own hands?

"Is that what you believe?" Pru asked.

"I don't, actually. For once I think he's got it wrong." Joe paused, possibly for dramatic effect. "See, I work with one of the lads from Tuckton Chiefs—he's on the same shift—and middle of the night, you chat about these things. I discussed it with him when Coach first got a bee in his bonnet, and he thinks it couldn't have been Osment driving because he's pretty sure he got a lift home that night. Not with the usual bloke who takes him to and from matches, but that's not the point. If he went home, then I can't imagine Osment getting his car out again to go back to where he'd been."

"Unless he left something at the club and needed to return for it?" Pru suggested.

"I suppose so, but I have confidence in the police, believe it or not. You probably treated me better than I deserved when I hit Kieran, and if you'd have been able to pin the blame on someone for the accident, then I'm sure you would have done. Fact is"—Joe swept the table over yet again, making Robin wonder whether he had a touch of OCD—"it could have been anyone, couldn't it? And they could have been heading home to Cornwall or wherever, taking their secret with them." He glanced up again from his table-cleaning. "I'll tell you the truth. If you proved who killed Jamie and if I ever met the scum, then they'd get the sort of thumping Osment must have got. You can write that into my statement alongside the part about my visit to the loo and I'll sign it, gladly."

Robin didn't fancy getting straight back into the car. He wanted to walk and walk until he could catch a glimmer of what the hell was going on in this case. Pru fell in with the suggestion, especially when the map on her phone suggested there was a park not too far away that would make for easier walking than a half-finished estate.

"Does he genuinely believe it wasn't Osment," Robin said, as they drove the short distance towards the park, "or is it a really clever way of showing us he has no motive to kill the bloke?"

"He seemed genuine enough," Pru replied, "although we've both heard right villains who sounded genuine enough. Probably practiced it from the time they first started to talk and began pleading they weren't the ones who'd been dipping their fingers in the jam tarts. They got away with it then and moved on to bigger things. Only I don't put Joe in that category."

"No, I don't either. But I've come away thinking he knows more than he's said." The offer to make a new statement felt like sleight of hand, misdirecting them from some vital point.

"I reckon they all know more than they've told us, old smooth-talking Derek Preese included. Closing ranks. Damn, here comes the rain." It had begun to drizzle, making Hartwood appear entirely lacking in charm. "I can't make out if it's about the training session or something else."

Robin, sighing in frustration, concentrated on the road. This was beginning to feel like a case that would slip through his fingers. Betteridge would sign off her drugs case, take the murder investigation over again, review the evidence, and gradually let it fade away. The inquest—already opened and adjourned—would return a verdict of unlawful killing by person or persons unknown, hampered as the police had been by a lack of forensic evidence and all the obvious suspects having alibis. *He'd* return to Abbotston and Adam with a stain on an otherwise spotless career.

Adam.

Robin had known he'd miss his partner emotionally, but hadn't realised how much he'd feel the need to discuss the case with him. Adam didn't bring much specialist knowledge—except when issues of child safeguarding were concerned—to the table, yet that didn't seem to matter. Sometimes his very distance from the minutiae allowed him to see things from an angle that the team had missed and his ability to ask pertinent questions often led to Robin making a leap of deduction that had moved the investigation forward.

He'd draw on that ability tonight. Maybe an independent eye was exactly what was needed to give the case a kick up the backside.

Chapter Ten

Thursday had dragged.

Each lesson had felt like it lasted hours, and the break times had been both interminable and filled with idle gossip, although Adam guessed the day was no different to normal. He was missing Robin, simple fact, and however hard he tried to not let it affect his work, it was a burden when he wasn't occupied. Still, he'd got a pile of stuff to do tonight, which he could plough through while Campbell snuggled at his feet.

Campbell was used to police hours, so didn't as a rule do anything daft like stare longingly at the front door when Robin was home late, no doubt knowing he'd see him—however fleetingly—the next morning. But this was different. He'd taken to sniffing around the place where Robin habitually sat on the sofa, or putting his front paws on the windowsill to gaze up and down the road. That morning he'd simply been sitting with a puzzled expression on his face, clearly wondering why the stool in the kitchen didn't have the usual bottom placed on it. All those pep talks Adam had delivered evidently hadn't penetrated his canine skull, possibly because they hadn't included food of any kind or possibly because he was feeling equally bereft.

When he got home late that afternoon, Adam made for the kitchen, where Campbell pounced on him rather than making a beeline for the back door and the chance to relieve himself. Adam tickled the dog behind his ear. "I know what you're thinking. I miss him too, you know. He'll be home as soon as he can be. Like I keep telling you, he's got a murderer to catch."

Campbell nuzzled his wet nose into Adam's palm; whether this was intended to dispense comfort or obtain it, Adam didn't know and couldn't be bothered to analyse. It felt good. He should be grateful that he had Campbell to snuggle up against, to hug and to share comfort with. Robin was on his own emotionally, even if he had a trusted colleague with him. Pru wouldn't be rubbing up against him or giving the benefit of a wet nose.

Hopefully.

As he let Campbell take his perambulation round the garden and got his own tea into the microwave, Adam reflected on not having to carry around the worry of a workplace romance going on in some hotel room in Hartwood. For a start, Robin didn't like women in a romantic way, and never had done. One of the lesser reasons he'd had such a miserable time at primary school was that he'd known at an early age that he was different, and by the time Robin had gone up to secondary school, he'd not only worked out why but had decided that he'd no interest in trying to conform. By then he'd apparently become best friends with Dan, the biggest lad in his year, who had kept an eye out for him. Anybody who picked on Robin would have had to answer to Dan, and the chance hadn't been worth taking.

Secondly, and crucially, even if he had been with a male colleague—and a gay one to boot—fidelity meant fidelity in Robin's language, as it did in Adam's. All of that added up to no concerns about what was happening in his husband's bed, despite his own bed being as empty as a pauper's purse.

Campbell came in and nuzzled Adam's hand with his nose once again, then gave him a sad-eyed, plaintive look.

"Right, I know you miss him, but can't take time off work to cosset you, you daft beggar. You've got Sandra wrapped around your paw, anyway." Sandra was the third worshipper at Campbell's altar. To the extent that she kept certain clothes just for wearing at their house so as not to take pet hairs home with her. Devotion indeed. "You can come to the choir practice tomorrow, okay? You like being my chaperone, so you can keep an eye on Sam Woakes."

Adam halted, then broke into an inane grin. *You silly sod.* Campbell was an intelligent dog, but surely not to the point that he could understand this meaningful a level of conversation. Irrespective of that, the Newfoundland certainly appeared reassured at the offer, giving him a final nuzzle before retreating to his basket, where he made himself comfortable, with his dog chew in his slobbery jaws.

Adam enjoyed his dinner, but no sooner had he sat down with a pile of books to work through than the phone went.

"How's my favourite deputy headteacher?" Robin sounded as though he was working hard to be cheery.

"Underpaid, overworked, and undersexed. You?"

"The same. Have you got a few minutes to listen while I put some thoughts past you? I miss our chats over dinner."

"Fire away." Schoolwork could wait for a while.

Robin, who'd kept Adam updated, gave an outline of what they'd discovered that day both from the interviews and the sheer slog of trawling through historical information. He finished with a word about forensics. "It *was* Osment's hoodie that got snagged on the wire and one of his thumbprints is on the cracked glass of the photo. A photo that shows the Hartwood team with a young Jamie Weatherell in it, as well as most of the guys I've spoken to here. The faces are too fuzzy to make out clearly, but the names were on the back. You can imagine how pleasant it was having to ring up the lad's father—he's the groundsman, remember—and tell him that."

"You have my every sympathy. Why was the dead bloke so obsessed? He must have known that stirring up trouble would put the spotlight on him. Which is ludicrous if there's a suspicion he did the hit-and-run."

"Park that thought for a moment, because it's not straightforward. He could have been doing what he did simply in order to get his own back on Dave. The bloke who he thought was having an affair with his missus."

"Oh, yeah. I'd forgotten that. Worse than a soap opera for trying to work out what's going on."

"Tell me about it." Robin groaned. "Let me deliver my warning about Joe Woakes. Best to keep your distance from his brother, Sam, until we can eliminate the pair of them. *If* we can eliminate them. Sam has no alibi for the time of death. The constable who spoke to him was told he went on a run, then had a shower and watched the telly while he played on his phone. Typical night for a guy who's still single."

"I remember those nights well. Glad that's not me anymore." Even though it wasn't dissimilar to life chez Matthews at present. "Do you really think he's involved, though?"

"Who knows? Sam's a dead ringer for Joe—I've been comparing photos—and he plays rugby. He's usually at centre, but Pru reckons he could be a utility back and so cover for his brother at a pinch. If anyone had questioned him about his play, he'd say he was having an off game. I bet he could have worked in how the vandalism to the bench had thrown him off-kilter again. Anyway, until we're clearer, you'd better warn Martin to keep his distance, as well."

"Will do. What motive would either of them have, though? Do they believe Osment was the hit-and-run driver?"

"No. Or at least Joe says he doesn't. That might be a clever deflection. Osment was certainly still playing at Tuckton Chiefs when the accident happened, and he gave the game up soon afterwards. We're trying to pin down if he played that afternoon and who gave him a lift home."

"Surely there were some forensic evidence at the scene?" There always seemed to be on the telly, but best not to mention that. Robin always got twitchy about the way fictional crime investigation rarely resembled real life.

"Barely anything. It wasn't the impact that killed Weatherell but his knocking his head against the wall. The car—or whatever it was—must have hit the victim in the back and given that he was wearing a thick coat, it cushioned the impact. Nothing useful like glass breakage or chipped paintwork, although the callous bastard—or bastards—could have stopped and cleared away what was obvious. The vehicle itself probably had a dent or two but that would have been easily dealt with. Or hidden by knocking the car about deliberately."

"Dumb question. How did they know it *was* a hit-and-run rather than him simply falling off his bike because he'd hit something in the road?"

"Not a dumb question at all. Pru and I have been going back to basics on all of this, including asking ourselves that very thing, because the evidence is mostly circumstantial. Injury to the back and position of the body consistent with being hit by a car, certainly, and the lad appeared to have been fixing a loose chain on his bike, given the state of his hands. Otherwise we've got no more than a seventy-year-old woman and her hearing."

"Oi! Don't diss old women." Adam could think of a few in Lindenshaw who could run the combined armed forces given half a chance.

"I wouldn't dare. But a defence council would. Mrs. Sanderson lived along the road and thought she heard an impact and then a car speeding off. She went out to see what had happened, but it's an unlit road and Weatherell's body had been knocked into the entrance to the drive where he'd stopped to repair his bike. She couldn't see him. It was only later when the emergency services arrived that she went out and told them what she'd heard." Robin paused for breath. "Seems the owners of the house came home to this gruesome find and called for help straight away. Which is better than the culprit managed. Anyway, we've been through all the statements and there's nothing to get our teeth into."

"I wish you were here to get your teeth into me."

"Don't think I'm not wanting the same." Robin groaned. "Did that make any sense? This case is making me incoherent. I'm starting to think it'll turn out to be totally random. A junkie chancing their arm that there's something worth nicking in the dressing rooms. Doesn't get spotted because everyone's in a state about the injured player. Happens upon Osment, who's there to cause trouble. Thumps him and legs it. Never to be tracked down unless he happens to confess."

Adam had rarely heard his partner sound so depressed. "You remind me of Kayla."

"Kayla?"

"Girl in my class. She was in a proper state today because she'd lost her favourite pen, one her nan gave her. When Susie, who works in the class, got her to take everything from her bag and turn the lining out, the thing appeared where it had got caught up in a seam. Same bag where Kayla said she'd already looked for the pen three times."

That made Robin chuckle. "Not sure how I turn the lining out on an investigation."

"Consider it another way?" Adam suddenly felt inspired. "Kayla kept accusing this boy called Dale of taking it and he was getting increasingly irate. He can be a total horror but in this instance he was innocent for once and he was narked about getting the blame. What if the only connection between Osment and the hit-and-run is that he genuinely had his car nicked that same night and all the rest is the *no smoke without fire* mob getting into swing?"

"Hm. That could be worth thinking about. We've been wondering why he would have targeted the fundraising because it brought attention to himself and he'd have to be completely stupid to think he'd go unidentified." Robin sounded perkier already. "If Osment heard that he was being put in the kangaroo court dock—and he might hear that through his wife's best mate—then I suppose he might decide to get his own back by causing trouble?"

"Especially if he suspected someone else nicked his car to put the blame on him." Adam was on a roll now. "Could that have happened?"

"I guess it's possible. Seems far-fetched but who knows?" A yawn came down the line. "Pardon me. Feeling bleeding knackered. I'm not sleeping well."

"Sorry to hear that. I'm finding the bed's too big without you, and I'm not letting Campbell fill the gap. It would be impossible to break the habit when you get home." Damn, now Adam's eyes were turning scratchy. "I miss you. Not only your cold feet on my legs."

"Same here. I only realised today how much I miss being able to talk about cases with you. You always have good ideas."

"Do I?" Adam felt quite chuffed about that. "I enjoy being able to give my input. It's a bit like watching a really good crime show and trying to be one step ahead of the detective on the telly."

"I wish real life was like that." Robin yawned again. "We don't have the luxury of the killer being the small and seemingly insignificant character who appeared at exactly five minutes in and hasn't been seen since."

Adam chuckled, recalling the fun they had playing *spot the murderer* and how often that simple formula led them in the right direction. Mrs. Matthews had banned them from doing it if they were all watching a programme together, the last straw having been when they'd both said, *"She did it!"* ten minutes into a show and had turned out to be correct. "You get off to bed. You'll have a busy day tomorrow."

"I always have busy days at the moment." A third yawn. "Right, I better jot some notes down before I crash. If the theory about Osment being framed for a crime he didn't commit turns out to be crap, I'll blame you. And if it's the key to everything, I'll take the credit."

"Ha bloody ha," Adam said, confident that Robin would do no such thing. "Let me know who gave Osment a lift home from that match, will you? This is better than the crime show reruns on ITV3."

"Fancy yourself as Miss Marple?"

"No, thanks. Being at one step removed from a murder is enough for me. I'll remember to warn Martin when I see him tomorrow, though. Too late to ring him tonight—he'll get into a panic and I don't want Sam accusing me of slander."

He'd have to hope the warning wouldn't come too late.

Chapter Eleven

By the time the team met in the incident room late on Friday morning, they had a further wealth of information, although still no clear direction of where the case was heading. Like having a pile of jigsaw pieces and no picture on the box to guide them, as Robin described it.

Laurence had finally worked through his list of keyholders: all could give an account of themselves for the Wednesday night and none appeared to have any connection to Osment other than ones the team already knew about.

"That ex-barman was rather sheepish, though. The reason he was late returning his set of keys to the club was that he'd lost them and didn't want to admit the fact until he'd had a chance of finding them again."

"Which he did?" Pru asked.

"Yep. He'd been out drinking with his mates, so he had the bright idea of going to the places they'd visited on the off-chance the keys had been handed in and not already returned to the club. He struck gold at a pub—The Red Dragon. I rang them and they confirmed the keys had turned up in line with what the barman said and they'd been put away safely, waiting to be reclaimed. The manager at the pub had the sense to make a note of when they were handed in, and there's a couple of days gap between the Friday night of the pub crawl and the Monday they appeared. Therefore, anybody who'd been in the pub during that time could have 'borrowed' them."

"Great." Pru snorted. "Why did this bloke have them with him if he was out on the lash?"

Laurence shrugged. "He says it was habitual to pick them up and put them in his pocket. I believe him, actually. My maths teacher at sixth form college told us that she'd once gone off with the keys to a National Trust property she'd visited because she'd automatically picked them up."

"That's that, I guess," Callum said. "Hundreds of people go to The Red Dragon. We'll never pin them down."

"Maybe, maybe not. They told me it had been particularly busy that weekend, including a darts match on the Saturday night. Osment's team, given the notes in the bookings diary, and I think he was playing because the pub manager says he has a good memory for faces and recognised Osment's when his death was reported in the local paper. Although I clearly need to double-check that."

Robin, whose eyes had been drawn to the incident board again, suddenly turned around at the mention of the darts team. "Might be coincidental, but it gives him an opportunity to take them, although how would he know they were from the Hartwood ground?"

"Ah, now that's where it gets interesting, sir. The barman swore they had a label on when they were in his possession, which is why he was worried they'd be returned to the club before he could run them to ground. He'd have been for the high jump in that event. But the label wasn't there when he picked the bunch of keys up. It wasn't a full set for all the club, just the ones he would have needed for his job. Main gate. External door to the bar area, which is incidentally a Chubb lock that's identical to the one to the changing room, so he could open that door too. Then a couple of keys for unlocking the grill to the bar itself and to operate the till."

Not the huge bunch that Robin had built up a mental image of. Easier to slip in a pocket unnoticed, for one thing.

"And that's not all . . ." Laurence paused theatrically. "Some of the guys from the rugby club were at The Red Dragon on the Sunday lunchtime. They were having a meal in honour of Dave's birthday—it was all in the bookings diary."

Sally whistled. "That broadens the field."

"It does." Laurence, tapping his notes, evidently had more to add. "Because it wasn't only the players who were there. Wives, girlfriends, boyfriends, whatever. What if Dawn laid her hands on those keys? Superintendent Betteridge always says that you start closest to home. If Melanie was sick of Nick's jealousy, she might have wanted shot of him, and killing him off home soil deflected attention. Especially when she'd given herself such a good alibi."

Another theory to add to the mix, and one as unprovable as all the others were, unless somebody broke ranks and spilled the beans.

"You've done well, Laurence," Robin said. "I'd like you to keep with that angle. Get hold of that set of keys and dab them for prints. It might not help now because I bet the things are either smothered or clean as a whistle, but it could be a much-needed piece of concrete evidence if we ever get a case to give the Crown Prosecution Service. Also ring round and see if a stray set of keys has turned up—and ask people to ring us if they do."

Laurence made a note. "Do you want me to talk to Dawn, as well?"

"Not yet. Don't want her twigging that something's in the wind. Okay. Pru, you've been working the Osment angle. Was he playing in the match at Tuckton the day Jamie was killed?"

"Yes, according to Melanie. Next day he told her all about some dirty work that Hartwood players were using in the breakdown." Pru grinned. "Probably another dig at Dave because he was one of them."

"That would eliminate the possibility of Melanie spending her afternoon with *him*," Callum observed. "I mean, we know she was out."

"Afternoon yes, evening no," Robin said, not unkindly. Best to encourage thinking. "After the match Howarth took Osment home?"

Pru shook her head. "Howarth's daughter was taken ill and he pulled out of the game. He got another player, Colin Cooper, to do the honours, because he'd stood in a couple of times before. Cooper no longer plays for Tuckton—got relocated with his job, according to Howarth—and I haven't yet found a contact number for him. I'm working on it."

"Good. I want to get the events of that night as clear in my mind as the events of the night Osment was killed. Howarth have anything to say about it?"

"No, sir. Apart from being understandably upset at a young life snuffed out. Everyone at Tuckton was upset about it. I think the team got together to send a wreath to the funeral." Pru consulted her notes. "Chrysanthemums, in as near the Hartwood colours as they could get."

Which was a nice touch, but what about the important stuff? Testily, Robin asked, "Did Howarth offer an opinion on who had done the hit-and-run?"

"He only said that *he* didn't think it was Osment. Even when the rumours started flying about."

Robin, taking a deep breath, glanced over at his desk, where he'd spent the morning working through case files for the hit-and-run and the carjacking. It had been a dispiriting exercise. "I've been through a hell of a lot of stuff, but I didn't see any of your names mentioned as investigating officers. Mind you, I got to the stage where I couldn't see for looking. Were any of you involved with either of those inquiries?" Robin scanned the three junior officers but was greeted by blank expressions all round.

"Before our time. You'll have noticed that Inspector Warner was the lead on those cases," Sally said. "He's retired, but I know Sergeant Harper, who was a constable on the team back then. He's in traffic division now and he could tell you about it."

Callum cut in. "What he'll say is that Warner was convinced the two lads who nicked the cars caused the accident. Harper told me that himself when I'd recently started here. Warner's attitude was that we were better to have a name in the frame and fail to convict them through lack of evidence than have no name at all."

"That accords with what I've seen for myself," Robin said. "No wonder people have strong feelings about it. I'm not convinced Warner got it right. The carjackers said *they* didn't hit Jamie, and for once I'm inclined to believe them. One of them put his hand up to nicking Osment's car but the other didn't, so God alone knows what was going on there. An attack of conscience by the first or deflecting attention from something else?"

"I've got an idea, sir. It's slightly left field, but . . ." Sally shrugged and watched Robin hopefully.

"Let's hear it."

"It's based on Osment having been the driver at the accident and why—in that case—he'd bring attention to himself with the vandalism and whatever. He goes home from the match with Colin Cooper, then immediately takes his own car back to the club, maybe to follow Dave. It would be in character for Osment to think Dave might have been meeting Melanie." Sally, who'd been rushing through her words, took a breath. "When Osment gets to the club, Dave's already gone, so he dashes back home again, in a mood. But rather than his hitting Jamie because of his own dangerous driving, the accident's partially caused by Jamie himself. Mending his bike in the road rather than on the verge but not showing a light so he can't be seen until it's too late."

Robin remembered something he'd noted and promptly forgotten. "Pru, do you remember that Preese told us Jamie had come off his bike before because he'd been on the sauce? Hold on." He nipped back to his desk, returning with the postmortem report. "Yes. A small amount of alcohol in the system. Unlikely to have been over the limit while he was cycling, but some people go silly on half a pint. What if Jamie was less than careful that evening because the shandies he'd drunk—if they *were* just shandies—had gone to his head?" He stopped. "Sorry, Sally. I'm stealing your thunder, here."

"You're all right, sir. Glad to hear you don't think this is all entirely stupid." She gave the others a glare, clearly daring them to challenge her. "I know that road and it's pitch-black on a moonless night. If a cyclist who'd stopped wasn't showing enough light while he was mending his bike, a car could be on him in a flash. Imagine Osment happens to hit Jamie, then panics and leaves the scene. Afterwards everyone's elevating the lad to an iconic status and that hacks Osment off because he knows the truth."

"Okay, in that case, why didn't he share that truth with other people rather than making a nuisance of himself?" Pru asked.

"And risk being banged up? He'd have faked the theft and torching of his own car so that all would have appeared highly suspicious. Then, when the inquest revealed that Jamie potentially could have survived if he'd had earlier medical intervention, Osment must have realised he would have been crucified, irrespective of who caused the accident. Who'd have had any sympathy with Osment in that case?"

The team took in Sally's theory without ridiculing the notion. It pretty well stacked up with what little evidence they had, but was it the correct picture for the jigsaw pieces to form?

Callum raised his hand, like one of Adam's year six pupils might. "Was Joe playing in that game against Tuckton? Has anybody considered if *he* caused the hit-and-run? Whether it wasn't so much that he was upset about Jamie's death but so racked with guilt afterwards that he lashed out at his boyfriend?"

"I suppose that's possible, but it's stretching credulity," Pru commented. "He's a trained first aider, and he had a soft spot for Jamie. Wouldn't he have been the last person to simply drive off?"

"What if he didn't know it was Jamie he'd hit until afterwards? Just thought he'd struck a deer or a large dog? Or maybe he knew he'd hit a person and simply panicked?" Callum sounded less and less convinced by his own idea.

"We can't discount anything," Robin said, even though he'd privately discounted this theory. Time for him to share his thoughts. "When I looked through that stuff this morning, I came away with one impression, which I've already stated. There was something else that nagged at me, though. What if Osment *didn't* run Jamie over, but when the rumour mill started to name him for the crime, he made it his business to find out who did it? And what if he *did* run the culprit to ground?"

"When the police couldn't?" Laurence rolled his eyes incredulously.

"I don't think we're infallible. Do you?" When no answer came, Robin continued. "It's possible he's always known who did it. Maybe he witnessed it."

Pru almost bounced off the desk where she'd been perched. "Colin Cooper?"

"Maybe. We shouldn't confine ourselves to Cooper, though. Osment was a passenger in the car, so he might have seen or heard things Cooper didn't if he was concentrating on driving. A vehicle ahead of them or pulled in at the side of the road." He turned to Callum. "Did you investigate Osment's financial affairs?"

"Yep, and there's nothing odd there in terms of incomings or outgoings. If you're wondering if he was blackmailing the person who killed Jamie, then the money involved has gone somewhere we've yet to trace it."

"Maybe he'd only recently attempted blackmail and it hadn't paid dividends yet," Pru pointed out. "He might have been concerned about losing his job if the company he worked for was reorganising the staffing structure. Perhaps he fancied a new source of income to tide him over. As a result of which, the victim turned the tables and killed him."

"This would all tend to rule out Dave as the hit-and-run driver, I'd suggest," Robin said. "Osment would have been crowing it from the rooftops, surely? Even if he couldn't prove Dave's guilt, it would have blackened the bloke's name. We need to talk to Melanie about this. If he had a suspicion or a lingering resentment, you'd have thought she'd know about it."

But she didn't.

Robin had a long telephone call with her, which started spikily, Melanie going off on a rant, which finished with, "Why do you policemen have such dirty minds? Why can't my friendship with Dave be simply that? A friendship."

Had Dave been in touch with her since they interviewed him? Time to cool her down. "Mrs. Osment, you're an intelligent woman. You know we have a duty towards the victim to explore anything that might be relevant to his death. Don't you want us to find the killer as soon as possible?"

"Of course I do."

"And don't you want us to ensure that we're being told the truth and not believe any old gossip?"

"Yes. Yes, I suppose so. Sorry," she added, grudgingly.

That led neatly into the other rumours circulating in the case. "People are saying that Nick was the driver when a lad called Jamie Weatherell was killed in a hit-and-run some years back."

The rumours clearly came as no surprise. "I bet that bloody coach at the rugby club, what's his name—Rhys, something Welsh—told you that. He needs to keep his gob shut. That's slander."

Robin didn't want to argue the case about whether you could slander a dead person. He'd come across the question before and still didn't know the answer.

"He's suspicious because the car was stolen that same night." He'd narrowly avoided the words *allegedly stolen*. "What do you know about that?"

"That Nick was a bloody idiot. He was always leaving stuff on view, inviting trouble. Bags, his jacket, the satnav. He'd got away with it in the past and even though I nagged him until I was blue in the face, he thought he'd always get away with it. I could have killed him—" She gasped. "You know I didn't mean that. Although I could have brained him there and then when I came home on the Sunday to find the car gone and us having to use public transport or rely on lifts to get in and out of work. We used to travel together and I'd drop him off and pick him up."

"So, if Nick wasn't the hit-and-run driver, did he know who was? Or suspect who was? Hello?" Robin thought the mobile signal might have gone down—like it used to mysteriously disappear around Lindenshaw school—but Melanie eventually replied.

"Sorry, you caught me on the raw. Yes, he did suspect, but he wouldn't tell me who it was. I wish he had now. I'm guessing you think that driver might have had something to do with Nick's murder."

"We need to consider it." Although if Melanie hadn't a clue who Nick suspected and it turned out not to be Colin Cooper, what chance had they of following the line through? "Is it possible he wouldn't tell you because it was somebody close to home? Somebody you both knew, perhaps."

"That's possible. It's the sort of thing he'd have done. Although if he'd suspected the driver was either Dawn or Dave, I'd have heard about it soon enough."

"Okay. Last question. Did he act differently in any way the last few weeks he was alive?"

"Funny you should say that. You know—well actually you don't know because you've not asked before—there was something he'd been pretty smug about the last few weeks before he died. Said whatever happened with work, we shouldn't be worried because he had irons in the fire. I assumed he meant he had another job lined up and he didn't want to say too much about it because it would jinx it." She sounded choked up, again. "That was him all over. Don't tempt fate."

Robin put down the phone. Was tempting fate exactly what Osment had done and was it what had got him killed?

The afternoon seemed endless.

Lots of routine legwork by the team and lots of frustration. Laurence had retrieved the keys the barman had lost but any fingerprints from back then were too smudged to be of use. He'd set off to do a round of the local key-cutting services with the bunch and a picture of Osment.

People on the darts team confirmed that Osment had been smug about something but had refused to say what it was. He'd not mentioned any suspicions about Jamie Weatherell's death, although one of the players recalled him getting worked up when a report of another hit-and-run had come onto the television in the bar where they were practicing. Osment had been moaning that the police were bloody useless and that unless somebody shopped the culprit, they'd have no chance of tracking him down. He'd finished the rant with a comment about people spreading rumours without any substance to them. All of which created the picture that Osment had felt that he was being unfairly suspected of causing Jamie's death. Equally, it could have been a clever way of covering his guilt. Rather like those who shouted loudest about same-sex relationships being a threat to family life sometimes being the very people cheating on their wives with boyfriends of their own.

Pru, who'd spent most of the day making a series of calls—and apparently chasing her tail most of the time given how exasperated she sounded—at last pushed the phone away and came over to Robin's desk. "Got some news about Colin Cooper, finally."

"Sounds like you've had your work cut out, trying to run him to ground."

"It's been, um, interesting. In that *may you live in interesting times* way." Pru grinned. "I started with Howarth and then spoke to a series of friends of friends, but I've got him pinned down now. He lives in Warwick—got a job at a pharmaceutical company based there, which is how I was eventually able to make contact. He'll see us ten o'clock tomorrow morning, although he doesn't sound happy about it."

"I bet. Good work. Maybe we can go and get some lunch in Stratford afterwards. We deserve a break."

"That works for me, sir. Although I need to be back here by late afternoon. I've managed to connect up with an old schoolmate who lives the other side of Tuckton, and she's going to show me the nightlife of Hartwood." Pru's delighted grin suddenly faded. "If that's okay? You can come along if you want."

"And have to listen to all that *my little home in the valleys* stuff? Nah, you have a girls' night out. Assuming nothing turns up in the meantime to spoil it."

"I've got my fingers crossed."

Robin stared at his computer screen—unseeing and wistful—when Pru returned to her desk. Shame he didn't know anyone around here to meet up with for a beer and a curry. Another night on his lonesome-ownsome, unless one of the team suggested meeting up. He didn't feel like making the offer, mainly because it would impose a burden on his constables, who might feel guilty about saying no.

There must be a constructive way of using the time. Perhaps he should go out to Tuckton and then drive back along the road where Jamie had been killed. Get a feeling for the lie of the land and then let his subconscious work on what he'd seen. Maybe there was an obvious question they'd left unasked or a link left unmade.

The Tuckton to Hartwood road, as Sally had asserted, was what Robin's granny would have called *black as your grandfather's moustache*. His car had strong headlights, but he couldn't make out some of the twists and turns until he was almost on top of them. If the visibility that night had been dodgy—and the reports spoke of intermittent drizzle—then it might have been possible to have missed seeing somebody at the side of the road. He went up and down the stretch several times, noting anything of interest. The place where Jamie had died was itself around a bend, so if the car had come along too fast it would have been, literally, an accident waiting to happen.

Before Robin had left the office he'd contacted Mrs. Sanderson, who still lived a couple of doors along from where the accident had happened and who said she'd be pleased to see him. Could he ring a few minutes before he arrived because she didn't like answering the door in the evenings and did he prefer Dundee cake or almond fingers?

He'd promised to ring, and said he'd be polite and eat whatever he was given and looked forward to meeting her.

He called from a lay-by, the other side of the road, fifty yards towards Hartwood from her house. Such a location would have provided a ringside view of what happened that night. A shame that no courting couples had seen fit to make use of it or pipe up if they had: the police appeal for eye witnesses had come up with a blank. A road sign, warning of the blind bend ahead stood mockingly ahead of him, with a mirror located behind it that someone must have put in place to aid leaving their own driveway.

Mrs. Sanderson had surely been waiting for the sight of his car turning into the drive, because the door was opened as he stepped out of the vehicle. Her house was no more than thirty yards away from the accident site and appeared, to Robin's untutored eye, to have single glazing. That meant the occupant should easily hear what was going on outside. His granny had lived in a similar property, and when they'd installed double glazing, she'd complained that it was too quiet without the road noise.

He was soon settled into a comfortable lounge with surprisingly modern furnishings, a mug of tea on a small table next to him with a large slice of Dundee cake on a plate in his hand.

"I'm so pleased you accepted my offer of refreshments," Mrs. Sanderson said, taking a seat opposite him. "On the television, policemen always seem to refuse because they're on duty. Although I don't suppose the television is like real life?"

"I'm afraid not. Or else we'd see which one of the suspects was played by the most famous guest star and arrest them straight away. That what A . . . my partner always says, anyway." Robin would have to watch himself. For some reason or other—fatigue, loneliness, and a sense of frustration on his part while a comfy chair, refreshments, and a cheery face worked their magic—he was at risk of letting his guard down.

Mrs. Sanderson giggled. "Then you wouldn't arrest me. I'd be played by one of those actresses that you'd recognise because she has bit parts in everything but you have no idea what she's called."

"No. It would be Dame Judi Dench, at least."

"Are you always so charming with witnesses? You're not here only to talk about that hit-and-run, are you?"

Worryingly perceptive. "Well, I am, but it's part of a bigger picture."

"I thought so. I wondered if it was to do with the murder in Hartwood. The rugby team. Do you think the deaths are connected? Or shouldn't I ask?"

"You can ask whatever you like, but I may not answer." Robin took a tactical sip of tea. "I'm investigating the murder, yes. Whether that's connected to the hit-and-run, I couldn't say. Because I'm here on secondment, I wasn't around at the time of that investigation, and reading statements and going through reports is never the same as visiting the scene or talking to witnesses. The nearest thing we have to witnesses."

She nodded. Likely very little got past her. "Yes. If you'd had an eye witness, you'd have been able to catch the driver by now. I don't think those tearaways did it, the ones who were convicted of stealing cars, and I suppose you don't either but I won't press you on that."

Robin couldn't have been further from the truth when he'd said that a defence counsel would have pulled Mrs. Sanderson apart in the witness box. Quite the contrary. "I've been along the road, and I can quite imagine how dangerous it could be if the driver wasn't taking care. I'm surprised you don't have dozens of accidents."

"Oh, we've had our fair share this last thirty years. Especially with deer. Drivers don't expect to have one bouncing out in front of them and even a roe deer isn't small."

"Quite right."

"There was one killed the same night that poor lad got hit."

"Really?" That hadn't been in the report, but maybe it had happened much earlier or later.

"Yes. My son only lives a few doors down. He'd been away that weekend, and he got a shock waiting for him when he returned late on Sunday. Not only those yellow signs appealing for witnesses to the accident, but also a deer on his front drive, dead as a dodo and starting to pong." She giggled again, face as cheeky as a schoolgirl's. "I shouldn't laugh. Thing is, my daughter-in-law's a lovely girl but you wouldn't believe how house proud she is. The thought that some wild animal had dared to expire on her property almost drove her berserk."

"It had been hit by a car?"

"So Adam reckons. That's my son, by the way, although you'll have guessed that. He thinks it was hit, then managed to stagger away from the road."

Adam. Why did the son have to be called by *that* name? Robin had almost managed to forget that he wasn't where he wanted to be on a Friday evening, and now thoughts of home flooded in.

"Are you all right?" Mrs. Sanderson asked.

"Yes. Sorry. I was reminded of something." Time to pull himself together. "Did your son happen to notice anything else odd?"

"No, or we'd have reported it, I promise. Naturally, there were the usual flowers and messages and soft toys left by where the lad was killed, so that meant a fair number of people were coming and going. Often they were simply standing looking at the spot, paying their respects. A number of them must have been rugby players." Her eyes twinkled. "You can tell by the ears and noses. And in case you're thinking that I have nothing better to do than be nosy, I was doing my neighbourly duty. The lady whose driveway the accident happened in is housebound, bless her, so Adam and I both do what we can to help out. She was extremely upset, understandably, especially with all the strangers lurking outside, so I'd go in to keep her company and try to disperse the groups when I felt they'd spent enough time there. She got rather worried about the younger people who turned up but, bless them, they just wanted to say goodbye to their friend. They turned out to be very kind."

Robin wondered if the local special constables fancied taking up a new recruit and whether they'd turn a blind eye to Mrs. Sanderson's age, rather like they sometimes turned a blind eye to prospective special constables' actual heights. "Your friend must have been grateful."

"She was. But that's what neighbours are for, isn't it? I met the young man's parents out there—we brought them in for a cup of tea." She shook her head. "Nothing we could say, though. I can't begin to imagine how they felt."

Robin nodded his agreement. He'd noted the mention of parents, plural rather than singular. Tom Weatherell hadn't mentioned a wife—or had he? Yes, there'd been something about him carrying around his late wife's wedding ring in his wallet. Robin had assumed she was dead, but he'd need to check whether she was very much alive and had simply left him, throwing her wedding ring metaphorically—or literally—in the man's face. Weatherell himself, like so many others in this case, might have an alibi for when Osment was killed but would the same apply to his wife?

"They had such dignity about them. No hint of rancour," Mrs. Sanderson continued. "If that had been my Adam, I'd have been beside myself. I count myself a Christian but I couldn't have turned my cheek in that instance."

"I'd have felt the same." Had that been Adam, Robin would have been on the warpath. The same—although to a lesser extent—if it had been Campbell.

"They came back some time later, after the inquest, because they wanted to clear away the tributes. I gave them a hand. They were going to chuck the cuddly toys in the bin because they'd suffered with the weather, but I said I'd give them a clean and donate them to the local school. I go and listen to the children read."

"My partner's a teacher. Or he was. Deputy headteacher now." Well, that was out in the open now. An Adam waiting at home, rather than a madam.

Mrs. Sanderson didn't bat an eyelid. "A very rewarding career. Like your own. Both of them hard work, though." She picked up the teapot. "I can wrest another one out of this, I believe."

"Please." Robin proffered his cup. "We enjoy what we do. It might sound old-fashioned but we like to think we make a difference."

"You do. And if you can find out who killed the youngster out there—" she gestured with her teacup in the direction of the road "—as well as solve your other murder, you'll have made a lot of difference to a lot of people."

When Robin had finished his tea and refused another slice of Dundee cake to eat there and then—although he did accept one all wrapped up to take back to the hotel for future consumption—he made his farewells. While he'd have been quite happy to sit and chat for another hour, it risked him falling asleep in the chair.

"You'll have been to see the site of the crash," Mrs. Sanderson said, as she accompanied him to his car. "Not that there's much to see now. Even if it were light enough to see anything."

"That's what I expected. Do people leave flowers on the anniversary?"

"Not that I've seen. But I suspect his parents would have asked for that not to happen. I don't think they were comfortable about the original tributes. Oh. I remember now." She paused, evidently trying to pin down an elusive memory. "There was one message they got rather annoyed at. We found it when we were clearing all the dead flowers and plastic wrappers away. It said, 'Sorry. I didn't realise.' That was all. It had been tucked in amongst the other stuff, but it hadn't been out there that long, because it was written in ink and there was no sign of the lettering running. It had rained on and off until a few days previously."

"You should join our forensic team." Interesting timing, of the note being placed there, if her reading of the situation was correct. "What happened to the note?"

"I assume it got chucked away, although I could be wrong. My grandson always says 'Never assume. It makes an ass of u and me.'"

Robin chuckled, even though he'd heard that before. "Did the Weatherells mention why they wanted to move the tributes at that point?"

Wearing a perceptive expression, she said, "They said things seemed a bit tatty—which was true—and that it was time for them to start to move on and knowing a sort of shrine had been created here wasn't helping. Which struck me as being a touch premature, but everyone copes with grief differently."

"You didn't believe them?"

"Am I that obvious? I must make sure I don't get drawn into poker games." The giggle emerged again. "I simply thought that I wouldn't have done that. Anyway, sometime afterwards, when I read the newspaper report of the inquest, I thought of that note. Did 'I didn't realise' mean the culprit had felt guilty that the lad could have survived if an ambulance had arrived earlier?"

"That crossed my mind too."

"I guess they panicked. Perhaps any of us would." Mrs. Sanderson peered out into the darkness. "I kick myself for not going out there when I heard something. Perhaps I could have seen him and called 999."

"Don't blame yourself. It might have been the impact with the deer you heard. If you'd been wandering around in the dark, *you* might have been the one the driver hit."

She nodded. "I suppose you're right. Although it's no consolation."

Which was an accurate—if depressing—assessment of the situation.

Chapter Twelve

Adam's plans to arrive mega-early for the Friday evening choir rehearsal were soon scuppered. Sandra had left a note asking if it would be all right to call and pick his brains on something, in reply to which he'd sent a text saying that would be fine so long as it was straight away. He could guess what it might be about, as she'd had a heart-to-heart with both him and Robin the back end of the previous year about whether she should worry if her daughter had put a science kit and a remote-controlled car on her Christmas list.

This time the call was fairly straightforward, concerning a gay couple in their fifties to whose wedding Sandra's sister had been invited and what would make a suitable present. He suggested, a touch more exasperation than he'd intended but it had been a stressful week, that she consult the wedding list, only to find that was the issue. There wasn't a list. Adam suggested John Lewis vouchers—boring but very welcome.

He came away from the call relieved that it had been so easy to deal with but reminded, yet again, of how he and Campbell were rattling around the house without the essential other side of the triangle. He put on some music in the kitchen—one of the bands Robin disliked and at a volume he'd have objected to—then heated up a tin of soup, ready for his riotous Friday night. Oh, the prospect of getting his tonsils around a selection of songs and warning Martin to steer clear of Sam Woakes.

As it turned out, he couldn't get the choirmaster alone before the rehearsal started, other people having turned up early, including Sam himself. The awkward air between the two blokes had returned and, if anything, had intensified. Eye contact was avoided as well as physical proximity, and Adam wasn't aware of any conversation directly between the two men all the length of the rehearsal. The singing went well, though, even if there was an embarrassing moment at one point when Campbell made his mind up to join in. Martin had decided at the last minute to give "Glory Glory Hallelujah" a go, at the suggestion of the fundraising organisers, Greg apparently being a huge Spurs fan. Adam should have warned him there was a risk of it setting the dog off, it being for some reason the only tune Campbell ever wanted to sing along to, but the whole Sam and Martin weirdness had put it out of his head. In the end he'd taken the Newfoundland outside for a stroll while the rest of the choir gave the song their all.

Once the rehearsal was over, Adam went into helpful mode, for which Martin proved grateful as the rest of the choir had cleared off, murmuring about pubs or Bosie's, the single gay bar in the area.

"You okay, mate?" Adam asked as they put back the last of the chairs to its rightful place and straightened up one of the flower arrangements.

"Yes," Martin snapped. "Why shouldn't I be?"

"Hey, don't bite me. I'm just concerned. You seem, um, rather preoccupied."

Martin gave him a sharp look, opened his mouth, shut it again, and finally said, "It's Sam. He rang me yesterday evening wanting to talk. It gave me the heebie-jeebies because I didn't recognise the number. I've been overly twitchy the last few months because I went through a spate of getting peculiar calls."

That would explain Martin's odd reaction when Adam had first rung in response to the appeal for choir members. "Nasty. Did you tell the police?"

"No. I eventually had the sense to block the number so they went away. Anyhow, once I knew it was Sam, I agreed to meet him at the pub. He wanted to know why the cops had been questioning him and was it to do with me talking to you?"

"How did he make that connection? And what did you tell him?"

Martin raised an eyebrow. "How did he make the connection? Everybody knows you're Robin's partner, so when he asked Del after practice on Tuesday who the fit bloke with the green eyes was, Del said that must have been you and that Sam needed to get his paws off because not only did you have a dog, you had a rozzer at home who'd come and sort him out if he misbehaved."

"Great." Adam would need to have a word with Del. Some people couldn't see a joke for what it was, and he didn't want Robin getting a reputation as a bad cop.

"Anyway, I told him Robin wasn't like that and he must only have been doing what he regarded as his job. You have to ask any and everybody when it's a murder enquiry, and the fact he was the twin brother of somebody who was connected with the case was enough to get folk interested. I managed to get him to see sense. After a couple of pints."

"Well done. Could have turned very ugly." But in that case, why the awkwardness between them? The expression on Martin's face bellowed that he had further things to say but wasn't sure whether he should. Best to ask him a question he could take or leave. "Are you sure you're okay?"

"Well." Martin glanced over his shoulder, towards the altar. "Can we talk about this outside? I know it's stupid, but I don't feel comfy discussing it in here."

"Whatever you want." They collected Campbell, then headed out of the door.

Martin's squeamishness at discussing whatever-it-was clearly didn't extend to the church porch. "Trouble is, I was feeling so relieved that nothing bad had happened that I asked him if he wanted to come round for a coffee rather than have another pint. I live five minutes from the pub, so it seemed the right thing to do."

"And?"

"And matters got a bit out of hand. You know, he's a handsome bloke and he seems genuinely nice so . . ." Martin shrugged.

"You got it on with him?" No wonder Martin—fastidious, cautious Martin—hadn't wanted to talk about it in the church.

"Yes. I mean, it was great and all that but when he left to go home it was one of those *Was that only a one-off or is this the start of something?* type of situations. He said he'd call me and I said that would be cool, but he hasn't and I don't know if I should ring him." Martin shrugged. "Given how uncomfortable it was between us this evening, I don't know what's going on. Sorry, I shouldn't off-load onto you."

"If it helps to talk, I'm happy to listen." And to pass on information to Robin, although that would remain unsaid.

"I worry that I was too needy. That I simply grabbed at the chance of having some fun without thinking of the consequences."

Adam's heart sank. "You did take precautions, didn't you? You didn't do anything stupid?"

"No, of course not. I'm not that dumb." Martin grinned sheepishly. "I'm not that worried about one-night stands, either. They happen. It's—it's . . . maybe Sam and I could have forged a proper relationship together if we hadn't dived in at the deep end. It's like he doesn't want to know, now."

"He might feel the same. In which case it's going to be stupid you two dancing around each other not speaking. Talk to him, get it out in the open. It can't make things worse." *Hold on. Maybe that's not the tack to take. Isn't it time to deliver the warning?* "Look, it might even not be you. It could be this case hanging over Sam's head. His brother is still being investigated for that murder. I'm not saying either of them are involved, because Robin reckons he's got a number of leads, but until Sam can be sure he's not under suspicion, he might be edgy. Especially given *our* friendship."

"Good point." A glimmer of hope lit Martin's face. "I'll text him and say I enjoyed our evening and if he wants to get in touch, he knows where I am. Or do you think that's unwise, given his potential involvement with Robin's case?"

"Texting him will be okay. It's unlikely he's a danger to you—or to anyone—but just be careful. If he's keen, you can always keep him on hold until the concert's over and done with. Plead pressure of work and not enough hours in the day or something."

"Will do. Thanks. See you soon." Martin, unexpectedly, put out his fist for a bump. Adam returned it with a grin and a "Good luck!" then headed to his car to put the dog blanket away. Rather than go straight home, he took Campbell to the little patch of ground at the back of the church, ostensibly to let the dog relieve himself. It made a great cover for messaging Robin to see if he was still awake.

Yep. Want to talk?

Only by message, unless you want to wait until I get home. Don't want to risk being overheard. I'll be about ten minutes by the time Campbell's all sorted.

Okay. Speak then.

When they finally managed to connect, Robin sounded even wearier than he'd been the previous evening. Time for Adam to put any guilt aside about adding to his woes, though; he'd know if this was important or not.

"I'll make this brief. I was going to deliver your warning to Martin but I was too late. Apparently Sam Woakes met up with him last night to give him grief. Reckons because Martin and I met to do some planning—all the choir know that because he mailed out about it—he'll have spoken to me and I'll have spoken to you and that's the reason the police questioned Sam. Which is true, but I'm surprised he didn't come around here and talk to me, in that case."

"He's probably scared of Campbell. Or frightened that you'd report his visit straight to me." Robin's tones felt reassuring. "Did he thump Martin or anything?"

"Worse than that. He sweet-talked his way into Martin's bed."

"He what?"

"They met at the pub, Martin defused the situation, asked him to come for coffee and then Sam seduced Martin. Or maybe it was the other way round. He's pretty lonely and Sam's dead fit." Adam blew out his cheeks. "Anyway, I had to hurriedly rewrite the speech I was going to deliver and simply told him as a friend—rather than flogging the rozzer angle—to make sure he didn't get in too deep while Sam was still a person of interest in the case. I felt a total bastard for spoiling love's dream, if they hadn't spoiled it already themselves, but what else could I do?"

"Nothing. You did the right thing even if it wasn't the easiest one. You'll get used to being a bastard, believe me—I have to do it all the time. Another job you can do for me"—Robin's tone morphed into his most serious one—"is to watch your own back. Sam might be totally innocent and just has the hump on that he's been questioned, but you can't be sure."

"I'll keep Campbell with me at all times. The choir seem to have adopted him as their mascot, anyway. Somebody brought him dog biscuits today. He's spoiled rotten."

"I got spoiled rotten tonight too. And don't panic—it was by that seventy-odd lady I told you about. I went to see her about the hit-and-run and was given a slice of the best Dundee cake I've ever tasted."

"Don't tell Campbell. Gran used to make that and she'd slip him a smidgeon when he was no bigger than a puppy." Lucky the dog wasn't in the room as he'd have no doubt sensed that cake was being discussed. He'd been allowed a smidgeon of wedding cake on the big day, but that had been a very rare treat. "Did you find out anything else about the accident?"

"Odds and ends. I'd hate to live on that road—taking Campbell for walks on a winter's evening you'd be taking your life in your hands. And it's a dangerous place to live if you're a deer."

"Like the road we lived on when I was younger. Mum said it was an absolute death trap, although my dad always swore that being in houses is more dangerous than being in cars, given the number of people who fall down stairs or off ladders. Or go and electrocute themselves while messing about with dodgy wiring."

"He could well have been right. As I've said until I'm blue in the face, you're likelier to be murdered or assaulted in your home and by someone you know than in a strange place by a total stranger." Robin snorted.

"Could be. Trouble is we can't really teach *Parent Danger* to the kids rather than *Stranger Danger*. Can you imagine the reaction?"

"In the case of a few of your families, it would be accurate, though."

"Too true." The situations some of his pupils were in, the sheer fecklessness and selfishness of their parents, and the potentially lifelong impact it would have on their offspring, beggared belief. "Anyway, Mum reckoned my old man only harped on about danger in the home because I used to hare down the stairs at a hundred miles an hour. Maybe he was more concerned about wear and tear to the carpet than injury to his only son."

Robin's voice softened. "I doubt that. Not from what your mum tells me about him. Apple of his eye, you were."

"I'm going to have to stop you two meeting up. You make me blush." Nice to be reminded of the affection they had for each other, though. "So, should Martin be worried about Sam not being in touch?"

"How do I know? I'm too busy being a policeman to be an agony aunt on the side. Sorry, didn't mean to sound so waspish. I'll be delighted for him if he can sort out his love life—might stop him making calf eyes at me. Only if he can hold fire on the romance side until we know how deep the Woakes brothers are involved, that might make everyone's lives easier." Robin yawned. "I need my sleep. Wish you were here, but as you're not, don't forget how much I love you."

"Miss you and love you too." Adam cleared his throat. "And that's enough of that, or I'll be a blubbering mess and Campbell will insist on comforting me. I'll end up slobbered to death."

"I'll slobber you senseless when I get back."

"Promises, promises. Good night. Sleep well."

"I'll try my best."

As he finished the call, the dog—who'd probably guessed that his other master was on the phone or sensed people were in need of comfort—stuck his nose in Adam's hand.

"Hello, you." Adam stroked Campbell behind the ears. "No, I've no idea when he'll be home. Yes, I do miss him. Yes, he misses us both too, and no, you're not taking his place in the bed."

Campbell tried his most appealing expression but it fell on blind eyes, so he sauntered off to the kitchen and his own bed, leaving Adam to wonder how he'd managed to be content for so long with sleeping alone.

Chapter Thirteen

Colin Cooper wasn't quite what Robin was expecting. For some reason he'd got it into his head the guy would be built like a brick outhouse but he was small and wiry, like a typical scrum half from the amateur rugby era. *You should have grown out of making assumptions about what people would look like from their names alone.*

Robin, hoping his face hadn't shown any surprise, launched into the questions.

"As Sergeant Davis told you, we're here about the death of Nick Osment. You knew him when he played for Tuckton?"

"Yes. Not the most talented player, but wholehearted. Put his body on the line. Are you sure I can't get you a coffee?" It was the second time he'd made the offer. *Enthusiastic host or nerves manifesting themselves?*

Robin glanced around the room. A typical lounge in a 1980s house and seeming much the same as it might have been back then: slightly cramped, although light and airy, with furniture and ornaments that were well kept if starting to show their age. Was there any conclusion to be drawn from the house needing some money spent on it? Or did Cooper simply like keeping hold of old things for as long as possible? It was sometimes a matter of choice rather than funds.

Of interest was a pot full of pens that stood on the windowsill and which Robin had made a mental note of as soon as they came in. Among the eclectic collection of biros was what appeared to be a fountain pen, although they couldn't jump to conclusions from that. Plenty of households still possessed one of those knocking about, even if they rarely used them.

"Tell us about your friendship with Osment," Robin said.

"I wouldn't say it was a friendship, *per se*. My giving him a lift was simply a case of helping out Ashley—Ashley Howarth—when he couldn't oblige."

"It all seems a lot of trouble to go to for one player. Especially one you described as not the most talented," Pru added.

"We'd have done it for any of the lads, talented or not. We were encouraged to car share, anyway, it being good for the environment and all that. Our coach at the time was heavily into the green agenda. Sometimes Ashley ran both of us home if the timings worked. He's no great drinker so it didn't bother him."

The environmental concern certainly made sense of why Osment had routinely been given a lift. "Why did Osment give up rugby?"

"One too many blows to the head, I'd say. He'd been knocked out twice in the previous twelve months. It's a dangerous game."

"Nothing to do with him being red-carded in what turned out to be his final match?"

Cooper shrugged. "That might have come into it. I really don't know."

Robin asked, "Did he say anything which you now think may have had a connection to his death?"

"Apart from his occasionally pouring his soul out about whether his wife was having an affair? Nothing." Cooper ran his finger round the ridges of his ear. "I did see the news about his being killed, so if I'd had information, I would have done my good citizen bit."

"And what about being a good citizen as far as the hit-and-run was concerned?"

Cooper appeared to flinch. "What hit-and-run, Mr. Bright?"

"Jamie Weatherell. The lad riding his bike home from the match Tuckton had against Hartwood. The match you played in."

"Oh. That was years ago. I thought there must have been another one. The roads are so dangerous nowadays." Cooper couldn't have been much older than Robin, but he gave off an air of being fussy and middle-aged, as though he were from a different generation. "That was a terrible thing to happen to such a young lad. Everyone was cut up about it."

"You must have driven along that road that evening, on the way home. Didn't you notice anything?" Robin couldn't press further as they still didn't have a clear timeline of who had left the club when and were unable to prove that there would have been a juxtaposition of Jamie's journey and Cooper's.

"I'll be honest with you, Mr. Bright." Cooper turned to Pru. "And Miss . . . Davis, was it?"

Pru nodded curtly. This was exactly the kind of witness with whom his sergeant had little patience, although normally they were thirty years older.

"I didn't see anything, cyclist or other vehicle, apart from once when a vehicle came in the other direction, with its headlights on full beam and almost blinded me. I had to pull into the side of the road until my vision cleared."

"You remember it well for something that happened years ago," Pru observed.

"I do. Because Nick kept nagging me to get going again. Said he needed to get home."

"Why the urgency?"

"He wouldn't say. Probably thought his wife was up to something. We'd left the club earlier than the rest of the players, anyway, so I told him to be patient." Cooper fiddled with a loose thread on the arm of his chair. "We'd get there when we got there."

That didn't strike Robin as something you'd have to make a big fuss about confessing. There had to be more to Cooper's *being honest.* "Is that all you have to say?"

Cooper sighed. "No. I've been clinging on to this for too long. I need to come clean."

Robin caught Pru's eye—was it too much to hope for that they were about to hear the big confession?

"About a hundred yards down the road from where I'd stopped, I hit a deer." Yes, far too much to hope for. "I know it's only a wild animal, but I felt terrible about it. I still do."

"Why?" Pru asked. "I mean why such a burden of guilt?"

"Because I should have taken extra care. I'd seen a deer earlier, running by the side of the road—I doubt it was the same one, but that should have been a warning to me."

"How do you know it was a deer you hit and not Jamie Weatherell?"

The bluntness of Robin's question made Cooper flinch again. "Because Nick told me. I stopped the car and he got out to have a look. He said he'd seen a deer staggering off into one of the driveways, so he guessed it was only bruised and winded. I think I suffered as much—I was really shaken."

"Was there any mark on your car? A dent? Blood? Deer hair?"

"Only a scuff and a small dent on the bumper. To match the one I'd put there the week before, hitting a gatepost." The grin Cooper had broken into disappeared as though switched off at the mains. He'd clearly realised, if a touch late, that this was no laughing matter.

"Why didn't you report this at the time? You must have seen the police appeals for information."

"I did, Miss Davis, but I couldn't see how my hitting a deer could have anything to do with things." Cooper went through what appeared to be a bad pantomime of light dawning. "Oh, do you think the deer I saw had something to do with the accident? A car swerving round it and losing control, for example?"

Robin sighed. Why was this such hard work? "I was thinking along the lines of you not reporting it because you were worried it was Jamie you'd hit, not a deer."

"No, Mr. Bright. Never." Cooper's expression contradicted his words.

"You're an intelligent man, Mr. Cooper," Pru said, switching into the soothing voice that had worked wonders with witnesses in the past. "Surely you're not expecting us to believe that you never considered that possibility?"

"You're extremely perceptive." His face hardened and the silly-ass veneer began to slide away. "Yes, I did consider that at the time. I'm ashamed now, in retrospect, that I didn't contact you, but I spoke to Nick, and he reassured me that I hadn't hit anybody. Are you saying I might have collided with that poor lad and Nick lied to me about it?"

"We have to consider that possibility." Robin also had to consider the possibility that Cooper had constructed and kept this story ready to wheel out at any point it was needed. Very convenient for him that the time had long past that forensic checks of the car could have yielded any fruit. And the witness to the supposed deer collision was dead. Except that there *had* been a deer killed on the road that night. *Coincidence or more than that?* He and Pru could discuss it on the way to Stratford. "Did you go back to the scene?"

"I'm sorry?"

"Where Weatherell was killed. People went to leave flowers."

"Ah, I see. No, I didn't know the lad, so that would have felt inappropriate. False grief and an intrusion on the real thing." That last piece sounded like a true reflection of what Cooper felt, much truer than much of what had gone before.

"You didn't leave a note among the flowers?" Pru asked.

"No. Why should I?"

"Guilt," she said.

"But I felt no guilt. I believed I'd hit a deer. I still believe that. You can ask—" He halted, flustered. "Sorry, that's stupid. You can't ask Nick to confirm it, can you?"

"Clearly not. But we do have to ask *you* about what you were doing the night he was killed." Robin raised a hand to stave off any protest. "It's purely routine."

"Glad to hear that. I wouldn't have wanted him dead, especially given what's turned up in this conversation. He'd have been the only person who could verify what I said."

Or disprove it entirely. Robin persisted, "Just answer the question, please."

"I'll need to consult my diary." Cooper crossed the room, opened the draw of a wall unit, and produced a slimline diary, bought from the Oxfam shop according to the logo, which was where Robin's mum always got hers. Would it contain the same messy scrawls and cramped writing that Mrs. Bright employed to cram in all the many commitments she had? He managed to catch a glimpse of the contents, which seemed remarkably sparse, but noted that several of them appeared to be written in ink. What he wouldn't give for a time machine, to be able to go back and get that original note for fingerprinting and forensic comparison.

"What date was it?" Cooper held his diary in one hand while he did the ear poking thing again with the other.

"Three Wednesdays ago," Pru said. "Between the hours of six o'clock and ten o'clock in the evening."

"I was away on business. I work in marketing for the Hepius Pharmaceutical Company, and we had a meeting in the Mercure Hotel at Banbury." Cooper tapped the diary, as though that concluded the matter.

"Somebody can vouch for that, can they?"

"Yes, Sergeant, my work colleagues would be able to. Let me get the contact details of one of the people at the meeting."

"Thank you." That conversation would be happening as soon as they left, before Cooper had the chance to influence what might be said. Assuming he hadn't already done so, getting all his story lined up.

Pru, leaping up, took the piece of paper on which Cooper had jotted the number down, keeping it in her hand. "We'll be back in touch should we need to be."

"I guess you will." Cooper ushered them towards the door. He made a point of shaking hands with them on the doorstep before saying, "God, I don't believe in karma, but if Nick lied to me about what I'd hit and that lad could have been saved if we'd rung for help, maybe fate caught up with him."

Robin didn't believe in karma, either, although he did believe in human wickedness. Wasn't it likelier *that* was what had eventually settled Osment's fate?

Ellie Harrison, the marketing executive who was supposed to be confirming Cooper's alibi, wasn't answering her calls, so Robin left a message for her to get back to him as soon as possible. Aware of Cooper watching him from his front window, he deliberately turned his back while on the phone. Let the man mull over what might be being said. Meanwhile, Pru had worked out that it was only thirty minutes' drive from the Mercure to the Hartwood ground—perhaps forty when the traffic was sticky—so it wouldn't have been outside the bounds of possibility for Cooper to have driven there and back, provided he wasn't conspicuously among colleagues at the relevant times.

"Do you believe that deer story, sir?" she asked as soon as the car doors were shut and the engine started. "It would seem rather a far-fetched coincidence to me except that Mrs. Sanderson told you that there was a deer killed on that road at about the crucial moment."

"Agreed, although either Cooper or Osment could have gone back to the scene—they'd not have stood out among the other visitors coming and going. If they spotted the dead animal, they might have decided that would be their backup story. Especially if they'd genuinely seen it or a similar one haring down the road either before or after they hit Jamie Weatherell. Bugger." Robin drummed on the steering wheel. "At last I've remembered what Cooper said about being able to have saved him if they'd stopped. How did he know that?"

"He'll have read about it in the stories covering the inquest, surely?"

"Maybe, but why take such an interest?"

"Think of how people like to be outraged, sir. You can imagine the furore that medical evidence stirred up. People would have been talking about it at the rugby club."

"Okay, I'll buy that. I'm getting suspicious of everything." Robin concentrated on a tricky junction that didn't seem to align with the directions his satnav was giving him. "Let's say Cooper was duped by Osment. He wanted to get home in a hurry so he pretended it was a deer that was hit. Stretching my Christian charity to its limit, let's even say he thought Jamie was dead so they couldn't have helped him anyway. All that would make him complicit in covering up an offence at the very least. And to continue covering it up if Cooper really did get back to him for reassurance it was a deer. Why bring attention to himself by making a fuss over the fundraising?"

"Double bluff? Sheer stupidity? Victim blaming?" Pru drummed her fingers together. "People do that all the time: try to shift things off the shoulders of the guilty. If Osment was carrying around a load of guilt about what had happened that evening, he might have persuaded himself that it was actually Jamie's fault for not making sure he was visible to motorists."

"Okay, we'll assume that's true for the moment. What about Osment blackmailing Cooper? He didn't strike me as being rolling in money, given the state of his furniture, although I guess he might just be the type who hoards his dosh rather than spend it."

"Maybe he's not rolling in it because Osment's been taking his share for years. In small amounts so it's not left an audit trail in bank accounts. Did you notice Cooper had a fountain pen in that pot?"

"I did. And some of his diary entries used ink." Robin negotiated another tricky junction, inwardly cursing the local road designers. "Don't forget there was a fountain pen at Osment's flat too."

"I'd forgotten that." Pru chuckled. "Should I write out fifty times 'Must do better'?"

"Only if it stops you from being bored."

"I might have to resort to it if we're cooped up in that hotel much longer. Okay, the note. If Cooper wrote it because he felt guilty after the inquest, then he might have told Osment he was coming to us."

"Wouldn't that have made him the potential victim, in that case? Osment wouldn't have wanted his part in the matter exposed, especially if Cooper could have persuaded us that it was Osment who was behind the deer story." Every time they got a lead, it seemed to evaporate in a haze of unbreakable alibis or illogical behaviour.

"Does it make more sense if Osment wrote it? He knew he couldn't come to us because his own part in it would be exposed but it nags at him. Maybe Cooper even threatens that if Osment brings it into the open, he'll say that he knew he'd hit someone and was all for dialling 999 but that Osment insisted they drove off. No, that's too weak."

"Cooper might have used a bigger threat. What if he said he'd swear to us that he'd had to go out again—back to the Tuckton ground because he thought he'd left something there—and saw Osment driving along that road? Or was out near the waste ground and saw Osment trashing his own car. The guy had a near miss previously, whereas Laurence has confirmed that Cooper's driving record is clear apart from the close encounter with the gatepost he admitted to. Who would people most likely believe to have done it? Preese already thinks it was Osment's fault and he's hardly been Mr. Popular."

"That might still make Cooper the potential victim, though. What's changed to make Osment vulnerable?"

"What if he found something that could put Cooper in the frame? I know—" Robin sighed "—it's a long shot, but if Osment turned up some proof, then he'd have grounds for blackmail *and* he'd give Cooper reason to kill him."

"What kind of evidence did you have in mind? I—" The sound of Pru's phone cut her off. "I'll take this now. It's Laurence."

Robin, torn between driving the unfamiliar roads and working out what the conversation was about from the snatches he caught, decided to focus on the car. There was plenty of Stratford-bound traffic, and not all the drivers were paying as much attention as they should. Once the call ended, he asked, "What's he turned up now?"

"Mrs. Weatherell. The late Mrs. Weatherell, to be exact. Laurence didn't talk to the groundsman—he managed to find his sister-in law, so asked her. Apparently, Jamie was an only child and his mum never really recovered from his death. The sister reckoned she'd had a weak heart since childhood, and about a year after her son's death she suffered a massive coronary embolism. Everyone said it was losing Jamie brought it on, although whether that's possible, I don't know."

"Neither do I, but his death won't have helped."

"Agreed. Something interesting turned up, though. Joe Woakes was her cousin."

"What?" Robin slowed to a speed at which he could concentrate on what he was being told but not risk the ire of the Saturday morning drivers.

"Bit of a stunner, isn't it? Joe Woakes—and therefore Sam Woakes—are first cousins to the late Mrs. Weatherell. Quite a difference in age between them, clearly, but it makes Jamie their second cousin. Or cousin once removed. I get those confused."

"So do I. Whatever it is, that's close enough to make me question why nobody's bothered to mention it, even in passing?" The *sorry, didn't think it was relevant* excuse would no doubt get aired again and, in this instance, it was wearing thin. "No wonder Joe got so upset about the hit-and-run. Did he explain his relationship to the victim at the time of the assault charge being dropped?"

"Not that I remember, but you know what it's like reading about a case at second-hand. Something might have been mentioned that didn't make the written record." Pru glanced into the side mirror. "The bloke behind's right up our backside."

"Let him be. I'm only just below the speed limit, and if he wants to overtake me on a dangerous bend, I'd be happy to play traffic cop." Maybe he'd gain some temporary satisfaction at having an easily identifiable culprit to deal with.

"I'll keep an eye out for people using mobile phones at the wheel. Sitting ducks." Pru snorted. "Joe Woakes, though. That relationship probably takes away any credibility of him being the one who ran Jamie over unless he's a totally heartless bastard, and he didn't strike me that way. Gives him—and Sam—a better motive for wanting Osment dead if they thought he was responsible."

"It does indeed. Assuming he was lying to us about not agreeing with Preese about Osment being the driver. It's a matter of fact that witnesses never lie to us." With a snicker, Robin sped up again and headed for the intricacies of the Stratford road system and the challenge of finding a parking space.

They'd parked, lunched, left a message for Joe—who was likely at work if what he'd said about his shift pattern was right—to contact them urgently about having another chat, and were walking along the riverbank when Ellie Harrison returned Robin's call.

"I'm sorry I missed you, but I never take calls on a Saturday morning if my boy's got a game. It's only under elevens but he takes it very seriously."

Robin explained who he was, while wondering if the younger Harrison took the game as seriously as the adults probably did. "I'm ringing to ask about the meeting you had at Banbury a few weeks ago."

"Yes? At the Mercure?"

"That's the one. Can you confirm when it was held?"

"The Tuesday and Wednesday. I'd need to check the actual dates but it would be three weeks ago this coming Tuesday."

Robin did a quick mental tally. "That sounds right, although if you could double-check I'd be grateful."

"Let me take the phone into the kitchen and have a look at the calendar. We're very low-tech here."

"Paper calendars can't crash."

"True. Yes, it was the fourth and the fifth."

"Was Colin Cooper at the meeting?"

"He was. There might have been a dozen of us altogether, so if you need that corroborated, I'm sure that wouldn't be a problem. I could give you contact details."

"Thanks, although we don't need that at this precise moment." It didn't sound a promising enough lead yet. "Did you stay overnight?"

"Yes. Had a smashing meal the Tuesday night, although the people who've been in the company longer than I have say the hospitality's nothing like it was in the past. I suppose companies have to consider cutting costs and getting rid of a huge jolly for the boys and girls seems an obvious place to start."

"It's the way of the world." Robin waggled his thumb at Pru, trying to convey that he might be on to something at last. "Which nights did you stay at the hotel?"

"Oh, sorry. I was prattling on and didn't really answer your question. Doh." Ellie laughed. "We only stayed the Tuesday night. We went home—or wherever else people were heading—after the meeting ended on Wednesday."

"What time was that?"

"It ended at about half past four, but I guess it would have been gone five by the time everyone got away. Some of the blokes went to the bar too. Said they'd not got away ahead of the rush hour so they might as well wait for it to clear. Just an excuse for having a couple of beers, I suspect. I hit the road."

"Was Cooper amongst those who stayed on drinking?"

"He told me that he was going to stay on until the traffic had eased slightly, which was a surprise." Ellie took a contemptuous sniff. "He's known as a bit of a tightwad. Usually after a meeting he gets straight into his car and heads off home, although one of the guys who did go to the bar could verify that."

"If you could give me a name and number, that would be great."

Once he'd got the contact details and thanked Ellie for her help, Robin ended the call and brought Pru up to speed. "So, assuming he got away around five and the traffic wasn't horrendous, he could easily have been at Hartwood in time to meet Osment."

"I'll call all the team in to start going through CCTV images. I made a note of Cooper's registration. Assuming the car on the drive was his? They can check that too, and if it's someone else's, then they should follow it up with him to get the right motor."

"Hold fire on that until we know for certain that he could have driven there. If we have three witnesses putting him in the Mercure bar ale-ing it up until ten o'clock, it'll be pointless." A waste of resources and the team's goodwill too. "At present we've only got a tenuous motive, evidence that he's stretched the truth about where he was on the evening of the fifth, and the fact I don't like him."

Pru kicked at a stone on the path, sending it hurtling into the river. "I didn't like him either, although that's no help."

"Let's see if..." Robin consulted his notebook, "Roger Crompton can shed some light on things."

He could and did, answering Robin's call at the third ring and confirming—somewhat long-windedly—that Cooper had been at the meeting and hadn't stayed afterwards. Crompton also confirmed that the car they'd seen on the driveway was the one Cooper had driven to Banbury.

"Is he in trouble, then?"

"It's simply routine enquiries. A matter of elimination," Robin replied blandly, knowing he wouldn't be believed.

"I bet that's what you always say. Let me know if I can be of further help. I always try to do my public duty."

"Thank you. Much appreciated." Robin made three further attempts to end the call, each one stymied by Crompton wanting to chat about how important it was to aid the police. In the end, Robin had to risk further cooperation by being little short of bloody rude.

"Typical salesman," he said when he'd eventually extricated himself. "Never use one word when six will do. Cooper didn't stay at the bar, so he's given us a flaky alibi. I wonder if he hoped Ellie had believed him about visiting the bar and that we'd believe *her* without double-checking."

"He either thinks we're gullible or he's buying time. Do you want me to get the local police to nip round and see if he's done a runner?"

"Might be worth it, even if that's only to see whether the bird has already flown. We'll also get your traffic-cameras plan into action with the team. See what we can find to put pressure on him."

Pru halted to let a small child on a scooter get past without taking out anybody's ankle. "Magic. There's only one obvious route to Hartwood from the Mercure, so we'll have to hope Cooper took that rather than some obscure rat run that only the locals know about. Although if we focus on the traffic cameras nearer the ground, we narrow the options—all roads must lead down to only one."

"That sounds deeply philosophical. We should head back and give them a hand, unless I can get hold of Joe, in which case we'll divert there. I'd like to talk to him, as soon as possible."

"He's probably at work now, given what he said about a new shift starting."

"Then he can make a time to see us tonight. If I can't be out on the razzle on a Saturday night, then he can't either."

Pru flicked him a quizzical glance. "Do you ever go out on the razzle on a Saturday, sir?"

"You'd be surprised." Although in reality she wouldn't. A wild Saturday night out for the Bright-Matthews household consisted of a few beers, a curry, and a taxi home.

And Robin would give almost anything to be doing that in a few hours' time, rather than poring through traffic camera footage or pinning down Joe Woakes.

Back at the station, Robin made time to step outside and get far enough away to be able to ring Adam without the risk of being overheard. After letting the phone ring several times, he was about to hang up when a panting voice answered.

"Hello?"

"What have you been up to?"

"Took Campbell for a run. We'd literally got through the door and I was bursting for the loo—he's okay, he can cock his leg against a lamppost anytime he wants to." Adam chuckled, still a touch breathlessly.

"I wish I'd timed my call better. I now have visions of you all hot and sweaty, and it's not doing anything for my sangfroid." Thank God he'd got away from the station to make the call.

"And there's me thinking you'd been tracking me on the Find My Friends app and deliberately chose the moment."

"I've never thought of doing that. Ten minutes later and you'd be stepping out of the shower. I better get that vision out of my mind too." That could have formed part of a wild Saturday night, as well. "I rang to give you a heads-up that I'm about to poke the Woakes wasps nest again. In case there are repercussions."

"Been a development?"

"Yep. Turns out he and Sam are some sort of cousins to the lad who was killed in the hit-and-run. Not that Joe bothered to tell us."

"It would explain why he got so worked up. I guess I'd better warn Martin that he might be getting another irate visit. Although I think he might be away this weekend at a family bash, so he's probably okay."

"Please make sure that if Sam comes around and bothers *you* that you slam the door on him and call the local police out."

"Happy to do the first, but isn't the second over the top?"

"Not while he remains a person of interest in this case." They'd both been threatened before, and Robin was determined to do everything he could not to have Adam—or Campbell—put at risk again. "If you see him lurking around and want to decamp to your mum's for the rest of the weekend, then do it."

"Point taken and batted right back at you. Don't put yourself at risk, either."

Robin forced a laugh. "I've got Pru to protect me. Speak tomorrow. Love you."

"Love you too. So does Campbell."

"Give him a hug from me."

"Will do. Once he's had a bath. *Eau de sweaty dog* isn't my favourite cologne."

"Ugh." At least the thought of that would act as a passion killer.

Once back at the incident room, Robin felt the buzz of excitement in the air.

"We think we have him, sir. Cooper," Callum said. "About quarter of a mile from the ground, at four minutes past seven on the Wednesday evening. I'm not a hundred percent certain, so we're tracking back to the next camera in the direction of Banbury."

"Thing is," Sally cut in, "he could have come in on one of two roads, and the camera on the probable one hasn't got him at the right time. As well as checking other options, we're scrolling back in case he parked up in between or went for a drive around."

"Great work. Pru, have you heard from Joe?"

"Yes, five minutes ago. He can see us in between getting home from work and going out. Seven o'clock-ish." Her pout showed her level of dissatisfaction. "I couldn't resist saying I was glad he could make time for us in his busy schedule."

"We'll have to think of lots of questions and ask them very slowly." As so often before, Robin glanced across at the incident board, to find a fuzzy picture of Colin Cooper there.

Laurence, who'd been hovering next to the display, said, "It's the best we could find, sir. I know it looks like it could be almost anybody."

"It'll do for the moment. Although we'd need something better if he did a runner."

"We'll have to hope he takes it as a good sign that we've not been straight back round there." Pru had come to join them. "I've asked the local beat officers to keep an eye, but we can't justify keeping him under close observation. Yet."

"With any luck we'll get another sighting of his car before we go to see Joe. Then we can head back to Warwick and spoil *his* Saturday night too."

Chapter Fourteen

Seven o'clock on the dot, Robin rang the bell of Joe's flat. When Joe opened the door, his expression was neither welcoming nor happy. He ushered them in quickly, evidently trying to demonstrate just how much of a rush he was in and how he'd put himself out hugely to be able to see them. Robin guessed he was going out on a hot date, given the intense wave of aftershave—the classiness of the scent tones being counteracted by their sheer quantity—coming from Joe's direction.

"We won't keep you long," Robin said, quite prepared to break that promise if the interview content reached a point where the standard caution needed to be given. "Why didn't you tell us that you were related to the Weatherells?"

Joe, whose jaw had dropped at the word *related*, quickly recovered his composure. "I thought you knew. I'm sure I told the officers I spoke to when I got questioned about the assault."

Robin was pretty certain Joe was either lying or stretching the truth to breaking point. Nothing said in their interview had hinted at such a familial connection, although he'd have to give Joe the benefit of the doubt in case a police officer back then hadn't done their job properly. Discovering the extent of the bad practice—let alone the corruption—going on at Abbotston in the previous few years had been an eye-opener. "Be that as it may, we didn't know. We could argue that you misled us with all the stuff about your soft spot for him. You can imagine how suspicious that seems."

Joe shrugged. "What can I say? I'm sorry you've had to come back on a wild-goose chase, but I didn't lie to you. I did fancy Jamie—I always had—and we weren't so closely related that we couldn't have had a relationship."

Pru's snort showed what she thought of the response.

"Look, I told you last time, I had no reason to murder Osment," Joe snapped at them. "I didn't think he killed Jamie."

"Really?" Pru said, in similar tones to those Adam must use when one of his charges has been caught red-handed doing something and denies all knowledge of the offence. "Easy for you to say that. How do we know that's true? Have you mentioned it to anyone else? Preese, for example?"

Touches of sweat were breaking out on Joe's previously immaculate T-shirt. "You don't argue with Coach. Everyone will tell you that."

"We *have* been told. But that doesn't answer the question." Pru smiled patronisingly. *Exactly the way to get the witness worked up.* "What about Sam? Surely you'd have discussed Jamie's death with him. And the rest of the family. You must have wanted to know who was responsible."

Joe waved the question away with a flick of his wrist. "We were advised to stop speculating. *I* was advised to stop speculating. Part of learning to manage my anger was trying to get over Jamie's death." He paused to take a deep breath. "None of this is helping me to keep my cool right now."

A sudden *ping* from Pru's phone, signifying an incoming message, clearly didn't help his situation, especially when she ignored it, leaving the thing to *ping* again midway through her next remark. "If that was a member of my family, I wouldn't be able to dismiss the matter so easily. I'd want to know."

"Maybe you would, but you're not me."

Robin, aware that the angrier Joe got the more he clammed up, said, "You've spoken for yourself but not for the rest of them. Is there not a single family member who wants to know who the driver was?"

"There used to be. Not that any of us would speculate on it in front of Tom, though. That would be digging in the knife. Anyway, most of us stopped wondering when you banged up those two hooligans who nicked cars."

"The family thought they were responsible?"

Joe shrugged. "Either that or they persuaded themselves it was the right outcome. Better to have someone to blame rather than not knowing. That awful feeling that you might be walking down the street and the culprit passes you by. Or you could get involved with them romantically and never know." He blanched. "Sorry, I don't want to talk about this. It's too painful."

Evidently closure still hadn't been found. Robin changed tack slightly. "I understand that, but we've got a job to do. Tell me about Jamie's dad. He seems to be coping pretty well. Is he in the *right outcome* camp?"

"Yeah. He's a legend. If I'd been him and had to cope with two deaths, I'd have gone off my rocker. But he's always been strong—go-to man in the family when there's a crisis. He held everyone together when there was the inquest on Jamie, and then again when the trial of those two carjackers happened. Sam went to pieces and—" Joe halted abruptly, tight-lipped.

"Yes?" Robin pressed him. "What about Sam?"

Joe gave a small, embarrassed grin. "Me and my big mouth. Don't tell him that I said this, because he'll ki— he'll go ballistic, but he got really upset when those yobs were being tried."

Fits of temper clearly ran in the family, although if the twins were identical maybe that was no surprise. "Want to explain what you mean by 'got really upset'?"

"He was sure their lawyer would get them off on a technicality or something. He kept saying what he'd do to them if they were found innocent and released. Both Jamie's dad and I had to talk the idiot out of it. Tom's always had the gift of the gab. Probably comes from being in sales, once. Luckily he doesn't have our side of the family's temper."

"So, when they do come up for release," Pru cut in, "I wouldn't want to be in their shoes if Sam gets hold of them?"

"I didn't say that." Joe cast her a malicious glance. "Why must you twist my words?"

Pru was evidently getting under the witness's skin, but to no avail. The days of "good cop, bad cop" might have been in the past, but it wouldn't hurt for Robin to emphasise how sympathetic he was being. They only wanted the truth, after all. "You said yourself that Sam made threats. We're clarifying whether those threats are still tangible."

"Of course they're not. Sam's a good bloke. Way better than me on lots of counts. He wouldn't harm a fly. All bluster." Joe flicked his hand again. "Anyway, this is irrelevant. Nobody's actually hurt the blokes who stole the car, have they?"

"No, but they hurt Osment." Robin leaned forwards. "Sergeant Davis, would you please take another official statement from Mr. Woakes to cover everything we've discussed here. And the answer to this. Did you and Sam swop places when you went to the loo?"

"Eh?"

"Did he take your place on the field and give you an alibi?"

"No, he did not. He was at home. I know because I rang him there when I got home from the hospital." Joe shook his head. "I guess you won't believe me, and I can't prove it."

Robin suddenly felt sorry for the bloke. "Is there nothing you can tell us that would help Sam? If we know he was at home, it probably puts you in the clear."

"No, I—" Joe studied his hands. "Wednesday night, he was watching the football, because he was slagging the Arsenal off when I spoke to him a couple of days later. I bet he was on Twitter moaning about them too. Always is on a match day."

Robin nodded. "We'll check."

He sat quietly, mulling over Joe's words, while Pru took the revised statement. *"Nobody's actually hurt the blokes who stole the car, have they?"* That effectively summed up Robin's thoughts at this point. They had potential motives but not for the right victim and were still no closer to knowing why someone wanted Nick Osment dead.

Once outside the block of flats, Pru checked her phone, then broke into a triumphant grin. "The team has found Cooper's car on a traffic camera feed again, farther away from the ground but close enough to suggest the other sighting was also him. Much clearer image this time so there's no doubt."

"Excellent news." At last, somebody without an alibi and in the right area at the right time.

"Fancy getting round there now and hoping he's at home?" Pru eyed the car. "I know there's the chance that he'll be out, but if we ring beforehand that risks him getting the wind up."

Robin gave the notion a moment's thought. "No. Let's make it tomorrow. If he's going to do a runner or destroy evidence, the chances are he'll have already done it. If we need to bring him to the station for questioning or get in a forensic search team, then tomorrow morning is a better time. Cold, clear light of Sunday when I've had the chance to sleep on what Saturday's turned up."

That included the revelations about Sam Woakes's temper. Should he be ringing Adam to issue yet another warning or was that being too mother hen–ish?

"We could go and see Sam Woakes, as well," Pru said. "He's only been spoken to on the phone so far, and I'd like to see his face when he answers the questions."

"Me too. He's about the only other person without an alibi."

The fact that interviewing Sam would take them so close to Lindenshaw that a night at home could be justified had nothing to do with it. Not at all. But Robin would pack an overnight bag on Sunday morning to stick in the car boot, just in case.

Chapter Fifteen

Sunday morning, Cooper was at home. Or, to be accurate, there was a light on inside and the car was on the drive so Cooper was likely at home. No hot date for him like there'd been for Joe the previous evening, unless he was still entertaining someone: Robin hoped they wouldn't find him and some woman—or bloke—in an embarrassing state of dishevelment. Fortunately, when Cooper answered the door at the second ring, he simply appeared a bit bleary-eyed.

"Oh. It's you. I was having a kip. I wasn't expecting to see you back so quickly." He rubbed his left eye.

"Really? Did you think we wouldn't find out that you left Banbury not long after five o'clock when your meeting finished on the Wednesday or that we wouldn't want to come and find out why you lied?"

Cooper's mouth flapped up and down like a fish's before he snapped it shut. He opened the door wider, stepping back to let them in. "You know where the lounge is."

"Thank you." Once all three of them were in there and seated, Robin pressed on, "Maybe you thought we wouldn't find a traffic camera image of your car in Hartwood, a quarter of a mile from the training ground at a few minutes past seven that same evening. But we did. We found another one, as well, to confirm matters."

Cooper slumped into a chair. "I've been an idiot. I should have owned up to being in Hartwood. This is going to sound awful, but it's not what you think, I swear."

Robin had heard that line before. Sometimes it turned out to be true. People did cover up what they'd done, sometimes for the most bizarre reasons, leaving the lie to escalate into something out of all proportion. He put on a soothing voice. "Why don't you tell us what happened? Make it nothing but the truth, this time."

"The truth?" Cooper shrugged. "Nick got in touch a few weeks back and said he wanted to meet up. I assumed he was bored and was thinking of knocking back a few beers for old time's sake, so when he suggested we get together that Wednesday, it fitted in perfectly. I could call into Hartwood on my way home from Banbury. It's not that far off the route."

And he'd have been able to claim part of the journey as legitimate business mileage, which would have been a real bonus to somebody so reputedly tight-fisted. No wonder the date had appealed. Robin nodded for him to continue.

"I asked which pub he fancied meeting at, but he said it wasn't a social thing and he didn't want to risk the conversation being overheard. He said he had important business he needed to discuss." Cooper, unnervingly, kept his gaze pointed anywhere but directly at Robin.

"Did he say what that business was?"

"Not directly. It was all rather cloak-and-dagger. But then he always had a touch of the overdramatic." At last Cooper faced them. "He said we couldn't use his flat because his wife was having a do with her pals but that if we met at the sports ground, we'd be able to talk without anyone listening in. Somehow, he'd got his hands on some of the keys. God knows how or why."

By now, Robin new how—Laurence had discovered that Osment had walked into a DIY shop on the edge of town, with a handful of keys to copy and a story about his dad starting to lose his memory and a spare set of everything being needed. He'd been utterly believable. The *why* he'd done it still eluded Robin, unless Osment had simply fancied keeping a copied bunch for the sake of the sense of power they brought. Perhaps that turned him on better than sex did. Or it could have been about nostalgia for those happy days when he'd been at the athletics club—access to a safe bolt-hole.

"Maybe he needed the keys because he wanted to cause more damage," Pru said. "We know he'd done some vandalism at the club."

"Had he? That sounds right up his street. He was a tearaway when he was younger, always in trouble at school. One of the other Tuckton players knew him from then and told us about it. Nick reckoned he'd grown up since then, but maybe a leopard doesn't change his spots."

"What reason did he give for wanting to meet there rather than finding a quiet car park or wherever? There are plenty of places along the road you used to take from Tuckton where you could pull in and chat without drawing attention to yourselves," Robin said. "Wouldn't you be seen at the ground?"

Cooper flicked away the point with a wave. "That's what I said to him, but he had his reasoning off pat. Training night for the rugby team. Plenty of cars there so mine wouldn't be noticed. Some rule about players not being allowed to go into the changing room once the session had started. So long as we didn't turn all the lights on or make a din, he said we'd be safe. Bloody stupid, if you ask me, although he always did have daft notions. Like he was living in a soap opera or something. Anyway, he'd got it into his head that was what was going to happen, and once he got an idea, he couldn't be talked out of it." He paused. "Here, you spoke about vandalism. Do you think he might have been trying to set me up? He goes and causes trouble but I'm the one found on site and get the blame?"

"Maybe." That was certainly a possibility, if a highly unlikely one, but not being able to read the dead man's mind, how could they tell? Best to focus on what they knew. "How did Osment know about the coach's rule that once players were on the field training, they had to stay there?"

"Through his wife. It was a story he told me years back, when I gave him one of those lifts home. Her best friend goes out with one of the Hartwood players. He's known the bloke who coaches them since schoolboy training days and he'd always had the same stupid rule." Cooper rolled his eyes.

"Who reckoned it was stupid?" Pru asked.

"This friend of hers, for a start."

"Dawn?"

"If that's her name, Sergeant, then yes. You wouldn't have got anyone at the Tuckton Rugby Club agreeing to act like they were a bunch of schoolboys in a PE lesson, afraid they'd be put in detention. Osment's wife was obviously going to make fun of it if her friend did."

Another—albeit small—niggle between Dawn and Preese. Would it turn out to be relevant or simply another one of life's dramas that had no bearing on the case? Cooper had remarked that Osment went around like he was living in a soap opera, but he wasn't the only one. Some of the behaviour Robin encountered or heard about in his job would make the average soap-opera storyline appear tame.

"Okay, so you decided to go along with Osment's plan. What next?" Robin asked.

"I drove over to Hartwood as arranged, but I got there early. Not the usual amount of traffic on the road. As a result I went past the ground and parked up." Cooper twisted his fingers together. "At that point, I nearly pulled out of meeting up. Having time to think made me start to wonder if I was being an idiot and getting myself into something I wouldn't want."

"What changed your mind?"

"Realising that if we didn't meet up then, it would be some other time." The fingers clasped each other again, almost fit to break. "See, I checked my phone and found he'd emailed me earlier, although it had only come through a couple of minutes ago, because the 4G cuts in and out on the local roads. He was telling me not to stand him up. If he was so determined to see me, putting it off wasn't a viable option—I'd just have to put on my big boys' pants and face him. Anyway, sod's law meant that I got held up returning to the ground. There'd been a prang between two cars at a junction and the traffic got backed up, so by the time I reached the ground, I was running late."

Robin suddenly remembered the damage to the photograph frame. Was it possible that Osment had got angry at thinking he'd been stood up and had taken it out on the nearest object? Or was Cooper right, that he was being set up for something and only Osment's death had prevented that plan coming to fruition—possibly death at Cooper's own hand, if he had realised what was going on and reacted violently.

"What then?" Pru asked.

"I turned my lights off and swung in, parking where I couldn't be seen from the pitch, then headed for the clubhouse door. As instructed. Nick told me there was hard standing near the bar entrance, which was used for deliveries. I used that."

"So, this was all in the dark?" Although Robin's instincts suggested that Cooper was telling the truth, this still sounded like the worst sort of bull.

"There was enough illumination from the floodlights to be able to pick my way."

"I didn't mean that. Given that there were to be no lights on in the bar, didn't you ever wonder whether you'd be in danger?"

"Ah." Cooper stared at his hands, which had at last disentangled themselves. "I'll come clean. It crossed my mind, so I took along my pitching wedge. I always carry a small set of clubs in my car boot, in case I get the chance to practice a few shots."

"Did you practice your short game on Osment's head?"

"No!" Cooper sprang forward in his chair, then flopped back down again. "No, I did not. And I'm happy to give you a formal statement making that plain. I never even saw him. When I got there, the door to the bar was unlocked, like he said it would be, so I went in. There was no sign of him. I used the light on my phone to take a look around, but the place was empty. I spoke his name but there was no reply."

"Did you try the door through to the changing rooms?"

"No. It would never have occurred to me to do that. I wouldn't have known where the door was, for a start, without putting the lights on and maybe not even then. Is it labelled?"

"Yes." Not a lot of point in pursuing that, given they had nothing to contradict what Cooper was saying. "What you're telling us Osment is that wasn't anywhere to be found. What did you do then?"

"I decided he was playing silly buggers with me, so I left and came home. I kept expecting him to get in touch, slagging me off for not turning up, but he didn't. Then I saw the story in the news and realised how lucky I'd been."

"Lucky?" Pru said.

"Think about it. There must have been a killer loose in the building. Maybe he was still there when I was and could have heard me shout or seen the light from my phone. What if he thought I'd seen something or could identify him? I spent that next week scared stiff to answer the front door in case it was him and he'd tracked me down." The frightened expression on Cooper's face gave credence to his words.

"Mr. Cooper." Robin shook his head. "I'm struggling here. Why the hell would anyone agree to meet a bloke he's not seen in years, in the dark and at a strange location, keeping it all hush-hush if he didn't know what they were going to discuss?" He waited for a response but none came. "I'm not leaving until I have the answer."

At last, Cooper said, "He reckoned he needed money. He didn't actually write that bit down. That first time he got in touch, he rang from work. Never gave me his mobile number because he did all the arranging by email."

"Have you kept those emails?"

"No, I deleted them. All they concerned were the ins and outs of meeting up. He didn't commit any of the money stuff to writing and neither did I." Cooper started wringing his fingers again, much to Robin's irritation. "I couldn't have paid him much, anyway. My ex-wife is fleecing me. Are you married, Mr. Bright?"

"Yes." How ironic that this was the first time Robin had shared the fact with a stranger.

Cooper snorted. "I hope you're luckier than I was. Self-centred, two-timing cow. Glad I'm shot of her, even if my bank account isn't."

Pru, perhaps sparing Robin any further questioning about his spouse, asked, "Why should Osment have expected you to pay him anything at all?"

"Given our conversation of yesterday, can't you guess? He said he knew who'd killed Jamie Weatherell and left him to die. Had proof. Given that we'd been in the car together that night and I'd hit what I thought was a deer, I guessed he had me in mind." Cooper put his head in his hands. "He said we needed to talk about it and work out a plan to his financial advantage. He wouldn't discuss it further before we met, but I supposed he was going to threaten to go to the police if I didn't cough up."

Guessed. How much of this was fact and how much Cooper's overimagination? Robin asked, "Can you be more specific about what Osment actually said to you during the phone call?"

Cooper raised his head, eyes welling. "Not really. It was like a bad dream, and when I tried to get the detail clear in my mind afterwards I couldn't. I just kept thinking 'Why now, if he had seen I killed Jamie that night?' And what proof could he have that he hadn't used before?"

"He didn't give you any clue to what that proof might be?"

"I've told you, no. I've racked my brains, but I can't imagine what he could have got hold of that wouldn't incriminate him too. Like if he'd taken a picture of the crash site, that would show he'd been there and he'd not called for help when he should have."

"Maybe he was simply calling your bluff," Pru said. "The threat being enough to get you to turn up. Are those emails in your trash folder?"

Cooper, frowning, fished for his phone. "I suppose they must be. Never thought of that. Assuming they haven't automatically been scrapped by now."

"If you would forward them to us right now that would help us verify what you've said." Pru provided him with an address to send them to, watching over him until the process was—as far as they could tell—completed.

"What email address did he send them from?" Robin asked, wondering why these emails hadn't been flagged up when the team had performed the routine job of checking Osment's mailbox, unless he'd double deleted everything.

"See for yourself." Cooper gave him the phone.

Mystery solved. The team had gone through Osment's Google account but this was a Hotmail address, and if Osment had only accessed it via his phone, they wouldn't have known about it. Searching through that would be another job for Ben—no, Callum, he corrected himself, forcing his thoughts away from home turf. Robin scrolled through the message threads but, as Cooper had stated, the conversation seemed concerned with logistics, his questions to Osment about what he was up to going unanswered.

"It says here that you were to meet him at seven. What time did you turn up at the ground?"

"I got there around quarter past, so I'd have been in the clubhouse bar maybe twenty past or so. I could only have waited five minutes, because I was back in the car before the Radio 5 Live news at half past."

If that was true and Osment had arrived when he was supposed to, then where was he at that point? Hiding? Being hid and kept quiet by someone else? Or already dead? Given that Joe had gone for a slash no later than ten past, the key time seemed to have narrowed considerably.

"Did you hear anything while you were in the bar? Or see anyone?" Pru's voice had an exasperated edge, quite understandably.

"Of course I didn't, or I'd have told you. What would be the point of hiding anything now?"

"No point, but people do it. Believe me." Robin eased out of his chair. "You'll need to come with us now, to make a formal statement. I'll get one of my constables to run you home." Assuming nothing further came up that meant they'd have grounds to keep him under arrest. And assuming he came voluntarily now and didn't force Robin's hand. "We'll need to see those golf clubs of yours, if you don't mind. To eliminate them from our search for the weapon used on Osment."

"Don't you need a warrant for that?"

"If you insist on me getting one, I will, but that will only put off the inevitable. Sergeant Davis here can stay with you until we've got a magistrate to sign one off." She could keep an eye on both the car and the house while she was at it, ensuring he didn't try to clear away any evidence, although if he was guilty and had any sense, that would all have been done. On the positive side, those grooves on a club were ideal for retaining fragments that the forensic team could get their teeth into.

Cooper spread his hands, resignedly. "Oh, take what you want. Doesn't make a scrap of difference to me. I didn't kill Nick Osment, and as far as I know I didn't kill Jamie Weatherell, so what is there to lose?"

Which sounded horribly like the response of an innocent man.

Cooper had been deposited with Laurence, the golf clubs had gone to the forensic team—with a note to make them a priority—while Robin and Pru had headed straight to the coffee shop, bringing their takeaways back to an incident room with only Callum in occupation, Sally having taken herself off somewhere. The constable had his head down over the computer, trying to get into Osment's

Hotmail account, aided—although not greatly up to that point—with a list Melanie had provided of the passwords and PIN numbers her husband was in the habit of using.

"So, we've got a motive for killing and a believable story—at last—for why Osment was poking around that clubhouse." Pru took a swig of coffee.

"I'd say it's half a story. He was meeting Cooper, yes, and from what those emails say it was clearly his idea to set the time and place, although I'm still not convinced we know what *his* motive was in picking that location. Apart from sheer bloody cussedness." Robin wrinkled his nose, like he might when encountering a strange smell. Certainly this case was proving as unsavoury as the other murders he'd tackled.

"I wonder if he was thinking that he could somehow frame Cooper if he refused to pay? Nick stuff from the changing room, then somehow plant it on Cooper?"

"Who knows what was going on in Osment's head?" Things were starting to add up but the final answer to the sum still eluded them. "What evidence do you think he could have had about the hit-and-run?"

"Beats me. He may have picked something up at the time of the crash, but why keep it all these years before using it?" Pru drained her cup. "Like Cooper said, why now?"

"He was at risk of losing his job. What else could have changed?" Robin peered into his cup at the last dregs of coffee, but they'd lost their appeal.

"What if the old stuff wasn't proof enough and he'd recently laid his hands on something new? Something definitive?" Pru asked.

"That's a good point. What if he'd been searching for that extra proof for years, stirring up pools of trouble to see what came to the surface?" As logical a reason as any for Osment objecting to the fundraising. "Do you think Cooper did it?"

"The hit-and-run or the murder?"

"Either or both." Robin turned to Callum. "What's your take on it?"

The young constable was evidently delighted to be asked his opinion, if his grin was anything to go by. That grin soon faded, as though he were dismayed that he couldn't produce some profound observation that would allow the case to proceed to a result. Robin could remember feeling the same way at the same stage in his career under Betteridge and how her encouragement—and allowing him to voice his opinions and thoughts, no matter how left field—had built his confidence. The fact that this team didn't appear to have been given the same opportunities was worrying but surely had to be laid at the feet of the officer who was currently unwell. Robin couldn't be distracted at this point by worrying whether his old boss was losing her touch.

"I think we're closer, sir. You've uncovered strands to the investigation that we hadn't."

"Thanks, but it's a team effort. *We've* uncovered them."

Callum's self-assurance visibly blossomed. "Thank you, sir. That means a lot. Sorry that I can't say for certain what I think about Cooper. DS Betteridge always tells us not to jump to conclusions."

"Quite right." Robin stretched his neck: hotel beds were never as comfy as your own. And the worries he'd had over what might have been going on with the team didn't help ease his muscular tension. "There's nothing much any of us can do until we have the forensic report on those clubs. Once you've finished with those emails, get off home. I'll do the same with Laurence once he's finished with Cooper, unless anything notable turns up. We'll take the statement with us while we're heading south to talk to Sam Woakes."

"The other person with a motive but without an alibi," Callum observed. "Although isn't it looking increasingly unlikely that Osment was the driver who killed Jamie Weatherell?"

"It is. But when did the truth always coincide with what people believe? I can imagine Cooper—or whoever—being banged up for death by dangerous driving and people still swearing Osment was responsible, if they disliked him enough. Proof wouldn't matter to them, even if it matters to us." Suddenly conscious that he was getting on his soap box to preach to the people who should least need to hear the sermon, Robin grinned. "I'm starting to sound like Winston Churchill. Anybody want a sandwich from the café across the road? My treat."

They organised who needed what, including something for Laurence, although nothing for Sally, who had gone off, so she'd told the team earlier, to do some poking around, having solemnly sworn not to get into trouble or danger while doing it. Robin appreciated the opportunity to get out of the station rather than sit twiddling his thumbs there. Simply revisiting the information he'd already gone through or dealing with the few emails from Abbotston that actually needed action was getting him nowhere. None of those couldn't wait until tomorrow: clearing his head was urgent.

Chapter Sixteen

Early Sunday afternoon, Adam had settled down with a large mug of tea to watch the start of the early kickoff before heading for choir practice at the church. Everyone had been told to be prompt as they had to be out by six o'clock or risk the wrath of the ladies of a certain age who mainly constituted the half-past-six evensong congregation. Not even Campbell would be able to face down their wrath at being held up.

The buzzing of his phone roused him from where he'd just about dozed off, which was a lucky escape given the precarious position of his still-half-full mug.

"Hello, you. How's life with my favourite rozzer?"

Robin chuckled. "Better than it was yesterday."

"Got the villain bang to rights as your equivalents say on the telly?"

"No, but getting closer. Getting closer to home too. We'll be in the Kinechester neck of the woods later today. I'll stay over."

"You'll be home?" Adam fleetingly wondered if he was still asleep and dreaming the words, given that he'd been aching to hear them.

"Only for the night. We're conducting an interview this evening. Not worth driving back afterwards when I'll be dog-tired."

"Too tired for some proper *R and R*?"

"Probably, so don't get your hopes up."

Adam resisted the obvious joke about getting anything up: Campbell had big ears and was easily shocked. "I'd be happy with a cuddle and your feet in the small of my back. Although won't it be a pain driving back up to Hartwood fighting the Monday morning rush hour?"

"We can leave a bit later. I know Pru wants to get home to wash and tumble a batch of clothes overnight. Otherwise it's using the hotel laundry and a bill as long as your arm."

"Music to my ears."

"That's a great cue to what I need to say next. Like we're a double act. You've another rehearsal this afternoon?"

"Ye-es. How did you know? And why do you ask?"

"We're interviewing Sam, and I want to do it face-to-face rather than down a phone line. Hence the reason it's this evening rather than clashing with your sing-song."

Sam. That sounded ominous. "Anything I need to be aware of?"

"Nothing other than what's been bubbling already. Seems Sam has rather a temper on him too. It must be in the genes."

"I'll steer clear of him at the rehearsal. Thank God you're seeing him after that or he'd be going ballistic at us." Time to concentrate on the domestics. "Will you need something to eat?"

"Probably. We only had a sandwich at lunchtime, so by the time I've dropped Pru off and got home, I'll be Hank Marvin. Don't put yourself out, though. And don't hold off eating for my sake."

"I won't, I promise. Singing makes me ravenous. I'll get something out the freezer so I can heat it up in the microwave. Can't promise anything more exciting than cottage pie."

"Sounds like bliss. I'll text when I leave Pru's. Can't wait to see you."

"Same here."

As the call ended, Adam became aware of a pair of big dark eyes gazing at him hopefully. "Yep, that was your other dad. He'll be home tonight. And yes, you can slobber all over him but, no, you won't be sleeping on our bed tonight. Never been into threesomes."

Campbell thumped his tail against the floor contentedly. For a few hours, normality would be restored to the Matthews-Bright household.

The rehearsal went well. The singing was better than it had been previously, and while there was still noticeable tension between Sam and Martin, it didn't seem as intense as before. Adam got his fair share of dirty looks from Sam's direction, but he'd been expecting them. In his turn, he treated the bloke with absolute courtesy. If they were entertaining a murderer in their midst, he couldn't show any sign that he suspected the fact.

At the end, Martin praised them all, checked they were happy with the next few rehearsal dates, and reminded them the concert itself was less than a month away. Adam, shooting up a silent prayer that the case would be settled by then and that Robin would be home, became aware that they were being given an important update on Greg's condition. Things were not as bad as first feared, and there might be a chance of his regaining the use of his legs with intense treatment.

The sharp reminder of why they were doing this and that somebody else had suffered irreversible consequences from the fateful night at the rugby club hit home. While it would send the choir out in a slightly sombre mood—there but for the grace of God went any of them—it also galvanised them again. They had to do this right; they had to succeed and make as much money as they could. Adam resolved to put a notice up in the staffroom rather than just mention the event over coffee. He could probably put something on the school newsletter, even if it risked outing himself to the wider parent community when the rainbow flavours to the event emerged. The kids were cool with him having a male partner, but some of the parents were as prejudiced as they came, and while the word was no doubt getting out, a trickle was preferable to a flood. Or would it be better to get the whole thing out into the open at once?

He'd sleep on it and maybe pick Robin's brains on the subject over breakfast, if that didn't add to the stress the bloke must already be feeling.

"Come on, boy." Adam picked up Campbell's lead and was heading out of the door when Martin called down the aisle, "Have you got a moment?"

Heart sinking, Adam forced a smile. "Yes, so long as it really is only a few minutes. Robin's back for the night, then off again tomorrow."

"He's here to talk to Sam?"

"Yes. But you clearly know that already."

"Hey, don't be so tetchy. I took what you said to heart. Played it cool."

"Okay. Sorry. I just don't want you to get mixed up until we're sure that Sam has got nothing to do with the case."

"I'm trying, but he nabbed me before he left." Martin jerked his thumb towards the door. "Said he was due for the third degree so he needed something to look forward to and was your boyfriend as hot as he's made out to be?"

"Blimey. Who told him that?" Probably Martin himself—pillow talk, maybe?—although Adam was prepared to give the bloke the benefit of the doubt.

Martin flushed. "I may have mentioned it. I hope I haven't caused any trouble."

"Robin can take care of himself." And he'd have Pru to guard his virtue. "Is that all you wanted to see me about?" Adam edged towards the door.

"Mostly. It's simply . . ." Martin squirmed as he struggled for the right words. "He texted me last night. Drunk text, I think, because he said he'd been to the pub and he wasn't that coherent. Said he was sorry. I assumed he was talking about that night he came over to mine, so I said he didn't need to apologise because we're both grown-ups and know what we're doing. He replied it wasn't *that* he was sorry about. He didn't regret anything about that evening."

"In which case, what *was* he referring to?"

"Something about what a pain in the arse it is to have an identical twin." Martin must have been wound up to even mildly swear in the church. "He said he wanted to explain in full but couldn't because his phone battery was about to die. I thought he'd text this morning once it was charged, but he didn't. Not a word about it now, either."

"Perhaps he was so rat-arsed he doesn't remember texting you." Although likely he was too embarrassed to mention it. "I wouldn't worry about it. If it's important, he'll mention it again."

As Adam would be mentioning it to Robin as soon as the right moment came up.

Campbell heard the car before it pulled onto the drive. At least, Adam assumed his acute canine hearing had picked up what must be a distinctive engine sound, rather than some super doggy sixth sense kicking in. The Newfoundland was waiting at the door, blocking any entrance or exit, seemingly determined to be first to deliver the welcome home.

"Oh, go ahead." Adam shook his head. "Only leave part of him for me, eh?"

Once the orgy of hugs, kisses, and applications of wet noses—those solely from Campbell—had been got out of the way, Adam went to crack open a few beers and get Robin something to eat. They all needed half an hour of quiet domesticity with nothing more taxing than a discussion of what the hotel in Hartwood was like and whether there were any decent restaurants.

Once dinner and a couple of beers had been consumed and they were sprawled on the sofa with Campbell keeping guard on the floor, Adam asked, "Any trouble with Sam? No hands on your knee or anything?"

Robin's brow wrinkled. "No. Should I have been expecting it?"

"He was asking Martin if you were as fit as people make out."

"Was he? I suppose I should be flattered. No, he kept his hands to himself. Maybe I'm not his type. Or he was scared Pru might lump him one."

"Definitely the Pru thing. You're everybody's type." Adam snorted. "He was probably just trying to get Martin to open up about what he knows concerning the case. Which is pretty well sod all as far as I can see."

"Martin's not tried that on with you?"

"He wouldn't dare, and I don't give him the opportunity. What did you get out of him?"

Robin raised his eyebrows. "You'd be rubbish at poker. There's a hidden agenda in that question."

"There is. I won't raise the point until you answer my question, though."

"To tell the truth, we didn't get as much as I hoped. He insists he was nowhere near Hartwood on the night Osment died and says while he was angry about Jamie Weatherell's death, he never thought

Osment was the driver. He admits he loses his temper at times." Robin shrugged. "I've got to say he seems to be a credible witness. We saw his Twitter feed, and he was moaning about the Arsenal backline all evening, so unless there's a third person involved, using his phone, then it's looking less likely that he covered for Joe. Although I can't pin down what's going on with him and the brother. Sam didn't like it when I took a punt and said that he should be able to understand why we were suspicious, given him and his brother being so alike. And I have to say, they're like two peas in a pod. If I'd met Sam in the street, I'd have thought it was Joe."

"He's edgy about something to do with their resemblance." Adam repeated the conversation he'd had with Martin. "Sorry not to have anything concrete to offer."

"I appreciate any and everything you turn up. No need to feel guilty, though. It's my job, not yours." Robin ruffled Adam's hair. "You start finding too many clues and I'll have to reciprocate by marking your pupils' books. Anyway, I'm getting one of the team to go through the traffic camera footage again to search for Sam's car."

"Rather my job than yours. Or one of your constable's. Too much routine and legwork." Not the glamorous profession that some of the television cop shows made it out to be, although not the slough of despond that others depicted.

"You can't get away from routine as a chief inspector. I need to read through Cooper's statement properly. See if his story changed at all from what he told me and Pru." Robin yawned. "I'll do it later, once I get my brain back."

"Would it be wrong for me to get a gander at it? I've only seen one statement before and that was mine." Sitting in the school library at Lindenshaw, being interviewed about the corpse that he and the chair of governors had found in the little kitchen where the children usually learned to cook. Adam remembered every minute as though it were yesterday, especially the young inspector who'd faced him over the table and got him all flustered. Truth to tell he could barely recall what his official statement had looked like, even though he'd read it and signed it. "I could say it's to broaden my education, but it's really my curiosity."

"It probably is wrong, but if I happened to leave it on the table where I placed it when I came in, while I go now and have a shower . . ." Robin grinned. "Maybe you can work your usual magic. Spot something we've missed. Spectator sees the game clearer than the players and all that jazz."

He got up, kissed the top of Adam's head, gave Campbell a rub behind the ear, then headed for the stairs.

The statement, as Adam soon found, didn't make riveting reading. Cooper's long explanation about how he'd ended up arriving at the sports ground late, what Osment had said—or not said—about meeting up: it was all rather underwhelming. Campbell coming over and insisting that he needed to be let out into the garden brought a good reason to put his reading to one side. He watched the dog do what was necessary, cleaned up the mess, washed his hands, and put the kettle on so that when Robin came downstairs—assuming he hadn't crashed out on the bed—there'd be a cuppa and biscuits waiting for him.

Both of them proved very welcome—lifesavers, as a freshly washed and dressed Robin said.

"What did you make of the statement?"

"Got bored with it, sorry. Himself wanted to be let out and I never got back to reading it through to the end. I'd be a rubbish cop."

Robin laughed. "If you were a cop, I doubt we'd have had a relationship, fit as you are."

"So give me the dénouement. Who did this Osment bloke think had done the hit-and-run?"

Robin glanced over the rim of his mug, frowning. "Cooper, of course."

"Doh." Adam mimed smacking his head. "See? Rubbish cop as well as rubbish at having a poker face. I read it as him saying he knew that the driver was somebody else and assumed he'd want Cooper to back him up."

Robin put his mug down. "Say that again, because I'm tired and I only have three functioning brain cells, but I think you said something significant."

"Did I? I think I said that I took what I read as Osment threatening to dob in a third party for the hit-and-run and how that would be to his advantage. I didn't take it as a threat to Cooper."

"Okay. I'm going to go over it again. Any chance of a top-up?"

Adam took the mug to refill it while his husband pored over the statement again.

"You could be right," Robin said as Adam returned. He grabbed his mug. "Thanks for this. Lifesaver. The drink I mean, not the idea. Or maybe I mean both."

"You're almost incoherent." Adam laid his hands on Robin's shoulders, gently massaging them.

"That's a lifesaver too. What I mean is that Cooper made an assumption and we've followed suit. It makes more sense—I think—if the driver was somebody else. It could explain why Osment didn't ask for money straight away or commit any details into his emails."

Adam, warming to both his roles as masseur and acting constable, observed, "It might also explain why they had to meet at the club. If the person Osment thought responsible was there. Maybe it was going to be a three-way meeting—during or after training. Cooper could have been asked there to act as wingman. Is he built like a minder?"

"Not one I'd choose. Not if I was tackling any of the blokes at a rugby club. Maybe he fights dirty. Don't stop." Robin patted Adam's hand. "I have no knowledge of anatomy but I'm sure that's making blood flow to my brain. Other parts, too."

"I'll hold you to that. I still haven't had my honeymoon."

Which was the cue to putting everything to do with work to one side. There was a bed upstairs, big and welcoming.

Adam took Robin's hand, to lead him to the bedroom. "Not you this time," he said to the dog, whose disappointment was evident in the comically sad face he produced. "What's going to go on up there isn't suitable for spectators, even of a canine kind."

"Promises, promises." Robin let himself be led up the stairs, interrupting their progress with kisses, much as he'd done in the early days of their courtship. Adam was grateful he'd never been a *wham, bam, thank you, man* type.

As they reached the doorway to the bedroom, Robin paused. "You have no idea how much I've missed you. Not simply the sex, although that's been on my mind at some awkward moments, but . . . *you*. Talking, lying having a kip on the settee, mending Mrs. Haig's fence. I'm turning into an old married man."

"Turning into?" Adam drew him closer. "We've been like this for ages. And it's great."

The time for words was over. Time to strip off the cares of the day and leave them discarded on the floor with their clothes. The bedroom was warm enough to take away the need for covering, other than skin on skin, but cool enough not to overheat as their ardour—as well as parts of their anatomy—rose. They took it slow and easy and when they finally reached the point of bodies merging into one, it was every bit as good as Adam had hoped when he'd been dreaming about having his husband back in his bed.

Afterwards, lying in each other's arms, Robin ran his hands through Adam's hair. "I needed that. I've been trying to be strong and professional on the outside, but inside I turn into a mess if I'm away from you too long."

"Same here. Been keeping it locked up inside, mostly. Thank God Campbell's a good listener." He hugged Robin tighter. "Need to clone him so you can take your own handy Newfoundland back to the hotel."

"I'd rather clone you. One Adam for home and one for work."

"That sounds positively obscene." Adam chuckled. "Almost as obscene as the state of us. Go and have a wash."

"How romantic." Robin eased out of the embrace. "I mean that, by the way. Been waiting too long for this particular excuse for a second shower."

Adam flicked his husband's backside. "You say the nicest things."

Chapter Seventeen

Monday morning, Adam felt a huge reluctance to get out of bed, and it wasn't solely due to going back to work and facing his class. They wouldn't be in, the school being shut to pupils for a training day. Exactly the kind of thing that Adam would usually have been chomping at the bit to get to, but the warm, comforting presence of Robin in the bed was a better prospect. Still, he'd have to be getting up soon to get ready to head northwards again and Campbell's bladder wouldn't stand for any delay in having its needs met, so Adam would need to shift himself as well.

By the time the dog had been let out into the garden and had returned indoors quickly—the morning being decidedly nippy—Adam could hear his husband pottering around upstairs. Robin was no doubt repacking his case with clean clothes, having deposited—with apologies—a batch of washing to be done. Adam would get the machine on before he left so Sandra could hang it out when she dropped in later. *More joys of domesticity*, he thought with a sudden surge of realisation that it *was* a joy to have Robin's clothes in the machine. They were a palpable sign that Robin was still part of the setup, even when he was miles away.

Once all the washing and dressing was done, they could concentrate on the business of feeding and watering. Campbell sat happily munching on a doggie chew, having wolfed down his breakfast as though starving. The humans of the household took a wiser pace.

"When will you start the journey?" Adam asked, between one spoonful of cereal and the next. "The local radio says the roads are sticky this morning."

"Nearer lunchtime than breakfast," Robin said. "Pru's getting a lift into Abbotston station, and I'm meeting her there. I want to touch base with Cowdrey before we set off."

"Need to keep the boss happy?"

"Need to keep me happy too. There might be something going on and, if so, I'd prefer to know about it, rather than returning home to a bombshell." Robin finished the last scrap of toast. "Nothing on the local news about major crimes?"

"Not a dicky bird. Therefore, unless something's going down that they're keeping quiet about, I'd assume it's all low-level stuff."

Robin wagged his knife in admonishment. "One of the witnesses I interviewed told me that when you assume, you make an ass of you and me."

Adam groaned. "I'll remember that. It's the corny cliché the kids love. How's work with Betteridge going, by the way?"

"Slowly. She's up to her eyeballs with other cases, but she's coming out the other side. Getting her sense of humour back, anyway. She seems happy with how we're handling the investigation. Relying on us to get a result, naturally." Robin made a face like he was sucking an acid drop. "Not sure how soon we'll deliver on that. Still, she says that she's heard the team is developing well with Pru and me at the helm."

"I'd expect nothing less. You underestimate your talents." Adam patted his husband's hand. "Only don't go getting a reputation for being the fixer. I don't want you being dragged all over the country to sort out people's cold cases or dodgy constables."

"God forbid. If there's one thing I've learned this last week, it's how much I value being in my own home with you and *himself*." Robin slipped off his stool. "Right, give us a kiss before I hit the road. Oi! Not you." He patted Campbell's head, the dog having suddenly appeared at his side as though teleported there.

"See? There's another person in this relationship. Thank God I'm not the jealous sort . . . Hey. What have I done to deserve that?" Adam had been clasped firmly on both cheeks and given a smacker of a kiss. Which was lovely if out of the blue.

"You've given me an idea. Another one." Robin grabbed his car keys. "I'm hitting the road before I lose my train of thought."

"Pleased to be of service. Tell me all about my moment of genius when you get the chance. I'm fascinated to know what it was."

As Robin headed out of the door, Adam cleared the breakfast things into the sink.

"Did you know you've got two masterminds for fathers?" he asked Campbell, but the dog was only interested in his chew. "Yes, I suppose it is distinctly underwhelming."

He settled the Newfoundland down for the day and got ready to leave for work.

Robin and Pru pulled out of Abbotston police station car park at a few minutes past eleven, which was later than intended because Cowdrey had been in an unusually loquacious mood. He'd confessed in the past that there was no other officer he could talk to like he could Robin, which probably explained the length of the interview. The content—a series of robberies and a fraud case—didn't.

They were barely a hundred yards up the road when Pru asked, "Did you get a chance to read Cooper's statement again?"

"Yes. It's in the briefcase on the back seat. You have a shufti and see if anything strikes you."

"Okay." Pru sounded bemused but she leaned round, got the papers, and read them. "Nope," she said, eventually, "nothing new striking me."

"Try this. Are we making a huge assumption here? The same assumption Cooper made. Look carefully at what he says Osment told him, supposedly as close as he can remember. It doesn't make a direct threat."

"No. You're kidding." Pru rifled through the statement again. "Oh shit, you're right. Not once does Osment say *you*. Simply refers to knowing who did it. He could be referring to somebody else entirely."

"Yep. We know Cooper feels guilty—because he knew he'd hit something that night, and he's been wondering if the deer wasn't a deer—he heard what he *thought* was being said to him."

"In that case, does it explain why Osment got himself copies made of the keys to the sports ground? He thought he might find evidence there?"

"It's as good a reason as any we've yet come up with." Robin paused as he negotiated his way around a wandering cyclist. "He might have been planting that evidence rather than picking it up. A good old-fashioned threatening note in a player's bag, for example. That would leave less of a trail than a phone message or email."

"You've got someone in mind, haven't you?"

"The obvious one is Dave."

"Dave?"

"Yep. I've been thinking about it all morning, since Adam talked about Campbell being the third person in our relationship. That's how Osment must have regarded Dave—the continued presence in Melanie's life. If he knew—or suspected—all along that Dave had killed Jamie, but he couldn't prove it, he might have kept shtum because people would have thought it was simply a matter of him causing trouble for the bloke and deflecting attention from himself, his own car having been stolen that night."

"Which in this case would simply have been a horrible fluke? Horrible for Osment, that is," she clarified. "If that's the case, I bet he was less worried about people in general thinking he was making up stories about Dave and more about Melanie herself thinking he was lying."

"Exactly." While this was all nothing but speculation, it was making sense. "Do you remember Sally having a theory Osment had gone back to the club to follow Dave? Melanie herself told us he'd done that before."

"What if she's right? Osment followed Dave from the ground that night, but instead of him hitting Jamie, he witnesses Dave swerve because he's hit something. Maybe Osment thought it was another deer getting itself thumped, and it was only later when he heard about Jamie and roughly what time he'd died that he put two and two together." Pru nodded. "Then why make a fuss now? If he didn't have any evidence at the time, what could he have turned up since?"

"I might have an answer to the first part. If he knew that Melanie and Dave had started seeing each other again, he might have been tipped over the edge. Decided to take action and that was the only weapon he had left to him." That sounded very thin, but people *did* do the stupidest things when they were overcome by jealousy. "As for your second question, that's the gaping hole in my theory. There's no proof Osment had any fresh evidence: no proof of anything at all."

"We have proof that he met somebody and was killed by them. Osment's dead body. I suppose we're now speculating that the killer was the same person who he was accusing of the hit-and-run. If that's Dave, then somebody's covering up for him." Pru exhaled loudly. "Andy, maybe. I got the impression he worships the ground Dave walks on."

"Maybe it's the other way round. Andy—or whoever—attacked Osment while sticking up for Dave and *he's* part of the cover-up."

"Melanie might have been inclined to cover for Dave, as well. This interrelationship between the Osment household and Hartwood Rugby Club—it's getting too complicated. And don't get me started on all these people with their watertight alibis. Is it me being oversuspicious, sir, or are you feeling twitchy about that too?"

"Twitchy as hell. I'm inclined to believe the people who *don't* have anybody to stand up and vouch for their whereabouts, but maybe I'm getting a twisted view of life. This job can mess with your mind."

"You can say that again." Pru sounded tired, despite the evening at home. Perhaps everyone was at risk of getting too tired to think clearly. "Like when I hear some bloke mouthing off that LGBT people are a threat to family life and the future of society. First thing I wonder is whether he's got a boyfriend of his own lurking somewhere."

Robin chuckled. "Adam always says that. Perhaps we should apply those words of wisdom to this case."

"I'm not sure I understand, sir. Not with you."

"I don't think I'm with myself, on second thoughts. I was trying to think if anybody had been trying to shove the blame for Osment's death onto someone else. Trying to hide their own guilt. But I can't recall anyone doing that."

"You're right. Not a sniff of some barbed remark supposed to deflect our attention. Plenty of that around the hit-and-run, though."

"Yes. Who's been so keen to point at Osment? Your mate Preese, for one."

"The silver fox?" Pru managed a giggle. "People would certainly believe it if he told them something was true. Thing is, if he's the sort of bloke who'd run over one of his players and not stop, he'd have to be a damn fine actor to get away with hiding it for all these years. Your character always shows in the end."

"But does it, though? Think of all those cases where somebody's been accused of an awful crime—child molestation through to murder. There's always a queue of people willing to stand up and say that whoever it was couldn't possibly be guilty, because they're such a great bloke or such a nice woman." Robin needed to calm down, this being a real trigger point for him and a huge one for Adam, who swore that the worst child molesters in education were often the most popular teacher in the school. Grooming the adults around them as well as the children.

"That could apply here too. Preese might have heard Osment was linking Dave to the hit-and-run and refused to believe it. 'Not one of my boys,'" she added, in a much broader Welsh accent than her own lilt. "So, he spreads counter-rumours. Joe would believe him, I bet, despite what he said."

"I agree, but unless we can break the Twitter alibi and pin Sam down as being in the area, then he joins the list of those we can't verifiably link to the crime scene at the right time."

As applied to everybody bar Cooper. Robin wasn't hopeful on that front, either.

Halfway through Monday afternoon, they bowled into Hartwood station incident room, ready to share their new ideas, although before that Robin wanted to find out whether Sam's car had been in Hartwood the night Osment was killed. This wasn't the time to be chasing the wrong hare. Sally was back in at her desk, seeming pretty pleased with herself.

Robin couldn't resist a barb. "Hello, stranger. Where did you get yourself off to yesterday while we were working our arses off?"

"I was working too, sir. I'd have rung in, but I dropped the bloody thing in the loo and it's been sitting in pieces in a bowl of rice." She waggled what Robin thought of as a Nokia brick. "Having to use an old pay-as-you-go until the iPhone dries out."

If that was a lie, it was an elaborate one, with all the right props. "I may have got a lead," she added.

"She wouldn't tell us what it was until you two got back, sir," Callum said. "She just sits there all smug."

"We might have got some leads too. Time to share them." Robin parked his backside on the edge of a desk. "First off, Sam Woakes seems to have got a guilty secret that's to do with how much he resembles his brother, although his Twitter story hangs together. And they really are identical, down to their haircuts. Laurence—his car?"

The constable shook his head. "No sight of it on the traffic camera footage yet, sir. Although as Superintendent Betteridge keeps telling us, absence of evidence isn't evidence of absence. He might have got a lift."

Robin grinned at the intonation, which was identical to the way he'd heard the phrase as a young constable. "You and I know that, but try standing up in court spouting that line."

"One other thing, though. We've got Cooper's car on the homeward journey. Given the timing and where he was, he must have left the ground no later than twenty to eight."

"Okay. That might still have given him time, if he was quick and lucky. Anything from forensics yet?"

Callum shook his head, then scribbled a note. "I'll chase them."

"Thanks. And while we're at it with theories and no evidence, here's something to mull over." Robin—with interventions from Pru—outlined the new theory. "If this is true, it could mean that Osment was killed by the person he was going to confront, and the reason he couldn't meet Cooper was that he was already lying dead. I wish we knew about the forensics on those golf clubs. I worry we're getting so convoluted we're missing the bleeding obvious."

"I'll chase them now, if that would help, sir," Callum offered.

"Yep, you do that while Pru and I update the team on what Sam Woakes had to say for himself." That update included the third-hand report of his apparently hiding something to do with their close resemblance. By the time they'd finished, Callum had completed his task, re-emerging from behind the small partition that did such a meagre job of making a cubicle. "The forensics people say they were about to ring us, sir. That may or may not be true, given that they say there's no sign of anything incriminating on Cooper's golf clubs. Although I guess we weren't expecting there to be."

"No, but it would be good to have some real, hard evidence for once. The only audit trail is from the victim." Robin had to keep believing that they'd end up in a position where they had solid stuff to base a case on rather than speculation. The murder of Nick Osment couldn't become that thing he dreaded—the great unsolved mystery. "Sally, give me some good news. What were you up to yesterday?"

"Getting pally with Melanie Osment's best friend, Dawn. A few days back, I realised that she and I go to the same gym and a couple of times we've chatted while we've been on adjacent equipment. She seems happier gassing than listening to music like everyone else seems to prefer. I keep thinking that she must know more about this—from both sides—than she lets on, so I thought I'd keep an eye out for her and see what I could find out away from a formal interview." She paused, eyes pleading for encouragement.

"I'm listening," Robin said, trying not to get his hopes up.

"Early Saturday I went in for a workout. She was there and I overheard her saying she'd be back late Sunday morning. So I decided to return yesterday, hanging around on the off chance and praying she hadn't changed her mind. When she turned up, I went on the cross-trainer next to hers, then started up a conversation. Said I'd heard through work that her fiancé had been injured and hoped he'd be alright." She paused, clearly aware that Callum and Laurence were sharing glances.

"Go on, Sally." Robin glared at the other two constables. "*I'm* still interested in what you have to say."

"Sorry, sir. Sorry, Sal." Callum seemed appropriately sheepish. "I'm dog-tired and I get silly with it. No excuse for being sarcy."

"You'll have to get used to being tired, in this job. You need to remember we work as a team, as well. Which means we don't do each other down. And we don't take off without informing other people what we're up to, after the event if we can't do it before," Robin added, with a sideways squint at Sally. "Right, sermon over. Your conversation with Dawn. Did it get further than chatting about Greg?"

"Yes. I was totally upfront about being a police officer, which I know risked putting her off but I'd rather everything was above board. Anyway, rather than her blanking me, she asked to talk. Had stuff to get off her chest and she reckoned pouring it into an independent ear—independent of her circle—would be cathartic. We finished in the gym, went for coffee, and the floodgates opened. She said she'd been so busy taking care of Greg and trying to make new plans for their life ahead that she hadn't really had time to get involved in other stuff. She felt guilty about not supporting Melanie, although less so than she had."

"Interesting," Pru said. "What changed?"

"Melanie gave Dawn a gobful. All the usual stuff like 'Why weren't you there for me when I needed you?' And when Dawn pointed out that she'd had other people who'd needed her there for *them*, Melanie played the *you don't ditch your friends just like that* card." Sally grinned. "Dawn apparently went apeshit. I wish I'd been there to see it. I think she started at 'Don't try to guilt me' and ended with the fact that if Melanie hadn't kept hanging around with Dave, then none of this might have happened. I've asked her to come in later and officially give a statement detailing what she told me."

Robin tempered his enthusiasm at what might be a potential breakthrough: he remembered the little inconsistencies between Dawn's account of the evening of the murder and that of Preese's. Was one of them lying, or was it simply the usual, innocent discrepancies that turned up when two people related an event? "You can't leave it like that, without giving us a heads-up on what she said."

"There's a lot of it."

"We've got plenty of time to listen. What about her saying she was going to sober up and drive but then calling for a taxi?"

Sally rolled her eyes. "Oh, that's an easy one, sir. She said that because she was scared Preese would offer her a lift. She says he's a bloody awful driver. Seems like there's an epidemic of them."

"Yes." That would account for it, though. "Right, let's have the rest of it."

"Long story short, Nick had been acting smug about getting his hands on some money if his job went arse up. We knew that, of course, but Dawn reckoned it involved Dave."

"How did she know that?" Callum asked, in a tone a little short of sarcastic.

"Because she and Melanie had been going out to lunch two Saturdays before Nick was killed, but had turned around a few minutes after they left because Melanie had swopped handbags and forgotten her pills. *The* pill. She takes them at lunchtime every day." Sally quickly hid a smug grin. "Which means that her sex life isn't as nonexistent as we were led to believe."

"Unless she takes it to regularise her cycle," Pru pointed out. "Although if Nick discovered she was taking contraceptives and knew that it wasn't for anything happening in *their* bed, he was bound to have assumed it was for Dave's sake, even if it wasn't."

Sally nodded. "Anyway, when they got back to the flat, she caught the tail end of a conversation Nick was having on the phone. He must have realised they were in the flat so he slammed the phone down, although not before she'd heard him say something like 'Don't ring me here again.' He stormed into their bedroom, he and Melanie sounded off at each other, and then he flounced out of the house. Dawn took the opportunity of surreptitiously ringing 1471 and noting the number. It was Dave's."

"He kept that quiet." Robin narrowed his eyes. "Pru, arrange for him to come in here today. We've got enough to justify a formal interview. Sally, any else to add?"

"Plenty. Dawn was well away once the seal burst. You know how Dave and Melanie just happened to meet for coffee in Morrisons on the Monday before Nick was killed? That was no coincidence. They meet up *every* Monday at that time, when she does her big grocery shop. It was one of Nick's darts nights, so normally they'd be safe. Thing is, he got wind of these meetups a few weeks back. Around the same time he got in contact with Cooper."

Laurence raised a tentative hand. "Remember how all the accounts of that night talk about Dave wanting to stay out on the pitch and watch what happened with Greg? And then go with him to hospital? He practically had to be ordered into the changing rooms. What if he was avoiding Osment? Hoping the bloke would simply give up and go home?"

"But something doesn't add up," Pru said. "Why arrange to meet Dave during training? Osment would have known—especially since he was aware of the coach's rules—that no players could leave the pitch."

"Because he could have arranged to meet him beforehand. In the clubhouse," Robin said. This was starting to hang together. "If that's true, there are two possible outcomes. Dave met him there and killed him—remember how he was last to arrive that evening—then somebody else moved the body into the changing room while he was giving himself an unbreakable alibi. Or Dave deliberately arrived late so he wouldn't have to meet Osment at all. Which might explain the damage to the photograph—frustrated at having been stood up so he took his feelings out on anything that came to hand."

"So, Dave's been counting his blessings ever since that whatever Osment knew died with him." Pru nodded, but her narrowed eyes told Robin she clearly wasn't convinced. He'd seen that expression before. "Two questions, sir. Why put the body in the changing room loos and what about Cooper? He was expecting to meet Osment around seven o'clock, not earlier."

Before Robin could summon up an answer, Laurence chipped in. "Whatever happened in the clubhouse that evening and whoever did it, there was one element they didn't factor in, because they couldn't have predicted it. The accident and the arrival of the ambulance. Whether Osment's death was planned or a spur-of-the-moment thing, having the emergency services arriving would have thrown anyone into a panic. The police could have been called in as well, for all they knew, so their natural reaction would have been to get out."

Pru shrugged. "Okay, but that still doesn't answer why the body was in the toilets, unless it was to buy the killer time. The loos aren't visible from the main changing area."

"Osment could have been mooching around the changing room of his own accord. Looking for something else to trash." No, there was a better explanation. "Or what if he got those abrasions when he hit the glass? He could have wanted to clean the wound at a sink and he'd have known there'd have been no players there."

"Apart from Joe," Pru pointed out. "If Osment walked into the changing room from the bar when Joe had nipped in to have a slash, there could have been a scuffle. The connecting door is right next to the loos."

"Unless Joe was the one Osment was intending to meet all along." Callum turned to Robin, hands spread. "This theory seems too complicated, sir. He goes to meet Dave, but even though Dave doesn't show up, Osment gets killed by somebody else. And where's Cooper while all this is going on?"

"Hold on," Sally said. "Osment might have asked Cooper to arrive later so that he could talk to Dave on his own."

"But why?" Pru asked.

Robin rapped the desk hard, then jumped off it. "That's enough speculation. Callum and Sally, can you get all the statements and work out a timeline of who was where and when at the sports ground that evening? With a note of where that information has been corroborated by other people. Laurence, can you concentrate on Osment's movements, so far as we know them? I know you drew a blank with checking the local CCTV before we got called in, so we're working off what Melanie told us about his leaving home and those emails where he's asking Cooper to meet him at seven o'clock. I want you to double—or triple—check that we haven't missed anything that can fill the picture in further. We'll touch base again when we've spoken to Dave, assuming that nothing major turns up in the interim."

About which Robin wouldn't hold his breath.

The interview rooms at Hartwood station might have been modern and airy, but they still held that distinctive atmosphere Robin had encountered in every one of their kind. Dave was waiting for them, scowling, clearly not best pleased at having been called in to the station. He made it clear that, in his opinion, calling him in from work had been out of order, causing him considerable embarrassment. Robin took little notice: he'd heard worse bluster from people who were guilty as sin. He and Pru went through the formalities of explaining how they'd be recording what was said, clarifying that they weren't pressing charges on anyone at the moment, and establishing whether he wanted a lawyer present.

Dave had nodded at the first, rolled his eyes at the second and shook his head at the last. "I have nothing to hide. Ask what you want, then I can answer and get out."

"Are you in a rush?" Pru asked, in her most insouciant voice. "Oh yes, it's your regular evening to meet Melanie, isn't it?"

"What do you mean?"

Pru smiled sweetly. "I mean that we know you and Melanie meet for coffee every Monday evening. Nick's darts night and her big shop. Very convenient."

"So what if we do?" Dave had flushed a hideous shade of red. "There's nothing wrong with chatting to an old friend."

"Nick didn't like it, though, did he? Especially when he found out it was still going on."

"Nick didn't like anything to do with me, frankly," Dave said, instantly appearing horrified that he'd made the admission.

"Did he have grounds for that?" Robin asked, pleased to see that they were getting under the witness's skin.

"Only his insane jealousy. There was nothing in it. It *is* possible for a man and a woman to be nothing other than friends," Dave added, with a sneer.

"Thing is, Dave, we've been told that Nick arranged to meet up with you the evening he was killed." That question hit home, as well, evidenced by the colour draining from Dave's face. "Is that true?"

"Who told you that?"

"Answer the question, please." Robin waited.

Eventually, Dave said, "Yes, he wanted to meet. I told him to stick his suggestion where the sun don't shine. I assumed it was going to be about Melanie."

"But it wasn't."

Dave shook his head.

"For the tape, please," Pru reminded him.

"It wasn't." Dave spoke exaggeratedly slowly and clearly. "He was at risk of losing his job, so he'd got some half-arsed idea in his head about me giving him money. I told him where to stick that too."

"Did he communicate by phone or email?" Pru asked.

"Phone. From work, I think. Why?"

"If it had been by email, you would have had proof of what was said. Otherwise we're relying on your word." Before Dave could respond, she continued with, "Why did you ring him at his flat?"

"To tell him I wasn't going to meet him. He said I had no choice but to come along."

"Where did he want to meet and at what time?" Robin asked.

"I thought you'd have known all this" Dave waved his hand towards the files laid on the tabletop. A real belief or bluster, playing for time so he could get his story straight? "Half past six, in the clubhouse. Somehow, he'd got hold of a set of keys. Typical. Melanie reckons he loved all the cloak-and-dagger stuff. Made up for the lack of other excitement in his life, I guess."

"See, that's another thing. We've been told about his lack of sex drive. How did Melanie feel about that?"

"She's stood by him when perhaps most people would have upped sticks."

"That's not answering my question." Time to go fishing, despite Robin knowing the bait wasn't foolproof. "Melanie seems to still have a sexual appetite, seeing as she's on the pill. Few people would blame her for occasionally satisfying her needs elsewhere, if that meant her marriage surviving. Were you the person to help her out?"

The bait got taken. "Did she tell you all that?"

"Answer my question, please. Was it you sleeping with her or someone else?"

Faced with the prospect of potentially labelling his old girlfriend as too free with her affections, Dave gave in. "Okay, okay. When they were first married, but only then. Melanie and I had the occasional time in bed and she really appreciated it. Said I was being a true gent. But it never sat easy with her—always aware she was being unfaithful to Nick. It seemed reasonable to give up the sex for just being social. It works for both of us." He shrugged. "I don't know if Nick ever found out for sure what we'd been doing, but even if we hadn't had the odd evening of passion, he'd have still been suspicious."

"Thanks for getting that into the open. It's always better in the long run." Robin glanced at Pru.

"Back to the meeting with Osment. You had no choice but to go," she said. "What did he have to say to you when you got there?"

"He didn't say anything, because I didn't go. I left it until the last moment to get to training—any of the lads can tell you that—and hoped he'd got the hint that I wasn't interested."

Pru carried on the grilling. "Must have been a shock to find him dead. Or were you expecting it?"

"What? Of course I wasn't." Dave grabbed a clump of his hair and tugged at it. "How the hell would I have been able to kill him and get his body into that cubicle without any of the other players seeing?"

"Maybe you had help." Robin made a show of consulting his notes. "The keys to the clubhouse that Osment had got hold of. If you knew about them, why didn't you tell anyone he had them? Given how keen the club is to guard the players' valuables, wouldn't it have been sensible to tell Mr. Preese that there was a rogue set in circulation?"

Dave's eyes flicked from side to side before focussing on the table. "I was going to; I simply didn't get the chance."

"Really?" Robin leaned forward, resting his arms on the tabletop, willing Dave to look him in the eye. "Isn't it a fact that Osment had a hold over you, and you'd not have dared report him in case you landed up in worse trouble?"

"Are you saying he wanted to blackmail me?"

"Yes. Which is why he wanted to meet and why he was wanting money from you."

At last, Dave raised his head, although he remained silent. Robin had seen that expression on a suspect's face before. It either heralded a last-ditch stand before the truth began to emerge or an entrenchment, burying the facts deeper below the topsoil of defiance. What would be the best strategy to ensure it was the former not the latter? To prolong the silence, letting it become so uncomfortable that Dave felt compelled to speak, or press on with the questions?

Pru went for the second option. "Dave, you're not stupid and neither are we. Tell us why Osment was so keen to meet you. It's because he knew you'd killed Jamie Weatherell, isn't it?"

"No!" Dave struck the table with his fist, then slumped back in his chair. "No, I didn't kill him, but yes, that's why he wanted to see me. Said he had something to sell me—proof of my involvement in the hit-and-run. I reckoned that was a load of rubbish. He wanted to cause trouble for me because of my friendship with Melanie."

"Let's get this clear. For the purposes of this statement, you're saying that you didn't hit Jamie Weatherell with your car?"

Dave didn't get the chance to answer, as a sharp rap sounded on the door. Robin, usually annoyed to be interrupted, welcomed the opportunity to get his thoughts in order as they'd not really learned anything they didn't already know.

"This had better be good," he said to Callum anyway, once he'd stepped outside.

"I thought you might like to know while you still have him in there. Osment's phone has turned up. The one he had with him the night he was killed."

"Where was it?"

"In someone's back garden. It must have been thrown over a wall and fell behind a bush. The houseowners found it while they were gardening this morning and rang the station to see if it had been reported stolen or lost." Callum wagged his finger in the general direction of the station entrance. "The constable who took the call had the sense to notice how close the address was to the ground, saw that the general description matched Osment's missing device, then got a patrol to pick it up."

"Good work." The solid, boring stuff that made up good policing. "We're sure it's his?"

"Ninety percent. The distinctive case Osment kept it in—R2D2, so the bloke had some degree of good taste—has gone, I guess because whoever slung it thought that lessened the chances of a match-up, but we had a description off Melanie to compare it with. Distinctive scratches on the back, under the Apple logo. SIM card's been removed too, but once the device has been checked for prints, it'll go down to the tech people. To see if they can get into it."

"Okay. That was worth interrupting me for." Not least because a notion was starting to form in Robin's mind. He doubted there'd be something on the phone like an incriminating photo of Osment's killer, taken as he was attacked—the killer would surely have taken a hammer to the thing in that case—but there could be other items of note. Like the elusive "proof" that Osment had allegedly possessed concerning the hit-and-run.

Robin re-entered the interview room, gave Pru a nod, and then settled himself while she did the formal interview-recommencing speech, concluding with, "Back to the night Jamie was killed."

Dave turned slightly, conspicuously to address the recording device. "I admit I left the Tuckton ground after Jamie did and I drove down that same road, so I must have passed the place where it happened, but I don't remember seeing anything at the time. Is that clear enough for your recording?"

"Have you come across a man called Colin Cooper?" Robin asked.

"Eh?" Dave wagged his head. "Never heard of him."

"Osment asked him to the meeting. The meeting he wanted with you."

"Did he?" Dave grunted. "Maybe you should be questioning him about the murder, then."

"We have. He was late arriving, which we know for a fact, so he didn't get to see either of you. He was the person who gave Osment a lift home from the derby game the day Jamie died." Robin rested his elbows on the table again. Time to go angling again. "Maybe *he* was the proof—the missing witness to the accident who'd be able to put the blame on you?"

"That's nonsense." The suggestion had got Dave riled, though.

"There's the phone."

Dave started forward in his seat—focussing on the hit-and-run, or anything linked to it was showing dividends in his reactions. "What phone?"

"Osment's. The one that disappeared the night he was killed. An old phone. One on which he might have kept pictures. Of you and Melanie, for example."

"I wouldn't put that past him."

"Maybe he had a photo of your car, the night of the accident."

Eyes narrowed and voice clipped, Dave said, "He might have done, seeing as I've admitted to being on the road that night. That proves nothing. He's always been—always was—a troublemaker."

Robin waved the remark away. "Anyway, we'll soon find out what's on there, because it's turned up, which is what my constable came to tell me. Did you get rid of it?"

"No. I've never had his phone. Like I said, I didn't meet him that night." Dave sat back again. "Are we finished?"

"For the moment. We need to take your fingerprints and DNA—for elimination purposes, unless you've already given them—and I'd be grateful if you'd give us access to your bank records rather than us having to get a warrant."

"Feel free on both counts. I suppose you're on the hunt for payments from me to Osment but you won't find anything." Dave broke into a broad smile. "I have nothing to hide on that front."

"I have a horrible feeling that I believe him," Pru said, once the interview had ended and Dave had been taken by Callum to have his fingerprints taken. "At least about the bank statements and possibly about not having the phone."

"Yep. He strikes me as the type who tries to be careful about what he says so when he's on firm ground, he wants to make the most of it. He didn't like me mentioning the phone, though."

"I noticed that too. Do we know there are pictures on Osment's phone, or were you taking a punt, sir?"

"Dangling a worm in the water." Robin shrugged: a policeman had to take a leap in the dark at times. "I wouldn't be surprised if there are. Strikes me that he must have had some reason for keeping it, despite it being an old device. And while that may have simply been so he and Melanie had a backup in an emergency, it might also have been because it had something on it that was worth keeping."

"Wouldn't he have backed the pictures up to his iCloud so it wouldn't matter what device he was using?"

"Not if he'd chosen not to. Might be as simple as his storage being full. Or maybe Melanie had access to his Apple ID and he didn't want her seeing them." Robin pushed his chair back from the desk, ready to be on the move. "We'll know once the techy whizzes have done their techy whizzy stuff."

They had the answer to Pru's question by five o'clock, at which point they also had a timeline, but the device took precedence. There were a number of pictures on the phone, time and date stamped with the night Jamie died, at around the time the accident must have happened, showing both the dead deer in the front garden and Dave's car near the fatal bend in the road. Some general ones had been taken a couple of days after that, showing the scene by twilight. There didn't appear to be any particular significance in those, but they must have meant something to Osment. Perhaps those pictures taken on the fatal night had helped him to work out who had been where and when in relation to the site of Jamie's death.

The most damning sat on the camera roll between the ones of the deer and the ones of Dave's car. A young man, oblivious to being snapped—Jamie, surely, given the clothes he was wearing and which Robin recognised from the pictures in the case files—fiddling around with a bike.

A shame that the photos on that Saturday evening hadn't been taken from the lay-by Robin had parked in and which would have given a clear view of the accident. But if Nick had parked there, Dave might well have spotted him. He must have found another place to hide his car. The sequence of snaps suggested he must have been on foot at some point, having got out of the car to poke around, unnoticed.

"Hardly cast-iron proof that Dave caused the accident, are they?" Laurence pointed out.

"No," Callum agreed, "but think about the timeline they construct. First a snap of the dead deer, then a big gap. That's when Nick's being dropped off and picking up his own car." He glanced at Robin, who nodded for him to continue. "He returns to the scene, gets bored waiting for Dave to drive by, so has a poke about by that deer. He spots Jamie and takes a snap."

"Why doesn't he go to help with the tyre or offer the bloke a lift?" Laurence asked.

"Because he's decided that's where he'll wait for Dave. Better there than nearer Tuckton, because those roads don't have anywhere you could tuck—excuse pun—a vehicle away unnoticed. He can't help Jamie because wants to be able to hare back to his car and get on Dave's trail." Callum drew breath. "He's returning to his motor when another car comes along, so he dives into the entrance to a drive and gets a picture of Dave going past. Timeline of photos."

"Okay, that works," Laurence conceded. "There was an old house along there which they were redeveloping at the time. I remember because my parents went to have a nose up there. Anyone could have easily nipped into the entrance to the site and not been seen. Maybe even parked there."

"Go on," Robin said to Callum. "Where do the pictures take us next?"

"Away from the crash site. Osment's clearly followed Dave about that night, maybe trying to catch him meeting up with Melanie." Callum pointed to a sheet of notes he'd made. "There are snaps taken a little while later at the chip shop on the outskirts of Hartwood. The timings of those show that Dave must have driven straight there from Tuckton. Osment mightn't have formed a timeline of what he thought had happened until later that night, if that's when he heard about the fatality."

"And maybe he also got his hands on other evidence that we've not tracked down and the pictures were only part of it," Laurence agreed.

"Um, sir." Pru, frowning, had apparently been struck by something on the incident board. "Osment's car. It was allegedly stolen before Jamie got run down. Did he lie to us about the time?"

"His original statement just gave a window of a couple of hours between when he last saw it and when it had gone," Callum pointed out. "He could have gone and trashed it himself before ringing us. Panic stations set in when he realised that he was in the wrong place at the wrong time."

"Or," Laurence suggested, "if he knew there were thieves in the area—which we all did at the time—he might have left his satnav out on display to tempt them."

"He might even have borrowed his wife's car to go back to the Tuckton road in case anybody recognised his vehicle," Pru said, "and by a classic case of Murphy's Law got home to find his own one had been nicked."

Robin raised his hand. Time to return to facts rather than speculation. "His wife didn't have a vehicle, remember. They shared one. Can we return to the Wednesday? We've established that he had the photos with him the evening he was killed, but that his phone was taken and thrown away. Any prints on it?"

"Blurry ones. Osment's, Melanie's, and a partial third set. No match for those as yet."

"Remind me whose prints were taken on the Wednesday or subsequently." Robin, irritated by the blank faces greeting his question, snapped, "Please tell me that somebody had the sense to obtain some for elimination?"

Sally swallowed hard. "Because the CSIs said there were so many at the scene, with most of them blurred and unusable, Inspector Robertson suggested we left it until we had something more concrete, like the weapon. Imagine all the comings and goings in a changing room, sir. Not to mention the loos."

"I take the point, but what about the door from the bar? Was that in a similar mess? Does nobody bother to clean the place?"

"The bar, yes," Laurence said. "That's part of the groundsman's job and he does it pretty well. The doorknob had been recently wiped, so it only had Osment's fingerprints on it; same with the bolt. The teams are supposed to keep the changing rooms clean. You can imagine that only gets done once in a blue moon."

Time to take a deep breath and try to calm down, or else he'd go mad with frustration. If he'd been running this from the start, he would have had Grace—possibly the best CSI anybody could hope to have—going over that place with a fine-toothed comb. Maybe she'd have turned up other things than simply the dabs of blood on and under the edge of the changing room bench and the snag of black plastic. Even if she hadn't, Robin would have felt more confident that there was nothing else to be found. Somebody had missed that broken picture first time around and the material caught on the wire.

"Shall we look at the timeline for that evening, sir?" Pru, in soothing mode, gave him a smile.

Robin, smiling back, turned his attention to what appeared to be old computer paper, the sort with perforated sheets. Laurence had apparently sourced that from some part of the station that was in a time warp. It ideally suited the purpose, though, being long enough and wide enough to carry all the relevant times, locations, and names.

Preese had arrived first, around about six o'clock, so he could unlock the access gates and get things set up. Most of the players had been there by quarter to seven, bar Dave, who'd appeared at ten to the hour. Somewhere in between those times, Osment must have sneaked into the bar; probably closer to twenty past six if he hadn't wanted to risk being seen by the players. At twenty past seven, everyone had been on the pitch awhile and remained there until well gone eight, so the only person they knew for certain to be in the building at that point was Cooper.

"What if we're barking up the wrong tree?" Laurence asked. "If Osment left that bar door open, then anybody might have come in there unnoticed. Somebody who's completely unknown to us, like a vagrant chancing his arm that he'd find something to nick. Or a warm place to spend the night."

"Seems unlikely," Pru said, "that they should try that door exactly at the point it's been left unlocked. If they watched Osment opening it, they'd have known somebody was in the building."

"Unless it was someone who deliberately followed him there, for whatever reason," Laurence pointed out, "not realising he'd arranged to meet people there."

"Sir." Sally's tones were not quite as tentative as earlier. "I've got a couple of thoughts. We've kept asking why Osment arranged to see Dave at the club and for Cooper to come there. Could it have been for his own safety? If things had got nasty, he could have nipped into the changing rooms, if he'd already unbolted and unlocked the door to give himself an escape route. If he found the players still in there, he'd have got some stick from them but that would be better than getting attacked. If not, he could have locked the door behind himself. In the event, he didn't have time to do so."

"I like that idea, Sally." Pru pointed at the photo on the incident board of the bench where Osment's blood had been found. "Where his head hit that wooden edge isn't that far from the entrance to the bar. If there'd been a scuffle in the doorway he might have fallen backwards as the door was pushed in, resulting in him whacking himself."

"He was still finished off afterwards," Robin reminded them. "So even if this started as an accident it didn't finish as one. It could have been a spur of the moment, red-mist-descending moment, using whatever implement came to hand, but it smacks to me of lurking intent to do harm. Sally, you said you had a couple of thoughts. What's the other one?"

"It was about Cooper, sir, and why he'd been asked to come at seven if Dave was due to arrive much earlier. Maybe they were never meant to overlap."

Callum said, "I'm sorry but I don't follow."

Sally didn't seem fazed by the challenge. "Maybe Cooper was right when he said that Osment wanted to get money off him. Perhaps he wanted to blackmail the pair of them, separately. 'What about all these pictures I took on the night when I went back there. I know you must have been the one who hit Jamie.' He'd have had some story ready that he'd have adapted for each of them and the sequence of pictures he showed would be different. It would have had to be backed up too. His own eyewitness account in the case of Cooper, something else we've still to establish in the case of Dave."

"That's possible," Robin acknowledged. "Does it take us any further forward, though?"

"It might if they weren't the only people he planned on blackmailing."

Callum snorted. "Are you suggesting he had a whole string of people he asked to turn up? A sort of extortion surgery? That sounds like it came out of a farce."

While it did seem far-fetched, Robin knew both from experience and reading up on cases that blackmailers went to ridiculous lengths to snare their victims and often relied on a simple threat of action being enough. "I wouldn't dismiss it out of hand. We know he tried the pitch on Dave and possibly on Cooper. If he didn't think he'd get anywhere with them, he might have lined up further potential victims. Either for the accident or something else."

He yawned, suddenly feeling the effects of the journey, the late night, and his eighth straight day of work. At least he'd had the previous weekend off—the team here had been on the case for longer.

"You look how I feel, sir." Pru gave him a sympathetic smile.

"I could say the same to you." Robin stifled another yawn. "Right, *we* need a break and you're all probably in a similar boat. Everyone go home, get a rest, and come back tomorrow ready to tackle this again. We have to believe we're closer to the solution than we were."

Maybe after a decent night's sleep, he could persuade himself that was true.

Chapter Eighteen

It was unusual for the doorbell to sound in the evening, especially on a Monday. The last occasion had been when Mrs. Haig, she of the wonderful fruit cake, had sprung a leak from one of her pipes and Robin had nipped round with a wrench to do some timely tightening up. While Adam wasn't quite as handy as his partner in the plumbing department, if their neighbour was in trouble again, then at least he could offer comfort and advice. He eased out of his chair, then headed for the door, at the point as the bell went a second time.

"Okay, I'm coming."

But rather than any of his neighbours being on the step, there was a tired and wan Sam Woakes.

"Can I come in?" he asked. "I'd like to talk."

"Can't we talk out here?"

"Oh, Adam, it's fucking perishing tonight. Give me a break." Sam broke into a rare smile. It was easy to see why Martin was so smitten.

"Okay." Adam reluctantly opened the door, then ushered him into the kitchen. That room had the advantage of both Campbell being in residence and a selection of potential weapons—carving knives and the rolling pin—should self-defence be needed. "Want a cuppa?"

"I'd not say no. Strong, please. Same as I like my men, as they say."

"If you're going to spout clichés, you can naff off." Despite the banter, Adam kept an eye on his guest while going through the tea-making process. While he wasn't too concerned for his safety, there'd been other potentially fatal confrontations in this property, one in the house and one in the garden. Another incentive for them to move, before the non–Mrs. Haig neighbours started a protest group.

Or was this all leaping to conclusions about Sam's motive? "What did you want to talk about?"

"This fucking business with my brother, Joe. He's not a murderer. Neither am I."

"And why are you telling *me* this? I'm not the police and even if my husband is, I don't have any influence on his investigations." Adam cast a glance at Campbell, who'd woken at the arrival of Sam and had been keeping a wary eye on him ever since.

"Yeah, but he'll listen to you, won't he? Tell him to get off my back." Sam drummed his fingers on the breakfast bar.

"You've got this wrong, Sam. I don't mix work with home and neither does Robin."

From the way Sam rolled his eyes, that argument clearly wasn't convincing, and the idea of sharing a cosy cuppa with him was becoming less attractive by the minute. What would it take to get him out of the door? Feign a kind of seizure or pretend he had just remembered that he was supposed to be at Mrs. Haig's house mending her dodgy toilet handle? Neither of those were going to seem convincing, but that wouldn't matter if they did the trick.

"No sugar in the tea, by the way," Sam said, staring at the still unpoured kettle meaningfully.

"Oh, yeah." Adam filled their mugs, bashing the tea bags with a spoon to get them to brew quicker. "Martin said you—" He paused, annoyed that, in his desperation to find a way to end the conversation, he'd spoken his thoughts aloud.

"Martin said what?"

"He said you'd had a chat at the end of yesterday's practice." Adam thrust a mug at his uninvited guest. "Said you'd been asking if Robin's as hot as he's made out to be. In my opinion yes, but you know that for yourself by now." Hopefully that would deflect the conversation away from the other part of yesterday's chat.

"He's okay. Not my type. Distinctly Martin's, I guess. He's mentioned him once or twice. You'd better watch out."

Campbell's growl at that remark made Adam wonder, yet again, whether the dog followed human conversations with an unnerving degree of understanding. "You've upset him," he told Sam. "Doesn't like his other dad being maligned."

"Sorry. I'm handling this all wrong." He was, but there was still no sign of him leaving. "How friendly are you with Martin?"

"We get on okay. Not bosom buddies. Why?"

"If I tell you something, would he need to hear it? Would Robin need to?"

"Depends what it is and what my conscience would tell me to do about it. I can't make a blind promise without knowing what I'm getting into." Was this going to be some great revelation that would help bring the murder inquiry to a swift conclusion? Although, in that case, what could Martin have to do with it?

Sam stared into his mug, as though he could find the answer to his mysterious dilemma written in the brew, like the way old women used to read the future in the tea leaves. "It's not the kind of thing I want getting around. Doesn't do me any credit."

"If I tell it to Robin, it goes no further, I *can* promise you that. Unless it's relevant to this murder investigation." With a sinking heart, Adam registered Sam's wince at the word *murder*. Making sure that the rolling pin—which Sandra must have used earlier and left drying in the rack—was within reach, he took a deep breath and asked, "Is this to do with your brother?"

"Yeah. Sometimes we used to swop places. Not often and not for anything important like cheating in exams or whatever." Sam looked up at last, defiantly. "And not so we could create an alibi for bumping somebody off."

"Okay, so why the angst if it's no big deal?"

Sam squirmed on his chair. "I didn't say it was no big deal. It's a huge deal as far as Martin's concerned."

"Martin? How does he— Oh, I get it." The light on the road to Damascus couldn't have been so starkly illuminating. "You took Joe's place on that blind date?"

"Yep. I shouldn't have gone, because I was already feeling ropey, but I'd promised him I'd cover rather than him stand the guy up. He didn't want to pass up his chance entirely, in the event Martin turned out to be fit, you know."

What a pair of a right charmers: Martin was well shot of Joe, whatever the circumstances and maybe Sam came into the same category. "Why couldn't Joe go? Did he have the runs as well?"

"No. He had a hot date. Guy he'd met in the queue at the sandwich shop that lunchtime." Sam glanced down at Campbell, reached out as though to pet him, but snatched his hand back at the dog's admonitory growl. Newfoundlands were good judges of character. "I really fancied him at the time, still do. That's why when I saw he was involved with this fundraising choir, I had to wangle myself into it. Wanted a second chance."

"If that's the case, you have to tell him at some point. The longer you leave it, the worse it'll be. And you need to tell Robin. Now."

"Why?"

Adam managed not to yell *Are you thick or what?* "Think about it. He knows you're hiding something, because Martin told me and I told Robin. Of course, you numpty, he thinks you're covering up that you doubled for Joe at the club when that bloke was murdered."

"That's going to land me right in it." Sam pushed his mug away. "Won't it make him increasingly suspicious given that we've worked the switch before?"

"If you don't tell him, I *will* and how suspicious is that going to appear? Let's face it, he's not interested in your love life and how you run it. His priority is to solve this case and get home as soon as he can. If you can give him a break by shutting off one dead end, we'd all be grateful." Assuming, naturally, this wasn't part of some elaborate cover up. Confess to the less misdemeanour to deflect attention from the bigger one. He picked up his phone. "I'll dial his number now. Explain that you're here and that you have something important to say. Then we can both get on with what's left of our evenings."

With clear reluctance, Sam nodded, then waited while Adam rang and explained the situation.

"Why the hell did you let him in?" Robin said. "Is he there? Can he hear us?"

"Because it seemed like the right thing, yes, and only me. In that order. He has something to say to you." Adam passed the phone over and watched, with a touch of schadenfreude, as Sam related what he'd said earlier. When that was done, Robin had evidently gone into interview mode, given the string of answers—meaningless without the context of the questions—that Sam was producing. Amongst the interview questions was there also a warning not to harm a hair of either his or Campbell's heads?

Sam's sudden guarded expression caught Adam's attention. Robin had evidently asked a question he wasn't happy about.

"I haven't seen him for weeks. That's not unusual—we only meet up a few times a year. Joe bumps into him a lot, obviously."

Intrigued at who they could be discussing, but not wanting to make Sam feel any more self-conscious than he already was, Adam picked up the Sunday newspaper—still laying where he'd left it the previous afternoon—and pretended to read.

"I know they go for the odd pint, start and end of the season. Sort of ritual, I guess. He goes to watch training sometimes, but he doesn't go to the matches anymore. He lost his appetite for those when Jamie . . . you know." Another pause as Robin must have put a further question, one that got Sam riled again. "I have no idea how often he goes along on a Wednesday. Ask him. Or ask Joe. I wasn't there." A further silence while Robin—talking loudly but not audible enough—laid down the law. "Yeah, okay. I've got you. I'll hand you back to Adam."

Adam took the phone, and said into it, "Sorry about that."

"No need to apologise. He might have told me something I needed to know. I gave him an earful about not bothering you in future and that if he needed to talk, he should contact Abbotston nick and they'd contact me. Tell him to sling his hook."

"I will, only I'll be politer. Oh, and when you do get home, don't forget the milk."

Robin chuckled. The milk line was their private code for saying *I love you* when they were being listened in on. Adam had often wondered if the other rozzers at Abbotston thought the pair of them had a dairy addiction. "Love you too."

Adam ended the call, then crossed his arms. "The chief inspector says you have to go. And when the police say you have to do something . . ."

Sam broke into a grin. "Yeah, I know. I've outstayed my welcome. See you at choir practice."

"Yep. Talking of which, tell Martin what you've told me. Same threat—if you don't, I will. Like I said, he knows you're holding back, and he'll only go and imagine it's worse than it is." Although how it could be much worse—short of the murder itself—Adam wasn't prepared to consider. "If he gives you a gobful of abuse, you've only yourself to blame."

"Yeah, you're right. Doesn't make it any easier, though."

Adam—and Campbell, who'd clearly taken a dislike to their visitor—accompanied Sam to the front door, watched him drive away, and then locked and bolted the front door, an action he rarely bothered to do.

"Can't be too careful, can we?" he said to the dog. "We've both had one too many encounters with criminals."

The healthy wagging of Campbell's tail implied that he agreed.

Robin had wanted to get his head straight about what Sam had told him—and the implications of it—before talking to the team. Sleeping on it always helped, because a theory that felt great at night, especially after a few beers, could seem like a load of cobblers' come morning. The suspect could wait too, given that he'd waited long enough and might have been lulled into thinking that the police weren't looking in his direction. Well, they hadn't been up until now, deceived by the smoke and mirrors of a seemingly solid alibi and maybe a little tampering with evidence. The tiny crumb of knowledge that he often attended training as a spectator, so would know what usually happened on those evenings, might be the breakthrough they needed.

Come Tuesday morning, as soon as it was decent to do so, he got on the phone to Betteridge.

"Hello? Robin? What's up?" She sounded as though she'd not been long awake.

"Sorry, boss. I've got an idea, and I wanted to talk it through with somebody before I go charging in with my size tens. Can I pick your brains?"

"What I have of left of them. Been up until two o'clock supervising raids. I'll make coffee while we talk."

Prick of the conscience—Robin wasn't the only person with a serious case on his hands. "I could ring later."

"No. You've bloody well woken me up now. Tell me."

"I've got an idea that's gone from being viable to bleeding obvious. Who better at Hartwood sports ground to be able to clear away any forensic evidence that we may have overlooked than somebody who knows those pitches and buildings like the back of his hand? Damn it, I was with him clearing stuff into a black plastic bag—the same sort of bag we found a piece of at the scene."

"Okay so far, but being blunt, those sacks are the sort any household has. I've got a roll of them in the kitchen."

"Yours might not be an exact match. We'll test his." The team could get onto that today. "He even told me he wanted to play at forensic officers and said he fancied himself as Hercule Poirot."

"Now that's interesting. Hold on." The sound of filling a kettle for that coffee Betteridge needed. "Right. Do you think he was playing at amateur detectives, rather than hunting for his wife's ring, when he was at the ground that Saturday night he kicked Osment up the arse? Somehow got wind there was likely to be trouble and lay in wait?"

"Maybe. Or that was the evening he first recognised Osment as the vandal and decided to try to catch him out on subsequent nights." Robin remembered his mother's mystery books he'd read when younger, how in some of them there'd been a particular witness very keen to help the detectives with their enquiries who had turned out to be the culprit and had been covering over their crime with a show of cooperation. Almost daring the police to catch him or her and gloating over their apparent inability to get at the truth.

"If Weatherell is so keen on amateur detection, I can imagine him trying to find out who killed his son, particularly in light of his wife's death. What if that led him to suspect Osment all along, as Preese did?"

"Could be. Or he'd truly given up on trying to find out who had been the driver—as Joe suggested—and the Osment thing came as a shock." Why did that last point resound around Robin's brain as though he'd missed something? Better to let the subconscious work on that for a while. "Anyway, the Weatherell angle's the one I'm going to pursue. I'll let you know where we get."

"Okay. Good work. Enjoy your hotel breakfast. I'm not envious in the slightest."

Once Robin was settled with a bowl of cereal and a glass of orange juice—eyeing with envy the usual plate of fried delights that Pru was about to tuck into and which never appeared to add half an ounce to her frame—he outlined what he'd discussed with Betteridge.

"Oh, I like that, sir." Pru gestured with her knife. "You reckon his mate Archie's given him a false alibi?"

"Not necessarily. Just because a call comes to your landline, it doesn't mean it has to be answered from there. It's easy enough to set calls to rollover to a mobile—lots of businesses do that so they won't miss contacts from customers. Weatherell might have found it necessary to do that in his line of work too, especially if he's the emergency contact for trouble at the ground. The timing of that call is pretty vague on Archie's part, so around half seven could have meant later. Weatherell would have had enough time to scuffle with Osment, finish him off, leave the body, and be starting on his way home." Robin rapped the table with his spoon, sending a spray of milky droplets across the cloth. "Sorry, I've remembered something."

"It must be good, then."

"Not so much good as weird. I had this dream in the wee small hours. Totally fit for sharing in polite company." He grinned, then finished off his orange juice. "I had arranged to meet Osment in one of our interview rooms, even though he was dead. Told you it was weird. Don't you dare tell the rest of the team about it."

"You have my word." Pru scooped up some sausage and bacon, then munched on it while awaiting the rest of the tale.

"It was nighttime, with no lights on, so the room was dark. He mistook me for someone else—his wife, I think, which is somewhat odder and possibly Freudian so let's not go there—and he got his phone out and started scrolling through the picture roll."

"As he must have been intending to do with Dave. The setting's odd but the actions make sense."

"Exactly. Therefore, thinking about that in the cold light of morning, here's another take on things. Could Weatherell have come into the bar, initially innocently? You know, he's there to see the training, spots the bar door's open or whatever, goes to investigate and Osment, who's expecting either Dave or Cooper to turn up, assumes it's one of them coming in? Not knowing what he's actually doing, he shows Weatherell the pictures. 'Here. Look at these, from the night Jamie was killed. I was there, I know what happened.' If I'd been in the same position as Weatherell at that point, I'd have gone mental, thinking that somebody might have been there, maybe even witnessed the crash and done nothing to help."

"Okay." Pru laid down her cutlery: this was clearly time for a serious discussion. "I'll be devil's advocate. If that happened, why didn't Osment ask who was there? Was he that stupid that he wouldn't check beforehand he was talking to the right bloke?"

"Maybe he did. Maybe Weatherell simply said a mumbled yes. Playing at detectives. Perhaps he interrupted Osment showing the pictures to Cooper and overheard their conversation." Robin felt less and less convinced by the moment. The dream was turning out to have been a nightmare.

"It might have started with him seeing Osment breaking the glass in that picture."

"He couldn't have done if it was dark. He could have heard it, though, and thought he was up to his vandalism again. Scuffle first and ask questions afterwards, only there wasn't an afterwards, because he'd seen a red mist. Or the team picture is simply a red herring. Osment broke it in frustration at being stood up or out of spite and it signifies nothing." Robin buttered a piece of toast, then slathered it with Marmite.

"Do we have to squeeze the murder into the time between Joe leaving the loos and Cooper entering the bar?" Pru asked. "Could it have been done afterwards?"

"It could. Although that doesn't explain why Weatherell wasn't simply watching the players practicing before then. He'd have been seen, surely—unless he felt the need to hide, and what motive would he have had to do so at that point?"

"True. I suppose it also begs the question of where the victim was up until that point, assuming Cooper has told us the truth and Osment wasn't in the bar at seven twenty."

"It does, but I like it as a theory. Neater. Gives the murderer a bigger window of time to get in, kill the victim, and get out again." Robin jabbed with the remaining crust of his toast. "The crime scene investigator had a feeling the body had been dragged off and discarded in a hurry. What if that was because the killer heard the ambulance approaching and knew he had to get out quicker than anticipated?"

That would have the added advantage of partly explaining the coincidence of Greg's injury and the murder. If the killer had heard the sirens, that could have precipitated a panic.

"Okay, so where does Cooper come into all this? Wouldn't Weatherell have seen his car and become suspicious?" Pru paused, cutlery back in her hands but now suspended above her plate. "Or do we think that's *exactly* what happened? Weatherell goes to check that everything's all right, tries the bar door, finds it's open, then goes in and stumbles across Osment up to no good."

"I think that's possible, although there's another line I'd like to explore. A hunch."

"A hunch? Is that what some of our less enlightened colleagues would call women's intuition if I'd come up with the idea?" Pru grinned.

"Something like that." Robin returned the smile. "Based on something Joe said about Weatherell. 'Gift of the gab because he'd been in sales.'"

"Ah. I'm with you. Sounds like we need to get the team back onto those traffic cameras again, as a matter of priority. See if Weatherell's car was in the area that evening and exactly when." Pru speared the last bit of sausage with her fork. "They'll be overjoyed."

The inadequately suppressed groans when Robin told the team it was time to scour the traffic camera footage yet again were understandable. It was such a thankless task, a mixture of intense boredom and repetition combined with the need to remain alert at all times so that a vital number plate wasn't missed. Callum tackled the first camera Weatherell would have encountered if he'd taken the logical route to the training ground, while Laurence trawled through the recordings from the one nearest the ground. Sally and Pru concentrated on finding out everything they could about the man himself.

That turned out to be very little, as he wasn't on social media, didn't have a criminal record—not even points on his driving licence—and only appeared on their records in connection with his son's death. About which one of the long-serving uniformed officers had said he'd acted with a lot more dignity and restraint than most people would have done in such a shitty situation. Acting on one of Robin's hunches, Sally had been despatched with a set of questions to ask the personnel department at the company Cooper worked for.

It didn't take long to get an answer about Weatherell's location on the Wednesday night, though. His car had been clocked five minutes from his home at six forty. So, assuming it was him driving, he could have left home at just gone half past. If his intention had been to watch training, he'd clearly been going to miss the start of it, especially so given that he appeared to have been snarled up in the same traffic jam that had affected Cooper. He'd been caught by another camera, quarter of a mile from the ground, at seven twenty-one, so would have arrived a few minutes later and possibly taken Archie's call while still in his car.

Callum piped up. "Wouldn't this Archie bloke have noticed his call had rolled over and was being taken outside on a mobile and not on the landline at home? It always sounds different."

"Depends what his hearing's like," Laurence pointed out. "Even if he did notice something, Weatherell could have said it was a problem with the line."

"You can go and ask him. He doesn't like being rung at work, so let's see what he thinks about us turning up at the place. Might jolt him into telling the truth. Ah, Sally." Robin glanced expectantly at the constable as she re-entered the incident room. "Any luck?"

"In spades. Tom Weatherell was a salesman for Hepius Pharmaceuticals, on the same regional team as Colin Cooper before *he* moved into marketing. They could have known each other."

"You're thinking the pair of them are linked, sir?" Callum asked, nodding appreciatively.

"Possibly." Robin still needed to exercise caution about this theory. "Several times we've asked ourselves if this has been a case of two or more people working together. Sometimes those gut instincts are right."

"But we've picked the right pairing?" It was less of a question from Pru than a statement.

Robin nodded. "If Weatherell knew his old colleague had been in the vicinity when Jamie was killed, he might have been in contact to see what he knew. Cooper can't help him, until the day Osment gets back in touch, saying he has evidence about who the driver was. Cooper contacts Weatherell to tell him and suggests he comes along to the ground as well. Maybe not for the initial part of the meeting, because Osment would be likely to clam up."

"That would explain why Cooper wasn't that worried about putting himself in potential danger," Sally pointed out. "He knew he'd have backup."

"It would also give him a legitimate reason to be there, if challenged," Callum agreed. "He was there to meet Weatherell, who often came to watch training himself, so it wouldn't be out of the ordinary for him to be seen. Maybe there was something around covering up why he had that pitching wedge too, in case he was seen with it. 'I was bringing it because my old mate said he'd redo the grip for me.'"

As earlier, Pru slipped into the devil's advocate role again. "I'll buy this as a theory so far, sir, although Cooper would have had to be absolutely certain he didn't actually hit Jamie when he thought he hit the deer."

"If I'd have been him, I'd have checked my car the next morning," Callum said. "And double-checked all the details from the news reports. I'd have had to satisfy myself. But then, I'm not him."

"Indeed." Nobody could put themselves into another person's mind and take the measure of *their* conscience. Still, this had the advantage of explaining why Cooper had so readily depicted himself to the police as the potential victim. "Let's focus on the night in question. Both Cooper and Weatherell are running late because of the prang on the local road and because of the phone call from Archie, that has to be answered so it doesn't appear suspicious what our friend the groundsman might be up to. Osment, who's been sitting in the bar since six thirty, gets cross because he's been stood up twice, so he lashes out at the photo. That's probably a few minutes after seven, because none of the players heard it."

"Assuming it happened that night, sir." Pru jabbed a finger towards the picture of Osment. "If he was in possession of the keys, I'd reckon he'd have used them before then. Trial run, maybe. And what happened to the keys, anyway? They weren't found on the body."

"They didn't turn up in the search of the premises, either," Laurence confirmed, "although nobody was particularly keeping an eye out for them. Mind you, would he have needed to do a trial run? If he used to train at the club, he'd have known his way around."

"Not behind the bar, I hope." Pru rolled her eyes. "Add the whereabouts of the keys to the list of unknowns. Like what Osment was doing between six thirty and when he died."

"When he was in the bar, I bet he would have had a poke around hunting for anything valuable. Was there a till?" Sally asked.

"We saw one when we looked around the clubhouse," Robin replied, "but it appeared to have had the cash drawer taken out for security. He could have nicked bottles off the optics, although they're not so easy to transport home. He'd have checked his phone, surely, for messages from Dave or Cooper."

"Maybe he fell down the internet rabbit hole," Callum suggested. "Like I said before, you decide to give your phone one last check for notifications when you go to bed and suddenly it's half an hour later and you're on some website reading about how they're trying to reconstruct mammoths from DNA."

"That's a good point. It could be used to account for any of the time gaps we're trying to fill up." The joys of modern life that the police of twenty years previously wouldn't have had to contend with. Robin turned back to the incident board, staring at the picture of the victim. "Whatever he was doing in that bar, he's out of it by twenty past seven. If you bet he'd rummaged round the bar, Sally, I bet he'd have done the same in the changing rooms, once he was sure they were empty again. Out for what he could nick, if he was so in need of money, or what havoc he could wreak, especially in Dave's direction. That's what he's doing while Cooper's in the bar. Maybe Osment has a good nose around in all the nooks and crannies farthest from the door so can't hear that Cooper's turned up at last."

"And then what?" Pru asked. "Osment simply sits around, maybe down the internet worm hole again?"

"Rabbit hole. Get your animals right. Maybe he did just sit around. He had time to kill before his darts match, he couldn't go home and it would have been warmer—slightly, anyway—than wandering the streets and less depressing than sitting in a pub being *Billy no mates.* He might have gone back into the bar to avoid being seen. You could even lie down on one of the banquettes there and have a crafty kip. Cooper, meanwhile, has gone home, thinking that *he's* been stood up twice over. Weatherell's either too late arriving to cross paths with him or for some reason doesn't notice the car."

Pru rapped a happy tattoo on the desk where she was perched. "Then Cooper hears the news the next morning and suspects that his old colleague might have had something to do with the murder. No wonder he kept it all quiet if he thinks there's a risk what he knows makes him a potential target. He certainly seemed worried about it when we interviewed him."

"Yep. I know we're indulging in speculation, but it's not all that wild. Weatherell goes to see if anyone's still hanging around—maybe he's angry, too, because he thinks he's been called out on a wild-goose chase. He discovers the clubhouse door open and Osment lurking in there. Confronts him, wanting to know what evidence he has about the hit-and-run. Things get out of hand." Robin puffed out his cheeks. "I have no idea what weapon he could have used, though."

"Maybe he went and got something after he found the door unlocked and before going through it," Laurence said. "One of his tools?"

"Could be." Robin shrugged. "Okay, I want both Weatherell and Cooper called in here today for further questioning. Pru, can you get onto that because I want them at the same time."

Pru grinned. "And you want them both to know the other is being questioned?"

"You've read my mind. Then lean on the forensics people to see if there's anything else they can tell us about the weapon used other than it not being that golf club. Laurence, you're going to see Archie to find out if he's deaf as a post and whether he can tell a call taken at home from a call taken outside. Add to your list finding out whether he rang Weatherell out of the blue or if it was somehow agreed in advance."

"In order to get himself an alibi? Will do, sir." The constable jotted that down.

"Sally and Callum, I think we've still got those keys to the sports ground in the evidence room. Take them, get down there, and have a poke around. Fresh eyes, focussing on this new theory."

"Do you want us to look for the weapon, sir?" Callum asked.

"Keep your eyes open for anything that strikes you, although if there had been something screamingly obvious in plain view all along, then we should all get the sack for missing it." Robin first out of the door, because he'd been to the ground twice. "Unless, of course, it's a totally commonplace object that Weatherell took away, cleaned up, and slipped back into where it belonged once we'd done our search. Hiding it in plain sight. Apart from the weapon, there's another thing I had in mind. If Osment had the spare bunch of keys, did they ever leave the premises—like the phone, to be chucked away somewhere they've yet to be turned up—or did he either mislay them or deliberately discard them, given that they might have outlived their usefulness?"

"Hunt the keys it is, sir." Sally gave Callum a wink. "What if Weatherell's there and sees us?"

"That's all to the good, as far as I'm concerned. He could do with the wind put up him."

Pru agreed. "What with you nosing about and us wanting to see him, he might get in a panic and do the kind of stupid thing he's avoided doing so far."

"I think he already has done something stupid." Robin, was pleased to find he could still be a step ahead of his sergeant. "He should have left the body, made his way out through the bar, and left everything unlocked in his wake. We've been so focussed on thinking about how Osment got in that we've glided over how the killer got out. Must have had his own keys."

"Unless he used Osment's," Pru said. "So if we *do* find those on the premises, that'll be another piece of circumstantial evidence."

Assuming—big assumption—that this wasn't another red herring.

"Why would anyone be so daft?" Callum asked. "Panic?"

"No," Laurence said. "Remember my teacher who picked up the bunch of keys automatically? I can imagine Weatherell automatically locking everything up. Routine. If he was in a panic to start with, autopilot might have taken over."

Robin nodded. "Let's see whether we can panic him again, either in here or at the ground. If he is there, when you've done, see if you can find somewhere to watch him from that means he doesn't know he's being watched, all to the good."

Callum nodded. "I know exactly the place. My aunt's house backs onto the ground, and she'll let us watch from the back window. Grandstand view of . . . the grandstand, actually."

And with the corporate groan that produced, the briefing came to an end.

An hour later, just as Robin rose from his desk to get in a swift loo break before ringing Betteridge for the daily update, Sally rang.

"We've got the keys, sir. Or I should say we've got *a* set of keys, although they appear to match the set of four the barman lost. There's a grating in the room where they clean boots. I guess they use it to swill any mud and grass into, because the holes in it are pretty large. Large enough to accidentally drop a set of keys down, we thought. Callum tried to raise it but he cut himself, even through his gloves. Like Osment might have done. Remember the marks on his fingers?"

"I do indeed."

"So, I went and got Weatherell, who was out on the pitch fiddling about with some patch of mud that he was trying to regenerate. He was annoyed to be interrupted, but eventually he said you needed an implement for hoicking the drain cover up, because it's set pretty solid. I went with him while he fetched it from his workshop-cum-shed. It was easy enough to find the keys once we had the cover removed, because they'd got wedged in a bend. Callum watched him while I pulled them out—he reckons Weatherell seemed really unhappy about it all. And that was *before* I bagged the drain cover for testing, which he didn't like, either. Made a right fuss about risks of clogging the plumbing with no cover to catch the muck. Not that I think we'll find much if we test the thing, but the whole rigmarole probably unnerved him. He went back to poking his pitch but he wasn't happy."

"Good work. That implement he used wasn't made of steel with powder-coated paint, was it?"

"No such luck, sir. Appeared to be too thin to have made the wound on Osment's head. But we've got a cunning plan about that. Sorry, got to go."

With that intriguing comment, Sally ended the call. Robin dropped her a quick text saying that if this cunning plan involved putting either her or Callum at risk, they shouldn't be executing it. The equally mysterious reply—that the only risk initially involved was overfeeding themselves on Callum's aunt's almond cake—only reassured him up to a point. Still, he couldn't stifle initiative.

By the time he was about to have another loo break—prior to going down to the interview rooms, that fostering enterprise had paid off. Callum was reporting in this time.

"Hello, sir. Got an update. I spoke to my aunt about using her room to observe what went on and she was dead keen. You remember she used to run there, so she feels a vested interest in the place. Struck me that I should ask her how well she knew the clubhouse. She said thirty years ago it was like the back of her hand, although she's not been in there since a do they held a few years ago."

"And?" Robin, already tensed up at the prospect of the interviews, found his patience was wearing perilously thin.

"She reckoned there was a secret hidey-hole that some of the teenagers used to use, back in the Stone Age." Callum chuckled. "Hid their ciggies there so they could have a quick fag after training without either Mum or Dad or the coaches knowing. Osment could have known about it but—this is important—so could Tom Weatherell. Groundsmen know the ins and outs of everything."

"Assuming it's still in use." Robin held his rising excitement in check.

"It is. Because we've been back there and opened it. We made sure we followed the proper procedures and took plenty of pictures before and after." Callum sounded rightfully pleased with himself. "Even better, we've got a third-party witness of Weatherell's actions. My aunt kept an eye on him while we drove round to hers. Apparently, no sooner had our car left than he abandoned his muddy patch and legged it round to his workshop. By the time we were in our observation place, he was nowhere in sight, but Aunty reckons when he emerged he was carrying something. By the time he was back on the pitch again he didn't have it. There was nothing else to see—he simply tidied his stuff away and must have set off to the station."

With not enough time to go home in between. "You went back?"

"Yep. Almost had to sedate Aunty Charity to stop her coming with us, although I noticed her still watching from her window." Callum's throaty laugh was almost deafening. "Anyway, you go into what the rugby club uses as an away dressing room, and there's a big metal cabinet that's divided into lockers. At some point in the past, a false top's been put on. Great big length of plywood, covering over where the outside rim is higher than the internal roof of the cabinet itself. I'm not explaining this very well."

"Do you mean like the top of a fitted kitchen cupboard where you get a decorative ridge around it?"

"Yes, exactly that. Somebody's made that void into a hidey hole. You can't see it from eye level, and even when you get up on the bench it'd be easy to think that top's meant to be there. But when you prize it up—bingo."

"Pru's just come in—I'm putting you on the speaker." Robin held the phone between them. "Let's have the punch line."

"In there, along with a packet of fags and a porno mag, there was this metal . . . thing. Like an oversize version of the gun you'd use to put sealant round a bath."

"I know the sort."

"This one must be used for marking pitches. Sally's going to send some pictures over."

"Great. Then get it bagged up and brought in for testing." Even if the object had been cleaned and subsequently used for its proper purpose, removing and obscuring evidence, there was always a chance the forensic boffins would be able to extract some tiny but telling piece of proof. Although, Robin reminded himself, forensic evidence didn't play as big a part in real life as it did on the small screen.

"Horrible-looking thing, isn't it?" Pru said, once the call was ended and they had the pictures to hand.

"Yeah. I remember seeing a television show where a suspect used one of those sealant guns to keep the police at bay. From a distance it seemed like an automatic weapon. I wonder if Osment saw it and got the shock of his life."

"I can imagine Weatherell getting this from his shed before going into the clubhouse. As you say, it would scare an intruder—and be useful to keep someone at arm's length. You could swing it like a club too."

"I get the picture." Robin sighed. "God, the sheer nerve of it. I think he might have had this out when I went to the ground that second occasion. And even if we had done a proper sweep of everything at the ground, it would be difficult to prove he struck the blow, simply from fingerprints. He had legitimate reason to handle it all the time."

"Thank God for Callum's aunt."

"Amen to that."

The divide-and-conquer stratagem was one Robin had used successfully in the past. One suspect in one interview room, another down the corridor but making sure that they saw each other—or were made aware of the other's presence—before questioning started. Breaks to compare notes with the other interviewing team or alternating between rooms, whichever best seemed to suit the purpose. Sometimes the force with which one party tried to shove the other under a bus left them both beneath the wheels.

Cooper, beads of sweat on his brow, appeared the nervier of the two; Tom Weatherell having the same no-nonsense, steady air about him they'd already encountered. The rock of the family, as Joe had pointed out. He could be left to stew in his own juice for a while, to see if the experience might fluster him.

"Mr. Cooper." Robin slapped a fat file down on the desk in front of him. In truth, much of the content was meaningless padding, but it produced a formidable impression and had the desired effect when the suspect blanched on seeing it. They went through the formalities, then Robin said, "I believe you used to work alongside Tom Weatherell, when he was at Hepius."

"Yes." Cooper cast a glance at the duty solicitor, without getting a response. "Must be ten years ago, now. I'd not been with the company that long, doing my stint in sales before I got into marketing."

That matched what they'd been told. "Did you keep in contact?"

"No. We weren't big buddies."

"When did he get back in touch?" Pru asked.

"He didn't. We ran into each other." Cooper sat back in his chair, relaxing slightly. "A group of us from the Tuckton club had gone to lay a tribute at the site Jamie died. A rugby ball, which we felt was appropriate. Tom and his wife were there, we recognised each other and got chatting. Hardly the best of circumstances, but what can you do except the right thing, which is to pay your respects and avoid clichés."

That showed a surprising degree of sensitivity and perception. "Did he know you'd driven along there the night of the accident?"

"Yes, because I told him so. I said I wished I could have helped him find out what happened."

"Can I clarify that?" Robin leaned forwards. "Was he asking for information about the accident or did you offer your help out of the blue?"

Cooper wriggled uneasily in his chair. "A bit of both. His wife had gone off to chat to someone, and I wanted to explain that I'd not been to the police because I'd not seen anything. There was a yellow sign right next to us, appealing for witnesses, which kept tugging at my conscience. Tom started to pump me, not that there was anything to pump, so he gave up when his wife rejoined us."

"Did you keep in touch after that?" Robin asked.

"Not really. He invited me to the funeral—to represent the club, he said—but I had a minor op scheduled for that day so I had to give my apologies. Ashley Howarth went instead." The expression on Cooper's face showed how grateful he'd been to have a valid excuse not to attend.

"So, who contacted who about this meeting with Osment?"

Cooper flinched at Pru's question, the intercutting between the two clearly unnerving him. "I'm not sure what you mean."

"When Osment contacted you," Pru spoke slowly, as though addressing a child, "to arrange to meet you at the club, Weatherell was due to be there as well. Did you tell him about it?"

The stab in the dark worked. "Yes, I did, the week previous to the meeting. I felt he needed to know if there was new evidence about his son's death. He was absolutely furious that somebody would want to make money out of such a tragedy. He wanted to come along and see for himself, but I only agreed to that if he promised to keep calm. Which he did. Promise, I mean."

"He'd be backup for you too, in case Osment turned nasty," Robin cut in. "In our previous interview, you said that Osment was going to fit you up for the hit-and-run. Is that true?"

The suspect flicked a glance at his solicitor, whose face remained impassive. "It's true that I assumed the likeliest person in the frame would be me. But I knew Tom would believe me when I said that I hadn't done it. Or if I had done it, I wasn't aware of the fact because I'd been lied to about hitting a deer. Tom knows that I would never have knowingly left anyone to die without summoning help. You can ask anyone that about me."

"We will, if it comes to that." Robin made a note, more for show than purpose. "Why didn't you tell us any of this before?"

"Because none of it came to anything. Tom didn't even turn up on the night. I was supposed to get there around seven, but you know I got badly held up in the traffic. Tom was coming along later, in case his being there from the start made Osment reluctant to talk. As it turned out, I saw neither of them."

"You'd swear to that?" Pru asked.

"I would. I saw and heard nobody in that building, from the moment I parked up to the moment I left. Ever since then I've been wondering if I was there at the same time as the killer, and how close a call I might have had."

Robin's turn. "Who do you think the killer was, that you so narrowly avoided?"

"Eh? How do I know?"

"Mr. Cooper, you're not stupid. You must have had a guess at what went on." Robin waited for a response; when none came except Cooper shifting in his seat uncomfortably, he said, "We need an answer. Did you suspect anyone?"

Cooper slumped in his chair. "Yes. I suspected Tom. Is that what you wanted me to say?"

"I want you to tell me the truth. Nothing more and nothing less. So, I ask you again. Did you suspect anyone and why?"

"The truth is that I couldn't get the notion out of my head that Tom might have got there early, encountered Osment, and then got into a fight with him. Maybe because Osment wouldn't share what evidence he had." He glanced at the solicitor, who nodded. "I was scared, so I didn't respond to the appeal for information."

"The thing is, Mr. Cooper, that Weatherell didn't get to the ground until later than you did." Robin tapped the file. "Those traffic cameras that picked you up caught him too. What they haven't shown is you leaving the ground when you said you did."

"That's because I went a different route. I couldn't be sure the accident had been cleared up, so I got my satnav to take me on the back roads."

"Are you certain of that? Sounds a good way to cover up your being at the ground and confronting Osment."

"I had nothing to do with his death." The force of Cooper's assertion seemed to carry a weight of veracity, although Robin had heard similar pleas of innocence from the guiltiest of suspects.

"Then persuade us that's the case by giving us some help," Robin pleaded. "You suspected Tom Weatherell. Was it only that?"

"I . . . I don't know." Cooper, head wagging, turned to his solicitor. "I swear to God, I didn't see him on that night—I didn't see either of them."

"And since then," Robin pressed. "Has he been in touch?"

"No, and I've been damned grateful for the fact." Cooper raised his right hand, palm outwards. "You can put me on oath and I'll say the same. I've turned things over in my brain ever since, but I honestly don't know what else I can tell you."

"I think I believe him, sir," Pru said, as they emerged from the interview room. "He's been riding his luck, hoping we wouldn't turn any of this up. Then he wouldn't have had to face the fact his old mate might be a killer."

"Yeah. Let's face that old mate and see where we get."

Weatherell had refused a solicitor's presence, despite repeated offers. He'd asserted that he had nothing to hide and—going on outward appearances—that could convincingly be the case. A good actor having recovered his composure following the encounter with the constables, or an innocent man with the police having backed the wrong horse? Maybe something else entirely that was outside Robin's ability to read on first impressions. Best to cut straight to the nub of the matter and let the answers guide them.

Once the proper rigmarole of setting up the recording had been gone through, Robin stated, "We want to talk to you about the evening Nick Osment was killed. He'd arranged to meet Colin Cooper at the Hartwood club."

"I believe so." The calm response was followed by silence.

"It's more than *believe*, though, isn't it?" Pru asked. "Cooper contacted you about the meeting."

Weatherell nodded. "What can I say? Yes, he did. We used to work with each other, years ago, but I suppose you know that too. I'd not seen him for years until he turned up after Jamie was killed. At the informal memorial people set up on the spot. I knew Colin played rugby, but I had no idea it was for Tuckton."

"Did you go to Jamie's last game?" Robin had chosen the words to be insensitive and provoke a reaction: they had the desired effect.

"No, we didn't. I've regretted it every day of my life since." Weatherell leaned his elbows on the table, head in hands. "If we'd been there, we'd have brought him home with us. He'd be alive today, and maybe his mother would, as well."

"That's understandable. The guilt of those left behind." Pru spoke kindly, seeking for a rapport with the witness. "Why weren't you there?"

"We got invited to a wedding. One of Lulu—my wife Louise's—friends. We got the call about Jamie at the evening do." Weatherell rubbed his forehead. "We'd had such a lovely time and then suddenly it turned into the worst day of my life. Can you imagine what that's like?"

"I can imagine, yes, although I'm sure I wouldn't get anywhere near what you've experienced." Robin had every sympathy for someone finding themselves in such a life-changing situation, but that compassion couldn't blind him to what had happened to Osment. He also had a father to whom he'd been close, who'd been devastated by his death. "You must have felt angry. Did you want to punish the culprit?"

"You bet I did. Wouldn't anyone? It was only Lu—Louise making me see sense that stopped me going on an all-out campaign to find whoever it was, especially when your lot were getting nowhere." He looked Robin in the eye. "I had to find closure. Not just about the hit-and-run, but about my own guilt. The fact I could have saved Jamie if I'd been at the game and driven him home. I got some professional help—I was dubious about that but my wife insisted—and it worked. Young Joe could have done with it too," he added, with a shake of his head. "He told me you'd been asking about his wobble."

"I'd hardly call assaulting your partner a wobble." The sympathy was starting to wane. "When your wife died, did your thirst for vengeance come to the surface again?"

"You don't miss anything, do you? Yes, it did, but I went to see the same counsellor another time, and he helped me get back on an even keel. Joe can confirm that."

"We'll ask him. Hearing that Osment wanted to see Cooper about the night your son died must have rocked your keel completely off-balance for a third time," Pru said, then waited for a response.

"It certainly took me by surprise." The cautious response gave no elaboration.

"Cooper asked you to go along to the meeting, with him?" she asked.

"He did."

Still the clipped answers. Robin couldn't get a grasp on what the suspect's stance would turn out to be.

"As a result of that request, you went along." Before Weatherell could comment, Pru pressed on. "We know that because we've caught your car on the local traffic cameras."

"Then you'll have the time I was seen by them, which would prove that at the point I got there, Colin had gone. If he was ever there in the first place." A combative note appeared amongst the air of caution.

"Oh no, he'd been there all right. He's told us all about it. Let's have your version." Robin, sitting back in his chair with arms crossed, smiled and waited.

"Nothing much to tell. I got to the car park, walked up to the clubhouse, found that nobody was around. I wasn't going to leave the place unsecured, so I locked up and left. You'll have a record of me heading back on your traffic camera, I assume?" The suspect must have registered the fact that neither Robin nor Pru jumped straight in with a confirmation of time and place. It was written in the relief flooding over his face. "Then you'll know I didn't stay long. I went home to watch the football."

Robin, determined not to let Weatherell gain the advantage, calmly said, "The same football you told us you were about to watch at home when your pal Archie's call came? Why did you lie to us about that?"

Weatherell spread his hands again. "Because I'm an idiot. I didn't want you to know I'd been at the ground. I never thought you'd be any the wiser. Archie always rings me on the landline, and I'm not sure if he realises it rolls over to my mobile sometimes. Poor old bugger's a touch deaf, so he wouldn't have known if I was at home or up the Eiffel Tower. I had the car radio on, so he'd have probably thought that was the telly."

All very convenient and believable, although bordering on overexplanation. Still, they had other evidence they could use to better effect. "So, you ended the call, then went to find Cooper. What next?"

"Like I said, I secured the site and went home."

Time for bluff-calling. "Only you didn't. You knew you had to meet him—and Osment as well—in the clubhouse. So when you found the door open, you went in."

Weatherell flicked a glance at the file Robin had in front of him, maybe thinking it held additional evidence of his presence. The bluff had worked. "Yes, I went in. The bar area was empty. I know because I shone around the torch on my phone to check."

"And that's when you spotted the cracked photo frame?" Robin asked. "The one Osment broke."

"No," the suspect bridled. "I promise you, I didn't see that until the day I showed you around the club. If I had found it that night and knew who'd done it, I'd have been fuming."

"Like you were fuming with Osment for having information about your son's death and trying to profit financially from it?"

That hit home. "Yes, Mr. Bright, I admit that I was very angry when I heard about that, but Colin calmed me down. Anyway, all this is irrelevant, as I never saw the young scrote. Although if I'd known it was him I encountered on the previous Saturday, he'd have got more than a kick in the arse. If he had evidence about what happened that night, he should have shared it long ago."

Such a strange mixture of honesty and dissembling, as though he was willing to admit only what Robin could prove—or what Weatherell believed Robin could prove—and nothing else. It also sounded as though he had not suspected Osment was the driver up to the fatal evening—understandable if those around him hadn't wanted to speculate about the accident in his presence.

Did this add up to a basically honest man caught up in a situation he'd never wanted to be in, overtaken by events and hoping against hope he'd get away with it?

A loud rap at the door made Weatherell glance up sharply, betraying his first real sign of nervousness. Presumably, this was one of the constables reporting back, and while Robin would usually be fuming and demanding the interruption prove worthwhile, in this instance it already appeared to be working in their favour. Like the thick file had unnerved Cooper, despite its contents being unknown to him, any conversation outside the room where Weatherell was being interviewed would produce an unsettling effect.

"Thought you might like to know this, sir," Laurence said, once Robin had stepped into the corridor. "Archie Spenser—the bloke who rang Weatherell—says he assumed the call was answered at home because he thought that's where Weatherell said he was but *now he comes to think of it*"—the constable rolled his eyes—"it could have rolled over to a mobile and what he took as noise from the telly might have been something else. He says he was too wrapped up in his own thoughts to notice."

"Okay." That didn't seem enough to warrant interrupting an interview, though. "Unfortunately we've already established that. Did Archie ring of his own accord or was it prearranged?"

"Own accord. Said he felt down in the dumps. He did add that Weatherell seemed a bit worked up when they spoke. Wanted to end the call."

Robin nodded. Verification of what they knew but still nothing fresh.

"Another thing," Laurence said. "Archie says that when they met for that drink—which is what the phone call was about in the first place—Weatherell was in a dark mood and knocked back too much. Archie drove him home, and at one point Weatherell muttered something about Lulu never being able to forgive him, now. I have no idea who Lulu was and I didn't have the chance to ask, because Archie's boss came along and had to talk to him urgently. I feel a right twit for not following that up."

"For once I'll let you off." Especially as that was another small weapon to put in the armoury.

Once back in the room, trying to appear secretly pleased, Robin got Pru to recommence the interview, then said, "Back to the night in question. You entered the clubhouse. Are you saying that you simply took a cursory look around and then left? After all the issues you've had at the ground with vandalism and theft?"

"The check I made was more than cursory." The words might have been glib, but the suspect appeared rattled. Had he caught any of the discussion with Laurence? "However, the rugby team were there that night—nobody would have chanced their arm at causing damage with them around."

"But Osment did. He went poking around with his freshly cut set of keys, in the certain knowledge that Derek Preese doesn't routinely let anyone off the pitch once training has started. As you'll know from watching the Wednesday sessions," Robin added. "You saw my officers retrieve those keys from the boot room earlier today, didn't you?"

"Is that what they were?" Weatherell shrugged, although it seemed a carefully careless gesture. "Your constables were being extremely secretive about what they were doing. I suppose it comes with the job."

"You were being mysterious too, after they left," Pru cut in. "We have a witness who says you were acting suspiciously. You took something from your shed, then went and hid it."

All colour drained from the suspect's face, but he rallied to say, "What witness? What are you talking about?"

Pru ignored the protest. "What were you hiding this afternoon?" When no reply came, she took a photo from the file and passed it across the desk. "I'm showing the suspect a photograph of what appears to be a line-marking device. Do you use this at the ground?"

"One much like it, yes." Weatherell, who'd picked up the photo, quickly laid it down, perhaps to hide the fact his hands were trembling.

"This was found hidden in one of the dressing rooms at the ground. We believe you put it there earlier today." When Weatherell didn't reply to that either, she asked, "Did you hide it there? An answer for the tape, please."

"Yes, yes, I did. It's another example of me being an idiot. I found it at the ground on the Thursday morning, and I panicked because of what had happened the night before."

Robin pounced. "What *had* happened?"

He anticipated hearing the classic *I know there must be forensics that I need to explain away, but why not divert attention from me and throw my mate under the bus while I'm at it* type of answer. Something along the lines of, *I thought Colin might have used it to attack Osment, and I didn't want him getting into trouble.*

But Weatherell wasn't following the usual line that suspects took. "Somebody could have used the aeroliner—that's the pitch tool in the photo—to commit the murder. On the spur of the moment I decided they might have had good reason to kill Osment and what if I muddied the waters? I took the pitch marker home and gave it a cleanup."

Again, telling enough of the truth not to be caught out. Still, he'd made a major mistake. "The entire ground remained shut for anything but police access on Thursday. The uniformed officer at the gate turned several people away." Robin consulted the list towards the top of his bundle of papers. "Including you."

Weatherell sighed. "Yes, I admit, including me."

"I think," Pru said, sympathetically, "we'd better go back to the Wednesday evening. What really happened?"

"When I found the door to the clubhouse was unlocked, with no sign of Colin outside, I decided to check the place over, exactly as I told you. But I didn't fancy going in there without something to defend myself with. What if I'd been set up and one or both of them—Colin and Osment—were waiting for me? I decided to slip into the shed, where I saw the aeroliner. I thought that it might appear to be a gun from a distance and put anybody off attacking me. If that didn't work, it would be long enough and heavy enough to fend someone off with."

"Or whack them over the head." Robin delved in the file again. "I'm showing the suspect a picture of the dead man, Nick Osment."

Weatherell winced at the photo, then turned his head away. "That's horrible."

"Yes, it is." Robin left the picture on display. "The medical and forensic evidence suggests that he hit his head on the corner of a bench, perhaps accidentally in the act of trying to get away from his assailant. Away from you." When the suspect didn't comment, he continued. "Tell us what happened. Everything this time, not simply the parts you think we can prove at the moment, because—believe me—we won't let this alone, even if that means tearing the Hartwood club apart brick by brick to find the evidence we need. We'll include your house in that, as well. One of my constables is getting warrants right now."

Still the silence, as Weatherell clearly wrestled with a deep dilemma.

If pressure didn't work, perhaps persuasion might. "Your pal Archie. He's been a good mate to you. He understands what it's been like. He knows Louise would have wanted you to be honest."

"Yes, she would. She deserves it." Weatherell sat up straighter in his chair and smoothed back his hair. "When I went in the clubhouse and found it empty, I suspected someone was arsing me about, and needed to check the rest of the place. When I found the door through to the changing room had been unbolted and unlocked, I decided I wasn't going in there unarmed. I went to get the aeroliner and some other things."

"What other things?"

Weatherell shrugged. "A plastic bag and a handful of rags. I thought I might need them too. You have no idea some of the filth I had to clear up when vandals have been visiting in the past. I collected them, then returned to the clubhouse and when I opened the interconnecting door, I could hear swearing coming from the boot room. Osment was in there."

"How did you know it was Osment?" Pru asked. "Had you met him before?"

"I didn't know at first, although I guessed, given that it wasn't Cooper. I clearly knew by the time the news broke the next day."

"Go on," Robin said.

"Osment was trying to get the drain cover off. I assumed it was an act of vandalism, because Cooper hadn't turned up, so I swore at him and told him to stop. He leaped up and barrelled into me, then headed off through the changing room." Weatherell rubbed his forehead. "I swear I didn't touch him, he just slipped on the black plastic bag on the floor. It must have fallen from my pocket when I came through. He cracked his head against the bench, exactly as you said and was out for the count. He'd dropped his phone."

"Yes?"

"It was unlocked where he'd been using it as a torch. I picked it up and saw there was a photo album open. I shouldn't have looked at it but I was curious about what he had to show Cooper. I noticed the label on the folder. The date Jamie died."

"What was in it?" Robin asked gently.

"A series of pictures. I— May I have a glass of water?"

Robin poured a glass from the jug on the table. He passed it across to the suspect. "When you're ready, Tom."

After a long drink, the groundsman said, "I saw the times on the pictures, the familiar road signs. I know that stretch like the back of my hand by now. I thought, 'he was there the night Jamie died.' Then I saw the photo of my Jamie with his bike. If Osment saw him trying to fix the tyre, why hadn't he helped? There might have been no accident, in that case." He took another draught of water. "That picture was the last insult. The last photo ever taken of him and it was this bastard who'd been keeping it, not me. Then he came round."

Robin waited while Weatherell took another drink. "Go on. He came round?"

"Yes, and he wanted the phone back. That's all he cared about. No mention of Jamie or any apology for taking the pictures, just him saying I had no right to touch his phone. I got angrier and angrier."

"What did you do?"

"I asked him what he'd been playing at, that night Jamie died. He told me to eff off." Another sip of water. "He got to his feet, lunged at me, but I dodged him. I said he wasn't getting his hands on the phone until I had an explanation."

"Did you get one?" Pru asked.

"No. He just sneered at me. Said if I'd been there that night, I would have seen what happened. That was the last straw." Weatherell pushed away his glass, then stuck his head in his hands. "I must have hit him. I don't remember, honestly, except that I came to and found myself with the aeroliner in my hand and him dead. I checked his pulse and he was gone, I swear to God. I dragged him into the toilets, because I couldn't bear to be around the body. Then I tidied up. There wasn't much mess because he'd slipped and his head was lying on the bag. Stroke of luck for me, given that I heard sirens at that point. I left everything and hid in the bar."

So luck—bad for Osment and fortunate for his killer—*had* played its part, time and again. Still, the clothes Weatherell had worn that night should tell as much of a tale as the murder weapon would, assuming he'd not got rid of them.

"Then what?"

"As I said several times, I locked up and went home. It was too chaotic out there for anyone to notice me. Persuaded myself I'd done the right thing by Jamie. Been in the right place at the right time, like he'd been in the wrong one."

"What did you do with Osment's phone afterwards?" Pru asked.

"I was going to keep it, so I had the snap of Jamie, but I couldn't. I stopped on the way home and slung it into a front garden. If I'd been thinking logically, I'd have taken it somewhere and smashed it into smithereens with a hammer. Trouble was I couldn't bear having the thing with me. Lulu always said I hadn't got enough common sense to fill an egg cup." Weatherell screwed his eyes shut, obviously fighting back tears. "She was right. The last few weeks have shown that. But I thought that maybe I'd been lucky, rather than smart. I should have known I couldn't get away with it much longer."

In other circumstances, Robin might have made a barbed response, but this didn't feel like the time and place.

"I'd like to show you something." Weatherell, eyes dewy, reached into his trouser pocket, brought out his wallet, then opened it to reveal a small, much-folded piece of paper he kept inside a small plastic case. This he took out and spread carefully so they could see it. Written in ink pen, faded and crumpled, the words were barely legible.

Sorry. I didn't realise.

"Where did you find this?"

"With the flowers left at the site of Jamie's murder." Interesting that Weatherell chose to use that word at this point. "I've kept it with me ever since. It must be from the driver, either saying they didn't realise they'd hit him or that if they'd stopped and rung for help they could have saved him. Only Osment didn't appear to be in any way sorry for what he'd done."

"I have to take that for evidence, I'm afraid. Please, could you put it back into the case?" Robin held out his hand. "You won't want to hear this, Tom, but there might be a good reason Osment wasn't sorry. We doubt he was the person who killed your son."

"No!" Weatherell slammed the table. "No. That can't . . ." He slumped into his chair, face ashen, muttering, "That can't be true. Lulu would never forgive me. It can't be."

Robin and Pru shared a glance: this job stank at times.

The evening post-choir-practice phone call from Robin—immaculately timed just as Campbell had gone into the garden for his final toilet visit of the day—turned out to be the one Adam had been longing to receive.

"We think we've got this Hartwood case sorted," he said, as soon as the initial small talk was done. "We need a couple of days to finalise everything and tie up a loose end or two, but I should be home this weekend."

Adam, feeling tears threatening to well up, took a deep breath. "That's the best news I've had in a long time."

"Yeah. Want the story?"

"Bare bones. You can give me the detail when you're back." Adam listened to a brief account of the solution—two solutions—that Robin's team had managed to work out. When Robin at last paused, he said, "I *do* need to hear the whole of that. Like something out of a book, choosing the wrong victim."

"It's certainly felt weird at times." Robin dropped his voice. "Anticipating being with you in our house. Then it'll be like I'm back in the real world."

"I can't wait, mate." Adam yawned. "Sorry. Been a long day."

"Yeah, I get that. I'm bleeding knackered as well. Before I fall into my bed, I want to say how much I've really appreciated your patience on this one. It's not been easy for either of us."

"That's what you get when you marry a rozzer, having to play the support card at times. I'll be glad when you're home and can do the same for me."

"I'll be glad to." Robin hesitated. "You've not got Ofsted coming in, have you?"

"Worse than that. This concert. The nearer *it* gets the jumpier *I* get. I had a real panic this evening at the latest practice, simply imagining being on stage. Stupid, isn't it?" The little knot of fear formed in Adam's stomach again. "Part of me feels like wimping out. Part of me says that if one of my pupils pulled that stunt, they'd be getting a talking to."

"*You'll* be getting a talking to." Despite the joke, Robin's voice betrayed his concern. "From my mum, for one. She's been messaging me saying she's almost as excited for the performance as she was for the wedding. She also wants a copy of the CD. When does your choir's track for that get recorded, by the way?"

"Next rehearsal. Some tech guru mate of Martin's is coming along. Phil something or other. He's done recordings for weddings, and he reckons he understands the church acoustics." Adam sniffed. "I'm not worried about that. Apart from Campbell disgracing himself and joining in."

"Hey, try not to worry about the concert," Robin said, soothingly. "You'll be fine. I know that sounds like the worst sort of cliché, but you will. I'll be there to have your back, and even if a mass murderer strikes that day, I'll refuse to let them call me in. They can sack me first."

"You big wazzock." Cliché or not, the comforting words had helped.

"And how are love's young dreams? Sam and Martin, I mean."

"Well, I knew you didn't mean me and Campbell." A happier recollection of the evening's rehearsal were the glances the two had shared. "The air's been cleared, it seems. Martin must have had a better sense of humour than I gave him credit for. He came up to me at the end of practice, at which point I was dreading some fresh revelation, but he simply wanted to thank me for talking some sense into Sam. Happy ending on that front, at least for the moment."

"Maybe they'll want you and the rest of the choir to sing at their wedding. Joke," Robin added, hastily.

"It had better be." Adam caught the yawning bug. "I've got to go and crash out. Love you."

"Love you too."

As the call ended, Adam brought the dog back indoors. "Good news, boy. Your other dad's coming home soon."

Campbell, in a move that was completely out of character, jumped up to lick Adam's chin.

"Save that for him, you daft beggar."

Adam would be doing the same.

Chapter Nineteen

The Wednesday afternoon briefing had Superintendent Betteridge in attendance. Despite appearing pretty tired from the drugs case, she was bright-eyed enough. She had some leave due, but was reluctant to take it until all the details of the murder case were with the Crown Prosecution Service and Robertson was being eased back into work.

Betteridge confessed to Robin before the briefing that the prospect of being away from the station didn't grab her. "When you're up to your arse in work, you think that a break would be great, but I'd get frustrated at being out of the loop, even if you stayed and I knew everything would be in safe hands. Talking of which, I'd like to have a word afterwards."

The team greeted her with genuine enthusiasm: Robin let them take her through the process that had taken them to arresting Weatherell. She gave the right amount of praise for what had been achieved and challenge for the robustness of the evidence accumulated so far and that in the pipeline. There was plenty still to be done in terms of fortifying the case—confessions could be rescinded and a guilty plea changed—but that could be left in the hands of the Hartwood officers who had their list of jobs to work through. For Robin and Pru, home was calling.

"You don't feel like delivering me a result on the hit-and-run while you're at it?" Betteridge asked, at the end of the briefing.

Robin grinned at his team. "We might surprise you, and not just along the lines of that series of photos. Osment worked for a phone company, so I've had Callum doing some digging there, while Laurence handled the other end of things. Want to update us, Laurence?"

"Dave has previous for using his mobile at the wheel," Laurence said. "Sergeant Davis got an order to access his phone records for the night Jamie was killed."

"You're thinking he may have been texting and lost control of his vehicle?" Betteridge asked.

"Something like that. There's a text went through—responding to one of Melanie's—at around the right time and from the right area. We also found a link between the supplier Dave uses and the mobile phone company Osment worked for." Laurence jerked his thumb towards Callum for him to take up the tale.

"We'd been wondering what proof Osment might have had. I asked myself what if he'd been able to poke around in the phone records himself and compared what he found to the time stamps on the photos of Dave's car? It seems he had. They got me into his computer, and I had a hunt through his files. I've downloaded what we need." Callum waggled a memory stick. "That's why nothing turned up on his home devices."

"That's a start," Betteridge said. "However, we'll need stronger evidence than this to get a conviction through, including any forensics we can get off that note. And there are still some things that don't entirely make sense. Like the whole business with the so-called stolen car."

"If I were a gambling man, I'd have ten quid on that situation being exactly what it was supposed to be. Nicked. He had a habit of leaving stuff on view and he paid for it. In more ways than one." Robin took one final look at the victim's picture still displayed on the incident board. "People always expect a link between events rather than nothing other than a chance of fate."

"I'll accept that as a possibility." Betteridge tapped her teeth with a biro. "Although he still might have wanted the car nicked if he suspected Dave might have seen it on the night in question and wanted to muddy the waters of who was driving. Park on the road, leave some valuables in full view, see what happens. I guess we'll never know for sure. Like we'll never know why Osment would have made such a fuss over the fundraising that went on after the accident."

Robin shrugged. "I'd have another tenner on it being a further dig at Dave. He was involved in the campaign following Jamie's death, and if Osment knew he was doing that while possibly being the person actually responsible, I can imagine he'd have wanted to stir up shite. Perhaps he hoped in some way that it would point the finger at his rival."

Betteridge chuckled. "Isn't that rather abstruse?"

"Is it? Haven't you ever been around someone who's in a mood with you? And when you ask them what's wrong, they simply say, 'If you don't know, I'm not telling you.'" Adam didn't do that, thank God, but the previous boyfriend had and it had driven Robin to distraction. "They think you'll work it out from obscure hints."

"I'm not sure if I buy that, although I'll bear it in mind. We've got a new direction to take, which is a start. Yes, Sally?"

"Well, ma'am, I'd like to pursue this with Dawn. If Dave did it, given that he's so thick with Melanie, I bet he's said something about it. Something that rang no alarm bells at the time, but which could make sense now?"

"You do that. I'm all for cracking cold cases and while you're fresh off this result, let's keep the momentum going." The superintendent turned to Robin. "You don't fancy staying on and seeing this one through, as well?"

Without a moment's hesitation, Robin said, "Thank you, but no thank you. As they say, my work here is done."

The work hadn't quite been done at that point, although there wasn't much to finish off. Pru and Robin debated whether to have another night in Hartwood or drive home late that evening, but the decision was made for them when a major fuel spill shut the motorway at the point the rush hour started. The time it would take to resurface and reopen the road meant gridlock on all the local rat runs, so they opted for setting out at silly o-clock the next day.

As they sat over a well-earned pizza and a couple of beers, Pru said, "We should have got onto Dave earlier, sir. He had a fountain pen on his desk that first time we interviewed him."

"Seems like everyone else had a fountain pen, so don't beat yourself up. Real life isn't like a mystery book where some tiny clue solves the whole thing, and anyway we didn't have the original note to compare it with at the time." Robin raised his glass to chink against his sergeant's. "Home."

"Isn't the toast 'Home and beauty,' sir?"

"That as well."

And Robin had the two most beautiful creatures in the universe—in his admittedly biased opinion—waiting for him.

As Adam pulled into his road on Thursday evening, the sight of Robin's car parked outside the house made him as excited as a child seeing their stocking on Christmas morning. Household back on an even keel.

He was no sooner through the front door, with a cheery shout of "Hello, wanderer!" than he found himself engulfed in Robin's arms, swiftly followed by Campbell joining in the family hug.

When they'd disentangled themselves, Robin said, "I've got dinner cooking and there's beer in the fridge. Whenever you're ready for it."

"My hero." Adam gave him a kiss. "I had the kids for PE today, so I'm going to change before I stink the house out. After that, feed me till I want no more." A flick on his backside from the tea towel which had been draped over Robin's shoulder accompanied Adam up the stairs. Yep, life getting back to normal.

Dinner—one of Robin's excellent stir-fries—eaten at the breakfast bar and with a cold lager to accompany it, tasted better than a meal at the Ritz. He'd given Adam a blow-by-blow account of the case-which-had-turned-out-to-be-two-cases, then laid down his cutlery, face suddenly serious.

"Rukshana wants me to relocate to her area. Lick the Hartwood team into shape."

"Oh." Was that one of the reasons behind this evening's dinner: buttering him up to get the right answer? "Is that what you want to do?"

Adam braced himself for the answer. He'd always known this decision might come up, that one of them might have to make a sacrifice for the other in terms of career development. His profession probably gave them flexibility in terms of relocation, as there were always opportunities for good teachers and school leaders, wherever in the country they ended up.

"Not particularly. Not now, anyway." The wave of relief Adam felt must have been written on his face, as Robin continued, "That much of a reprieve, is it?"

"That obvious?" Adam took Robin's hand. "Hey, if you're saying no simply on my account, you don't need to. We can make relocation work."

"I know, and I appreciate it. But I've had enough of sorting out other people's messes for the moment."

"Okay, but let me say this. If we had to move in order for you to get promotion, it wouldn't be a problem."

Robin grinned. "It might not come to that. When I was back on my fleeting visit here, Cowdrey dropped a hint or two that he's ready for retirement. May be on the early side for me to get his job, but if they draft in a whizz kid who only stays a year or so, things could turn out perfectly."

In a year or so Adam could be thinking about his first headship, or at least being head of school in a confederation under some executive headteacher from whom he could learn a ton of skills. By then they'd have completed their long-planned house move too, so they hopefully wouldn't be tackling too many changes at once.

"What will you tell Rukshana? She won't be happy."

"No, she won't, but I've got a crafty plan. Stuart Anderson could do with a change of scenery, I hear. Helen wants to move into a bigger house and has been bemoaning the stupid property prices around here. Hartwood's a lot cheaper." Robin snickered. "I'll give Rukshana the lowdown on him, tell her I took him under my wing like she took me under hers and recommend that she gives him a whirl. Cowdrey will put in a positive word too."

"Excellent. It'll do Stuart the power of good." Robin's old sergeant had matured a lot over the last few years, due to a combination of following his boss's example, being given some responsibility of his own and, on the personal front, becoming a father. Adam raised his beer glass. "Here's to a quiet— No, I won't say it. We tempted fate before and look what happened. I need you on routine cases at least until this bloody concert is done with."

"We'll drink to the concert, then." Robin chinked his glass against Adam's. "To a clear voice, no laryngitis, and no stage fright."

Epilogue

Adam took a deep breath. He shouldn't be feeling like this: he'd stood in front of a hall full of children time and again—and their parents too—without blinking an eyelid, even on the occasions he'd been addressing them all on a controversial topic, prepared for a ton of flak. He wouldn't be on his own tonight, he'd not even be in the front row of the choir, and the audience was bound to be far more receptive, so why was he in such a state?

Because this is the first time you've been performing with Robin in the audience. Remember what it was like at school when you were five and took the part of the innkeeper in the nativity play? Both your parents and gran were in the audience?

He'd nearly wee'ed himself with nerves back then. And while there was no risk of him disgracing himself in the toilet department tonight, that sickening attack of butterflies—great big ones wearing hobnail boots—jiving about in his stomach was almost as debilitating. He missed having Campbell hovering around somewhere, providing his calming presence as he'd done at rehearsals. The dog had become a talisman for the choir, although they couldn't have him either backstage or front of house this time. Instead, they'd got a picture of him on one of the music stands to bring them luck, but it wasn't the same.

Bugger. Martin was briefing the choir from on top of a convenient box placed in the wings, and Adam had missed whatever the first bit of the team talk had been.

"—you're feeling nervous, that's natural. Remember, the first song's been chosen to let us get our voices up to speed, so if your throat's feeling tight, don't worry. It'll soon loosen. And if you're still worried after that, just imagine the audience sitting there in their old baggy y-fronts. That'll soon calm you down."

Robin in y-fronts, even baggy ones, was hardly the kind of mental image to calm anyone down, although one ray of sunshine was that Martin was unlikely to have *him* in mind anymore. Things on the Sam front appeared to be still going along swimmingly, if the continued shared smiles and little glances were anything to go by. Ah, the heady days of new fledged attraction, the sighs and pauses when together, the mental testing of whether what one person meant was what the other did, and the agony of being apart even for a day.

You can stuff that. I'm glad that's all long past me.

Martin was making what appeared to be the final announcement, given that the music track that served as an overture was coming to an end. "Everyone wants this to be a success, audience included. They're not going to be looking for any little mistake. Come on. Let's do this." He jerked his thumb towards the stage and they began to file on, to enthusiastic applause.

What seemed like fifteen minutes later but was actually an hour of choral and instrumental items, the first half came to an end, to thunderous clapping. Adam, who'd been scanning the audience whenever he could, hadn't been able to spot Robin, nor either of their mothers. All three had to be there, no doubt ramping up the volume of the applause. Suddenly, a loud whistle from the audience caught everyone's attention. There was Mrs. Bright in the middle of a row, fingers in mouth, producing the sort of ear-piercing noise Adam had never been able to manage. There was Robin, seated between her and Adam's mum, wearing a proud-as-punch expression. Adam's heart leaped at the sight. He'd not let down the team—choir or family—at all.

Robin appeared to be egging Mrs. Bright on to do her whistle again, much to the amusement of the young men they were sitting amongst. By the expression on his own mother's face, she was struggling with whether to be appalled or amused. Maybe when she'd got a glass of interval wine inside her she'd be giving it a try herself.

Adam could have done with a stiffener himself but made do with water to cool and lubricate the vocal chords.

The second half commenced with some of the solo acts, then the choir returned for a final set, after which—following prolonged, rapturous applause and a whole series of whistles not only from Mrs. Bright but those sitting around her—they returned for their encore. A wholehearted rendition of "All that Jazz," with jazz hands and jazzy hats, brought proceedings to an end. The applause was still audible as the choir made its way to the deepest regions backstage.

"You were brilliant." Martin, on the verge of tears, could barely get his words out. "We've raised a higher total than expected, with the CD sales still to add on. People have been asking about a copy of the music from this concert, so after we've had another encore, can we arrange a date to get together? I'd like to make a high-quality recording of our entire set, not solely the tracks for the main CD. We've been offered the use of a proper recording studio the other side of Kinechester, if that's an incentive."

"No incentive needed for me." Adam wasn't sure if he spoke for all the choir, but his views must have been fairly representative, given the chorus of approval. "I'm going to miss this. Maybe we should get together once a month for an informal session. Or whatever."

Another hum of endorsement and offers of finding locations to host the group broke out, at which Martin's tears really did start to flow. "You lot. You're great."

Sam came over, put his arm round the choirmaster's shoulders, then kissed the top of his head. "Well done, mate. What about three cheers for Martin, lads?"

Adam naturally led the *hip hips* and joined in loudly with the *hoorays.* He caught Robin's eye, getting a huge thumbs-up for him alone, and returning it with a blown kiss. The evening had been bloody brilliant, and Robin had been absolutely right, as usual. Only Adam wasn't going to admit that if he could possibly help it. Prospective detective superintendents didn't need any further encouragement at the moment.

Explore more of
The Lindenshaw Mysteries series:
riptidepublishing.com/collections/lindenshaw-mysteries

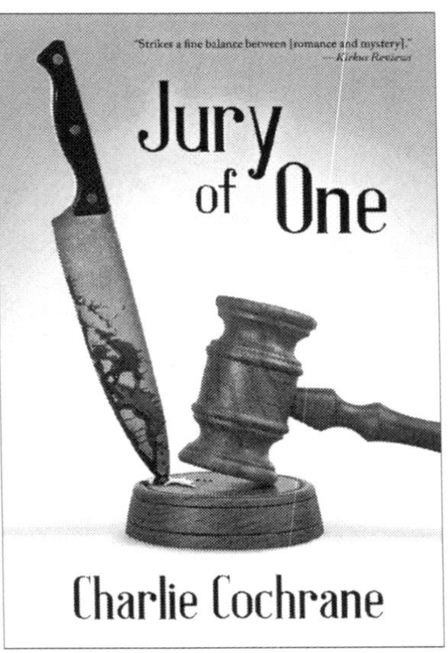

Dear Reader,

Thank you for reading Charlie Cochrane's *A Carriage of Misjustice*!

We know your time is precious and you have many, many entertainment options, so it means a lot that you've chosen to spend your time reading. We really hope you enjoyed it.

We'd be honored if you'd consider posting a review—good or bad—on sites like **Amazon, Barnes & Noble, Kobo, Goodreads, Twitter, Facebook**, **Tumblr,** and your blog or website. We'd also be honored if you told your friends and family about this book. Word of mouth is a book's lifeblood!

For more information on upcoming releases, author interviews, blog tours, contests, giveaways, and more, please sign up for our weekly, spam-free newsletter and visit us around the web:

Newsletter: riptidepublishing.com/newsletter
Twitter: twitter.com/RiptideBooks
Facebook: facebook.com/RiptidePublishing
Goodreads: tinyurl.com/RiptideOnGoodreads
Tumblr: riptidepublishing.tumblr.com

Thank you so much for Reading the Rainbow!

RiptidePublishing.com

Acknowledgements

Many thanks to the person at Fleet Pitch Markers who answered all my questions about aeroliner devices, what they were made of, what they weighed, and whether you could kill someone using one. Research can be a bizarre experience at times.

Also by Charlie Cochrane

Novels:
The Best Corpse for the Job
Jury of One
Two Feet Under
Old Sins
Lessons in Love
Lessons in Desire
Lessons in Discovery
Lessons in Power
Lessons in Temptation
Lessons in Seduction
Lessons in Trust
All Lessons Learned
Lessons for Survivors
Lessons for Idle Tongues
Lessons for Sleeping Dogs
Broke Deep
Count the Shells

Novellas:
Lessons in Loving thy Murderous Neighbour
Lessons in Chasing the Wild Goose
Lessons in Cracking the Deadly Code
Lessons in Playing a Murderous Tune
Lessons in Following a Poisonous Trail

Collected novellas:
An Act of Detection
Pack Up Your Troubles
Love in Every Season
In the Spotlight

Standalone novellas and short stories:
Second Helpings
Awfully Glad
Don't Kiss the Vicar
Promises Made Under

About the Author

Because Charlie Cochrane couldn't be trusted to do any of her jobs of choice—like managing a rugby team—she writes. Her mystery novels include the Edwardian era Cambridge Fellows series, and the contemporary Lindenshaw Mysteries. Multipublished, she has titles with Riptide, Carina, Lume, and Bold Strokes, among others.

A member of the Romantic Novelists' Association, Mystery People, and International Thriller Writers Inc, Charlie regularly appears at literary festivals and at reader and author conferences.

Where to find her:
Website: charliecochrane.wordpress.com
Facebook: facebook.com/charlie.cochrane.18
Twitter: twitter.com/charliecochrane
Goodreads: goodreads.com/author/show/2727135.Charlie_Cochrane

Printed in Poland
by Amazon Fulfillment
Poland Sp. z o.o., Wrocław